RESPECT
the DEAD

SHAWN MCLAIN

Respect the Dead

For my wife, who has always believed in me. I love you.

End of the Day

The sun had already begun its slow descent behind the mountains as the Jeep twisted along the familiar path home. Gravel spit as the back of the vehicle fishtailed. The driver jerked the wheel to regain the pavement. Dan had been feeling tired, lethargic, and unwell for most of the day. His head was pounding and his mouth was a desert. Bile churned in his stomach as he pulled onto the long, wooded drive of the house he shared with his longtime girlfriend.

Lisa put down her book and eased herself off the couch. She had been slowly recovering from the flu and moving made her want to throw up. A small smile crossed her face as she heard the familiar crunch of Dan's old Wrangler on the drive. After such a terrible week, she was happy to have him home for the weekend.

Slowly she made her way from the living room to the kitchen. Pouring herself a glass of water, she leaned heavily on the sink, thinking about what Dan could make them for dinner. She was pulling out ingredients when she paused, wondered what was keeping him. He usually made it quickly from the car to her arms, making sure she was doing OK. He was always worried about her. She had been having health problems for months. They had only had a brief phone call over lunch to talk. He had a very busy day, so she expected him to be through the door already. She wondered what was keeping him.

Dan stumbled getting out of the car. His legs betrayed him with weakness. His head felt as if it were about to split open and then burst into flame. The pounding in his skull brought him to his knees. The only sensation greater than the blinding pain crashing through his brain was the burning hunger in his stomach. He needed to eat. He had to eat.

Lisa looked out the front window. The glass slipped from her grasp, shattering on the floor. Dan was almost doubled over. He stumbled, crawled, then limped onto the porch. She rushed to the door. Throwing it wide, she was greeted by groans from Dan.

"Dan! Oh my God, are you ok? What's wrong, honey?" She yelped, moving to catch him.

Dan looked up, eyes bloodshot, mouth hanging slack and drooling. The only thought screaming in his burning mind was "*FOOD!*" Lunging forward, he no longer recognized his love; he only saw a meal.

His nails scratched at her bare skin and his teeth sank into her outstretched arm. Blood gushed over his teeth and chin while her screams filled the small house.

Lisa was terrified of the man before her, a man she no longer recognized. She fell back, slipping on the spilled water as the thing that had been her lover crashed down on top of her, clawing at her legs. She kicked at the door, but Dan's torso was already across the threshold.

Pain exploded through Lisa's leg as Dan sank his teeth into her left calve. She kicked at his once kind face; a face contorted in hunger. His head snapped back as she kicked free. Lisa grabbed at the furniture, trying to regain her feet, desperate to escape. Pain hobbled her, sending her crashing forward. A lamp smashed to the floor and stars exploded in front of her eyes while her head rang. A red stain appeared on the corner of an end table. The thought that she had always hated that lamp flashed through her mind.

Dazed, she rolled away, trying to regain control of the spinning world. Warm sticky blood streamed down her face from a deep gash above her eyebrow. The cut began to swell, obscuring her vision. Dan was on his feet, the side of his face bruised from her kick. Throwing a hand out, she found the overturned lamp. Dan's gaze followed the trail of blood from his feet to her freely bleeding leg.

Releasing a long, low moan of longing, Dan shambled forward, his teeth bared. Using the couch to steady herself, Lisa struggled to her feet. She turned, swinging the lamp. Blood and saliva splattered her face as Dan's head snapped to one side from the blow. Glass and wire from the shade pierced one of Dan's eyes. Stunned, he wildly grabbed for her. She swung again. "CRACK!" The lamp broke. Dan fell backward over the overturned table.

Lisa dragged her damaged leg as quickly as she could down the hall toward the bedroom. Not daring to look back, fear drove her forward. She could hear Dan stumbling to his feet. Throwing herself through the door, she slammed it shut. Her trembling fingers scrambled for the lock. With every attempt, the lock popped open. Panicked at its defiance, tears streaming down her face, she gave a small laugh when the lock finally clicked. She slid down the door slumping against it. Tears rolled freely down her face to mix with Dan's blood.

Dazed and bloodied, Dan slowly clawed his way over the shattered table. The one eye that could still see followed the trail of blood to the bedroom door. Raising his battered body, he stumbled forward. Confusion clouded his mind. Where had it gone? Cocking his head to the side, he could hear weeping. Food was behind that door. His prize was hidden behind this obstacle. He pushed against the barrier, and frustration filled him at its resistance. Raising his fists, he slammed on the flimsy hollow core door, rattling it in its frame. Dan had been meaning to replace this door for months with something more substantial. Now he just needed to get through it.

"GO AWAY!" Lisa screamed as the door bucked against her. Her head was pounding. Her stomach was churning and her blood was pooling around her torn leg. She turned her head to the cracking sound coming from the frame and around the handle. He would be through soon.

"Go *away*," she said. The frame splintered and the door inched forward into the room. His frantic pounding mixed with the sounds of breaking wood and guttural growls. "Go 'way," she whispered, as her head exploded in agony.

Dan threw his weight against the broken door. It moved slightly against a heavy object and then swung free. He began to raise his hands, then paused. A low frustrated, mournful moan escaped his lungs. Lisa, slack-jawed and hollow-eyed, stared back at him. Her moan met his.

Together they turned toward the door. Limping and staggering, they wandered out of the house onto the porch. Darkness had fallen, and the woods were barely visible beyond the pool of the porch light. Their dead eyes stared into the darkness, and then turned to each other. Slowly making their way up the long, wooded drive, they could sense it. Somewhere out there was food.

Last Date

Seventeen-year-old Beth McDaniel's annoyance grew as her boyfriend Corey's car left the main road to turn down a side street. They were getting further and further from town. "This is not the way to the theater," she grumbled as Corey took another turn.

"It's a shortcut," he replied, grinning.

"I know how to get to the movies, and this isn't even close. Where are you taking me?" she demanded.

"Relax, this is going to be better than the movies." He patted her knee, an act that only added to her growing annoyance. She wanted to see the movie. She had been anticipating it for weeks. In the end, she had agreed to see it with Corey instead of her best friend, as she had promised. That was a decision she was regretting more and more by the second.

The houses were getting fewer and fewer and the landscape more wooded. She began to recognize the landmarks. The large black barn that sat close to the road, the fork with the gnarled old tree with the huge branch pointing the way—this was not going to take her anywhere near where she wanted to be.

"Why are we out here? The movie starts at 7:30," she huffed, checking her watch.

"I wanted to show you something." He said this with that annoying smirk in his voice, that one that at first was so endearing, and now was just tiresome.

"I've been out here before. I know all about the *"haunted"* bridge."

"I know." He smiled. Something about the way he said it made her extremely uncomfortable. The smile on his face was illuminated by the dashboard light. It made him seem ugly and slightly creepy. "Seriously, I've been here before." She was getting nervous, "We can still make it. You know the previews take forever," she added hopefully.

"Come on, this will be more fun than some stupid fantasy movie," Corey said, using what he thought was a sultry tone. It made Beth's skin crawl. He pulled the car to the side of the road and flipped the lights off.

"I want to see this movie," she insisted, backing further away as he advanced. One of his hands was gripping her knee, the other was snaking around her shoulder. The harder he pulled her to him, the harder she tried to pull away. Unfortunately, she was pinned against the car door. "Corey, stop! I mean it! I want to see this movie."

"I have something planned that is so much better than..."

"Stop it right now! I told you once, and I won't tell you again."

Ignoring her demands, Corey leaned in and started kissing her neck. Beth pushed him off, but he grabbed at her hands, laughing. Beth's annoyance was now starting to fight with fear. He was holding her wrists in one of his hands, while his other hand was on the back of her neck, pulling her toward him. Freeing her left wrist, she grabbed at his face, pushing away hard.

"What the hell is wrong with you?" he cried. rubbing his cheek. Her handprint still visible on it.

"I want to go home, now!"

Changing his tack, he smiled sweetly, "Come on, baby, don't be a tease. It'll be fun," he whispered, leaning in again.

She pushed him back, angling herself with a knee between them. "Stop it right now! Take me home."

"Oh, I'll take you somewhere, honey." Before Corey could move more than a few inches...*smack*! Beth's hand connected painfully with his smug face.

"What the hell!" he screamed, massaging the spot where she had hit him.

"I said take me home right now!"

"You bitch! What the hell did you hit me for!?"

"I told you to stop!"

Anger flared in Corey as he reached over and grabbed at Beth's hands. "You don't hit me, EVER!" he growled. Beth fought back, slapping his hands away. She fumbled behind her for the door latch with one hand while keeping him at bay with the other. Corey's voice rose with each word, anger contorting his face. "You think you're man enough to hit me? Then I'll treat you like a man!" His fist cocked back, the door popped open, and Beth spilled out onto the gravel road. His fist hit the seat where a split second before her face had been.

Crawling over the seat, Corey grabbed at her feet. She pulled them out of his reach. Kicking hard she slammed the door it in his face. When it appeared in the window a second later it was full of rage.

"Fine!" His muffled voice screamed through the window. Beth scooted further from the car, "Fine! Stay out there, bitch!"

He disappeared, but the engine revved. Beth scrambled to her feet and out of the road. Gravel and dirt spit from the tires as Corey sped forward. Shaking with anger, Beth watched as the brake lights came on. The car skidded to a halt. There was a pause. Suddenly the reverse lights illuminated the road. The engine whined in reverse. The vehicle swerved, whipping around, and gravel shot out from the tires again. Beth stepped further off the road, shielding her eyes from the bright headlights as the car spun. Fearfully, she stepped back as the vehicle hurtled toward her. Mere feet away, the brakes locked up again, skidding to a stop. Beth stumbled back away from the car, ready to run. Corey got out, slammed the door and advanced on her. She stood her ground. Out of the car, in the open, she knew she could take him. He noticed her stance and faltered.

Beth had shown more than once she could take care of herself. The memory of gym class when she had protested the sexism of girl's sports versus boy's flooded back to Corey's mind. She had seriously embarrassed one of the school's top wrestlers that day. Still, he was going to make it clear she was in the wrong. Pointing an accusing finger, he said, "You said you've been out here before when I brought it up. What the hell is so important about a stupid movie?"

"What... huh... what?" Beth sputtered in her anger and confusion. "I came out to the haunted bridge, so what!? What does that have to do with, with..." She couldn't comprehend how her being out here before constituted it being acceptable for him to assault her.

He backed up with a look of contempt on his face. "Is that what you think this place is?" He sniffed his disdain, "You just missed your chance. You should stay with the geeks, not try to date outside your league." He turned back to his car. Flinging open his door, he turned and pointed at the passenger side. "Get in."

Beth stood still. "I prefer to walk." Disgust dripped in her voice.

"Just get in. We'll go see your stupid movie."

"I don't want to go anywhere with a pig like you."

"Just get in the damn car!"

"No."

Angry, hateful words echoed through the dark woods surrounding them. In the end, he had sped off, calling her several names that ensured they would never speak again. When the taillights faded away, Beth was alone with three choices: walk home in the dark, call her brother, or call her best friend, Wesley Davidson. Her brother, Steve, would be at work. She cringed at the thought of making him leave work. On top of that, he would be more interested in beating Corey to death for picking on his sister. He had never liked Corey and was very vocal about her choice of dating him. "Still an option," she muttered. "Maybe tomorrow."

She decided on Wes. She prayed he wasn't too angry with her for ditching him for Corey to see the movie. It was his favorite series, after all. They had seen all the others together on opening day. She took a deep breath as she remembered the excitement they both had about it. Then she remembered the look on his face when she told him she was going to opening night with Corey instead.

"Yeah, hey cool, maybe we can see it some other time" he had said in a too-cheery way that told her he was highly pissed. She cringed at the memory, and several other things she had done, including but not limited to ignoring him at school, and laughing as Corey's friends made fun of Wes. She really hadn't been much of a friend to him since she started dating Corey.

Way to be an ass, Beth, she chastised herself. Shaking the memories from her mind, she opened her phone and placed the call. The phone rang and rang again. She started to fear he wouldn't answer. Maybe he found someone else to go with. The thought caused her stomach to tighten. She realized it wasn't because she might have to walk home or call her brother.

Finally, she heard the familiar sound of Wes' voice. "Hey, didn't expect to hear from you. What's up?" he asked. She could hear the concern, yet coolness, of his tone.

"I...Wes..." She knew he was going to be upset. "I need a ride. Can you come to get me?" She winced as she asked.

"Yeah, sure. Where are you? You OK?" He knew she was out with Corey.

"I'm out at Troll Bridge," she said with a sigh.

She waited, listened to silence, until he said, "Why are you out *there*?" His voice was strained, annoyed.

"Listen, it wasn't *my* idea. Can you please just come get me?" she replied, slightly angry.

"What happened? Do I need to bring *Corey* some gas?" He sneered the name.

"Nooo." She replied through gritted teeth, her anger began to bubble up again. Taking a deep steadying breath, she blew out her aggravation. Rolling the tension in her shoulders, Beth hesitated, then explained, "No...he...well, he sorta left me here."

"WHAT? ALONE? What the hell?" he yelled. Wes was now upset, and she hated when he got all worked up. "I'll be there in ten minutes," he said. Through the phone, she could hear him crashing around. She could see him in her mind's eye, searching his cluttered room. She couldn't help but smile when she heard the keys jingling, followed by a loud swear. He had tripped on the nightstand...again. He did that every time he was in a hurry.

"Ten minutes, Wes? Really?" she asked skeptically. "You'd have to do a hundred miles an hour to get here, and your car doesn't do a hundred."

"Stay on the phone so I know you are OK," he demanded, a little irritated at the dig at his car. "And don't knock the car that is coming to get you." She stood in the middle of the road, listening. The engine on Wes' third-hand car struggled to life. She shook her head. Wes urged and threatened the car to start. Beth smiled as he whooped when the engine finally engaged. "Ok, where are you exactly?"

"I'm almost all the way to the bridge. Honk when you get here. I'll be by that tree with the big hole in it." Her anger was subsiding, leaving her tired. "You remember the one you said a gnome lived in." She sighed and a tear ran down her face. She brushed it away.

"Beth, I said stay on the phone so I know you are OK," he growled angrily, gears crunched audibly through the phone.

"Wes, you can't shift and talk. I've seen you drive *without* distractions." She shuddered. "Just be safe and come to my rescue." She tried to joke, but the effect was ruined by an escaping sob.

Thankfully Wes was too preoccupied with driving to hear it. "Fine! I'll hang up but you have to text me every minute, OK?" he demanded. She could tell he was already having trouble driving and talking.

"OK", she conceded and heard the phone thud, swearing, and then silence. He must have hung up, she told the darkness. Looking through the swaying leaves at the moon, she tried to figure out what she had done to deserve this. Anger flared. Corey is such a dick. She berated herself. What were you thinking? And she slapped herself on the side of the head. Somewhere off in the distance she heard the moan of the trees in the breeze, and the cry of a hawk, or maybe it was a cat. Beth wrapped her arms around her shoulders and nervously stared into the darkness.

A chill began to creep up her spine when she heard the weird cry again. She couldn't tell where it came from. With shaking fingers she scrolled to Wes' number. She hesitated, and then closed the screen. It's only an animal, nothing to worry about—but she was edging slowly off the road. She could hear the running water of the creek under the bridge. Carefully, she eased down the bank toward the water.

Getting a better view with the help of moonlight, Beth got her bearings. She wasn't far from the gnome tree, as she and Wes had dubbed it. It was a huge tree with a hole at the base large enough for a small person to fit in. They had come out here a few weeks ago. She had heard a couple of the girls at school talking about it and asked Wes if he knew it. He, of course, had been rather interested in a haunted bridge, and the name Troll Bridge had been the topper.

Of course, those girls came out here. A thought hit her like a slap in the face. For just the reason Corey wanted. Damn it! Her fists and teeth clenched. This is a make-out spot! She stamped her foot in fury, but immediately her foot slipped. Throwing her arms wide for balance, she caught herself before she fell to the soft earth. The creek was swollen from a late autumn rain and the air still clung to the chill and wetness. She looked out over the fast-moving water and at the moon reflected in it. When she had been out here with Wes, it had been to look for ghosts. That night had been a lot more fun.

How the hell did I let this happen? she growled. I knew he was an asshole— good looking and popular—but an asshole. She sighed again, taking a step toward the tree. Her foot caught on a root. The ground rushed up to meet her. Throwing out her hands to break the fall, her phone flew into the darkness.

"Sploosh!" Her head, arms, and body were instantly submerged in cold swift water. With her legs still on the bank, she was covered from her head to halfway down her back. The freezing water felt like daggers on her skin. Pulling herself out, her knees sank into the mud, soaking the legs of her jeans. Cold water ran down her back from her long sopping hair. Beth sat there shivering for a moment. The shock of the fall and the cold caused her to shiver uncontrollably. It all became too much, Beth burst into a wailing cry.

She hated Corey, hated him. Angry, frustrated sobs wracked her body as she shivered, wet and cold, on the muddy bank of the creek. Her cell rang. She couldn't see where it was. Throwing aside leaves and twigs, she found it several feet away in the grass. Her fingers shook with the cold, and tears clouded her sight. Her crying made it hard to answer.

"Beth! Why haven't you texted? Are you ok?" Wes shouted into the phone.

"I'm....I'm.....oohhhh godddd….." Beth wailed.

"Hold on." Wes cried. The familiar thump of the phone on the seat was followed by the whine of the engine. Snuffling, she tried to catch her breath. She looked at the phone, trying to figure out how to put it away in her soaking clothes. She was freezing. Slowly, she half-crawled, half-walked over the muddy ground to the tree. Slumping against it, she let the tears fall thick and fast. This would never happen to her again. She swore it. Sliding down the rough bark, she shimmied into the hole. It was only slightly warmer out of the breeze. Hugging herself tightly, she willed Wes to hurry.

Several long minutes later, Beth heard a car racing toward her. Headlights flickered an unusual pattern on the road and trees. Risking a peek out of the tree, she recognized the headlights. The right one was bouncing a little. No matter how much Wes tried to tighten that one it always came loose. A breath of relief escaped her lungs. Extricating herself from the tree, she wrapped her arms around herself and headed to the road. Just when she crested the hill, the beat-up car skidded to a halt. It was barely stopped before Wes was holding her at arm's length to make sure she was ok. She was soaked, cold and crying. His arms encircled her. She felt their warmth and comforting embrace. She clung to him, letting the tears flow. She felt like such a fool.

Still Hungry

Glass sliced into Dan's arms and ripped his hands as he clawed through the shattered window. The woman inside screamed as she ran for the front door. Throwing it open, she ran straight into Lisa's grabbing arms and hungry mouth. Blood flowed freely from the fresh wound torn in the woman's neck. A gory chunk hit the floor with a splat as it was wrenched free from Lisa's open mouth. She lurched in for more. The terrified woman struggled to free herself pushing against Lisa's face with one hand while grabbing at the wound on her neck with the other. Blood coated her hand instantly. She stumbled back, only to emit a gurgling scream as two fingers parted company from her hand, lost in Lisa's chewing mouth. More pain burst through her body as Dan's teeth sank into the other side of her neck. Blood sprayed across a picture on the wall of a calm lake, its waters now stained permanently red.

Gray-faced, the woman was able to push free. Dizzy and weak, she stumbled across the room. A weak cry sounded in her throat. She watched her severed fingers fell from Lisa's mouth. Cold; the woman was getting so cold. The horrid pair slouched ever closer. The woman leaned heavily against the wall, sliding down it. Her damaged hand fell to her side, and even as she tried to stem the tide of blood from her throat, her heart stopped beating. A pool of blood grew around the body. Dan and Lisa stopped; Dan's head cocked to one side as if asking Lisa a question. Her head bowed. She stared at the cooling thickening blood. Dan's moan was answered by Lisa's. Their prey was gone, dead. They moaned again. As if in response, the woman's moan joined them from the floor. One hand still clutched at the wound on her neck, while the other left a thick trail of red on the wall. The woman raised herself slowly. The three stared at each other with grey-colored eyes. Their hunger burned. They needed to feed.

Blinded by fear, the husband ran, ran from the house, from his wife. Those people…those things attacked her, bit her, his mind screamed. He was crashing through the underbrush, heading for the road. Somewhere nearby he heard a car skid to a halt. Someone was there. He could get help. Tree limbs smacked and slashed his face. His legs protested and his lungs screamed in his chest. Years of heavy smoking, fatty foods, and watching TV took their toll. Gasping, he could see the taillights. His chest burned. He couldn't breathe. Falling face first down the gully, his heart gave out.

Back at the house, three heads snapped up in unison, turning to the sound. The skid of tires on the road not far from away rang like a dinner bell. The only thing that separated them from the car was the woods and the creek. These obstacles meant nothing. Darkness, cold, and freezing water wouldn't get in the way of what they needed...

Warm, living, food.

Not All Bad, Yet...

"Are you okay?" Wes whispered.

"Yeah...now." Beth hiccupped.

Wes just held her for a moment, rubbing her back, and to her surprise, he kissed the top of her head through her wet hair.

"Come on, you're going to catch a cold out here," he said, taking her by the hand and pulling her to the car.

They got to the door when Beth stopped. "I'm going to get the seats all wet and dirty," she said with a sob.

"I don't care. I mean, look at this thing," Wes said, exasperated. Beth shrugged at him. "Fine, wait a second," he said. Holding up a finger, he reached into the back and pulled out a hooded sweatshirt. He held it out to Beth. She looked at it and smiled.

They stared at each other for a second until Beth arched an eyebrow at him. Wes jumped quickly, then turned his back to her and closed his eyes. Beth laughed as she pulled off her soaked shirt. She pulled on the sweatshirt and zipped it up. It was warm and dry.

"I'm sorry," she muttered.

"For what?" he asked, confused.

"For dragging you out here." She sighed. "It's just...all Corey wanted was sex and... I don't know... I just thought he would realize that wasn't going to happen. I thought he would chill out and be cool. I mean, why can't more guys be like you?" She smiled at him. "I mean you never try any of that stuff with me." He tried to say something, but she wasn't paying attention. "I mean, they start out all nice, and then it turns out they have other intentions…" She was rambling and starting to cry again. Then she stamped her foot and swiped at her cheeks. "That is enough, Beth!" she chided herself.

Wes took her wet clothes from her and pulled her into a hug. "I came here to get my best friend. That was my only intention. " He swallowed nervously. "So, all Corey wanted was…never mind, I…I don't want to know," Wes muttered, hurt in his voice. He swallowed hard, holding her soggy shirt out to her. She pushed her wet hair out of her face. She gave Wes a smile. He inclined his head to the car.

"He wanted it." She placed a hand on his arm. "He never got it from me." Beth headed for the door. Wes made his way around the car. They stared over the roof while she opened the door. Wes looked at her and smiled.

Once inside the Beth relaxed. It was warm and she was safe. Her legs were still cold, but Wes turned up the heat for her.

"You OK?" he asked.

She nodded. "Thanks."

"So, what happened?" Wes asked, looking at her.

Beth sighed. She didn't really want to tell him. She knew Wes hated Corey, and this wasn't going to help. Yet once she started to tell the story, she couldn't stop. Everything that Corey had done, everything he had said, everything. She had been keeping it to herself and it had been driving her crazy. As she finished, she couldn't meet Wes' gaze. She felt ashamed and shallow.

She knew his question would be, "Why are you with him?" But she didn't know the answer. To her surprise, he didn't ask.

She looked up at Wes and saw the anger and hurt in his eyes. "Just know…" he started, then looked away.

"What?" she asked.

"Nothing," he sighed.

"Wes?" she said, taking his face in her hand, pulling him to face her, "Really, what?"

Wes shook a little but kept her gaze. "Um…just know…I would…never do that to you…um…You deserve better." He hesitated, "You know if you are looking for a nice guy… um, well, you know where to find one." He finished almost in a whisper as he lost his nerve. He looked away.

Beth sat for a second and then replied, "I know."

Wes turned back to look at her. She put her hand on his cheek and leaned forward. Wes leaned in, and their lips met.

Something slammed onto the hood of the car. The two sprang apart. They stared at the man standing in front of the car. The headlights illuminated him as he stood reaching toward them, his arms outstretched over the hood. His face was just barely visible in the dim light, looked bruised and beaten but pale. The man's hands came down onto the hood again, his nails scratching at the paint.

Wes got the message, quickly putting the car in reverse. He pulled away, leaving the man lurching after them. With shaking hands, Wes spun the wheel, trying to turn the car around, Beth squeaked, hanging onto the seat belt as she tried to put it on. Wes slammed into first gear, praying it didn't stall. The car lurched, then caught. He pushed his foot to the floor, and left the man stumbling after them in the fading red of the taillights.

"Damn," he said, shaken by the man's anger. He checked his rear view mirror again and again. "That dude was pissed."

Beth placed her hand over his. "Karen said that when she and Dave were out here last week, they were chased off by a crazy old guy. She said he was screaming about kids and music and stuff." She laughed nervously.

"Yeah, well knowing Karen, the old dude had a point." Wes laughed. "I guess she'll have to find a new place to...um...hang out?"

Beth sat back in the seat and laughed. "Maybe she should hook up with Corey."

"I heard she already did." Wes laughed.

Beth spun in the seat to face him, "Really? God! That lying bastard," Beth spat out.

They spent several minutes thoroughly trashing Corey. When they pulled into their development, Wes glanced sideways at Beth. "What were you thinking?" he asked.

"I wondered when you were going to get there." Beth sighed. "To answer, I guess I wasn't." She shook her head. "I went with looks and popularity over personality. I just hope my new boyfriend will always like me for me and not because I look good with his car." She laughed as Wes pulled into her driveway, "Then again, I'm not sure anyone would look good with this car."

"Funny, you were happy to see it earlier," Wes grumbled, pulling into the driveway. Beth began to unclasp the seat belt. She reached for the door handle when Wes spoke up. "Um hey, Beth?"

'Yeah?"

"Would you like to….um….ya know, I just kissed you and stuff… Damn it!" Wes took a deep breath as Beth smiled at him. "Can we start dating? I mean… yeah…I want to be more than…you know friend-zoned…" Wes stumbled. Cringing at himself, he looked hopefully at her.

"Wes, I don't kiss guys I'm not dating, just so you know," she stated, trying to act angry but failing through the laughter. She leaned over and kissed him again, laughing through the entire kiss.

"No…no, I didn't think you would." Wes smiled. He leaned over and kissed her. She reached into the back seat and grabbed her wet clothes.

"Come over tomorrow to get your hoodie?" she asked, turning back to face him.

"Yeah, sounds good. What time?" He smiled.

"Come by for lunch. Maybe we can catch the movie tomorrow," she said, and kissed him goodnight. She was barely out of the car when her phone rang. She looked at the number, then over at Wes.

"It's my ex. I think I'll let it go to voice mail. See you tomorrow." She closed the door. Wes watched her go through the front door. Sure she was safe, he headed home, a huge smile on his face.

Wes' head was spinning with the night's events as he pulled up to his house. His room was above the garage, an addition that was built in the sixties and still retained some of that character. Outlines of huge flowers could still be seen in the paint of what Beth had dubbed the Scooby Room. The rest of the house was a small post-Second World War ranch. It wasn't as big or nice as the houses in Beth's part of the neighborhood, which was built in the nineties. He had always been slightly embarrassed about the place, but tonight he could only sit and smile at it.

"Finally! Finally, she sees me. I can't believe she likes me!" He told his car, rubbing the faded and cracked dash affectionately.

It wasn't until the front porch light flicked on that Wes turned the key. He smiled as he listened to the tired engine sputter and die.

He leaped out of the car, bounding to the front door. He gave his mom a kiss on the cheek as she moved out of his way to let him in.

"How's Beth?" Wes' stepfather, Reggie, asked as he gave a small cough. Reggie rubbed his throat and grimaced.

"Great! Just great. I'm gonna call it a night." Wes bid his mother and stepfather good night.

"What? I thought there was some kind of trouble...," his mother yelled after him, as he took the stairs to his room two at a time. He thought about seeing Beth tomorrow, which made him smile all the more.

"There was, but everything is great now."

More of a Bad Night

Corey's little red sports car screeched to a halt, causing several of the people standing around the parking lot to jump out of the way. Lance slapped Wayne on the back and nodded toward Corey's car, the outline of a lone occupant silhouetted by the security light of the nearby building.

"Guess she *could* resist him," Lance laughed, while grabbing a couple of beers from inside his own car.

"So, how was she, studly?" Wayne laughed as Corey slammed his door harder than was necessary. Corey responded by giving Wayne the finger as Lance pressed a beer into his other hand.

"So, the date ended early? She didn't even want to come to Linda's party, huh?" Lance asked, downing his drink.

Corey opened the beer and took a long drink. "Don't know. I left her ass out at Troll Bridge."

"Dude! That is cold," Wayne laughed.

Corey just gave him a disgusted look. Lance cocked his head to one side. "Dude, that was uncool, you need to go get her." He finished his beer and then reached for another.

"She made it clear she did not want to be in the car with me." Corey drained his own beer, flicking away the empty can. Wayne continued to laugh as he passed him another.

"Come on, man. Let's go get her. If she doesn't want to ride with you, I'll drive her home," Lance said, with a slight slur followed by a long loud belch.

"Or maybe she'll come to Linda's and we can change her mind," Wayne ventured, an evil grin spreading across his face.

"Dude, you think she will ride with you? You're already half drunk." Corey frowned. "You know how she is about that stuff."

"Yeah, but only half. So we should do it before too much longer."

"You guys have fun." Wayne waved. "I'm heading over to Linda's." The engine growled to life then sped away. Soon his thumping music faded. Corey frowned at the place where Wayne's car had been.

Several other people left. The crowd thinned while Lance and Corey opened a bottle of bourbon. After several shots and a couple more beers, the two decided to have one more drink and go back to pick up Beth. Corey figured she would have calmed down. "She'll be grateful for the ride," Corey shouted. Lances burped his agreement. Getting shakily into his car, Corey took the lead. He watched Lance weaving slightly in his rearview mirror. He could tell that Lance hadn't stopped drinking while they were on the way. Corey was having a little trouble keeping his own car between the lines, a task made harder by changing songs on his iPod and drinking another beer.

The drive back to where he had left Beth only caused Corey's annoyance to resurface. He had tried to be patient, he thought, but they had been dating long enough. The more he thought about it, the angrier he got. He had been more than patient. He had taken her out, bought her things. He deserved it. The more he thought, the more he blamed her friend Wesley.

"That little geek was always hanging around her." He yelled at a passing car. "Then there's her stupid brother. The hell with her!"

He was considering turning around when the thought of Beth's brother came back to him. The former captain and quarterback of the football team would not be pleased if anything happened to his baby sister. Corey threw his empty beer can out of the window and concentrated on the road.

About a mile from the bridge, Corey swore and swerved across the road. His tires screamed as he nearly lost control. Looking quickly in the mirror, he watched as Lance also barely kept on the road while narrowly missing the woman who had stumbled out from the woods. Corey was sure it wasn't Beth, but this only annoyed him more. He swore loudly again, punching his steering wheel. "What the hell? Is everything against me tonight?" By the time they reached the bridge, Corey was in a towering temper.

Beth was nowhere to be found. The boys called out for her. They had tramped around near the creek and across the bridge. Corey was inspecting some skid marks when Lance spoke up.

"That wasn't her that I almost hit? Was it?" he slurred, trying to focus on Corey's face.

"No, that was some crazy old bitch." Corey pulled out his phone. He called Beth; she did not answer. "I bet she got that little emo puke to come get her." He snarled. "This was a total waste of time." Corey advanced on his friend. "You thought she might go for you, didn't you?"

"Wha? Dude thas just shtupid, you better hope it wash... Wesh and not her brother," Lance defended, while backing away. "I'm just lookin out for ya, Bro." He weaved over to his car and grabbed the half empty bottle of bourbon.

"You know it was Wesley. He is the only person who wouldn't have anything else to do tonight." Corey grabbed the bottle away from Lance's lips. Taking a burning swig of the amber liquid, he surmised, "How else would he get out here so fast?" Lance merely hiccupped and shrugged, taking back the bourbon. He shook the bottle, frowning at the little that was left.

"Like he has a chance with her." Corey grabbed the bottle back from Lance and drained it. He threw the empty into the woods. A frustrated yell erupted from him. "What the hell is wrong with her?"

"Yeah, how coulds shom one reshist your charm?" Lance laughed.

Corey opened his mouth but stopped, He glared at his laughing friend. His attention was caught by the sound of an animal crashing through the brush just out of their headlight glare. He strained his eyes to see what it was. Only darkness stared back.

"Well, you didn't get anywhere, maybe she prefers..." Lance started but was silenced by a hand held up by Corey. Smirking, Lance decided to get a fresh bottle. This thought drowned out the previous one, so instead he asked, "So what do you want to do about it?" An innocent look crossed over Lances' face as he blinked repeatedly, trying to clear his vision.

"Oh, we'll get him. I doubt the tires on that hunk of shit he drives are long for this world," Corey spat.

"We'll do it tomorrow night." Lance pushed himself off the side of the car. He swayed for a second. "I want to hit the party tonight." He continued stumbling over to the edge of the road.

Corey nodded. "Come on man, let's go! I need to get wasted after this crap."

Lance waved over his shoulder, "I'll catch up. I gottsa take a piss."

"All right, I'll meet you over at Linda's." Corey was in his car a moment later and he sped off.

Lance listened as the car rumbled down the road. Swaying slightly, he began to relieve himself. The snapping of a fallen branch reached his ears. He looked up as something large moved around in the brush. Straining to see through the darkness and his alcohol-impaired vision, he staggered slightly, losing his balance for a second. Shaking his head, he decided it was nothing. He turned to stagger back to his car. His foot slipped on the spot where he had made the grass wet. Trying to recover, he tripped over a log.

"Shit!" he laughed. "Guess I'm pretty messed up."

"UUUUNNNGGHHHH," cried out the darkness. Lance flipped over, staring around for the cause of the sound. Even in his stupor, fear gripped his heart.

"Who's there?" he shouted. Another groan, followed by the heavy rustling of leaves and brush, answered him. A figured appeared in the pool of light from his headlights. His head snapped around to the shadow cast across his vision.

He looked up and saw a woman, the woman he had almost hit, shuffling toward him. She was dragging a leg that was covered in blood. The front of her shirt was also stained deep, dark red. She held out one arm toward him. She was moaning as she continued closer and closer.

Lance pushed himself up to his feet, staring at the woman. "You OK, lady?" he asked in a whisper. He began to back away. He prayed her injuries were not of his making.

A crashing sound to his left alerted him to the presence of a man. His face was bruised and bloody. His teeth were bared as he moved toward Lance. Lance began to edge toward his car when an arm grabbed him by the throat. Pain shot through his shoulder.

He wrenched himself free. He was shocked as he looked into the gaunt face of another woman. Fresh blood, his blood, dribbled down her chin. Now the man grabbed him as Lance tried to back away from the shriveled woman. Fresh pain burst forth from his arm as the man bit into his flesh. Lance screamed to the trees and empty bridge as the pale woman from the road joined the other two.

A couple of hours later, Corey mumbled something about Lance, and that he never made it to the party. Then he passed out. Linda and Wayne didn't notice.

It Started as a Nice Day

Lying in bed, Wes relived the events of the night over and over in his mind before falling into a fitful sleep. His dreams began with Beth but ended with the man banging on his hood. The man was coughing, pounding and scraping on his door, trying to get him. Wes woke up terrified. It took a few moments for his eyes to adjust to the dim light. He stared around the room for a moment before he realized it was morning. He was safe at home.

Wes hurried down the stairs feeling happier than he had in months. The morning couldn't move fast enough, knowing he had a date with Beth that day. Reaching the bottom of the stairs, his good mood met its first trial.

His mother got quickly up from her chair in the living room, hushing him. His stepfather was sleeping on the couch. "He couldn't sleep in the bed last night. He kept coughing," she whispered, leading Wes into the kitchen.

"I was going to go over to Beth's later." Wes looked back into the living room at the back of the couch. "Do you want me to stay home to help take care of him?"

His mother gave him an appraising look, then smiled. "No, no. I'll call if I need you. He seems to be sleeping finally. It might be better if I got you out of the house for a while, actually. You are always such a troublemaker."

"You know me, Mom. Loud and disruptive." He gave his mother a hug, "Seriously, Mom," he looked her straight in the eye, "call me if you need me, OK?"

"You're such a good boy." She smiled, giving him a kiss on the cheek.

Making a gagging noise, he smiled at his mother and slipped out of the house. His good mood disintegrated almost immediately. In the driveway sat his car, with four flat tires." Asshole Corey," he muttered as he crept back into the house. His mother was still in the kitchen. She looked at him questioningly. He whispered his explanation, and then retreated to his room, anger making him shake from head to foot. Pacing his room a few times to calm himself, Wes dialed Beth's number.

"Hey, when are you coming over?" she asked happily.

"Not for a while; it seems that someone flattened my tires. Mom wants me to call the police," Wes explained.

"Oh Wes, I'm so sorry. Do you think it was Corey?"

"I would bet anything. Tell you what—let me call the call cops and get this sorted out. Shouldn't take more than an hour or two."

"Do what you need to. I'm not going anywhere. Oh, and just so you know, I told Steve about what Corey did. He is pissed. I'll let him know about your tires. He may have an old set in the garage."

"Thanks, I'll call you in a bit." Wes hung up, took a breath, and then dialed the police. There was no answer. He didn't think this warranted a 911 call, but after he had tried all the extensions the automated service would allow, he tried again. He had been at it for twenty minutes when his mother knocked on his door.

"Reg is worse. We are out of cold medicine. I am running out to the store, so please stay home and keep an eye on him until I get back." Wes could see how scared his mother was. He hadn't seen her look like this since before they left his real father. He nodded as she quickly descended the stairs. Wes followed her. As soon as he stepped into the living room, he could see his stepfather looked very pale, and he was sweating. He was asleep. Wes' mother was out the door, so Wes crept back up to his room. Closing the door, he called Beth.

"What did the police say?" She asked.

"I never got through. Reg is really sick, so Mom went out to get some meds. I'm going to hang out 'til she gets back, then head over, if that is cool?"

"That seems to be going around. Dad said several guys didn't make it in to work. So he had to go in today," Beth explained. "Not enough people to handle the work."

"Yeah, Reg is coughing and feverish. Mom is really worried." Wes felt better talking to Beth. He always felt better talking to her. The McDaniels had always been there for him and his mom. Beth's dad had actually introduced Reggie to Wes' mother.

"Apparently it is some kind of an epidemic," Beth explained, recalling Wes to the conversation. "Steve is out and Dad is at work, so I've been watching TV. It is on all the channels."

Wes turned on his own TV and began to flip. He quickly changed channels until he found the news stations, a block he usually skipped. All of them were reporting on the illness. There had been several reports of violence; people attacking each other, sometimes for medicine but most others seem random. There were even unconfirmed reports of people being killed in horribly violent ways. Speculation that fever from the illness was leading to a kind of insanity or maybe a new form of airborne rabies was at the center of the attacks. The more he saw, the tighter the knot in Wes' stomach grew.

His fear for his stepfather grew worse with every report. When they saw a live report out of New York get cut off as people ran screaming from the subway, Wes was near panic. Beth was trying to calm him when Wes' mother called from downstairs for him to come help her. "I gotta go. Mom's back."

"Go" Beth replied. Wes hung up.

"The news says all the hospitals and emergency clinics are overwhelmed with sick people." Wes told his mother as he reached the bottom of the stairs.

"I know. The stores have been picked over. I almost got mugged trying to get this out the door." She held up a tattered box of daytime cold medicine.

"Take the gun next time. That will show 'em," Wes half-joked. His mother was not amused. Reg began to cough and moan.

Horde Beginning

The woods were normally full of sound. Birds chirping, the leaves rustling with animals scurrying about. Today it was silent. All the animals could sense there was something there that shouldn't be. Something very, very, wrong. The group that was wandering through the forest definitely did not belong there.

Several were covered in dried mud and blood. Some were in nightclothes, others in clothes that were torn and filthy, and one wore nothing at all. Then there were the ones with just a grey pallor and no sign of injuries. They might have just wandered into the woods for a walk and met up with these other folks. The group was mixed, young and old, black and white, all searching for the same thing, all lumbering at the same plodding pace.

Reaching the edge of the woods, the group paused momentarily, blinded for a second by the bright morning sun in their clouded milky eyes. They moaned. The ones in the back pushed the ones in the front forward. The group began to cross the open ground.

Confusion crossed the disfigured faces of the leaders as they reached a barbed wire fence. The wire cut into their waists, stopping their progress. As more ghouls pressed from behind, the wire cut deeper and deeper. The fence's wooden posts snapped and protested against the growing pressure. The top half of a woman parted company with her legs. Free from the fence, she began to crawl ahead of the others. The posts snapped, and several bodies fell when the resistance disappeared, pulling the rest of the fence down with them. The ones from behind did not notice the ones they stepped on and over on their way to the farmhouse.

The horse in the paddock whinnied and stamped the ground. The group was crossing a field of harvested corn. Stumbling through the uneven rows. Near the back of the group one of the ghouls was struggling to move forward. A section of fence dragged along behind it. The barbed wire was caught in the thing's large torso. Even further behind, the half-woman crawled along, leaving a trail of gore and innards that led back to its trampled and broken legs. Where the fence once stood, there lay a body that did not stir.

As they approached the pen the horse became more panicked, the wind bringing with it the unmistakable reek of death. The trapped animal bucked and neighed, banging on the fence and gate.

Jim rubbed his weary eyes as he walked to the window. The horse was making a terrible racket. He worried it would wake the boys. He and his wife had spent a sleepless night with their two sons, who had come down with the terrible flu. They were sure it was the one that they were hearing about on the news. The high fever and stomach cramps had kept the boys in terrible pain all night. No matter what they tried, the boys found no relief or comfort.

Finally, near dawn, the older boy fell into a restless sleep, followed by his brother. Both boys were drenched in sweat. Jim's wife kept replacing the damp cloths on their foreheads with cool ones. Jim had taken an early morning shift so she could get some rest. She was back now, at the boys' bedsides.

"Jim, we're going to have to take them to the hospital if this fever doesn't break soon," she whispered. Jim cringed but nodded. Money was very tight, and their insurance was not very good, but this was his boys.

His mind filled with worry for his sons. He was at the door without realizing it. How are we going to pay for a hospital stay? he thought, turning the knob. Stepping out into the sunlight, his thoughts swirled. If his attention hadn't been so distracted, he might have noticed how wrong things were outside his door. Pulling on his hat to shield his tired eyes from the bright sun, his eyes were down as he headed to the paddock.

Reaching the fence, he called to his frantic horse. "You need to be quiet. We just got the boys to sleep," he scolded, walking over to the gate. The animal stamped impatiently on the ground. As soon as the gate was unlatched the horse reared. Jim was thrown back as the horse burst through, running as if the devil were chasing him.

"Not what I need now, damn it!" Jim swore, pulling himself to his feet with the aid of the fence. "Great, not only do I have the boys to worry about, now I have the horse to find," he grumbled. Halfway through a swipe at his pants, Jim caught a glimpse of the oncoming crowd. They were three quarters of the way across the corn field, somewhere between twenty or thirty people.

They must... must have been in a bus crash or something. They had to be something other than what he swore they couldn't be. Terror fought with disbelief, rooting him to the ground, until a scream from the house pulled him back to reality. His wife burst through the back door as he ran to it. She was bleeding from her arms and hands.

"The boys, the boys," was all her panic would let her scream. Behind her, Jim could see his boys clawing at the screen door, blood covering their mouths and teeth. Seeing the oncoming horde, his wife let out another scream. Jim pulled her along to the truck parked beside the house. Frantically he grabbed at his pockets. "Keys! Where were the keys?" he shouted. A memory flashed through his mind. He had tossed the truck keys onto the table when he brought home the cold medicine. His wife screamed again as a blonde spiky-haired kid with a torn shirt and torn face appeared at the back of the truck. Jim turned, pulling his wife toward the barn. The sight of his oldest boy halted their movements. He was on his mother before Jim could even react. The blonde boy was now ripping into her neck as his son bit into her leg.

Jim ran to the barn, the screams of his wife chasing him. Skidding to a halt, his way was blocked by three of them. Turning, he ran to the house, his footsteps thundering on the wooden porch. He slammed the front door behind him. Jim clicked the lock and pushed the large chest by the window in front of the door. He spun on the spot: windows, too many windows. The noise was too loud...the back door! Jim ran to the back of the house, where the back screen door stood torn and open. Several undead approached. Jim slid across the bloody kitchen floor, crying out he slammed the door shut in the faces of the ghouls.

He gasped for breath, his blood pounded in his ears. He never heard the soft footfalls of his youngest son. The pain ripped through his upper thigh, and blood flowed heavily from the wound. Jim threw the child from him. Limping, he grabbed the keys from the table. He was at the front door, the chest was moved, the door opened. He could hear his son behind him. They were in front of him, beside him. Black tunnels obscured his vision. He was cold, dizzy, and then he was on his back. Horrid faces were staring down, and hands began to grab at him. He could feel the tugs, and then the pain was far away.

The ranks of the group were now swelled by four as the man, his wife, and two children, bloody and torn, wandered down the road toward the town.

Getting Bad

Even before entering the living room, Wes could tell that Reg was worse, much worse. "I asked you to watch him," his mother hissed. She hurried to her husband's side. Placing a hand on his forehead, she called to her son, "Get me a wet washcloth."

"How is he?" Wes asked his mother, placing a hand on her shoulder. She hugged it with her face and shoulder while she held the damp cloth to her husband's forehead.

Reginald Baker lay on the couch, gripping a blanket around him tightly. He also had three other blankets covering him. Sweat poured off his head while he shivered violently under the heap of covers. His skin was pale, his eyes half closed. Suddenly he erupted in a fit of coughing. It was a harsh, dry, hacking cough. It sounded like it was ripping at Reg's throat and lungs. It hurt Wes' chest just to hear it.

"Do you need me to go back out and get try to get something?" Wes asked his mother.

"I don't know. No. There was nothing left when I was just out. I just don't know when they'll get more. It seems everyone is sick, " she sighed. "It just... nothing seems to help. I don't want to give him anything else; he's had these and these already." She motioned to the open boxes of cold relief pills and bottles of cough syrup. "I was just hoping to find something better."

"Well, this is something to look forward to." Wes shuddered and rubbed his chest. Walking around the couch, he knelt down to check on Reg. "How you feeling, old dude?"

Reg gave a weak smile, which turned into another coughing fit. "I don't feel the best right now, kiddo," he wheezed. "But I'll be fine soon." He tried to give his wife a reassuring smile. He then shivered and wrapped himself more tightly in the blanket.

"Grab another blanket from the closet, will you?" Wes' mother asked. He hurried to the closet, and with every step the concern within him grew. Returning to the couple, he held out the last blanket they had. Reg seemed to be covered in all the others.

"What else can I do, Mom?" he asked. She sat on the floor next to the couch, helping her husband to drink. She looked up at him, shaking her head. "I can get the comforter from my room."

"I'm okay guys, seriously. Just a bad bug." Reg tried to calm them. He coughed, and then smiled, "Besides, that thing will only get me sicker. When was the last time you washed it?" His laugh turned into more coughs.

"If you are not better by tomorrow I am taking you to the doctor and that is that." Wes smiled as his mother laid down the law. "Now get some sleep. I'm just going to read for a bit. Wes, I'm sorry, but I need you here to help and... I... I'm just happy you are home. In case I need something."

"It's okay, Mom. I'm worried about the old guy too." He knew she didn't need him home to help but needed his support. He headed up to his room, listening as Reg broke out into another fit of coughs that ended in a moan. As soon as he closed the door to the bedroom his phone rang. It was Beth.

Downtown

Dave and Bridgette had just finished unpacking the last of the boxes in their first apartment together a couple of days ago. It wasn't much, but it was theirs. Located above a dance studio on the third floor of an old building downtown, the rent had been just right for the young couple, who were moving in together right after graduating college.

They liked the location downtown and the lack of neighbors. Of the four apartments, only two others were occupied. This suited the young couple just fine; they liked to play their music loud and have a good time. Today the apartment was quieter than normal. Bridgette had come down with the flu that had been going around. Dave watched the news nervously. The commentators posed theories, argued over the causes, and showed maps projecting the spread. The east and west coast were already covered in red dots. New York was completely covered in solid red. He looked from the TV to his laptop. The stories on the internet did not help calm his fears. The web was reporting deaths and some weird stories about people suffering from heavy fever that caused them to act crazy and attack doctors and loved ones.

Swine Flu, Bird Flu, whatever flu, Dave didn't really care. What he did care about was Bridgette and she was very sick. She was cold, no matter how many layers of clothes and blankets covered her. She also complained of a horrendous headache and stomachache. Dave was staying home from work to take care of her. She had always been a bit sickly and frail. Dave was not surprised when she got ill. She was lying in their bed coughing. Dave gave up on the news. He went to the kitchen to make her some tea.

"Dave..." she called. Her voice was very weak. He wasn't sure he had heard it at first. When she called out again, he hurried to the bedroom. "I really feel terrible. I think I need to go to the hospital." She moaned, and started to cough.

"I'll get your coat, okay? Be right back." He ran to the hall closet, but her coat wasn't there. He remembered she was already wearing it to beat the chills. Shaking his head in frustration, he grabbed his coat for her to wear, too. He hurried back to the bed-room. It was quiet.

"Bridge? Bridge!" he yelped at her motionless figure.

The coat dropped from his hand onto the floor. He rushed to the bed, feeling her wrist. She didn't seem to have a pulse. He leaned over her ear, close to her mouth, to check for breathing. He couldn't feel anything. He put an ear to her chest, praying to hear a heartbeat. No sound came. "Bridge? Bridgette?" he asked, finally yelling her name.

Her eyes flew open, and relief washed over Dave. Her eyes watched him as a sound escaped her throat. Dave leaned over to hear what she was saying. She lurched forward, sinking her teeth into his neck. His relief turned to terror. Blood sprayed over her lips and across the wall. He jerked away in agony and fear. Stumbling back, he stood straight up, and his hand flew to his neck. He tried to cover the severed artery that was spurting blood over the walls and bed. Dizzy, he turned to run from the room, but she caught him by the arm. Her weight pulled him back to the bed. He fell over across it, knocking free of her grip. Yet then she was on him in a second, biting him in the face.

He tried to fight off the small woman. His blood flowed freely from his neck onto the comforter. His eyes focused on the floral pattern he hadn't liked to begin with, now covered in red. He didn't even notice when Bridgette grabbed his hand. He had tried to keep her away, holding her at a distance. She was biting off one of his fingers, chewing the digit like a chicken wing. Dave's eyes darkened as he died.

Down the hall, an older couple watched the news. The burning buildings in Pittsburgh, mixed with the reports from New York and LA, had them frightened. The screams, then absolute quiet coming from the new tenant's apartment was enough. Frantically they packed. Now was the time to get out, to get out before panic made it impossible.

Bad News

"Hey, how's your stepdad?"

"Not so good. Man, he is really sick."

"I just heard that school is canceled Monday. Can you believe it? The news was saying this is a pandemic or something. People are sick all over the place." There was a hint of fear in Beth's voice.

"Yeah, Mom said the stores were running out of cold medicine and water and all kinds of stuff. You'd think there was a snow-storm coming. People fighting over eggs, bread, and milk. I guess French toast will get you through anything. How did Steve's meeting go?" Wes asked, trying to change the subject.

Beth sighed. "Not too good, I think. Steve was really down when he got home. He and Dad had another fight about it."

There was a long silence on the phone then Beth spoke again. "Wes, I...I'm sorry..."

Wes stomach dropped. She was going to dump him, already. He knew it.

"Wes?"

"Yeah I'm here," he morosely replied.

"What's the matter?"

"You're gonna end it, aren't you? You realized you just want to be friends, but I don't know if I can be just friends now," Wes huffed.

"Wait.. what?" Beth asked, confused,

"Um so...you're not dumping me?"

"Okay, listen!" Wes cringed at the annoyance in her voice. "Let's get something straight right now. Your self-doubt has never been one of your endearing qualities. I am not going to spend our relationship validating you.'

"Um right, sorry. ...You were saying?" Wes cringed. He had been dating Beth for almost fourteen hours. In that time, he had blown off a date *and* made her angry.

"What I was saying...Well, I hadn't been much of a friend to you since I started dating Corey and I wanted to apologize for that."

Wes interrupted, "Beth, you don't have to..."

"Wes, I have to explain things, okay?" She took a deep breath. "I made a mistake to go for popularity over substance. I'm sorry."

Wes smiled. "Cool! I have substance. Okay, you're right. I'll work on the self-esteem thing."

"You better."

Several seconds ticked by. Finally, Beth broke through the awkwardness. "We've been watching the news. Dad is getting really worried."

"Yeah, I get that." Wes tried to sound casual. "I keep trying not worry about the coughing and hacking coming from the living room." Even as he said this, he watched the pictures on the TV. Hospitals overrun, stores picked clean, pharmacies looted and burned, people protesting outside of pharmaceutical companies, demanding drugs.

"Listen," Beth paused to collect her thoughts. "Dad thinks it might be a good idea to get out of town. He says to tell you that if things don't get better soon, we are going to come get you guys."

"I don't know. Reg is really sick. I don't think we can move him." Wes frowned as a fresh wave of coughing erupted downstairs.

"I think Dad meant... um..." she took a breath, "only you and your mom." Beth hesitated. Wes didn't answer. She hurried on, as if it would be easier faster. "Wes, the stuff on the news. The sick people have been doing stuff...They've hurt people." Her voice trailed off.

Silence stretched again. When Wes spoke, he was calm. "No Beth, no. Not Reg. He would never hurt us. Never." Beth tried to interrupt. Wes spoke over her. "He promised!" It was her turn to cringe. When Wes spoke again it was with finality. "Let me know where you are. We'll meet you if things get bad and Reg is better." Wes shook his head. She couldn't be serious. The silence on the phone only accentuated the coughing from the living room. "Beth...I gotta go."

Worse News

"The CDC is now discouraging the public from using hand sanitizer, as it seems to speed up the rate of infection," the male news anchor stated, and the female anchor took over in a dramatic, serious tone. "Coming up next on your six o'clock news, our top story is the continuing team coverage of the flu epidemic. We'll have all the latest closings and cancellations, including this evening's game between the Pittsburgh Steelers and the Detroit Lions."

Steve McDaniel glanced up at the clock. With a frown, he confirmed it was getting to be almost time to go to work. His father sat with him in the living room, watching the end of the 5:30 news. "This is crazy," Mr. McDaniel muttered. "This new flu epidemic is completely out of control." He thumbed through a couple of channels, all showing "Breaking News" or "Special Report." He frowned. "The government should have had some kind of plan in place." He flipped past pictures of Baltimore burning. "Two weeks ago, there were reports of this thing in Asia, then last week it showed up in New York." He pointed to a shot of the Brooklyn Bridge jammed with traffic and people. "Then in a matter of days it has spread across the country." The image changed and an advertisement spoke of whiter teeth in just two weeks.

Steve shrugged. "The speed that this thing has spread, and the lack of information, has a lot of people panicked." Then he laughed. "But you still need a nice white smile."

His father frowned at him. "So many people are already sick. I heard local hospitals and governments can't get help to people who need it." He pointed to the crawl running along the bottom of the screen. "Look at that—a lot of businesses and services are already closed. Man, that is only causing more people to panic." Mr. McDaniel's annoyance was clear in his tone.

"I heard there were reports of riots in some of the larger cities." Steve shrugged, slowly rising to his feet to stretch out his back. "There were strange rumors coming out of Europe and Asia, I heard." He headed toward the closet. "Something about a complete breakdown in law and order. Some of the more populated places, like Mexico City, are under martial law." Steve didn't seem to feel much concern.

"Your new car is waiting for you at Draydon's Ford!" The cheerful advertisement concluded, followed by the theme music for the newscast.

The six o'clock pm news started with reports from Moscow. The international reporter explained the situation there. Anyone trying to leave the city, or those who were out on the streets without a pass, were being shot on sight. Tokyo's uninfected were being evacuated to the other islands, and even to Korea. Rumors had spread about a terrorist attack gone wrong. This led to violence in Detroit against its Muslim population. That in turn led to rioting and the fortification of several city blocks by the Muslims. The Detroit police were unable to respond because so many officers were too ill to come in to work. The fires had been burning for three days already. The mayor and governor had requested help from the National Guard, but they had received very little assistance as the military was spread so thin already.

"Where are you going?" Steve's father questioned, concern evident in his voice. He eyed Steve as if he was trying to get away with something.

Steve laughed. "The schools might be closed, but the distribution center is open."

"I really think you should stay home," replied his father. "I think we need to be ready to get out of town if things go bad. I told Beth to have Wes and his mother ready, but since Reg is sick, they don't want to leave."

"Dad, I'll be fine," Steve shrugged.

"Things are starting to get bad. I want to be sure you're safe."

"Seriously, Pops, we live in the most boring city in the state. What do you think is going to happen?" Steve gave his father a smile and a pat on the shoulder, Steve ignored a few muttered protests as he opened the hall closet. His coat wasn't in there. *Must have left it in my room.* He walked the short hall to his bedroom. The door to the room next to his was halfway open. Steve pushed it the rest of the way and leaned against the door frame. He looked in at his younger sister and shook his head, smiling. She was lying on her back, one knee up, with her other leg crossed over it, bouncing her foot. Her long hair lay in loose curls fanned out on her pillow. She was reading.

"Are you still reading that?" he asked. No answer came. "I thought you'd make it through a kiddy book like that quicker," he goaded. Beth looked over the top of the book. Steve was smirking at her. He knew calling it a kid's book would annoy her.

"This is the third book in the series, and it is NOT a kid's book," she responded with a growl.

"I thought you girls were into the mopey vampires, not the kiddy wizards." An aggravated huff was her reply. He knew he was getting to her, so he persisted. "Ya know, I hear the vampires are all sparkl....ow!" He was hit by a pillow thrown with excellent aim.

"You know I think that whiny girly stuff is crap!" She gave him her most menacing look. "Now knock it off!"

"Just kidding, Sis, relax!" He laughed. Now that he had her annoyed it was time to finish the job before he left for work. "So, uh, did Wes loan you that one too? By the way, I never did ask, how did your date with him go?" He asked in a would-be casual tone, picking at a spot on the door. She shut the book slowly. For a moment she glared at him but then her face softened.

"Since you seem sooo interested?" Now it was her turn to annoy him. "Feeling a little lonely?" There it was, the flicker of annoyance. She did not feel the need to press it. "If you must know, yes he did loan me this one as well." Then she sighed, "As far as the date, we didn't get together." His eyebrows rose yet before he could ask she explained. "Corey flattened his tires, then his mom wanted him to stay home to help her take care of Reg." She seemed to deflate as she spoke.

"So that Corey asshole messed with Wes' car?" He replied angrily,. "His brother was a dick too. Never liked that family. Seriously—you don't mess with someone's car."

She returned to her book. "The immature jerk. Because that will win me back, destroying my friend's property."

"That asshole."

"Yeah, he is." She sighed.

"So why did you date him?" Steve fired up at once.

"What does it matter? It's over now," she shot back. She wasn't about to be lectured by her brother.

"Well, let's see. He acted like he owned you. I never liked the way he treated you, and he always looked down on us. You know all he wanted to get from you…."

"Yeah, well he never got it!" she shot back angrily. "And even if he did, it is none of your business!"

"That only made him try harder," Steve huffed. "And it is my business. I'm your BIG Brother." He straightened up to emphasize his height. She laughed at the gesture.

"You…um, I can trust you and Wes, right?" Steve asked

"What do you mean?" She set her book aside, staring questioningly at her brother.

"I mean the more you… You and Wes have known each other forever… and you decide that he's the one. But believe me, Sis. I mean, Wes is great and all, but he may not be the guy for you for forever and…I just don't, um, think you should."

"NO!" She cut in. "Not that… which again, is none of your business, I…yes you can trust us. Not that you have any authority." This was getting weird. "I am not discussing this with my brother."

Steve began to turn toward his room. "I'm supposed to protect you. You know that, right?"

She rolled her eyes. "You've never been too good at that."

"Oh, please. I only lost you… what, three times?" he laughed.

"Four," she replied "and I am not a kid anymore, so you don't have to try to play big brother. Try taking care of yourself."

"I'm doing fine, and I think you guys are good together." He smirked.

"And why is that?" She waited for it.

"Because he is a total nerd. Just like you." There it was.

"I am not a nerd! Neither is he!" she shouted. "We are geeks."

"Steven! You're going to be late for work!" yelled their father. "And since you're not going to college you need this job."

"Don't start, Dad! I'll go next year," Steve grumbled.

"Great! So I can have two of you at school at the same time! Thanks for that."

"I thought you wanted me to stay home today?" Steve responded.

"That was before you started to fight with your sister," their father sighed.

"We're not fighting!" Steve and Beth both called. Then they started to laugh.

"We'll talk when I get home." Steve eyed his sister.

"Like I have to wait that long. You'll call me on your lunch break. Get a girlfriend, loser!" She laughed.

"Love ya, Sis. Maybe I can set up a *Lord of the Rings - Star Wars* date for you and Wes." He laughed and ducked out of the doorway as another pillow flew at him.

"Only if you play *Dungeons and Dragons* with us afterwards!" he heard her yell. "I know where you keep your twelve-sided dice!"

The smile that had played on her lips slowly slid off as she picked up her book. Finding her page, she stared, but she couldn't start to read. Why had she dated Corey and not Wes? She always told herself it was because Wes never tried to move forward. She guessed it was easier to convince herself that he just wanted to be friends. How had she missed it? Was she really that shallow?

What is Going On?

The group had already surrounded the cabin, with more of them coming out of the woods. John loaded his shotgun and watched as they closed in. He heard their thumping shuffles on the wooden porch. Spying through a gap in the dusty blinds, he noted that the main group continued past the tiny house along the wood's line. John slowly inched his way back from the window. A cool breeze stirred the dust in the room.

Fingernails scrapped across the old metal screens. He readied the gun, aiming at the open window. There was a thump on the door, followed by another. A slow pounding started on a window, and the continued scraping on the screen had John aiming from door to windows. He backed further and further into his room. The curtains rustled in the breeze, causing John to spin back toward the open window.

The breeze brought with it a foul stench of decay into the room. A ragged finger was caught in one of the holes in the screen. As it was withdrawn green-grey skin peeled off. Flies buzzed in through the hole as they crawled off the ragged flesh. Several pieces of skin clung to the barred metal. John blew out the breath he was holding. Metal screeched as the screen tore open. The hand the finger was attached to slid into the room. Sheets of flesh tore off while reaching in. Gagging on the stench and disgust, John's mind filled with terror. Rushing forward in panic and desperation, he slammed the window with all his might. The hand broke free from its owner, flopping uselessly to the floor. The pounding on the windows and door increased.

Surveying the hand, John smiled. His relief was short-lived as a window cracked. He waited for a moment, but the window held. He hurried down to the cellar. He returned with a small rifle and a handgun as well as several boards and a hammer. He hastily barricaded the door and windows. Grabbing boxes of shotgun shells and .22 bullets out of the closet, he loaded the guns to capacity. Shoving the barrel of the shotgun to the broken pane, he waited until one of them pressed their face against the glass.

Suddenly the air was filled with exploding flesh and the smell of gunpowder.

This is Not Going Well

"Dammit!" Wes grunted as he perused several websites advertising tires. Even the cheapest set was more than he could afford.

"Honey, I need your help, please," his mother called form the living room. Wes wearily walked over to the couch to check on Reg. He was pale and sweaty. "Can you make some more tea, please?" she asked.

Wes watched from the kitchen. His mother was attempting to get Reg to drink something. Wes hurried back to his mother's side, handing her the warm beverage.

"Reg, honey, try to drink this. It will make you feel better."

"My head… hurts so bad…" Reg moaned.

Wes ran to the bathroom to grab a bottle of aspirin. Shaking several bottles on the counter and floor, he found they were all empty. Frustrated he ran a washcloth under some cold water. He found his mother on the phone, tears in her eyes. "I'm on hold. The recording says the wait time is 2 hours!" she cried, hanging up. Tears spilled onto her cheeks. She swiped them away, trying not to let Wes see. He pretended not to notice while he knelt down next to Reg.

"I'm sorry, we are out of aspirin," Wes explained, placing the cloth on Reg's sweat-soaked forehead. "I will run out to get some later." Wes covered his nose, pretending to scratch, because Reg's putrid breath turned his stomach. Reg's skin was like marble, grey and white, hanging slack on his face. His lips were white and chapped. A shudder ran through Wes as he felt the cold hand of his stepfather take his hand.

"I'm okay," his words were barely a whisper. "You shouldn't try to go anywhere."

"Unbelievable!" Wes turned to see his mother's look of anxiety and anger. "How can I get an ambulance if I can't even get someone on the phone for several hours?"

Wes remembered the news and his talk with Beth. Looking from his mother to his stepfather, he made his way to the kitchen. Standing next to his mother, he turned his back to Reg. He whispered, "I heard this morning… they said there is no room in the emergency rooms so we can't take him there. The hospitals are all full."

"So what do we do?" she whimpered.

Their whispered conversation was instantly cut short when Reg sat up. They waited, but he simply moaned and lay back down on the couch. "My stomach… so hungry," he groaned.

"I'll make you some soup." Wes' mother perked up. "He hasn't eaten since he got sick."

"Anything I can do to help?" Wes asked.

"No honey, I…no, that's okay." She patted him on the arm and began to bustle around the kitchen. Wes looked over at Reg. His eyes were closed as he lay motionless on the couch. Trying to shake the fear building in him, Wes wandered back upstairs to his room.

Sitting on the edge of his bed, he became lost in worries. A vibration followed by a familiar tune caused him to jump. Frantically he fumbled in his pocket to extricate his phone.

"Wes, have you seen the news?" Beth demanded without preamble.

"No—well, I heard the hospitals are all full. Mom was told it would be hours before even 911 would answer. What have you heard? What is happening? Have they made any progress in finding a cure? Dad is really bad off."

"No, in fact, they don't seem to know anything. People are locking themselves in their houses or trying to get out of the cities." Wes could hear the strain in her voice. "It is crazy out there. People are walking around with surgical masks on. They said people should avoid contact. Then the CDC said something about hand sanitizer seeming to speed up the infection." As Beth spoke her tone became more panicked.

"Yeah, Mom heard that already. She threw out every bottle in the house. I swear she was a junkie on that stuff. She was always on me to use it. She must have thrown out like ten bottles." Wes sighed. He rubbed his face with his free hand. "Beth, I don't know what Mom'll do if something happens to him."

For a second neither spoke. "He is my dad, you know? More of a father than that other bastard ever was," Wes continued as a tear ran down his cheek.

From downstairs a painful hacking cough traveled to Wes' ears. He listened as his mother fussed over his stepfather. "I'm worried."

"I know, but he'll be okay." Beth's gentle voice soothed him, but something sounded as if she didn't believe it.

"He's never hit us or gotten drunk; I think I've seen him have like two beers the entire time they've been married." Wes was rambling and Beth let him. This was all information she already knew. Wes had basically lived at the McDaniel house when he was much younger. Beth's father had actually beaten up Wes' real father at one point, right after Wes' mother finally got the courage to kick him out. Reg loved Wes' mother, and Wes loved him for being so good to her.

"Thanks for always being there for me." Wes smiled into the phone.

"Thanks for being there for me. I will never forget what you did when Mom died. Without you Steve would have done all the cooking, and that might have been the end of us all." She gave a laugh. squelching the sob that threatened.

A long silence stretched, interrupted only by the sounds of coughing and moaning from downstairs.

Beth broke the void, "Aunt Marge just arrived."

"What? Oh, the book! Yeah, it starts to get fun from there."

They spent several minutes discussing the books and the first two movies they had watched together. The conversation was enjoyable. Both forget how worried and scared they were. That was until Reg started coughing again, a dry and rasping cough that sounded truly painful.

"I gotta go. I need to help Mom. It sounds like we need to get Dad to a hospital, even if we have to take a number."

Beth tried to talk him out of going, but in the end, she could only wish him luck. "Remember, if things get bad, Dad will get us out of town." She said goodbye. Wes sat in his room, listening as Reg coughed and coughed then moaned. With each cough, Wes grew more scared. His mother called for him. He was on his feet at the top of the stairs when he heard Reg start coughing and coughing, and then suddenly stop. Wes froze with his hand on the rail, his foot hanging in the air above the next step.

Another Night at Work

Steve got into the car and turned the key. The engine purred to life. The radio came on. It was news on all the channels. Nonstop talk about the illness and how the cities were having trouble with rioting. Steve selected his iPod. After that he was happily oblivious, off in his own world for the rest of the trip.

So far, the ride across town to the distribution center had been uneventful. The roads were empty, with very few people daring to venture out. The few people Steve saw hurried about wearing surgical-type masks. He shook his head as he saw them. That sanitizer stuff would just make people susceptible to this kinda crap. See, he looked at the steering wheel, I rarely wash my hands, and I feel fine! He scoffed, holding up his hands as if that proved everything.

"Beth, I hear you calling." He smiled to himself as the song began to play. He was happy his sister was done with Corey. "That guy was a douche," he muttered. He passed a car parked oddly on the sidewalk. He knew Wes has been in love with her for forever. More importantly, he trusted the guy. Even if it didn't work out, Wes would show her how a boyfriend should treat her.

Something caught his eye down a side street. He slowed slightly. It looked like a fight. There were three or four people all crowding around someone on the ground. Steve reached for his phone. He was about to dial when he heard the police siren. I guess someone already called that in. He accelerated and thought no more about it.

At the next block the light was turning red. As he slowed to a stop, he was surprised by two Harleys thudding loudly to a stop next to him. He glanced over at the steel and chrome-covered machines. One bike was covered by a burly bearded guy who looked the part. The other bike had two people on it. The rider was a smaller guy. His jacket looked almost new. On the back of the bike was a girl. Steve admired her figure. She was covered in leather from head to foot. She shouted something at the big guy and laughed. Steve noticed she was kind of pretty; at least he imagined she was. All he could see were her eyes under the full-face helmet.

She had the visor up to be heard. She had intensely blue eyes. His mind began to wander. The thunder of the engines startled him. The bikes roared off, leaving Steve staring at the green light.

He watched them ride away, the taillights getting smaller and smaller. His mind still on the girl, he pushed in the clutch and shifted into first gear. Beth was right, he seriously needed to find a girlfriend.

Letting out the clutch, he began to accelerate, thinking about catching up with the bikes. No more than the thought had crossed his mind , "SHIT!" he yelped, jerking the wheel hard to avoid hitting a woman who stumbled out into the intersection. Jerking the wheel straight and barking the tires angrily, Steve gave the woman the finger. "Watch out, you fucking drunk!" he shouted through the closed window as he pulled away. The woman stumbled after him for a few paces, then continued her slow shuffle across the street.

"Moron," he muttered angrily. Accelerating down the road, he scanned ahead for the bikes, but saw nothing. Disappointed, he cursed the stumbling woman out again in his head. He really wanted to see the face that held those eyes. Then the idea of the huge brute on the other bike made him think maybe he was better off not finding them. The fact that they were nowhere in sight was one thing. The complete lack of anyone else out and about was something else entirely. This started to bother him. Maybe things were as bad as they were saying.

Making his way down the empty streets felt eerie. Normally this trip should have taken longer. Shops were closed. There was no one out, no one at all. The last person he had seen was the drunken woman. He began to wonder where the bikers had been going and whether he should follow. To his surprise, he arrived at his destination.

Steve pulled into the parking lot. He found a space easily. Surveying the lot, he noticed how many spaces were empty. His mood soared. Even though he was early he knew the lot was more sparsely populated than normal. That meant more work to be done. It also meant possible overtime. Hitting the fob, he smiled as the alarm beeped. The headlights winked at him. Checking his phone, he saw he was at least ten minutes early, even with leaving late. Imagine how early he would have been if he hadn't been bothering Beth! He headed into the front office to clock in. He decided to grab a cup of coffee before jumping into his day.

As soon as he walked into the building he was met by Rachel Smyth, who was coming down the hall. Rachel was one of the managers. She was in her early fifties, a little plump but with a pleasant happy face. She was one of Steve's favorites. No nonsense and tough as nails, but she was fair and actually a lot of fun to be around if you did your job and didn't whine. Being a hard worker, Steve was one of those employees she got on well with.

"Hi Stevie, how are you doing this late afternoon?" she asked with a smile.

"Just happy to be alive," he responded.

"Glad that is the case. How is your family? Anyone sick?"

"No, we are all fine. How is yours?"

"My husband has called complaining of a bad headache. He wants me to stop and pick up something on the way home." She shrugged.

"Better raid the medicine cabinet here. I hear all the pharmacies have been cleaned out."

"I got it covered." Rachel winked, reaching into her pocket to reveal a handful of aspirin packets. "Are we going to see your sister again this summer? She was such a help last year," she continued as they moved down the hall. "I wasn't sure what her plans were."

"Well she is headed to college next year so I guess she might try to get something here part time. You know, to pick up some extra money before school starts," he shrugged.

"Well, she is always welcome. Have a good shift if I don't see you before I leave." She gave him a wave as she headed off to her office.

"Yeah, have a good night, talk to you later." Steve returned her wave with a smile, then headed outside to the loading area. He sighed, kicked a few rocks across the pavement, then swung into the seat of his forklift. Do I really want to work here the rest of my life? He thought, maybe I should get my act together. Suck it up and go back to school. Community college maybe, to help Dad out so Beth can go to State like she has always wanted to. He frowned bitterly as he lifted a container off a truck. Yeah sure, maybe this time you won't screw it up, Steve.

City Hall

Devin Kranser left the conference room shaking. "How in the hell could we evacuate the entire city?" he muttered, walking over to the huge picture window looking out across the town. His head rested on his arm. He looked down at the street. "This town is in a bowl," he sighed, "there is no easy way out of here." He gazed up from the street to the mountains.

The valley stretched out between two mountains, which that sloped steeply after a few hundred blocks of housing. That limited the access on two fronts. Added to the mountains were the rivers. Three of them converged into a rapids, which cut off a third exit. This was an old steel town, built here for the raw materials more than for ease of access. The mills had used the railroads. The railroads were already becoming disused before highways made trucks the preferred form of transport. Nowadays only rarely did a train leave on the remaining line. "Train might still be an option." Devin rubbed his face as he thought of the plans sitting in his office. It was a proposal asking the state to finally connect the town to the interstate—and the rest of the world. He sighed.

There were really only two ways in or out of the valley. Both had bridges to cross. One led to a two-lane road up into the mountains. The other road was the one that led to the highway. It was two lanes in either direction. There was a bottleneck in a small town five miles away. After that it was smooth sailing for two miles, where it then met up with the interstate.

That was a long way to go, and that bottleneck was going to wreak havoc. He slammed his fist on the windowsill. One access to the highway that slowed down on the best of days. Frustration pounded behind his eyes. Sure, some roads went up the mountain, and eventually some other roads would lead to the highway. He pinched the bridge of his nose, trying to quell the pressure. If people panicked, and they would, they could easily get trapped. They were going to get trapped! He closed his eyes, letting his arms fall to his side. Devin rested his head on the cool glass. The memories of what he had just heard crashed back over him. "We are going to have to evacuate the city. The rioting is out of control. People are attacking and killing each other. The police, and even what little help the national guard has sent, have been completely over-whelmed." The strained voice had crackled through the speakerphone in the middle of the large oak conference table. The faces of those sitting around it were pale and tight. "The CDC is saying the epidemic is causing people to go crazy and get violent. The police have started shooting the rioters. We are trying to get the uninfected citizens out."

A female voice broke through on the speaker, "One of our evacuation sites has already been overrun. The Army...started shooting everyone there. Then they...they just took off, leaving hundreds."

Another voice cut in. "It is the same as in Philadelphia. Riots and people going crazy."

The first voice was back. "You need to get a plan in place. Start moving people out before things blow up there."

A man's rushed voice broke in. "We are packing it up here. The Governor has already been moved. I have a helicopter to catch. God help us all." There was a click, followed by a moment of silence.

Then voices were talking over each other. The conference call continued even after the emergency management director in Har-risburg hung up in a panic. They had lost contact with the Altoona mayor halfway through Philadelphia's explanation of the situation. They had heard screaming, and then the line went dead. The Gov-ernor had been in Washington that morning and informed them the President had already been evacuated. Now she had also been moved and could no longer be contacted. They were on their own.

Devin looked down at his hands. He had no idea where to start. It was time to take action. So Devin decided he had damn well better find the start. He had left the meeting when the mayor and some senior staff began talking about acceptable losses. Devin had to get some air.

These were people he knew, people he worked for. How could there be...no, there is no such thing as acceptable losses. "This is crazy," Devin told his reflection. Taking a deep breath, he headed back toward the door. Before his hand touched the knob it flung open revealing a rather disheveled mayor.

Mayor Martin Griggs had been mayor for as long as anyone could remember. He had once been a professional athlete. He now enjoyed the finer things in life and his waistline reflected it. As a good mayor, no one said he didn't work hard. He been a champion for the city, attempting to bring in new industry and attractions to his town, sometimes by questionable means, it was rumored. Although charges of corruption were often made by his detractors, they never stuck. Nor did they keep him from being re-elected. No one actually doubted he truly cared for *his* city.

"Devin! Christ, you gave me a start. We need to handle this and fast. How long do you think it will take to organize an evacuation?" the mayor asked, pulling a pack of cigarettes out of his pocket.

"To where?" Devin' questioned.

Mayor Griggs lit the cigarette, inhaled deeply, and stared at Devin for what felt like a full minute. "I don't have any idea. What do you suggest?" he asked, the smoke rolling out as he spoke.

From behind the mayor, the deputy mayor spoke up. "We have the national guard post just outside of town. We have been very, uh, accommodating to the soldiers over the years." He adjusted his tie uncomfortably. "The base commander knows this. We should contact him." He rolled his shoulders. "You know, find out what the military is doing. Maybe they can help the evacuation."

Griggs scratched his temple, flicking ash unto the floor. The deputy mayor gave him a disapproving look. "Fucking sue me," the mayor grumbled.

"We need a plan." He took another drag from the cig. Clapping his hands, he said, "So! Devin, go to the traffic control center. Get one in place. Report back to me in...20 minutes." Mayor Griggs puffed, "You," he jabbed the cigarette at the deputy mayor, "Get Colonial Miller on the damn phone. I want to talk to that son of a bitch." He dropped his cigarette on the marble floor, crushing it out with his shoe. The deputy mayor wrinkled his nose at the act but said nothing. Mayor Griggs rolled his eyes. He shook his head at the other man's back. "Fucking kids," he muttered.

Devin headed down the hall while the mayor returned to the conference room. Before the door shut Devin heard, "Miller, its Martin, what the hell are you gonna do to help us out?"

Devin's thoughts were scattered. So he focused on the task at hand, getting the control center up and running. The control center, what a joke! He frowned and stopped outside a door, glancing up. An old sign hung out over the door. It read "Cafeteria". Pushing the door, open he could still smell the old cooking grease. In the darkened room, he looked around at the blue glow of the monitors set up around the room.

The monitors were fed by the five traffic cameras that had been placed around town. Devin glanced at the large logo of the local TV station. It was lit up. A chair and tripod sat in front of it. The station had helped to pay for the cameras. This of course was done so the station could use the cameras for "exclusive" traffic reports. This always made Devin laugh. They were the only TV station in town, so of course it was exclusive. The other two stations were in the bigger towns, twenty miles to the east, so why would they care about this town's traffic?

He focused his attention on the main camera, which showed the interchange for the connecting road to the highway. Devin slumped onto a chair. What was the best way out of town for Cheryl and the kids? He pondered.

It must have hit the news. The traffic heading out of the city seemed to have doubled in the brief time he'd sat there. He glanced around at the other monitors. Something caught his eye. He couldn't help but stare at the screen in wonder.

The downtown square was full of people. The square had been empty for the last two days as people hid themselves away to avoid getting sick. It was never this full on a Monday, even when everyone was healthy.

What are you all doing do there? Devin asked the monitor. The crowd was acting strange. They were just milling about. No one seemed to be talking to each other; they were just walking around, some even bumping into each other, but they didn't seem to notice. Devin thought back to what he had heard from Philly and Pittsburgh about violence and rioting. People here just seemed confused.

Picking up the phone, he pressed the three-digit extension for the mayor and waited. "What have you got, Dev?"

"I...well, it is already getting bad. People are streaming out of town. We should open up the incoming lanes to outgoing traffic...Also, and this is weird, the square is full of people." Devin stood to get a better look at the scene. "It's really strange. They just seem to be wandering around, you know bumping into each other, but no one is fighting. Not like we heard about in Philly."

"Shit!" the mayor gasped. "Get SWAT down there as fast as..."

"No! They aren't rioting. They are... well, they are just, they're... they look drunk." Devin tried to reassure his boss. "They are just wandering around and stumbling over each other." Devin spoke fast. "If we send in more people it might start a riot. Or do you think they'll get worked up and start attacking each other?" Devin blurted, now unsure what to do.

"Dammit, Devin! Figure out a way to get people out of town," Griggs yelled over Devin's growing panic. "Make sure you avoid the square! We'll send the police to block off the area. Get barricades set up in a one block radius. They won't hurt each other, but God help anyone who goes near them!" The phone clicked dead. Devin stared at the silent receiver and returned it to the cradle.

"What is going on?" He spoke to the empty room, fear bubbling in his stomach. "What did he mean they won't hurt each other, but will hurt anyone who gets near?" he asked the monitor. His attention was captivated by the people in the square.

He did not notice the screen in the lower left. It showed a car barreling toward the camera. A woman was desperately fighting a thrashing child. It clawed at her, with pure rage on its small face as it fought against its restraint. The woman's silent scream was not observed as the child lurched forward, ripping free of the seat belt. The screen suddenly went blue. The words "No Signal" appeared in the corner.

End of a Chapter

Beth realized she had been staring at the first three words at the beginning of the new chapter for about ten minutes. This is ridiculous! she thought, slamming the book shut. Everything is going to be fine! This is no different from Swine Flu, West Nile, SARS and all those other epidemics or pandemics or whatever. This is America; we don't die from that kind of stuff, Beth told herself, fighting the thoughts of death.

Giving up on reading, she lay on her bed staring at the book's cover. A smile crossed her face as the words she had just thought met her ears from the TV in the other room. "Damn right," she breathed. Reopening the book, she found her place. It was at the beginning of the chapter.

Five minutes later she had made it half a paragraph in. "Errgh!" Roughly stuffing a bookmark between the pages, she slammed the book shut. In frustration, she sat up exclaiming to the stuffed rabbit beside her, I've had enough of this. I'm going over there to settle this. His stepdad is sick, but he'll be fine. Just like when Dad and Steve get sick. They are men. She grabbed the bunny by the shoulders, staring it right in the eyes. They act tough until they get the sniffles and then they need all the help they can get. We'll load him up and head out of town until this all settles down.

She dropped the bunny when she got up. She grabbed her backpack off the floor, slipped the book inside. "Hey Dad, I'm going to walk over to Wes's and hang out for a little bit," she yelled down the hall. She threw on her jacket, about to grab the backpack.

"I really don't want...." the crash of shattering glass interrupted her father's response. "Who the hell are you?" her father yelled. "Get the hell out of my house!"

Beth ran into the living room. Her sneakers skidded to a halt at the entry. She stood frozen, as the scene before her eyes was impossible. Two men, covered in blood, were wrestling with her father. A woman stumbled through the shattered sliding glass door after them. Her bare feet crunched and cracked the broken glass. It was their neighbor Mrs. McGee, but there was something very wrong.

Her face was torn and bloody, her arm had a piece missing and blood oozed from her cut feet with each step. She walked slowly, seemingly unaware of any of her injuries. The commotion of the struggle caught her attention. She turned. The bloodied woman shuffled quickly towards Beth's father to join the others in the attack.

"Beth! Run! Get out! Get out!" her father screamed. One of his attackers bit him in the face. Mr. McDaniel threw the man off. The body crashed onto the coffee table, sending broken wood splintering across the room. Beth screamed. She took a step toward her father. He turned, pointed behind her. "BETH, RUN!" he screamed with ferocity.

Mrs. McGee turned her grey eyes on Beth, lunging at her. The woman who had once been her babysitter, the woman who had never missed Beth's birthday, who waved at her as she left each morning, was now coming at her with teeth bared. Her face was a mask of anger and hunger.

Mrs. McGee raised her arms, reaching out for Beth. As the limbs came up her left arm cracked at the elbow. Beth cried out as Ms. McGee's forearm fell free of her shirt to the floor. Beth was pressed against the wall and saw past the approaching woman to her father. The man who had been thrown onto the coffee table had a large chunk of wood sticking out of his shoulder. He leaned in and sunk his teeth into Mr. McDaniel's throat. "Beth... Gooooo ARRRGG." Blood sprayed the white living room wall. It looked like the two men were ripping him apart even as he fought them.

If it wasn't for Mrs. McGee's fingers pulling at Beth's hair, she would have stood there watching the horror. Her heart pounding in terror, Beth ran for the front door. She heard more glass breaking. Her head turned to the sound. In Steve's room she saw a girl from down the block trying to getting through the window. This girl was also covered in blood. Beth's shaking fingers fumbled with the dead bolt. It clicked free. Beth threw open the door, to immediately freeze at the scene from a war movie before her eyes.

Cars screamed down the street and people were running from their homes. Some people stumbled about bleeding. Across the street there were three people crouched over a fourth, who was still clawing to get away. It looked as though they were trying to eat him. Their hands, covered in blood, seemed to be pulling bits of him to their mouths.

Beth was pulled off balance as the shoulder strap of her backpack tightened. She didn't even remember throwing it over her shoulder. Beth stumbled into the door frame. Spinning around, she saw Mrs. McGee lose her grip. Reality hit her hard in the face. Beth let out a scream. She shot ran from the door, the backpack now swinging from her arm. Out in the yard she looked left and right and had no idea where to run.

A car tore around the corner. It sped straight toward her. It was coming fast as it jumped the curb and went into a skid, sliding on the grass. The tires threw mud and grass into the air. Beth's feet slipped and slid as she stumbled backward, terrified of being hit yet not wanting to back up too close to the house.

The well-manicured lawn was shredded as the station wagon skidded to a halt right in front of her. The passenger side door flew open. "Get in! Beth McDaniel! Get! In! The! Car!"

Beth took a step cautiously. A howl from behind her snapped Beth out of her shock, and she jumped in, slamming the door. Immediately she was thrown back against the seat. The car accelerated for a moment. She was thrown forward as the vehicle suddenly stopped. More dirt and grass flew in the air as the tires clawed at the lawn, trying to get traction.

Beth urged the car forward as Mrs. McGee approached. The woman's face smacked against the window. Beth yelped, jumping away and knocking into the driver, who barely noticed. The front tires bit into the concrete of the driveway and Beth was again thrown back in her seat. The car lurched forward as it squealed back onto the street, leaving a muddy, bloody streak on the window from Mrs. McGee's hand.

Beth watched her former neighbor grow smaller in the side view mirror as they sped away. Turning from the mirror to the window, she watched the road as cars and people flew by. She looked down at her lap. She played with the clasp of backpack. Realizing she was in a speeding car, she looked over at the driver.

"Mr. Reager?" she stuttered in shock.

"Are you hurt? Did they bite you?" he asked frantically.

"No...... Oh God, no, Dad!" She turned in her seat to look out the back window. She couldn't see her house. All she saw was a chaotic street and an empty backseat.

"Where is Denny?" she asked, turning back to the front. Mr. Reager didn't say anything as he hurled the car down the road, missing an oncoming truck by inches.

"Dead," he finally replied. He turned the car toward downtown and the road to the highway.

Nice Night for a Ride

Kate was curled up in the large chaise lounge in the living room. She was reading a heavy leather-bound copy of *The Lord of The Rings* her father had given her.

"You've got to be kidding," she said to the man standing in front of her. He held out her jacket. She let the book fall into her lap.

'What? Why not?" Martin asked his daughter.

"I don't know…It just feels inappropriate." She shrugged but had already put in the bookmark. She slipped on the thick black leather jacket. "Was this your idea?"

The rumble from outside answered her question. She shook her head, smiling all the while. "Bear's idea, then? Are we going to be making any stops along the way?"

"Maybe, why?"

"Because if we are traipsing all over the war memorial, these," she pointed to the purple Converse high top canvas sneakers, "are coming with us."

Martin crossed the room, heading back to the closet. The front door opened. A huge hairy man entered the room. "Bear" grunted a greeting. Kate barely straightened up from untying her shoes to give him a wave in return. He passed Martin as he headed straight to the kitchen. Martin dropped a pair of boots by Kate's feet as he followed Bear. Pulling on the boots, Kate threw her shoes into her pack then joined the two men.

"Totally empty out there," Bear was explaining, "Should be a great ride up the mountain to the memorial."

The memorial was the huge monument to the fallen soldiers from the area who had been killed in war. Bear's father's and Kate's grandfather's names were on that monument, as were several of Martin and Bear's friends.

"Are you sure this is a good idea?" she asked, even as she zipped up the jacket and pulled the straps of the pack over her shoulders.

Bear downed his glass of water, his smile barely visible through his thick beard. Patting Kate on the head, he said, "Kit, when isn't a good idea to ride?" He was past her and out the door before she could answer.

Kate laughed, shaking her head at his back. She knew Bear owned a car, but in all the time she had known him, he never drove it. "I swear he would ride in the snow if he could."

"I think he has," her father laughed. Martin held the door to the garage open for his daughter. Kate thanked him with a laugh. He gave her a short bow. She hit the button to open the garage. She passed the expensive German luxury car. Martin stopped at the shining Harley Electra Glide. Kate hurried around her older Honda Accord to grab her helmet. Pulling her hair back in a ponytail with several bands on it into a faux braid, she watched her father get the bike ready. The huge cycle roared to life and then purred loudly. Kate allowed herself a second to listen the rhythm of the pistons.

Adjusting her hair, she slipped the helmet over her head. Martin clicked the remote to close the garage door as Kate hopped onto the bike behind him.

"Ready?" he shouted over the rumbling engine.

She bonked her helmet against his in affirmation.

Martin pulled in the clutch, clicked the bike into first. As they eased down the driveway a smile broke out over Kate's face. As the bike accelerated, she yelled, "Swing by the Harley shop." Her excitement was growing. "I want to see my girl."

Martin nodded. Bear pulled up next to them. The two bikes rumbled down the empty street of the neighborhood. Reaching a stop light, Martin told Bear of the side trip downtown. "Getting anxious to get your own?" Bear laughed.

Kate just smiled at him. "I don't want to hang on to my dad forever."

"I'll miss having my girl with me." Martin smiled over at Bear.

"Don't worry; I'll still ride with you, just on my own bike."

"They gotta grow up sometime, Marty." Bear gruffed. "But Kit, don't be so quick to let your dad go."

"Seriously, I'm twenty and it might be time I..."

"You'll always be an itty bitty princess to me, and a daddy's girl," Bear laughed. Kate's reply was drowned out by the roar of engines when the light turned green. Bear pulled quickly away. Slapping down her visor, Kate chuckled at him. "Coward, you knew you were going to get an earful," she thought.

The smile on Kate's face faltered as they continued toward town. Empty street after empty street flew by. They had not seen another vehicle on the road since they left the house.

"This is just eerie," she thought. A small laugh escaped as she thought, "But this is the safest I've felt riding through town." She looked at all the empty cross streets. Nobody on a cell phone, looking in the wrong direction, or not stopping at a stop sign. Tonight it was just two bikes rumbling through a ghost town.

The light ahead turned red. Martin slowed to a stop; Bear pulled up next to them in the same lane. A beautiful red Mustang eased to a stop next to them. Kate glanced over at the car. "Not bad," she thought about both the car and the driver.

"So when we pick up your bike, do you think they'll have training wheels for you?" Bear laughed, grabbing Kate's attention.

"I just figured I'd borrow the ones you took off your bike last week." Kate shot back with a laugh. She glanced over at the Mustang driver. He was looking at her. "He *is* cute," she thought as her eyes caught his.

Bear's barking laugh was covered by the roar of the bike's engines as the light turned. Martin followed. Kate noticed the Mustang didn't move. "I wonder if he is thinking about following us?" The thought quickly left her mind as she noticed they were only a couple of blocks from the Harley shop.

A few more minutes on the empty streets, and then they were pulling into the completely empty lot. The store's sign was off, the inside was dimly lit; it appeared to be closed. This was not a surprise, as most businesses had closed early; some had been closed for a couple of days due to the illness.

Even though she was disappointed at the dark shop, Kate was off her father's bike in a flash. All thoughts of empty streets and cute boys in cools cars were gone. She only had eyes for the glistening chrome and steel with the sold sign that she knew was just inside the door.

She peered through the huge picture window searching for her bike. Her hand found her wallet in her jacket. She could almost see the motorcycle endorsement printed on her license. She had passed the safety course a couple of weeks ago. She had picked out her bike. Worked all summer to save up for it. On Monday the three of them would return to pick it up. A long and twisty ride was planned for that day.

Her imagination had her twisting the throttle through a turn, the road rushing by her feet. She didn't even hear her Martin and Bear walk up behind her.

"I haven't seen her this excited since that Lego set came out a few years back," Martin laughed.

"I still can't believe she went for the blue one. I thought sure she wanted a pink one."

Kate spun around to glare up at Bear. He took a step back, holding up his hands in mock defense, a broad smile playing under his beard. "I have never," she poked him in his broad chest, "and will never," another poke, and the large man backed up a step, "liked pink." Kate emphasized her point by punching him in the shoulder, repeatedly.

"Call her off, Marty, call her off!"

Martin laughed, "You got yourself into this, you get yourself out."

"Okay, okay, you don't like pink," Bear laughed. "I'm still buying you a basket for the front."

"Dork!" Kate said, shaking her head. She was trying and failing to not let the smile break out. With one last punch she turned back to the store. A flash on chrome caught her attention. A light appeared through a doorway in the back of the shop. "Hey look, Dusty is here." She pointed the light out to the two men. Banging on the window to get his attention, she yelled for him.

Dusty Rhode's head snapped up at the noise. He looked to the window. He saw Kate, and she smiled and waved at him. He hesitated for a second, looked down at his hands and shirt. Without returning the wave he disappeared back through the door.

Kate turned to look at the other two, who wore the same confused expression she did. "That was weird."

"Maybe he isn't supposed to be here?" Bear wondered.

"Huh." Kate she stared back into the ever-darkening store.

The crunch of gravel told her that the two men were heading back to their bikes. A cold wind whipped her hair over her face. She shivered slightly but wasn't entirely sure it was the wind.

"Come on Kate, let's get going," Martin called over the starting of his machine.

Kate stood staring between her bike and the closed door. Something was amiss. When they had been here on every other occasion, Dusty would go out of his way to talk to them, to the point that they had to make excuses to get away from him. Now he didn't even return a wave?

A bike revved. "We can pick you up Monday if you like," Bear shouted over the engine.

Kate returned to the bike. "Hold on a sec." Another cool breeze had caused her to zip her jacket up all the way. She opened one of the hard bags on Martin's bike and pulled out a pair of heavy leather pants. She pulled them on over her jeans and jumped on the back of the bike. Pulling on her helmet, she bonked her dad to let him know she was ready.

"Can we go now?" Bear complained, throwing his hands in the air. Kate waved him off while Martin put the bike in gear.

In the back of the store, Dusty peered through a small gap in the door. He watched the taillights disappear from the lot. He looked down at the bloody wrench on the table and his blood-covered hands and shirt. Would they have believed him? Behind Dusty, the service manager lay on the floor. The front of his head was caved in. Dusty's fingers rubbed lightly on the blood-soaked cloth covering the bite he had received from the slain man. He flinched at the pain. The wound was already feeling very hot while Dusty's head began to ache.

Back on the road, Bear's unease grew with each block now. He had noticed the small group of people as they left the Harley shop. They had been slowly wandering down the block. Something about the way they moved bothered him. They just…weren't right. "Probably bunch a meth heads," he grumbled to the wind.

The further they rode the more they saw. Up ahead was a woman hanging onto a signpost. Down a side street there were four or five of them wandering down the middle of the road.

"What do you reckon? The sick have started wandering about?" Martin shouted the question at the next stop light.

"What the hell is wrong with everyone?" Bear returned. His eyes went wide, "Marty! Kate! Look out!" He was pointing behind them.

Martin's head snapped in the direction Bear pointed. A bloody man in a suit stumbled off the sidewalk toward them. He reached out, grabbing Kate's forearm. It felt like a vice closing on her. Kate screamed. Martin revved the engine and let go of the clutch. The front wheel of the heavy bike left the ground. Kate fell back painfully against the metal of the backrest. Her free arm held tightly to her father, his left arm holding tightly to hers as he felt her being pulled sideways.

Kate cried out in pain as she was being wrenched from the seat. The bloody man stumbled to keep up but lost his grip, falling hard on the pavement. Kate could still feel his hand gripping her. She knew her arm would be bruised. Even with the pain, she wrapped it tightly back around her father as the bike increased in speed.

The two bikes flew down the road. Everywhere they looked, bloody and battered people seemed to be materializing out of nowhere. Bear nearly ran down a kid who was blindly wandering across the road dragging a skateboard behind him with one arm. His other arm was missing.

Martin was ahead now. He motioned to take a side street. They barely made the turn when they were faced with a wall of people. Smoke billowed from the bike's rear tire, rubber screeched, and Martin shouted while Kate screamed. The heavy Electra Glide slammed into the bloody wall of the stumbling horde. The handlebars snapped out of Martin's hands, twisting sideways. The bike lurched. Kate lost her grip on her father. For a moment she was airborne, leaving the back of the bike. Time slowed. She twisted in the air while hands reached out, grabbing at her and Martin. Then time caught up. Pain exploded in her back and fireworks burst before her eyes. She slammed onto the pavement, rolling painfully, her shoulders slamming one then the other onto the ground. She slid from there, until she was stopped by knocking down a woman who had been standing in the road.

The woman fell heavily across Kate's legs. Kate's helmet slammed into the ground again. She was sick and dizzy. She had landed in a reclining position due to her backpack, and her neck ached as it hung in the air, unsupported. The world spun. She felt as if she were just waking—that had to be it. That was the only explanation for what had just happened. It was a dream, a nightmare.

Reality crashed down in the form of pain, a pain that was shooting through her leg. The woman Kate had knocked down now had a grip on her thigh. The woman's teeth pinched the flesh like a clamp. She was trying to bite through the thick leather pants. Kate's knee felt like it was being ripped off. Then her arm was in a vice and being pulled up to a man's mouth. Fingers dug at her chest, trying to rip through her jacket.

Then in a blur of motion and sound, the woman at Kate's knee flew backward. The woman's head nearly separated from her body. To Kate's horror, the eyes still followed her every movement. A huge arm reached down, lifting Kate off the ground, into the air, then hard onto her feet. Hands still clawed at her, and fingers tangled in her hair. Her arm was still being held by a disheveled man. Kate screamed in agony. Her shoulder felt as if it was separating from her body.

Another blur of motion, and the ringing of metal like a bell. The man lost his grip on Kate's arm. She was in the air again, and then her breath was gone as she slammed onto Bear's shoulder. She fought to gain air as she was bumped along. Her back cried out in protest as she was slammed onto the back rest of his bike. She barely got her leg over before she was smashed between Bear and the sissy bar.

"Dad! DAD! Where's Dad?" Kate pounded on Bear's huge back. She could see her father's bike on its side. She watched his boots twitching next to it. Her father was completely covered by people.

The engine roared, tires screamed, dirt and gravel spit while the tires fought for traction. The front wheel left the ground for a second; Kate was crushed between the huge man and the seat again. She tried to turn to look back as Bear flew down the road. Tears streamed down her face from the pain of her body and knowing they couldn't help her father.

Time to Clock Out

Steve rubbed his eyes, then the back of his neck. So far the early part of his shift at the distribution center had been its usual mundane repetition. He was using one of the larger forklifts to stack empty shipping containers. The work was boring and Steve's mind was wandering. He was back on the football field; the stadium at the college roared. He was dropping back to pass. It was first and goal with seconds left on the clock. This pass would win the game and the division. CRASH! The container he was moving slammed down harder than it should on the loading dock.

Shaking out of his fantasy, he tried to play off the blunder. "Damn! I need a break. Hey Brad, let's get a cup a coffee." He shouted to the man who was passing on another forklift.

Brad Stevens was an older man. He had a short grey ponytail that framed the bald top of his head. He slowed his lift, thought for a second, then grimaced, "Yeah, alright, be right there."

"Well, only if it isn't too much trouble," Steve laughed, and jumped down from his machine. Brad waved him off as Steve passed by on his way toward the office. Halfway there, Brad jogged up to join him, slapping Steve on the back.

"Figured it was about break time. You woke me up with that last container." Brad laughed.

Steve looked over at Brad's ponytail and bald head. "When you gonna cut that thing off? You look like a bowling ball wearing a hula skirt."

"You can..." But Steve never heard what he could do. Their conversation was interrupted as an office window exploded. Glass and an office chair tumbled to the ground at their feet.

Steve stopped short, throwing out an arm to stop Brad. Their attention was drawn from the chair at their feet to the shattered window. Screams erupted through the opening. A hand shot u,p then another, grabbing onto the glass-splintered ledge. Rachel was trying to claw her way out of the shattered window.

"Help me, dear GOD! Steve, Brad! HELP!" She screamed. Her eyes were full of terror. They glanced at each other, then ran to the terrified woman. Steve searched for smoke or fire. He couldn't see or smell either. There were no alarms, just Rachel's pleas.

Each man grabbed an arm, trying to pull her free of the window. No matter their struggle she remained stuck, screaming louder and louder for help. Steve could barely keep a grip on her arm. Her hands and arms were full of cuts from the broken glass. Her skin was slick with blood and she was flailing in terror. They tugged and pulled, and each time she cried out in pain and fear. The more they pulled the more she seemed to be pulled back.

Her face was pale with terror. Her screams became more frantic by the second. Suddenly her grip her grip tightened painfully on their arms. "Pull me out pull me out NOW!" She struggled with all her might. She wriggled her feet, kicking hard. Her cries increasing in pitch and intensity, she was truly panicked. She grabbed and clawed at the men, blood oozed down the wall where the broken glass cut into her stomach. Steve heard crashing from the room. He had to cover his head as she thrashed and pulled. Steve tried to calm her, to get her to work with them to free her from the window.

"They...They...They're getting in! Get me out! Pull PULL, PULL! Get off GET OFF AAARRGHGGGH GET ME OUT NOW!!" Rachel screamed at them. Tears streamed down her face as her eyes bulged. Steve and Brad pulled with all their might, urged on by her panic. With a sudden lurch, like a cork being pulled from a bottle, she slipped free from the window.

Steve knew in an instant that something was terribly wrong. Rachel was far too light. Looking down, Steve cried in horror, "Sweet Jesus!". Lying at his feet was only half of the woman. She gasped as red covered her lips and ran down her chin. Blood was draining quickly from just under her rib cage. Her spine was exposed, and her intestines made a trail from her torso to the window.

Steve's eyes followed the gruesome trail from the ground to the gaping shattered glass, "Holy shit!" he cried, stumbled backward and tripping over Rachel's sputtering torso. Gaining his balance, he grabbed Brad's arm. The men were shocked with horror. The watched as the woman's intestines were pulled back through the window.

Rachel gurgled blood. It spurted from her mouth with each gasp. She reached for Steve. He never knew if she was trying to tell him something. He moved closer to her as her eyes rolled back into her head. Brad let out a howl and pushed away from Steve. He pointed at the window, and then ran toward the parking lot.

Steve's head whipped from his retreating friend to where he had pointed. In the window was the face of a man. It was the shipping manager, except that his right eye socket was empty and bloody. He was pulling the intestine back through the window. He pulled bits into his mouth, slurping greedily as he did so.

Steve watched the hideous display, unable to make his feet obey his command to run. Something grabbed his ankle, breaking him out of his shock. Not wanting to, but unable to stop, he looked down. Rachel had one hand on his boot and the other was clawing at the gravel. Her eyes showed no pain or recognition—just hunger. He kicked her off. He ran blindly after Brad toward the parking lot. Screams and more shattering glass chased him from the office.

Find Safety

Bill Reager slowed the station wagon slightly through the red light at the bottom of the hill. Beth clung tightly to the seat belt, not out of fear over the older man's driving but to fight the grief and panic that was threatening to overtake her. It was her lifeline, the only thing that seemed real at the moment. Every time she closed her eyes her father's face, contorted in terror and agony, swam before her vision. It was all that she could see. She *had* to talk to her brother. She needed to know he was okay, and he had to know not to go home.

Releasing the belt, her fingers ached from the grip. She moved her shaking hand into her jacket. It wasn't in the inside pocket where she kept it. "Where is it?" Beth fumbled through her pockets. Bill glanced sideways at her.

"Where is it?" She slapped at the jacket. She felt her pants pockets, then returned to her jacket. "WHERE IS IT!" she shouted.

Returning to the inside pocket, her fingers curled around the familiar shape of the phone. Pulling it from her pocket, she laughed, while several tears escaped her eyes. Hitting the speed dial, she put the phone to her ear. "Damn it." She hung up, scrolled through the contacts. She hit the name but then instantly dropped the phone, grabbing the seat belt again. Bill jumped a curve to avoid a motorcycle. The rider was out of control, tearing out of one yard then heading through another. Several people stumbled after him.

Recovering herself, she grabbed up her phone, frantically unlocking it as she tried to make another call. The car bounced and swerved around a burning truck. She hit the wrong contact. Quickly hanging up, she dialed another number. One hand held tight to the belt, the other held the phone to her ear. Anger swelled up in her. She jerked the phone from her ear, hitting the red "end" button. She tried again. Frustration boiled into anger. She pulled the phone from her ear, yelling into the receiver at the calm robotic voice. She called it the name she reserved for the most vile of her hatred.

Bill glanced over again. "What?" he asked calmly. He swung the car around a bend, out of the path a minivan. The van careened out of control through the guide rail and down an embankment. Beth spun in her seat to stare out the back window at the mangled railing. Bill did not slow down.

"All the circuits are busy or something." Beth turned back in her seat. She started to text Steve. "Damn it! The text won't go through either," she yelled, slamming the phone against her leg. "I need to find Steve! Can you take me to the distribution center?"

Bill glanced at her. "I have no idea where we need to go." His eyes followed a police car that screamed by in the opposite direction, lights flashing and siren blaring, ".... so why not?" He shrugged.

"What the hell is happening?" Beth asked angrily, holding up her phone as if it would answer her. "Why was Dad attacked? Why did they...kill him? Why is Denny dead? What the hell was wrong with those people? Mrs. McGee was, she was, I mean—she was all messed up!" Beth continued getting more hysterical with each question.

"I don't know. All the news said was that people needed to stay in their homes, not to panic. Something about the people with the flu getting violent. Denny had been sick for a couple days." Bill paused to twist his arms through a pretzel move as he swerved around a wrecked Mercedes. "I went to check on him and he wasn't breathing... but he got up... He got up and attacked me." Bill gripped the wheel tightly. "He was trying to bite me. He was dead but he got up and tried to...kill me." Bill was almost pleading with Beth to understand.

"I hit him. I hit him and he fell back against the nightstand." Bill clipped a mailbox as he skidded around a body in the road. "I heard his head hit the corner. His neck must have broken. He couldn't move but his eyes followed me. They followed me all over the room. The body was paralyzed, but... he should have been dead! He was dead!" Bill burst out. "He kept watching me even though he couldn't move. His mouth tried to bite at me... he was still trying to get to me." Bill looked over at Beth, who stared back, her eyes brimming with tears.

Bill stared straight ahead, his eyes barely seeing the road. Bursting across the outbound lanes, horns blared as several cars swerved out of Bill's path. They pulled onto the main road into town. The opposite lanes were streaming with traffic.

"I couldn't leave him. So I, I... I ended his suffering." Tears ran down Bill's face. He swiped at them, trying to clear his vision.

Beth turned to face the front of the car, staring blankly out of the window, trying to understand what she was hearing. She became aware the radio was on but very low. To drown out the silence she turned it up a little. For several minutes Beth and Bill said nothing, listening to the radio repeat the same constant loop. "The emergency management department urges citizens to remain in their residence. Please keep the roads clear for emergency personnel...stay tuned to this station for further information."

Soon Beth heard the recording as nothing but background noise. The sounds of the car's engine, along with the screech of the tires through the turns, began to fade as she became more lost in her thoughts. She made several more attempts to reach her brother and Wes. She hung up the phone, letting it fall into her lap. She decided to try again in a few minutes. The monotonous drone of the radio ceased. There was a click followed by crackle and indistinct voices. Suddenly there was a thumping, "We on? We're live, go."

The harried voice startled Beth. Reaching forward, she turned the volume up. She looked over at Bill, who was looking at the radio. "The Mayor's office, along with the Pennsylvania National Guard, have ordered an evacuation of the city and surrounding suburbs. Citizens are instructed to report to the Point Ball Park, The Richland Mall, or the Hilltop Movieplex. Whichever is closer to your... Hold on a moment, I have just been handed an update. What? Um...any individuals that are currently...is this right? Any individuals that have the flu are not to be taken to the evacuation areas. You are instructed to leave them as soon as possible. Secure the sick individual and leave them where they are. Medical attention will be sent when you give your information at the evacuation sites." The announcer tried his best to remain calm.

"Those evacuation points again are: The Point Ball Park, Richland Mall and Hill Top movies. By order of the National Guard the following policy is in effect for evacuation. If someone is sick, or has been injured by someone who is sick, they are to report to the medical tent upon arrival at the evacuation point." The announcer's calm voice began to crack. "Anyone with the flu will be evacuated separately...but it is recommended that they be left in your homes until help can be sent to them. CAN WE CHECK THIS PLEASE!" The voice on the radio was becoming more agitated by the second. There was a crackle, an emergency tone, then a recorded message saying exactly what the announcer had read. Evacuation points and report; leave the sick or injured.

Bill changed the channel, but it was on every station. "Leave the sick, or drop them off at the medical tent... They know what is going on," Bill grumbled.

Beth looked at Bill. "The Mall is closer, but the Point is only a few blocks from the distribution center," she said hopefully.

Bill jerked the wheel as several cars jumped the median to head back to town toward the ballpark. "Shit!" Bill yelled, avoiding a woman who looked out of her mind in panic.

Beth saw three children in the car, all crying and screaming as a man rose up from the back seat. "Oh my God!" She screamed, pointing at the car ahead.

"Hold on!" Bill yelled, throwing an arm across Beth. The woman's car jumped the curb, glanced off a telephone pole, and flipped over. Bill clipped the rear of the car, spinning it as he accelerated past it.

"Mr. Reager! We have to stop! We have to help them!" Beth screamed, grabbing his arm and trying to turn to look back.

Bill was shaking his head, mumbling as he drove on. "Too late for them... too late. Can't stop, too late. We'll find Steve and we'll leave. I'll find your brother; I said I would, but no more. Too late to help them." He pounded the wheel.

Beth was torn between wanting to get to her brother and helping. She closed her eyes as she turned back to face the front. She cursed herself and Bill. "Yes. Let's get Steve and get the hell out of here." Tears stained her face. She hated herself and her old teacher. Looking down at her phone, she frantically typed in another text. She had to retype it several times as her fingers couldn't find the right keys through the blur of tears. She sent the message to her best friend. She waited. The indicator read. "Message sent." She got excited. Immediately typing another text to Steve. With excited fingers she hit send. The progression indicator displayed "Sending." She urged it to go, "Come on, come on." She shook the phone.

"Sending."

"You can do it," she pleaded.

"Message failed." The failure notice burned into her chest. "Damn you! You worthless piece of sh..., um, uh. Sorry, Mr. Reager."

He glanced at her and laughed. With all this?" He gestured out the window, "You think I care if you swear? This fucking sucks and you damn well earned the right to say so."

Beth was shocked at the language. Then she laughed. She looked down at her phone, waiting for a reply from her friend.

Into the Fire

Steve slammed through the gate separating the lot from the loading area. "What the ???" The building across the street was completely engulfed in flame. Steve watched three flaming bodies fall from the second floor. His attention shifted immediately to the front door as it was flung open. Three people ran from the flames. One who ran toward him was a young guy Steve had seen a few times in passing. The young man fell, and Steve stepped forward to help him. He heard the man scream. One of the burning bodies had grabbed the guy's ankle. The other two burning bodies got slowly to their feet, advancing on the downed man.

The top windows exploded, sending glass raining down on other escaping workers. Steve looked back at the distribution center. His co-workers were also running from the buildings. He saw several friends attacked. The attackers were, to Steve's horror, also his friends and co-workers. "This can't be happening, this can't be!" They were killing and eating each other. "This is like some messed up horror movie!" Steve shouted, as if this would make it all go away.

Smashing through the gate, he turned back toward the parking lot, running for his car. He dodged several cars that sped past. Jumping over the hood of his boss' car, Steve barely avoided being hit. The BMW he slid over was not so lucky. Shakily regaining his feet, he jumped aside again as a pickup truck skidded to a halt in front of him.

"Steve! For fuck's sake, boy! Get the hell out of here!" It was Brad. "Oh shit, boy, run!" The truck's tires screamed, the engine roared, and the glow of taillights were all that was left.

Sparing a glance over his shoulder, Steve saw several bloody creatures stumbling toward him. "Fuck this!" He ran for his Mustang while digging in his pocket for his keys.

He had parked further out in the lot, thinking it would be easy to leave later, but it now felt miles away. He regretted the decision with every step he ran. "Seriously! I swear I didn't park this far away." He gasped as another car squealed out of the lot.

Finding the keys, he hit the fob unlocking the door. Slamming into the door a second later, he wrenched it open, flinging himself in. "What the hell is going on?" he breathed. His hands were shaking so badly it took several seconds before he was finally able to get the key into the ignition. The engine roared to life.

Taking a moment to clear his head, he tried to rid the vision of half-Rachel and the burning corpses. "They got up and were walking," he stuttered, rubbing his eyes. He could still see them, he could see them every time he closed his eyes, "This can't be happening, this can't be, can't be," he repeated, still trying to will it to be true. He shut his eyes tight, pressing them with his palms so all was black except the geometric shapes. He tried to block out the sound. Opening his eyes, it was all still there; the running, the screaming, the burning—were all still there.

"Beth, Dad!" he cried, reaching for his phone. "Holy SHIT!" The office manager crashed against his passenger window and slid down it. He was beating on the glass with torn hands, leaving bloody streaks.

Steve screamed again, throwing himself in the other direction, as a face slammed against the window next to his. The owner held up a bloody hand that was missing several fingers. The dead eyes locked on Steve's; they stared for a moment. Suddenly the corpse opened its mouth, calling out a long howl.

"WAAAAAA FUCK YOU!" Steve screamed, throwing the car into gear. His foot slammed down on the gas. The car lurched forward, sending Steve back into his seat. Suddenly he was thrown forward. The front wheels were blocked by the body of the business manager. The rear tires squealed in protest as they tried to gain traction. The corpse writhed, trying to claw away. The rear tires of the high-powered performance car grabbed the asphalt. The front powered over the body, pushing it along the ground. Then with a mighty lurch, the front wheels were over, and the back wheels spit flesh and muscle as they crushed his spine and sped off.

The gate to the lot was already off its hinges, and the guard shack was empty. The building across the road was sending flames fifty feet high into the air. Several flaming people were stumbling out of the burning building. Steve sped past. A couple made a feeble attempt to grab at the car.

"What the hell? What the FUCK! They should have been dead!" Steve screamed and pounded the wheel. "You should all be dead!" he yelled at a flaming man who was missing his lower jaw.

Steve returned to searching his jacket for his phone. The engine revved high. He fumbled with the phone dialing his house. Pressing the phone to his ear with his shoulder, he shifted gears. "All circuits are currently busy. Please try your call again later" was the phone's reply.

Fear bubbled up in his stomach. He tried his father's cell. It was the same taunting response. Panic rising, he tried his sister. Still the computer voice mocked his growing terror. "LET ME TALK TO SOMEONE, BITCH!" he screamed. The phone flew onto the passenger seat.

WABAM! A dark color flew over the hood of the beautifully maintained sports car and out of Steve's view. He had been so distracted with his phone that he had stopped paying attention the road.

Smoke billowed from the wheels as he slammed on the brakes and jerked the wheel. The gleaming car skidded to a halt in the middle of the empty road. Heart beating in his throat, he looked out of the window. The sight that met his eyes was the mangled remains of what only moments before had been a man.

Steve was glued to the vision of the broken body lying in the street. One leg was twisted backward and up, the foot lying next to the head. The left arm was pinned under the body, the other flung out to the side. As Steve tried to slow his panicked breathing, the body on the road raised its head and moaned at him. Steve looked past the crumpled body down the street. The road was filling with shambling dead. They were shuffling to the car as if answering the moan.

Steve swore, pushed in the clutch, slammed the car into gear and sped down the road toward his home. He prayed that the man he just hit had been dead before he had shattered him. That thought nagged at him. He pushed his foot harder on the gas pedal.

Dragons

Wes stood with his hand on the knob listening to the silence in the house interrupted by the noises coming from outside. Through the closed window seeped sirens and yelling. Whatever was happening was close. This didn't bother him, but the lack of coughing did. "Reg must have fallen asleep," he tried to convince himself, but another little voice said, "So suddenly?" Shaking the thought, he opened the door.

"Reg? Reg? Reggie!" Wes could feel the panic in his mother's voice.

Hurrying out of his room, he flung himself down the short stairway then down the hall. His mother's screaming urged him faster into the living room. He was unprepared for what he saw as he skidded to a halt on the beige carpet of the living room. His mother was screaming, but he found he could do nothing for her. The scene that met his eyes stole his breath and froze his limbs.

Reggie was on his feet, and blood covered his face and his hands. He clung to Wes's mother by her upper arms. Even from where he stood Wes could see the fingers starting to break the skin. Blood starting to run down her arms. She was struggling to free herself from his steel grasp. The wound on her neck was gushing blood, soaking the skin of her neck and shirt.

Wes could see she was fighting for her life. This was something she had done many times with his father, but never with Reg. She was hitting her husband with everything she had. She kicked him in the shins, stomped his feet, kneed him in the groin and clawed his eyes. Nothing seemed to affect him. Wes stared, frozen in terror and shaking with anger as he watched the scene.

"This can't be happening," his brain screamed, "Not again!" He ran at his stepfather screaming, "You promised! You promised never to hurt her! You promised! You bastard!" Wes flung himself onto the man, hitting every part of him he could reach. Reg either didn't notice or didn't care. Finding his efforts had no effect, Wes changed tactics. He began trying free his mother. He tried to break his Reg's grip, but his stepfather's fingers only dug in further. Wes pulled with all his might. His mother kept her hands on Reg's chest to keep him away. She pushed the man she had loved as far from her as she could, while his teeth chomped the air between them.

Helpless to free his mother, Wes backed off scanning the room for anything he could use as a weapon. She cried out again. Wes abandoned his search, backed up several steps, and ran, hurtling himself with all his might. He smashed into Reg just below the arm. Wes heard a crack but couldn't tell if it was Reg or himself. Stumbling back, pain shooting through his shoulder, Wes jumped on his stepfather. He pulled Reg's head back, trying to snap his neck. Reg did not seem to even notice he was being attacked. He just kept trying to bite the woman he had in his grasp.

Reg's face was cold and covered in sweat. Wes' hands slipped, and losing his grip, he fell to the floor. All he could do was watch wide-eyed as Reg lurched forward, biting into his mother's arm. Her scream pierced Wes' heart. Reg began to chew on the lump of flesh he had just torn from the limb.

"MOM!" Hold on, hold ON!" Panicking, Wes ran from the room. In the hall, he turned left, then right, then left again. "SHIT!" Flying up the stairs, he slammed through the door to his room. Crashing into the wall, his hand gripped the hilt of a sword he and Beth had bought one year at a Renaissance Festival. He ripped the weapon free from the wall. Bits of plaster fell to the floor as the metal hangers clanged across the room. Spinning on the spot, he hurtled from the room back down the stairs three at a time. Bouncing off the walls, he sprinted back down the hall. Skidding back into the living room, he held the sword high over his head, screaming, "Leave her alone!"

The blade swooshed through the air. The weight of the steel pulled Wes off balance as the blade crashed through Reg's back. Wes fell forward as Reg staggered, releasing Wes's mother. Relief washed over him as he watched his mother leave Reg's grip.

A moment later terror replaced that feeling. Reg was slowly turning to face him. Scooting away from the thing that loomed over him, Wes looked up into a face he did not recognize. It wasn't the face of the man Wes had come to know, the man he had come to love as a father. It was distorted, hungry, angry and covered in blood.

Wes knew in an instant that this wasn't his stepfather; this was evil staring at him. It lunged at Wes with arms outstretched. Wes grabbed at the sword laying inches away. He raised the blade, closing his eyes. He waited for the pain to come but it didn't. Opening one eye slightly, he saw the bloody fingers mere inches from his face, clawing at the air.

The sword was buried deep in Reg's chest, which kept him from his prey. The hilt dug into Wes' stomach. Reg swung his arms, letting out a moan of confusion and anger. Wes mustered all his strength, pushing Reg over. The man lay on his side looking down at the sword buried in his rib cage. It would have been comical had it been something other than real. Reg tried to roll one way, then the other, only to have the sword stop him in each direction.

Wes thought for a second that it was all over. He waited for the man to close his eyes, like in the movies, and die. That did not happen. As Wes watched the look of confusion left the face. It looked back at Wes, and the hunger was back in its eyes. Reg gave up on rolling; instead he pushed himself up to his knees and then to his feet. He swayed, off balance from the heavy weapon still sticking out of his body. What had been his stepfather lunged forward again.

Wes stumbled backward, falling over an armchair. His arms swung wildly while he fell. His hand found the hilt of the sword again. He instinctively grabbed it as he backed away, pulling the sword free, but pulling Reg closer with it. Blood oozed freely from the gaping wound. Reg didn't notice the damage while he continued after Wes.

Looking from the sword to the open wound in the man's chest, Wes dropped the weapon. He scrambled to his feet, running to his Mother's bedroom. He knew where she kept the gun. The gun she'd bought to protect them from his real father. He slid into the nightstand on his mother's side of the bed. He threw open the drawer, pulling out the black semi automatic. Wes cursed the fact that his mother never kept it loaded. Thankfully there was a full clip right next to it.

Wes fumbled with the clip. "COME ON!" he shouted as it bounced between the sides of the opening. Finally, he slammed it home, chambered a round and clicked off the safety. It was just in time. The room suddenly darkened as Reg filled the door frame. "Stay away, Reg, I mean it! Don't you come any closer! I will kill you! Don't make me shoot you!" Wes pleaded as he raised the gun with shaking arms.

What had once been a caring, kind man came at him. Bloody hands reached out for him. The creature's teeth were bared. It groaned as it entered the room. Wes pulled the trigger, and the bullet smashed into the man's chest. He staggered back a step, but just like the sword it had no effect.

"Stop! Damn you, why won't you stop?" Wes demanded. A second round slammed into the advancing thing's torso. Again, Reg stumbled back from the impact but didn't stop. Wes adjusted his sights. He took the breath and exhaled as he squeezed the trigger. His stepfather dropped to the floor. A small hole appeared between his eyes. Blood seeped onto the light blue carpet of his mother's bedroom.

The gun still clutched in his hand, Wes blindly walked back to the living room. His mother lay slumped against the couch. Blood covered her shirt, pooling on the carpet next to her body. Wes stood over his mother, staring. He knew she was dead.

This can't be happening. It was all he could think. "Dad was the one that was going to kill her, never Reggie, never," he whispered as tears began to prickle in his eyes. He looked down at his mother and thought bitterly, *At least she didn't have to know I was the one who killed Reg.*

Wes' heart leapt when he saw his mother twitch. He swiped the tears from his eyes and stared, "Mom? " He took a step toward her. Her eyes snapped open. Slowly she turned her head toward him, staring.

"No. No way—No! Mom! Not you!" He wept as she began to slowly push herself off the floor. "NO NO NO. Come on Mom, not you!" Wes screamed, backing away while keeping the gun aimed at her. "Stay away!" he cried.

The same look of hunger and anger contorted her face. Shaking, still pleading, he pulled the trigger; her shoulder exploded. Awkwardly she continued to push herself up. Gaining her feet finally, she stumbled toward her son. Wes watched the muzzle flash. The wall behind his mother changed instantly from white to red and brain matter grey.

Tears streamed freely down his face. He watched his mother crumpled in front of the couch. Closing his eyes, he sank to the floor in the living room and cried until he was completely drained.

The light was fading when it hit him like a slap to the face. I have to get out of here, get to somewhere safe... I have to find Beth. We have to get out of town. He got up and hurried back to his mother's bedroom. Stepping over Reg's body, he went to the bed. Throwing open the nightstand, he pulled out the extra clip and a box of bullets. "God, please don't let Beth leave before I can get there."

He stood with his back to the doorway. They were zombies. Unfuckingbeleivable. Zombies. He turned, looking at the body of the man who had taken care of him and his mother. The man who had loved him like a son and had always been there for him was now dead at his hand. Grief crashed over him again, bringing back tears he thought could not fall, forcing him to sit on the edge of the bed to keep from collapsing. Finally regaining his composure, he pulled the sheets from the bed. He covered Reginald Smith, the kindest man he had ever known.

He made his way back into the living room. He knelt down next to his mother. He couldn't look at her face. He covered her with the comforter he pulled from the couch. "You were always cold, Mom. This should keep you warm," he muttered, wiping his eyes with the back of his hand.

Picking up the sword, he grabbed a towel from the kitchen and cleaned the blade. He mounted the stairs slowly, returning to his bedroom. He grabbed the scabbard for the sword from the back of the closet. He fashioned a way to attach it to his back with an old belt. Real Conan-like, he told his reflection in the mirror. Looking closely, he grabbed an old shirt and scrubbed at the blood on his face. He rubbed until he was raw. Checking the reflection again, he breathed a sigh, noting his features were clean.

Next he found his backpack. Throwing out the schoolbooks, he looked around his room for "important things". Grabbing a couple of books and some pictures, he threw them into the pack. Something caught his attention out the window. A neighbor's house down the block was on fire. People were running in the streets while cars raced by. Thundering down the stairs, he jogged into the kitchen, looking around for a second. He thought about what he would need. He filled the backpack with as much canned food and bottled water as he could. Now with the heavily laden pack, sword on his back, the extra clip in his pocket and gun in hand, he headed to the front door.

He never once looked back into the living room. As he turned the doorknob he spoke. "I love you, Mom. I love you, Reggie. You were the best. I'm sorry. So sorry." He paused to let one sob shake him. Then Wes pulled opened the door, stepping out into utter chaos.

Get out of Town

Devin stared down to the phone in his hand without really seeing it. He had been trying to get a hold of his wife for the last half hour. His thumb hovered over the call button. He pressed it without thinking about it. He hadn't been able to reach her the last two dozen times; why should this be different?

His attention was drawn back to the traffic cameras. The crowd in the central park had grown over the last few minutes. Cars were speeding down the road. The drivers were erratic, driving wildly with no regard for the pedestrians. There had been several near misses already, along with several not-misses. Those who got either hit skidded along the pavement or went flailing through the air. The result of each incident was the same. The person would lie motionless for a moment, and then get up, or crawl. or stumble. Limbs would be at weird angles, legs and arms not working or completely missing. This is what caught Devin's attention. A car had just flown through the intersection, throwing a small person cartwheeling over it.

"Hello? Devin?" He jumped at the sound, quickly putting the phone to his ear.

"Cheryl?" Relief flooded over him.

"Devin what is going on?" Her voice was strained, holding more than a hint of panic.

He pulled the phone from his ear, closing his eyes. His heart ached. Biting his lip, he returned the phone to his ear. Fear threatened to overtake him. "Honey, listen, and don't ask questions, just do what I say, please! Get the girls and get out of town. Go to your mother's in Altoona."

"Why, what is going on?" she asked frantically.

"Please, just go. Things are going crazy. I want you and the girls out of…" Devin's attention was drawn back to the central park camera. The phone slowly dropped from his ear. He couldn't believe what he was seeing. A car careened around a corner, straight into the crowd.

Several people were thrown through the air. Several others in the park fell like dominoes, others sliding across the grass. Just as before they all just got back up, like nothing had happened. Except this time, they all began to converge on the car. Devin watched as the crowd began attacking the vehicle.

The driver was trying to back up, but he didn't seem to be gaining any traction. Then the wheels found traction. The driver gave it too much gas. The car swerved, smashing into a tree. He tried to drive his smoking car through the crowd.

He was driving into a wall of people. They barely moved, piling up on the hood or falling under the wheels. Devin half rose from his chair, the phone forgotten in his hand. He cried out when the driver's window was smashed. There was nothing he could do but watch as the driver was ripped from the car. The passenger door was wrenched open. Someone was trying to run but she was overwhelmed by the mass of people, who instantly surrounded her.

"Devin! Devin, what is going on?" Cheryl cried.

"Oh sweet mother of pearl!" Devin exclaimed as he watched the crowd rip the driver and passenger to pieces.

"Devin! What it is? What is going on? Devin, answer me!" Cheryl was truly in a state of panic now.

Returning the phone to his ear, he yelled, "Get the girls and get out of town NOW!" He watched the parts of the passenger being dragged in different directions from the car. Sinking back into a chair, he thanked God there was no sound with the picture. Putting his hand to his face he felt drained and defeated.

"Cheryl, I love you. Tell the girls I love them, and I'll see them at Grandma's," Devin whispered into the phone.

"Devin, what is going on? Come home and we'll leave together." His wife half-wept.

"Please, honey. Go now, while you still can. I love you." Devin spoke into the phone, his heart breaking as he did. He knew he couldn't make it home. All his routes were blocked; everywhere he looked there were people in the streets running.

"I will see you at your mother's, I promise." He lied.

"I love you." His wife's voice hitched as she called for the girls.

He heard his youngest say, "Mommy, there is a man at the door, he looks hurt." Like ice water pouring down his spine, Devin pictured a bloody man at the screen door. He heard his daughter's scream and the phone clattered to the floor.

"Cheryl! Cheryl!" Devin screamed into the phone, jumping to his feet. "CHERYL!" There was no one on the other end. All he could hear was banging, shouting, and the diminishing sound of someone running away.

"Cheryl…" He moaned into the phone. Hanging up quickly, he tried to call his house again. All he heard was a recorded voice telling him all circuits were busy. He tried his wife's phone—nothing. He tried his oldest daughter's phone, but heard only the same recorded voice telling him all circuits were busy.

Sinking back into the chair, all he could do was pray his family made it out of the house and were all right. A feeling of helplessness overwhelmed him as he looked from the useless phone to the monitors. The bridge out of town to the highway was clogged with cars; none of them seemed to be moving. Devin did something he hadn't done since the birth of his first child.

"Damn it!" he screamed as his phone flew across the room, smashing against the cinder block wall.

Not the Best Idea

The garage door rose too slowly. Gerry revved the bike's engine impatiently. Rolling his shoulders and neck, he readied himself. The hastily attached tree trimmer shook across the handlebars, the twine taught and straining. Slapping down the visor, he checked the machete duct-taped to his arm, extending past his hand. Heavy kitchen knives were strapped to his knees and boots.

The door was halfway up now. He could see several pairs of legs approaching, drawn by the sound of the opening portal.

"Vreee Vreee, pllt plllt plltt." The bike purred. Zipping up the camouflage jacket, a smile broke across his face. Finally! Finally, after years of playing the games, after years of being told he was wasting his time, he was going to prove them wrong. He would survive, and why? Because he *had* been playing the games, training for just this day.

The door was all the way up. He grinned as he watched them moving toward him. Graying skin stretched over tight muscles, teeth bared. His smile grew bigger. *Just like in the games.* With the open door came a cool fall breeze. Unlike the games came the stench. His eyes began to water behind the visor and his lunch jumped into his throat. The putrid stink of excrement and rot threatened to overpower him. "God," he gasped, "How did you get so smelly so fast?" Fighting through the urge to vomit, he slipped the bike into gear. The engine whined and the rear tire squealed. Gerry kicked out at the undead as he passed.

The air in the helmet cleared. The stink was still there but in the open he could at least breathe. Blinking away the tears he regained control of his stomach. Not being overwhelmed with the urge to hurl, his euphoria returned. Seeing another undead ahead he leaned toward it. Making contact with its right leg, the serrated bread knife ripped free of his shoe. It stuck into the thigh of the zombie he passed. It took no notice as it tried to follow him. He turned the throttle, leaving the ghoul with only the knife and his laughter.

He sped down the road. "Ten points! Ah, we can do better..." He searched the street for another target. "Oh yeah, gonna be a head shot!" he cried, pumping his fist in the air. Gerry smiled up at the blade of the machete strapped to his arm. Twisting the throttle, he leveled the blade. Eyeing the female coming across the grass ahead, he adjusted the height. "This is gonna take your head clean off." He grinned.

Pain like he had never known shot through his arm and shoulder, as his fist snapped back, hitting him in the kidney. Stars exploded before his vision and his lunch returned to his throat again. Wobbling dangerously, he fought to control the bike. Pulling his arm forward, he tried to put it on the handlebars. Fire shot through his forearm and fingers.

Eyes streaming, he only caught a glimpse of the limping man before the tree trimmer hit him in the midsection. The trimmer ripped free of the handlebars, hitting the kill switch as it dislodged. The rear tire seized into a skid. Panicked, he flipped the switch back to run. He flailed his broken arm, attempting to pull in the clutch. Bike and man crashed to the ground.

Lights again exploded before his eyes as his helmet smacked on the ground. Screaming in agony, he tried to push himself up with his broken arm. Bloody battered knees protested the attempt to stand. A zombie was limping toward him. It had his tree trimmer halfway buried in his torso. The woman he had tried to decapitate was approaching too. Her head wobbled on her slashed neck. Every step she took tore it further. The closer she got the more it threatened to fall off completely.

Terror drove him. He clawed at the ground trying desperately to escape. More pain shot through his leg. Rolling over, he kicked off the small boy who had appeared out of nowhere. Blood and a piece of leg fell out of the child's mouth as the boot and knife smashed the little skull. A bite on the shoulder, one on an arm, more in the legs, screams amplified in the closed helmet. Blood spurted over the visor as his head left his body.

The wobbly neck barely held on as the woman looked down at the helmet and head she had in her hand. Moaning, she dropped it.

The limping man stood up, dropping the liver he held. He looked at the woman, she stared back, and together they moaned as they began to wander down the road.

Moving the Barriers

The call had come from headquarters less than two minutes ago. To the officers stationed at the bridge it was a godsend. "Open all the incoming lanes to outbound traffic." The words were relayed down the line. The few officers assigned to the traffic control hoped this would alleviate the cursing, screaming and reckless behavior they had been dealing with for the last hour. Three city workers had just arrived on the scene. It took them a long time to push through even with the motorcycle police escort. Now their truck was blocking a lane, forcing drivers further into a bottleneck. Through the cacophony of shouting and horns, the trio quickly unloaded the small forklift from a trailer. This was hampered by drivers getting too far into the lane. Several times they had to force drivers to move so they had enough room to put the ramps down. The police stood by with weapons ready and sweat streaming. Any second the honking and swearing could erupt into total anarchy. Finally, the crew started to work.

The plan was to move several of the concrete barricades to make an off ramp to the other lanes. Several police cars screamed past, going outbound in the incoming lanes. Angry cries and calls of expedited movement came from the creeping traffic next to the workers.

"I hope they are stopping traffic, not just running for their lives." Larry Smith shouted to his coworker, nodding to the back of the speeding police cars. A few civilian cars now blew past.

"Let's just get this done. My wife is packing up the kids right now. We're just heading up the mountain." Barry Kline spoke as quietly as he could, trying not to be overheard by the third member of the team. "We're heading to the cabin. Get whatever you need and meet us there."

Larry nodded then motioned for Theresa Barnes to push the barrier with the forklift. A police bike rolled up, stopping just past the workers. Another police car pulled up on the other side of the barrier and turned around. The barrier scraped across the inbound lanes. The workers positioned it so it sat at an angle to the guardrail of the incoming lane.

The police car pulled into the opening, blocking access to the empty lanes. It moved slightly to allow the lift back through. Several more officers were now on the scene, trying to keep things moving and orderly. Even with the additional police the cars barely crept by. The pace of the traffic allowed the suggestions of what the officers and the road workers could do to themselves and each other to be heard clearly. More than once a bottle or other debris bounced off a police car or the cage of the forklift.

The second barrier slowly moved into place. A rock smashed the windshield of the waiting police car. The crew didn't need any additional encouragement. Immediately they began to move to the third divider. The plan was to block this expansion with another cruiser. They wanted to wave vehicles over in an orderly way. The police were not quick enough.

Barry hurried to the front of the forklift as the engine whined. A tieback had gotten caught in the lift's gears. He tugged at the fraying nylon, trying to free the forks. Barry had a second to recognize the complete panic in the eyes of a driver before he was smashed into the cage of the forklift. The car scraped along, trying to squeeze between the barrier, the lift, and the advancing police car. Blood poured down Barry's face as he clung to the cage. His screams were a howl of agony. The car continued to force its way past. The driver's attention was only on the open road ahead. Barry twisted against the rear bumper as the car broke free. He clung to the forklift's cage. Both of his legs were broken and torn. He was bleeding badly. In extreme pain and shock, Barry's head began to spin. He lost his grip. Larry ran toward his fallen friend. There was nothing he could do except watch as a truck ran over Barry. Blood spurted from Barry's mouth onto Larry's face and clothes as tried to pull him out of the way.

Theresa jumped from the forklift as another car hit it pushing it further out of the way. She ran to the truck they had arrived in. Larry was running toward her. She gave him the finger, "You didn't think I heard you and Barry? What, no room for me and my family?

Screw you!" she screamed, slamming the door shut. The large truck rumbled to life. Metal scraped and screeched as she smashed her way through the line of waiting cars. With a final crunch she pushed through the barriers, the police cruiser, and out through the opening. Breathing heavily, she took the open road in front of her at an ever-increasing speed, a trickle of other cars followed.

One of the officers ran to help Barry. Larry grabbed the officer, pulling him back. He had seen that his friend was gone. He had watched as the thing on the road became one of them. He consoled himself that it was only for a moment. He watched as his friend's body became unrecognizable as car after car streamed over the ground meat that had once been a human.

"Come on!" A voice called over the traffic. It was the officer he had pulled away. He was sprinting to his car. Seconds later the cruiser was on the other side of the barrier. The car was dented and battered. An officer was hanging out of the back window yelling for Larry. Shaking out of his horror, he waved them off, jumping the barrier. The police hit their siren, speeding off as Larry ran back to town.

Theresa's breathing slowed. The truck's engine whined with the strain of the heavy trailer. Even without the weight of the fork-lift it was a substantial burden. Several cars had already screamed past her. She found this irritating. They were going to get there first. Where they were going to get to was a mystery, but she was having none of it. Easing to the side of the road she slipped the truck into park. Jumping from the cab, she hurried to the back. Frantically she began unhooking the trailer. Her impatience grew as four more cars flew by. She hectically tried to get the trailer unhooked. As she did, she also tried to not get distracted by the increasing stream of cars.

"One of you bastards could stop and help," she yelled, pumping the handle to lift the heavy trailer. The hitch left the ball. "Yeah that's right!" she exclaimed, pointing at the hitch. Then her wide smile ran from her face. Tires squealing, metal crunching, engine growling, a black Volvo banged through cars, swerving across lanes. Theresa's eyes locked onto the driver's. Every detail seemed magnified as time slowed to a crawl. The grey pallor, the dark wet stain across the neck and clothes, the hand held to the wound. She watched as the life left the eyes and the head drooped.

Theresa's reaction was too slow. The car barreled down the road straight at her. The trailer caught her in the thighs. Oven the scraping crunching metal she heard the bones in her hips shatter. The pain was intolerable. Screaming, she pushed at the heavy wood and metal deck, trying to free herself. The driver of the Volvo lay only a few feet away. A gaping hole in the car's windshield told how the body arrived. Tears streaming down her face, she fought the tunnels that darkened her vision. Theresa struggled against the weight.

The body twitched. Theresa panicked. She pushed, pulled, and screamed. The trailer didn't move. The driver of the Volvo was another story. It crawled closer and closer. The fingernails scraped Theresa's face. The hands gripped her shoulders tight, and teeth tore through her nose. Theresa's dying screams gurgled through the streaming blood.

Caged

Doctor Gillian Olsen sat in her office rubbing her eyes. It had been a long day. She glanced at the note pad on her desk. The logo of Noah's Ark Animal Hospital emblazoned across the top of the paper made her sigh. She had always meant to change the name when she took over the practice. By the time she got around to it, the clients all knew it. On top of that it had a good reputation, so what could she do? The only places with Noah's Ark on them are day cares and veterinarians. she thought.

Stretching the day out of her spine, she put the last of the files away. The noise in the kennel concerned her. The room was always active with barking, meowing and whining. Tonight the animals were louder and more...anxious than usual. Her patients had been skittish all day, whining, barking, meowing, howling and pacing in their cages.

"What is with you guys? It isn't even a full moon." Gillian stood up stiffly. She was heading into the kennel when the front doorbell began ringing.

"I didn't think anyone was picking up late tonight," she told the poodle in first cage. The dog whined at her as she turned to check the schedule on the wall. Running her finger down the blocks, she confirmed there were no pickups scheduled. The familiar tightening of her stomach at the thought of an injured animal sprang up.

Must be an emergency! She grimaced, and the poodle barked in response.

Rushing out of the kennel to her office, she grabbed her stethoscope. Reaching the door that separated the examination rooms from the lobby, she skidded to a halt. The sound of shattering glass followed by the bang of the front door made her take a step back. .

"Oh shit! I'm being robbed!" she yelped, immediately covering her mouth with her hand. She always talked to herself and to the animals. Today was the day it would get her into trouble. Reaching into her lab coat pocket, she pulled out her new cell phone. Dialing 911 with shaking fingers, she edged quickly and as quietly as possible into one of the examination rooms. Cautiously closing the door to the slightest crack, she listened through the space as two voices began to argue.

"Dude! Why did you break the window? Now they can get in!" exclaimed the voice of a young man.

"What the fuck man, you rang the bell? Like anyone was gonna answer or even be here this late!" replied an angrier male voice.

"All circuits are currently busy. Please try your call again later" was all the help Gillian received from her phone.

"Let's get into the back. See if we can find some stuff to barricade the door."

Oh no! Not back here; don't come back here. Gillian panicked. They're going to find me, they're gonna find me. She scanned the room for anything she could use as a weapon. Her eyes fell on the plastic cutout of a dog's skull. It was a heavy model, solid. Grabbing it, she held it high over her head like a club. Break into my office and mess with me? You're gonna wish you hadn't!

Trembling, she waited by the door. Out in the hall she heard voices.

"Dude! What the hell? That bitch bit me."

"Man, this is totally messed up! Those people were crazy! What are we gonna do?"

"Shit," a voice exclaimed, followed by the sound of cabinets opening then slamming shut. "This won't stop bleeding. Help me find something to bandage this up with."

"What should I get?" questioned a different voice, a voice with a hint of resentment.

"Dude, I don't know! We are at a vet, so they have to have something around here for like dogs that have been hit by cars and shit."

Gillian listened to the two voices argue just on the other side of the door. Okay, she thought, Sounds like two boys, and one has been hurt. She wracked her brain, trying to remember the self-defense course she had taken in college. Aim for the eyes and the balls, she thought, psyching herself up for a fight. I think I'll forgo the screaming. No one will hear it anyway, and it's dumb. She let out the breath she was holding, then took in a deep one to steady herself.

Without warning the doorknob turned. In the second it took her to realize what was happening, the door swung wide, slamming Gillian in the face. Grabbing her head, she staggered backward. The plastic model clattered to the floor. She swore loudly. The side of her face throbbed. Through streaming eyes, she spotted a young man standing in the doorway, wide-eyed. He was about five foot two and utterly shocked.

"Hey lady, I'm so sorry, are you ok?"

Lowering her hands, Gillian stared at the young man. "Yeah, I think so," she said rubbing her face. Remembering that this guy shouldn't be here, she said, "Wait! You broke in! What the hell are you doing here?" she demanded.

"Hey Jeremy, man, come here."

A taller young man poked his head around the corner. Gillian noted his arm was bleeding at the shoulder. She also noticed he wore an unkind sneer. The shorter man spoke up, "Hey, sorry about the front door, but we had to find a place to hide. Are you a doctor? Can you help Jeremy?" he asked in rapid fire.

"Who are you?" Gillian demanded, rubbing her face. She backed slowly to a drawer. Opening it clumsily behind her, she felt around for an ice pack. Wincing she held it to her face. The sting reminded her she was angry. "This is so going to bruise," she grumbled. "Now! Who are you and why did you break in?"

The short man blinked at her for a second then replied, "Oh, hey, right. Sorry. my name is Matt, and that is Jeremy."

"And just who are you hiding from? The police?" She was still wary, in pain, and she wanted some answers. She could hear police sirens and wasn't about to trust two guys who just broke into her clinic. On top of that, one of them was bleeding onto her floor.

"Who are we hiding from? Dude! Seriously? Everyone! All those crazy fuckers out there," was Jeremy's shocked reply. "The whole damn town has gone nuts... Shit, this hurts." He grimaced, clutching his shoulder. "You're kinda like a doctor or something, right? Can't you give me something for this shit?"

Gillian stared at Jeremy. "Nice," she replied sarcastically.

"Sorry, Jeremy is kind of a dick," Matt muttered, leaning toward Gillian. "Uh, Doctor Olsen? Can you help him out?" he asked politely, while giving Jeremy a reproving look. Jeremy just shook his head in disgust.

"How did you..." Gillian stammered. Matt pointed to her lab coat where her name tag was.

"Right, well you can call me Gillian." Embarrassed by her own forgetfulness, she waved Jeremy over to a small wicker couch by the wall. "Let's have a look at that shoulder."

Jeremy pushed past Matt, aggressively stepping into the room. Gillian shook her head at his rudeness, but Matt just shrugged. Jeremy sat down in a huff. Gillian began to lift the sleeve of his blood-soaked t-shirt. "What do you mean the town has gone nuts?"

Jeremy's head spun to give her a look, like she was crazy. He turned a glare on Matt. With a sneer he spat out, "Well now that we've all been so properly introduced and all that shit. Haven't you been paying attention to the radio and the TV and shit?"

Gillian looked from Matt to Jeremy, confused. Matt shook his head. Shrugging He opened his mouth to explain but Jeremy gave an annoyed huff. "All the sick people have gone nuts. They have just gone fucking crazy. They are attacking people and trying to kill them."

Matt took a deep breath and answered Gillian's questioning look, "We were going through downtown when a whole group of them came out of this building and..."

"And just fucking came after us!" Jeremy interrupted, starting to get worked up. "Then... this girl," he paused with a glance at Matt, "She just bit me. I had to beat the shit out of her to get her off me, OW! Watch it, that hurts, dammit!"

Gillian was trying to clean the oozing wound. Jeremy spared Gillian a glare before continuing, "Well, the rest of them just looked fucked up. Some were all covered in blood... and they were just... the shit was all messed up." Jeremy trailed off, staring down at his hands.

Gillian looked to Matt to explain but he just pretended to look at a poster of proper weights for cats. She returned her attention to Jeremy's shoulder. With a slight gag she noticed the smell. "How long ago did this happen? This wound looks infected."

"About a half hour ago," Matt replied, with concern.

Gillian went to the cabinet to retrieve several items. Jeremy watched her the whole time. She began applying some antiseptic cream, which caused Jeremy to jump away, cringing. "Damn! Bitch, what the hell did you just put on my arm? God, that hurts!" he shouted.

"A half an hour ago?" Ignoring the insult, she stared at the arm in disbelief. The wound was green and black and there was a truly foul-smelling puss already leaking from the ragged wound. She could see the teeth marks. It was definitely a bite. Gillian frowned as she noticed the rest of the arm was red and hot to the touch.

"I need to get some antibiotics from the kennel. I'll be right back." She moved toward the door. Matt made to follow her when the sound of breaking glass made them all freeze.

Shaking with fear, Matt pushed past Gillian to the door. He opened it a crack and peeked out through the tiny gap. Glancing back at the other two, he opened the door and edged into the hall. Moving slowly and as quietly as possible, he crept to the door separating the hall from the waiting room. Gillian followed him. He held up a hand to stop her, then slowly eased that door open a crack.

It took just a glance for his fears to be answered. Jumping back, he closed the door as quickly and quietly as possible. He turned too quickly, smashing right into Gillian and banging his head into the already swollen side of her face. She whimpered, but Matt's hand flew over her mouth. "There are two of them in the front. I think they just stumbled in. I don't think they know we are here," Matt whispered, looking scared yet relieved.

"Two of whom?" she asked, pulling his hand from her face. Matt hushed her.

Jeremy answered her by vomited loudly all over the floor. Gillian turned her attention back to Matt. Before she could ask, he grabbed her arm, pulling her toward the back of the clinic.

"We have to get out of here now!" he urged in a desperate whisper. Gillian turned to face him. She was shocked at the absolute terror on his face.

"What about your friend?" she asked, turning back to Jeremy's room. They heard something crash to the floor from the counter in the waiting room. Gillian took a step toward the examination room. Matt pulled her arm, urging her to follow him. She ignored him, watching the door to the lobby as she crept forward. "It's too late," Matt hissed. She looked back at him, confused. "Come on, we have to go. We have to leave him," Matt pleaded.

Gillian was at the door. Jeremy was on the floor moaning. Suddenly he started convulsing. Foam was coming from his mouth. She moved to help but found her way blocked by Matt. He grabbed her shoulders. Using his whole body, he forced her away from the room.

"He is going to attack us," he whispered. "Just like Sarah did." Matt tightened his grip on Gillian, pushing her backward. "Please, we have to go now. Is there a back door?"

"I need to help your friend." She hesitated. "Who is Sarah?" Gillian asked as she tried to pull away. The door to the lobby rattled open. The world blurred into one point of focus. At that point all thought except escape left Gillian's mind. Two men entered the hall. One was missing his lower jaw, and the other had most of his left arm shredded.

Live Update

Tamera Allen had been working for six days straight. She was practically living at the station, having slept there for the last two nights. She was the newest member of the news team and the youngest. She was determined to prove herself to the other reporters and management, so that she could move out of this town as soon as possible. She had it all planned out. Harrisburg in two years and Pittsburgh in five.

Mike Hillman was a twenty-year veteran of the station. He had seen pretty much everything, from steel mill strikes to horrible accidents. He was as jaded as they came. His cynicism and apathy bothered Tamera. Today was no different. Mike was his usual grumpy self as they bumped and jostled down the road in the old Ford van that was converted to a Live TV truck. Their assignment for the day was the hospital.

The closer they got the more Tamera got excited. The road was packed with cars, and people in robes, pajamas or street clothes were either stumbling toward or being helped to the cots or areas on the grass with blankets. Police were directing traffic away from the front of the building, trying to keep a clear path the entrance. Mike saw an officer he knew, gave him a nod, and was waved through.

Tamera couldn't contain herself any longer, "Finally we are going to go live from some action. Not our usual... The area is clear now but that's not the way it was an hour ago! Look at this, it's a freakin' zoo."

"Glad the suffering of others can bring you such joy," Mike grunted.

Tamera chose to ignore him. He pulled the truck up on the curb as close as he could get to the hospital. There were people everywhere. Some were covered in blankets, other in coats. Doctors and nurses hurried through the sick, trying to reassure relatives and loved ones.

The late afternoon sun began to lengthen the shadows as Tamera took the camera out to start shooting some video. Mike was busy setting up the transmitter for their live update. Tamera returned with the camera. Mike continued to get set up as Tamera hooked up her mic and put in her earpiece.

Talking to the studio, Tamera asked, "What was that, Jim?" She had to force the earpiece tighter into her ear. "Yes, Mike and I will be ready in two minutes," she said into the microphone. Mike frowned at her and continued setting up his tripod and then cued the video she had shot.

"Jim! Jim! I think you need to come to us sooner—something is up!" Tamera shouted into the mic, causing her photographer to pull his headphones away from his ear. "They are coming to us now!" she yelled. Mike could not hear the producer, but knew they were on when Tamera started talking.

"We are here at County Hospital, where patients have been arriving for the last couple of days. As you can see the emergency room has spilled out onto the street." Mike reached behind him and rolled the tape, then flipped the switch from the live feed to the deck while Tamera kept talking. "Officials are asking the public to please stay in their homes and to only bring loved ones to the hospital for emergencies. Hospital staff have been overwhelmed with... Mike, come back to me," Tamera shouted. Mike clicked the feed back to the live camera shot. He panned around to what Tamera was pointing at. "It appears the National Guard has arrived to assist the medical staff..." A scream behind Tamera made both her and Mike turn quickly back to the hospital.

Several people were struggling to their feet or clumsily easing off cots and gurneys. People were fighting each other, and many were bleeding. Between the screams came shouted orders, as soldiers pushed past the news crew, knocking Tamera over. Mike began to protest, but she waved him off to keep shooting what was happening.

Doctors, nurses and civilians ran toward the soldiers, who raised their guns and fired. Tamera screamed from the ground. Several of the fleeing people dropped, shot dead, while others turned and ran from the soldiers back toward the fighting. The soldiers fired into the crowd. "I don't understand what I am seeing,"

Tamera reported, crouched beside the live truck. "The army has opened fire on the sick and the hospital staff. It appears the...um... the sick and... Oh my God, some of the people who were shot are storming the soldiers."

Mike had taken his camera off the tripod and was moving toward the soldiers, who had formed a line of two rows. It reminded Mike of a movie about the civil war, with one line firing while the second reloaded, except instead of one shot the soldiers were emptying magazine after magazine.

An explosion sent several bodies into the air and across the pavement. A soldier had lobbed in a grenade. Mike kept filming, watching through the eyepiece. It was impossible. He watched as a man whose legs had been blown to pieces by the grenade clawed his way toward the line of soldiers. Mike zoomed out to catch film of bullets slamming into the oncoming people, who did not stop or fall. Arms blew off, chests opened into a sea of red, yet only when a head burst did a body fall and stop moving.

A mass of people still moved forward, and calls of "I'm out!" began to erupt from the line of soldiers. Handguns were drawn and fired until the line began to collapse. The first of the crowd reached the National Guard soldiers. Their second line began to run, while the first line disintegrated. Several soldiers were on the ground being torn apart by the angry mob. Mike saw through his lens that they were not only being torn apart, they were being eaten.

The camera fell. Mike tried to run, but came crashing down next to his camera. Tamera screamed from the door of the van she was trying to close. A man had a handful of her hair, and blood sprayed across the white paint and station call letters. Tamera's scalp began to part from her head. A woman bit the back of the reporter's hand that still held the microphone.

Pain shot through one of Mike's legs he spun to see a soldier chewing on his calf. Mike kicked at the man's face, and even through the screams he heard the nose break. The soldier lay still. Mike crawled under the news van, dragging his camera with him, the cord still tangled around his leg.

No Way Out

Devin sat on the edge of his chair, transfixed by the monitors. He couldn't believe what he was witnessing. A man had just been killed right before his eyes. Run over as he tried to remove a barrier to allow people safe passage out of the city. They just left them, the police just left. These were people he saw every day, people of his hometown. These were the people he would say hi to on the street and get a pleasant response. Could it really be falling apart so fast?

His attention was diverted from the monitor. The door flew open, slamming hard against the wall. Lacey Warrington rushed into the room carrying several heavy binders. She took a seat a few chairs down from Devin, letting the binders scatter over the counter. "The mayor told me to come help you," she stated, fingers clicking keys as she logged onto a computer. "I can't believe what is happening. Have you called Cheryl?" she ended her question with a cough and a shake of the head.

"I tried, but we...we... we got cut off." Devin tried not to let his imagination run wild.

"Yeah, I can't get through to anyone either. All the cell and landlines are absolutely jammed. The cops have to use two-way radios and even then the static and interference from other users is crazy." Lacey coughed again.

For several minutes the only sound was Lacey's typing and her occasional cough. Then with a flourish, Lacey clicked the enter key. "That's all of them. All the traffic lights are flashing green for the way out of town. Now we just need to get the word to people," she wheezed. In a second the wheeze turned into a painful sounding hack. Devin looked over, concerned, but she just shook her head, waving him off with a smile. "I'm okay, just normal allergies."

"Shit it is totally falling apart out there," Norman Baker exclaimed as he banged into the room, looking up at the screens. "The scanner is going nuts. Did you call home?" he asked Devin.

"I was...something happened, and I can't get a hold of anyone." Devin repeated, as Lacy coughed again.

"Did you tell them to get the hell out of town?" Norman demanded. "You need to get your family out, man."

"I tried." Devin shrugged. His resolve that his family would be fine was evaporating quickly as he watched another group attack several people running from a building. "I told Cheryl to go; I'm sure she did, that must be the reason I can't get them." He wasn't sure if Norman believed this or if he even did.

"I'm sure they are…" Norman began. A crash of metal on tile made both men jump.

Lacey's chair toppled to the floor as she jumped to her feet. "Oh my God, the fools! What are they doing?" she screamed, pointing at the monitor that showed the bridge.

Cars were scraping through the barriers, trying to get across to the inbound lanes. Sparks flew off a small hatchback that was trying to barrel down the shoulder after a motorcycle. A motor home muscled its way through the breach, pushing a minivan out of its path. Both drivers sped down the open road. Without warning, the van crossed over in front of the RV. It clipped the front bumper, sending the van into a spin. It flipped over in front of the larger vehicle. The RV was now pushing the van, sending sparks flying. There was no sign of stopping. The RV swerved, trying to shake off the van. Then a bright green sports car tried to fly past the obstacle. The RV swerved back into its lane. "Look out!" Lacy cried, pointing at the back of the RV, where there was a platform carrying an extra cooler and two propane tanks. The car sideswiped another car, then slammed into the platform. The propane tanks erupted from the impact. The green car was now a rolling ball of flame. It glanced off a second car, lost control, then embedded itself into the retaining wall.

Flames were quickly eating away the rest of the motor home, and the driver was becoming more erratic. With a lurch, the huge RV skidded to a halt across the lanes, bouncing to a stop against the safety rail. Drivers slammed on their brakes, and others swerved, trying not to join the expanding flames. Black smoke billowed from the tires. Reverse lights flashed on. It was too late—the cars behind were coming up fast. They smashed into the cars trying to get back through. One small car flew over the wreckage, sailing off into the river below.

The trio in the control room watched in horror as a large jacked-up pickup truck smashed and swerved its way to the front. Picking up speed, it plowed straight ahead to the burning RV. Devin urged the vehicle on, hoping it would make an opening. The truck smashed into the burning wreckage. Its rear bed lifted into the air, only to crash down again. The truck had only added its hulk to the flaming barricade. The driver of the pickup truck jumped from the cab. In flames, he ran several feet before collapsing as a smoldering corpse. Now cars and flaming debris totally blocked the inbound lanes.

Burning bodies began to emerge from the charred skeleton of the RV. "Good God! It's like a fucking clown car." Norman shouted. "There must have been ten or fifteen people in that thing." He fell silent, watching the flaming undead. They were heading into the mass of crashed vehicles. People were climbing out of windows, leaving possessions and people behind. They scampered over hoods trying to escape, pushing others out of the way. "Oh my God," Norman whispered watching the chaos.

Now the outbound lanes were in panic. The arms of the burning corpses flailed over the wall. People ran between cars and over them. Vehicles tried to force past each other on the bridge, three abreast until the inevitable happened. No one was willing to back off; they became lodged against each other and the railing. The road emptied out in front of the blockage on either side. Several people jumped the barrier to run down the bridge.

Devin watched as others tried to get out of their cars. He saw the panic as the flames spread across one side and the dead closed in on both. Both kinds of doom were getting closer to the people trapped by blocked doors or wrecked cars. People tried to smash their windows to escape while others jumped from the bridge to the shallow river below.

Many were now running back to town, only to be met by another wave of people trying to get out. But this group did not have the same urgency. They were not running or pushing.

Reality dawned on Devin as he watched the group running from the flames falter. They began throwing rocks and debris at the oncoming crowd. "What are they doing?" he asked, gripping the back of a chair, denying what he knew.

The second mass of people steadily advanced. The rocks fell uselessly to the ground. Now there was running back to cars—or in any direction. Devin, Lacey and Norman stood stock still, watching. The group from town began advancing through the sea of wrecked vehicles. They were banging on windows. They attacked people as they tried to get away.

"Sweet mother of pearl!" Devin exclaimed.

"What the fuck is happening?" Norman whispered.

Get Home

Steve followed the slow progress of the little Toyota Prius as it passed along the front of his Mustang. In the driver's seat of the highly efficient car was a woman. She turned her dead eyes to meet Steve's. She contorted in the seat, both hands clawing at the closed window. She was missing a couple fingers on her left hand and her forehead had large gash in it.

Steve just watched the creature as the car continued its slow journey across his bumper, creaking and scraping as it went. Finally free of the front of his car, it drifted slowly into the wall of a building. The zombie inside the car turned in the seat to stare at Steve the entire time it traveled. She was trying to climb over the seat to get at him, but was hindered by the still-buckled seat belt. Steve watched as she clawed, strained, and growled. Shaking his head from his stupor, he gave the woman the finger. As soon as the vehicle was clear he pushed the accelerator.

I have to get home. Just get home, Stevie, he berated himself. In the rear view mirror, he could see the creature pawing at the passenger window.

Steve loved his Mustang. He had skimped and saved for this car for over a year. It had custom wheels, a deep blue paint job that he lovingly washed every week. The interior and exterior were spotless. The oil was changed regularly. Every care was taken to keep his girl looking beautiful. This thought flitted through his mind as he smashed into a garbage can, splattered a zombie across the wide hood, and sent sparks into the air as he scraped a building as he sped down the sidewalk.

He swung the car around. It fishtailed, then bounced off a light pole as he mounted the pavement of the road leading up the hill to his neighborhood. He saw smoke rising off in the distance. Oh God, please let them be okay. Please let me be able to get to them.

The familiar road was barely recognizable through the smoke. Abandoned possessions mixed with sights of gore. Red patches stood out bright against the grey concrete of the sidewalks. Some still contained mementos of what had happened there. Here a leg, there an arm, there an unrecognizable twisted pile of horror. Steve passed a group huddled on the ground. A hand shot up from their midst, curled, then sunk slowly back down.

Steve urged more speed out of the high-performance engine. He had a clear shot to the neighborhood. A zombie shuffled off the sidewalk up ahead. Steve didn't even swerve. The creature bounced off the hood while one of its limbs went flying. "I'll run over every fuckin one! Run every one of you bastards down! You can't stop me from getting home," he screamed as he clipped another one. The creature pirouetted on one leg while the other leg twisted in the air, shattered. It fell. Steve glanced in the rearview mirror. It was trying to crawl up the street after him. Steve's attention moved back to what was in front of him. He was heading straight at another one. Both feet stood on the brakes as he recognized that the creature was running toward him. This was different from the others. This one was alive.

Finding a Friend

Wes had covered two blocks. The pack on his back became heavier with each step, and he still had several blocks to Beth's house. It was taking longer than he had originally anticipated. The neighborhood was in total anarchy. Every house he passed seemed to be either broken into or out of. He had seen several people running. The few cars that passed barely slowed, even with his frantic waving. He had been following the street for about a block before coming to the conclusion that this was an incredibly bad idea. The zombies seemed to think the street was also the best place to be. After ducking several grabbing hands, he decided to make himself scarce.

Keeping to backyards as much as he could, he wondered if he should have stayed in his house. Then a sound other than screams caught his attention. Peering over a tall fence, he spied a dirt bike lying on its side, the engine still idling. Gun in hand, Wes found the gate to the yard. He edged forward along the wall. At the corner he saw the owner of the bike. He was missing his head. The rest of the body had been literally torn apart, leaving chunks on the sidewalk and lawn. Approaching the bike, he saw the helmet. The visor was up. Wes blinked, and the head inside blinked back.

Wes raised the gun, hesitated, and then lowered it. If he fired, he was sure it would just draw unwanted attention. The eyes followed his every movement. Wes tried to ignore this. He kept telling himself that there was nothing he could do for him. "I'm sorry," Wes mouthed.

Looking up and down the street, he assessed the situation. There were a few zombies a little way down the block. They were close. Thankfully they were wandering in the opposite direction. The road ahead looked mostly clear of the undead. The only obstacles were luggage and a couple of abandoned cars.

Might make it easily enough, Wes tried to convince himself. Of course, that might be what he thought. The eyes blinked back at him. Wes clicked on the safety. He tucked the gun in his belt. Readying, he rocked back and forth, took a breath, let it out, and ran to the bike. He quickly righted it. Jumping on, he twisted the throttle. The engine screamed. The zombies up the block turned, moaning their disapproval. Wes panicked. Sitting on the bike in the middle of the street, he kept revving the engine.

The engine cried out its power, but he wasn't moving. Several more zombies stumbled into the road from a nearby house. He was drawing a lot of attention now. Slapping himself hard in the head, het thought, Shit! Clutch!

Pulling in the clutch, he snapped the bike in gear. He rolled his shoulders, letting the clutch out. The bike immediately lurched into a wheelie. Wes screamed, letting off the throttle. The front wheel came down hard. Wes hit the pavement harder. More ghouls were converging now. Wes was quickly becoming surrounded. Painfully he scrambled up. He righted the now-stalled bike. He could feel their eyes on him as he got back on. With a shaking hand, he pulled in the clutch. His foot found the kick starter. The path in front of him was closing fast. He kicked the starter down. The bike roared to life at once.

Stunned, he sat for a second. That never happens in the movies. He laughed.

The smile slid from his face quickly. Slowly this time, he let out the clutch, twisted the accelerator and headed for the closing gap. The horde that was heading straight toward him. Shifting gears with more grinding than grace, he sped past the clawing hands.

Wes swerved around two wrecked cars. One had a zombie struggling to get at him through a half-open window. Several heart-pounding minutes later the bike skidded to a halt in front of Beth's house. Wes' heart sank. The door hung open. A trail of blood ran down the walkway.

"No, No, NO!" he shouted, jumping off the bike. He let it fall. The engine sputtered and died. Cursing under his breath, he pulled the gun from his belt. Cautiously he crept up to the door. Stealing a glance inside, he couldn't see anything further than the foyer.

Taking a steadying breath, he slipped into the house. Blood was smeared along the walls of the front hall. Edging his way deeper into the house, Wes paused, listening for movement.

"Beth?" He barely whispered. He wanted so badly to find her, but he was terrified he would.

He crept deeper into the gloomy hall. Wes heard the emergency broadcast on the living room TV. He edged slowly toward the sound. A man was standing in front of the TV. "The public is instructed to go to the following evacuation points: Richland Mall, Point Park, or the Cinema on the Hill..." the electronic voice rattled off, "Avoid anyone who is sick, has been bitten, or is injured by those who are sick. If someone has died in your home, leave them and evacuate immediately."

"Mr. McDaniel?" We' asked through a trembling whisper. His heart sunk, as he knew even before the man completed his turn. It had been Mr. McDaniel. He was missing an eye and most of his cheek. His body cavity was ripped open and most of his entrails were missing. His remaining eye focused on the Wes.

Wes whimpered. He stumbled backward as the creature raised an arm, reaching out to him. Raising the gun, Wes took aim. He found it hard to pull the trigger as he backed to the wall. The zombie McDaniel let out a groan. Before the groan could turn into a howl, Wes fired. Mr. McDaniel was no more.

Again, guilt and grief filled Wes. He stared at the corpse crumpled on the floor. Wes remembered the many times he had talked and laughed with the man. The many nights he had spent in this house when his real father had been in one of his drunken rages. He remembered all the times Mr. McDaniel had protected him and his mother. "Damn it," he muttered as he swiped at his eyes.

Turning his back on the scene in the living room, the thought hit him. Living room... Wes let out a humorless laugh. He did a quick inspection of the house. There was no sign of trouble in either Beth's room or Steve's, other than a broken window. He paused for a second at Beth's door. He noticed her jacket and backpack were missing. His heart jumped in hope. Gazing around the room, he spied a stuffed rabbit he had given Beth for her birthday. It had been a few years, but she still said it was her favorite. Grabbing it, he stuffed the bunny into his backpack.

On his way back outside he paused at the front closet. He knew Steve kept his hunting rifle in there. Frowning, he pulled it from the closet. He had hoped it would be gone. He slung it onto his back, next to the sword. Reaching up his hand, he scanned the top shelf and grabbed whatever ammo he could. He tried to stuff several boxes in his already overloaded pack. He pulled out the stuffed bunny, replacing it with the ammo. Throwing the pack over his shoulder he stood up, ready to move. He looked down and saw the stuffed animal smiling up at him. The bunny stared up with happy blue eyes. Wes turned, hesitated, buttoned his jacket, grabbed the bunny and stuffed it in. "You just had to be so damn cute," he grumbled.

Heading toward the door he caught a glimpse of himself in the hall mirror. His reflection forced out a laugh. There was blood splattered on his clothes and face. He held a gun in his right hand, a rifle muzzle and sword hilt poked out above his shoulders. The best thing was that peeking out of the front of the stained, torn and dirty jacket were two bunny ears. He addressed the ears, "Ok, bunny, let's get up to Richland Mall." Smiling he gave them a pat.

Turning back to the door, he found his exit blocked. Wes aimed and fired. The zombie crumpled, revealing several more filing in behind it. Wes fired again and again, but the noise only attracted more and more. The way out was now clogged by a pile of bodies. The only good thing was that he seemed to have made a barrier with the corpses. Even so, the living dead were beginning to push and climb over.

Not waiting to fill the breach, he ran to the back of the house. Vaulting over the body of Beth's father, Wes ran through the shattered sliding glass door. A little boy shuffled toward him as soon as Wes was free of the house. The child's ashen features and guttural growl told Wes all he needed to know. The boy began to moan loudly.

Not wanting a repeat of the house, and aware of the fact that the gun's ammo was low, Wes pulled the sword from his back. With a sweeping upward slice the child's head snapped back. Its bottom jaw was now limply hanging in two pieces. Still the boy moaned. Several dead were now shuffling through the broken sliding glass door. Others were creeping around the corner of the house.

"Dammit! Little bastard!" Wes huffed. He ran to the road in front of Beth's house. The dead covered the entrance. The motorbike was on its side, zombies tripping or falling all over it. "Damn!" He was spotted. The moan went up, raised by one and joined by others. The undead turned to face him.

Wes dropped the mag from the gun and checked it with a frown. He threw the sword onto his back. He dug in his pocket, slammed a fresh clip into the gun, and ran to the main road of the neighborhood. He heard the roar of an engine coming up fast. As the car crested the hill a smile broke out on his face. He knew that car.

Out of Control Center

Lacey gripped the console, breathing heavily. She stumbled backward as she began to wheeze. She grabbed at her chest while fanning her face. Fear filled her eyes as the wheeze turned into a cough. She was gasping for air, coughing non-stop. Norman rushed to catch her as she lost balance. Slowly he lowered her to the floor. Her hand now gripping his arm tight. Her eye bulged as her legs gave out. She fought for any tiny gasp of breath.

"Dev, grab me some water!" Norman cried. "Lace, Lace...Where is your inhaler?" He grabbed the woman's purse. Wallet, keys, and a compact flew out. Norman dug for a few frantic seconds before dumping the entire contents on the floor. Hands flew over the detritus until he found the small inhaler. Norman forced it to her lips.

As the purse's contents scattered across the floor Devin ran to the water cooler in the corner. While he poured water into a paper cup Lacey's wheezing ended in a long groan. Devin stood hunched over, his finger on the button for water, as he listened for her to catch her breath. There was nothing.

"Lace? Lacey!" Norman shouted. Devin straightened up. The cool cup of water felt foreign in his hand. He stared at the blank wall behind the cooler. This couldn't be happening. Slowly he turned back to see Lacey on the floor. She was staring at the ceiling. Devin knew she couldn't see it.

Norman held her in his arms. "She just died," Norman stated calmly, "Just died." He looked down at the woman. "I tried to give her the inhaler but it didn't work. How can asthma kill her?"

Devin closed his eyes. With all this, she dies from an asthma attack?" he thought. Hoping this was all just a dream, he kept his eyes shut tight. He listened for the familiar sound of morning in his bed. There was no mistaking the sound of the control room. Slowly he opened his eyes. The scene was as he left it seconds before, Norman cradling the body of their co-worker.

Norman slowly laid her on the floor. He reached out to shut her eyes. She blinked. Norman's hand flew back as if burned. She sat up, staring at him. Norman backed away and stared back in stunned silence.

"Lace, you're okay!" A relieved smile broke over Norman's face. Slowly Lacey raised her arms like she wanted to hug him. When her hands grabbed Norman, his smile was gone in a flash. She lurched forward, sinking her teeth into his neck. His blue shirt blossomed with red.

Norman's screams began to gurgle through the blood. The water flew from Devin's hand as he jumped backward. Pain and wet covered Devin's back as he rammed into the water cooler. The huge plastic bottle toppled to the floor, sending water cascading across the tile. Devin's cries mixed with Norman's screams. Norman grabbed Lacey by the hair, throwing her off. She skidded across the tile floor. She spun, cat-like, and turned quickly and crawled back toward him. Norman tried to back away. She caught his leg. He kicked at her, sending her reeling. Her small frame smashed into a table leg, rolled over, and came at him again. He threw up his arms to protect himself from her clawing and biting.

Devin watched the scene unfold before him, his mouth hanging open. He realized he was screaming. Without thinking, he ran forward. Grabbing a folding chair, he smashed it across Lacey's back. Devin's hands stung from the impact, but she didn't seem to notice. Norman was kicking and punching at Lacey, landing blow after blow. She kept coming.

Lacey groaned, struggling to get at Norman's face and neck. She was biting and clawing anywhere she could. Devin grabbed a laptop. Raising it high over his head, he brought it smashing down on her skull. He had hoped to knock her out. The first blow did nothing. Devin was screaming again, adrenaline taking over. He brought the computer down on her again and again. It was working; she seemed dazed. Now her attention was on Devin. Norman crawled away, leaving a wide streak of bloody water behind him.

Now that Devin had Lacey's full attention he faltered. Taking a step back, he recoiled as she gained her feet. Blood covered her neck, face, teeth and chin. Devin raised the computer. With a cry he swung it as hard as he could. Her head snapped to one side, but she still came at him. He hit her again and the computer began to break, as did her face.

"SMACK," several teeth left her mouth. "CRACK!" An eye socket smashed, the fluid from the ruptured orb oozed down the bloody cheek. Dropping the broken computer, he grabbed a monitor. In a fluid motion he ripped it from its connectors, raised it above his head, and "CRUNCH!" She fell backward, the monitor like a crown on her head. She teetered, swung forward then back. The monitor shattered when she hit the floor.

Her legs twitched. Her good eye was staring up at the ceiling once again. Devin grabbed another laptop. He couldn't stop; it was like a nightmare, and he hit her again and again. Her face was unrecognizable. It was a bloody pulp on the floor. He was drained, exhausted. Breathing heavily, he hit her three more times.

"Stop… STOP!" Norman was yelling. Devin held the computer over his head as reality raced back in. Devin looked down at Lacey's mutilated face. He dropped the computer into the spreading pool of blood. Her brain splattered as the case hit it. Devin backed away in horror.

"What the fuck?" Norman gasped, clutching his heavily bleeding neck. "What the hell just happened?"

Need a Lift?

Steve's eyes widened, seeing a young man run into the road. He was frantically waving his arms. Slamming on the brakes, the car went into a skid. Steve turned the wheel to avoid running over the guy. The huge grin Wes wore when he had seen the car ran from his face as the car slid sideways. It stopped mere inches from him. Steve couldn't believe his eyes. Wes stood there, a gun in his hand, a rifle and sword on his back, a huge backpack slung over his shoulders, with bunny ears sticking out of his jacket and a huge smile now back on his face. Steve couldn't help but smile himself as he threw open the passenger side door. "Wes! Get in."

Wes pulled off his pack and threw it over the seat, followed by the sword. He swung the rifle off his shoulder and jumped into the car, keeping it in front of him. He shut the door. They both sat in silence, their smiles evaporating. After a few seconds Steve began to pull forward. "Dude, we can't go that way!" Wes gestured out the front window, "It is swarming with zombies." He jabbed his thumb behind them. "There is an evacuation point up at Richland Mall."

Steve got the car turned around. They were heading back down the hill toward the road that would take them to the mall. He looked over at Wes, who was staring straight ahead. Steve recognized the rifle as his own. "That's my gun, isn't it?"

Wes did not look over at Steve. "Yeah," he muttered, still without looking over.

"Beth?... My dad?" Steve asked.

Wes took a deep breath. "I don't know about Beth. She... she wasn't at your house." Wes looked out the side window. "Your Dad. He, well,... he's... um."

"He isn't one of them, is he?" Steve asked frantically, turning to look at Wes.

Wes swallowed and whispered, "Not anymore."

Steve knew what happened just by the look on Wes's face. Anger, grief, sorrow, and pain all crashed over Steve. Wes seemed to crumble into the seat next to him.

"I'm so sorry," Wes sobbed.

Steve glanced at the young man sitting next to him. Then he returned his attention to the road. Several long seconds passed. "Thanks... thanks for not letting him... for not letting him stay one of those things," Steve whispered, tears rolled down his cheeks. Wes only nodded, keeping his face turned to the window. He didn't want Steve to see him cry.

Steve stared out the windshield, letting the tears run down his face. He reached over, placing a hand on Wes' shoulder. "Really. Thanks," he croaked, giving Wes a shake.

Wes looked over and saw the tears. "He was always so good to me...I couldn't leave him..."

"Your mom and stepdad?"

Wes shook his head.

"Did you?"

Wes nodded.

"I'm sorry." Steve's heart broke for Wes. Silence again filled the car as they turned onto the main road that would lead them up the mountainside to the Mall. The only sound was the hum of the engine until they came around a bend in the road.

"Whoa!" Steve cried, slamming on the brakes for what felt like the hundredth time in the last hour. Wes grabbed the dash to keep from flying into it. The road ahead was completely blocked. They could see a huge wreck involving at least ten cars. "Back the way we came," Steve grunted, putting the car in reveres. A commotion from the stopped cars caused Wes to point needlessly. People began screaming and running toward them.

"We're too late!" Wes gasped.

A few cars had already turned around. They were barreling straight toward them. "Shit!" Steve yelled, throwing the car into reverse. Spinning the wheel, he slammed on the gas. The car spun around, and Steve slammed it back into first gear. The tires braked and they were heading back the way they came. Other cars flew by. They were only ahead for a moment. The mini vans and SUVs were unable to out-strip the high-performance Mustang engine for long.

While Steve weaved his way in and out of traffic, Wes watched terrified faces pass in a blur. "The Point!" That is the next place they said to go," Wes yelled, grabbing onto the dashboard again as the car swung violently.

The Fall of City Hall

Devin stared down at Lacey's broken body, then to his blood-soaked hands. "What the hell is going on?" he demanded of the shattered skull. He turned to Norman, who was growing paler by the second. Blood was pouring from the man's neck. Dropping the shattered computer, Devin knew Norman was in trouble. "Hang on Norm, I'll go get help."

Wrenching open the door to the hall, he was greeted by more screams and yelling. The mayor and his assistant Trevor Smyth came running down the hall. Mayor Martin Griggs was yelling, "Devin! Come on, we have to get out of here!"

"They're already in the building!" Trevor screamed."

"The National Guard is on the way!" Martin called. "We have to get to the ballpark. That is where they are going to evacuate us," the Mayor continued, grabbing Devin by the arm.

Devin wrenched his arm free. Martin skidded to a halt, eyebrows raised. "Norm's been hurt. Lacey...Lacey went... she went, well we thought she died, but..." Devin tried to explain but the Mayor cut across him.

"Good God, did she bite him?"

"Yeah, he is losing a lot of blood, and we need..." The door behind him burst open. A blood-covered Norman lunged at them, arms outstretched and teeth bared.

Martin grabbed Devin again. "Too late! COME ON!" he shouted. Trevor was several feet ahead, urging them to follow. Daring a glance back at Norman, the three men ran down the hall. Crashing down the stairs, they rushed across the maze of cubicles to the doors to the lobby. Pushing through the doors, they were met with bedlam. The security guards were screaming at a group of people to stay back. The group was trying to break through the front doors. Devin saw streaks of blood covering the glass. The people looked like they had been through a meat grinder.

"Aim for the heads, boys!" Martin yelled. "Don't try to reason, just shoot and run!"

"The side door!" screamed Trevor.

The three men sprinted across the lobby, with Trevor in the lead, followed closely by Devin and the mayor, huffing, bringing up the rear. Glass doors shattered, guns blasted. The security guards fired and yelled as the men ran by. Devin covered his head, running like mad after Trevor. Martin yelled over his shoulder, "Shoot 'em in the head, or fuck it, run for your lives, damn it!"

Devin slid around a corner after Trevor. "Keep up, Marty!" Trevor called over his shoulder. Martin exclaimed in very explicit terms for them not to wait for him. Trevor skidded to a halt at the emergency exit to the alley. Devin slammed into the door next to him. The two men stared at each other. Both thinking the same as the other. What was waiting to greet them on the other side?

Martin barked at them as he ran full out, "Get out of the way, boys!"

"Mayor, what if they are out..." Trevor started.

"Then you two either better save my ass or run the other way," Martin shouted as he spun to slam through the door, back first, into the alley.

Out of the Cage

Gillian grabbed Matt's arm and pulled him to the back of the clinic. All of the animals were straining and crying in their cages. She hesitated for a moment, wanting to set the animals free. What would happen to them if she did? What would happen if she didn't? Would the creatures follow the animals, or leave them alone? Could she live with herself if she used them as bait? Could she live with herself if she left them in their cages to their fate? Her internal struggle ended with the clang of a metal dish falling from a counter.

Now it was Matt's turn to pull Gillian to the door marked Exit. Letting go of her arm, he pushed on the door. Nothing happened. Gillian looked back down the hall. The two undead were progressing slowly toward them. They were already passed the examination room where Jeremy was. Gillian threw a chair down the hall, tripping one of the ghouls. She picked up a large cat carrier, holding it at the ready. Behind the advancing dead, Jeremy stumbled out of his room. His movements were jerky and stuttered. It looked like he was having trouble making his limbs move.

Gillian saw the look on his face. The boy she had been treating was no longer behind the eyes. It was time to go. She threw the carrier at the dead man who was closest. It bounced off his chest, not slowing his progress in the slightest.

Matt glanced over his shoulder. Seeing the approaching ghouls with his friend close behind sent him into a panic. "Oh shit oh shit oh shit," he screamed, pushing at the door.

The jawless man was furthest down the hall. Jeremy was not far behind. The one who fell was thankfully having a difficult time extricating himself from the chair. Jeremy let out a howl like nothing Gillian had heard before. It was a low mournful cry that was answered by a gurgling from the jawless man and a lower howl from the chair man. Matt was pushing and pulling at the door, whimpering and pounding.

It started in her toes, working its way to the top of her head. Terror like she had never felt boiled within her. She flung whatever was in reach at the creatures. A pair of scissors flew from her hand, embedding themselves in the chest of Jawless. He did not falter.

Giving up on throwing things, she ran to Matt's side. "Deadbolt!" she screamed, trying to turn the knob. Matt, in a panic, tried to push the door open.

"Let go of the door so I can turn the deadbolt!" she yelled at the boy.

"What! Let me out! Let me out!" Matt screamed back.

Pushing Matt out of the way, she cranked the deadbolt, twisted the doorknob, and kicked the door open. She flung herself and a panicking Matt out into the street. Turning, she saw the jawless man right on top of them. The same stench she had encountered from Jeremy's wound accosted her nose. Gagging she slammed the door on the jawless face. The slam of the door barely hid the crunch of a nose as the door met his face.

Cool evening air flooded into her lungs. The smell of decomposition still haunted her sense of smell. Drawing deep heavy breaths, she slumped against the heavy steel door. The cool metal felt safe and sturdy against her back. Matt was looking up and down the alley. Gillian became aware of a scratching coming through the door. Suddenly the door rattled in its frame. Gillian jumped away, ready to run.

Matt grabbed her arm. "We, we should be ok. They don't seem too good with doorknobs." He panted, still scanning the alley.

She turned to ask one of the million questions screaming through her mind but only one came out as she saw the street, "What the hell is going on?"

Withdrawal

Wendell Phillips glared at Archie Snowden's back as he mounted the steps to the bank. The two men had worked together for the past seven years. Wendell had never really liked the man. Wendell's former partner had retired. That is when he got stuck with Archie. In Wendell's opinion, Archie was a foul-mouthed lazy grouch. He complained incessantly about the job, their supervisors, and the weight of the "other people's" money they carried.

For Archie, Wendell was a bore. All Wendell wanted to do was make the runs and get back without incident. Archie prayed for the day when someone would start something. Today could finally be that day.

Wendell had never even had a bullet in the chamber of his gun. This had earned him the nickname Barney Fife from Archie. Today the gun was out of the holster, loaded and ready. His head snapped to the left as a scream floated from a building across the street. A car jumped the curb and tore across the sidewalk, but kept going. Wendell's arms were starting to ache from the tension. He needed to get home to his wife. They needed to get out of this town.

Dispatch had ordered them to the main branch of the First County Bank. When they had arrived the manager opened the vault in a hurry. He told them to take the money to one of the branches in the suburbs. That was the last they had seen of him.

In the bank Archie wiped the sweat from his balding head. Grabbing three large bags and grinning from ear to ear, he moved his large frame out the door to the back of the armored car. Throwing the bags into the truck, he slapped Wendell on the arm and hurried back up the stairs.

"Hurry up, I want to get this done and get home," Wendell shouted at Archie, who just gave an irritated wave over his shoulder.

"Just have to get the rest of my retirement," Archie said to himself. He stepped over the reason for the manager's flight. The woman's eyes stared up at the ceiling. The top of her head was all over the floor and the desk behind her. Archie looked down at her.

"Boom! Head shot." He held his fingers like a gun with his thumb coming down. "You were a mess when you came in, oooo, all bloody and growling," he taunted. "Well, you're more of a mess now, aren't ya?" Archie laughed as he huffed back to the vault.

Grabbing three more heavy bags, he turned to head back out. He was in the lobby when he stopped. Dropping the bags, he pulled his gun. A window shattered. An arm thrust through the broken glass. The arm was cut up, the muscle and suit material hung from the shredded appendage. It flailed around in the window, but the height and bars kept the owner from getting in.

Dancing just out of reach, Archie shook his enormous backside at the grabbing hand. "OOH you like that, huh?" he laughed. Holstering the gun, he grabbed the bags and hurried out the door.

The look on Wendell's face told Archie there was going to be a problem. Next to Wendell was the corpse of a man in a suit. It was obvious that he had been like the woman in the bank, and the flailing owner of the arm.

"I've had enough! I am taking the truck, I'm getting my family, and I'm getting out of town. Let's go," Wendell demanded, pointing to the door of the vehicle.

Archie stared at Wendell. The last seven years burned in his stomach. He had always hated Wendell. Whining about his family and boring him with stories of his old partner. This scrawny old bastard was not going to keep him from this windfall.

"The world is falling apart," Archie growled, "and by the time they get this straightened out I will be long gone and forgotten. So will this podunk town bank's money." His hand dropped a money bag. It edged toward his gun. He eyed Wendell's weapon. It seemed heavy and awkward in his hand. Archie trained weekly, and he doubted Wendell even liked to carry the gun, let alone fire it.

"I am taking the truck, and you can come along. I will drop you somewhere but we are leaving now. You can have all the money as well. I don't...." Wendell's attention was distracted by movement on the side of the bank. A man with one arm missing was approaching them.

"Fuck you and fuck your family," Archie spat.

Wendell turned back, ready to tell Archie what he thought of the fat lazy...His eyes went wide as saucers. The look of total amazement was priceless to Archie. Three rounds hit Wendell in the chest, and his gun clattered to the ground. Archie stood over him for a moment, trying not to laugh at the look of surprise still etched on Wendell's face. Blood spread out from the body as Wendell gasped for breath, reaching out to Archie. His eyes rolled back in his head.

"They won't miss a rent-a-cop either, or figure out I did it." Archie laughed as he ran back up the stairs to the bank, shooting the one-armed man as he did.

Disintegration

The sun burned blood red as it began its descent behind one of the mountains. The glow was brightened by the addition of the several buildings burning out of control. Sitting alone by one of the infernos was a fire truck. Copious amounts of water spewed from a hose no one attended. The flaming lawyer's office next to the truck collapsed, sending sparks high into the darkening sky.

Gillian and Matt peeked around the corner. At the end of the block the road was clogged with cars. They were smashed into each other or stood abandoned with doors hanging open. Nothing was moving and there was no clear path. They retreated to the other end of the alley. A light burned in a window straight ahead.

Gillian recognized the café across the street. She had just had lunch there yesterday. The front window was streaked with bloody handprints. Open mouthed, Gillian stepped off the curb toward the restaurant. A car screamed around the corner, and two hands yanked her from the road back onto the sidewalk. The car never slowed as it passed.

"Be careful!" Matt hissed.

She glanced over her shoulder, giving him a nod of thanks. Breathing heavily through the adrenaline, her attention was drawn back to the window. A figure slowly stood up. Its back was to the glass. Slowly it turned. For a moment it just stood there staring out the window, swaying slightly. Then it saw them. Gillian backed up until she ran into the wall. Bloody hands slammed against the window. Teeth scrapped at the glass while loose skin dragged across, leaving streaks of makeup and blood. Half of the blond hair of the waitress was missing along with part of her scalp. Blood stained the pink and white uniform.

Gillian's hands covered her mouth as she forced back a scream. The waitress kept trying to get through the glass at them. Matt appeared at her side again, grabbing her arm as several people ran past on the other side of the street. They took no notice of the ghoul behind the glass. It slammed its fists against the glass, making it rattle dangerously.

"She'll make it through eventually," Matt nodded. "They don't seem to get tired. Just keep banging away until they get through."

Her attention followed the retreating group. "Where are those people going?"

Looking at the direction they came from, they did not get an answer. Instead they saw three ghouls kneeling over a prone figure. One raised its head. Blood covered the mouth and front of the suit shirt. Another head came up, looking in their direction. Its green Mohawk was half flattened against the head with dried blood. Its mouth was also covered in dripping red.

"Come on, we can't stay here." Matt whispered.

"Right, my car is this…" Gillian faltered, putting her hand in her pocket to search for her keys. The memory of earlier in the day played back in her mind like a film. She had taken them out of her pocket and put them by her lunch bag so she wouldn't forget them. Slapping herself in the forehead, she couldn't look over at Matt.

He read the look. "No keys?" He moaned.

"Come on. We are three blocks from the city building. They have armed guards there and police," Gillian said. Matt stared at her.

"We have to walk? Dude, that sucks!" Matt frowned.

Gillian smiled, "Dude? Really?" Matt smiled back. They both chuckled nervously, regaining their composure. "We have to move. This way." She pointed away from the three ghouls and their prey. The suit and the punk were already on their feet, heading in toward them.

Matt and Gillian moved quickly down the block toward the city building. Gillian trying to block out the screams and blood that seemed to surround and follow them. A man passed them, running in the other direction. He stutter-stepped, and reaching them, he faltered just long enough to grab Matt by the shoulder and yell, "GET TO THE BALLPARK! The Army is going to pick us up!" He released Matt and ran away. Gillian made to follow the fleeing man, but Matt pulled her in the direction they were previously going.

She began to question him. "That is the way Jeremy and I were coming from. There are too many… uh, zombies that way," Matt stated flatly.

She hesitated, then let herself be led away from the direction of the ballpark. "Who was Sarah?" she asked.

Matt stopped took a breath as he looked down. "She was my sister." He started moving again but did not look at Gillian. "My dad was sick, ya know, with the flu. My mom called from the hospital where Dad was. She told us things were going crazy down there and to leave. Jeremy, Sarah, and I were trying to get out of town."

Coming to a corner Matt pressed himself flat against the wall. He took a quick look then finally met her gaze. "That way looks okay." Gillian nodded. Matt however didn't move.

"Jeremy was driving, and we got hit by a truck. It just blew through the light. Sarah got bounced around pretty hard when we got hit. We tried to run to the ballpark like the radio told us but she was really hurt. Jeremy had been helping her, but she fell down and we couldn't get her to get up. That was when we saw that group come out of the building. Jeremy tried to pick her up. That's when she," Matt took a deep breath and swiped at his eyes. Gillian acted like she hadn't noticed by looking up and down the street.

It took a moment then he continued, "She attacked him. She bit his shoulder…her eyes… her eyes were all crazy. He pushed her away, but she came at him and he pushed her again. She wouldn't stop coming after him. I tried to grab her and oh god." Matt wiped his eyes again. The tears were rolling free. Gillian placed a hand on his shoulder. "She just wouldn't stop. Jeremy had no choice. He loved her, ya know. They had been together for two years." Matt looked up at Gillian, his eyes pleading with her to understand. He dropped his gaze.

Matt stepped around the corner, keeping close the wall edging down the street. "They are together now, I guess." Not knowing what to say, Gillian followed Matt to the next corner, where they stopped. Across the street was a bank. A guard was rushing out of it carrying money. Matt nodded to Gillian, agreeing silently they should make for the building.

The sound of gunfire caused them to stop instantly. They watched, stunned, as an older man sunk to the ground. The words said by the shooter lost in the chaos that surrounded them. "It is really going to hell, isn't it?" Matt questioned. The fourth shot caused him to jump. Looking back at the scene, he could see a retreating figure entering the bank.

Gillian shook her head, "I can't believe we are turning on each other already."

"Well we need a ride, and I doubt one will be offered. I think it is okay to steal a car from a murderer," Matt noted nervously. Gillian couldn't think of anything wrong with Matt's reasoning.

"We heard four shots. So he only has two bullets left," Gillian surmised.

"Assuming he has a revolver and not a semi," Matt explained. A look of panic passed between them. Without a word they hurried from the corner they were hiding around, across the street to the armored truck.

"We need the keys. Check his pockets." Gillian said, glancing into the cab. She grabbed the gun from the ground. Anxiety brewed in her stomach. This was a semi-automatic. She figured out how to drop the magazine out. It was full. She grabbed all the extra ammunition from Wendell's belt.

Matt stood staring down at the man. Gillian saw the fear on the young man's face. "Fine!" she grunted, quickly shoving her hand into a pocket. Finding keys, they jingled free. She tossed them to Matt, who hurried to the passenger side door. Wendell groaned. Gillian jumped back.

She could see the blood pool. She was surprised he was still alive. There was no way they could get him to the hospital. She also knew there was very little time before the other man returned. Gillian cursed, closed her eyes, then checked the back of the truck for any weapons they might need. She only found several sacks of cash. She allowed a moment to muse over the bags, thinking she had only ever seen them in movies. She also tried not to think about putting the dying man out of his misery. He seemed to have passed out. Shaking the thoughts, she returned to searching. Nothing in the form of a weapon reveled itself. With a curse she slammed the door shut.

Running to the driver's door, she found it locked. Standing on the running board, she looked through the window. There was the top of Matt's head outside the cab at the other door. Gillian swore again and ran around the front of the truck, trying not to look back at the legs twitching behind the vehicle.

"What is the problem?" she demanded.

Matt fumbled through the keys, trying each one. "There are like a hundred keys on this ring."

"Come on, come on," Gillian urgently whispered.

Inserting several keys without luck, Matt whooped when the button clicked up. "Ha! Got you, bitch." Matt threw open the door and scrambled up into the cab. "Uh, sorry." He smiled sheepishly at Gillian. She shook her head, then spun toward a shouting voice.

"Hey! Hey! Get away from there!" Archie came lumbering down the bank's front steps, dropping one huge bag, then another. "Get the fuck out of my truck!" The third bag hit the ground with a thud. Pulling his gun, he watched the woman scamper into the cab.

Gillian pushed Matt over to the driver's side. Two loud clangs hurt their ears as bullets bounced off the armor. Archie fired another shot. It struck the side mirror, shattering it. Matt fired up the engine.

"What about him?" Matt jabbed a thumb over his shoulder. Through the broken mirror Gillian could see Archie trying to reload his gun while running after them.

"Leave the murdering bastard," Gillian replied flatly.

Matt nodded, slipped the truck into drive. Gaining speed, he watched as Archie stopped running after only a few feet. He aimed at them, getting off three more shots before Wendell stood up behind him.

Wendell's teeth ripped into Archie's shoulder. Spinning in pain, Archie backed into a man missing an arm. He had a hole in his chest that oozed thick coagulated blood. His remaining limb encircled Archie's neck as the man bit off his ear. Archie emptied the gun into Wendell even as the one-armed man bit through Archie's face.

Matt lost sight of Archie when he turned the corner into the alley next to the city building.

Passengers

Martin slammed into the wall on the other side of the alley. Trevor and Devin spilled out behind him. The rumble of a large engine stopped Trevor in his tracks. An armored truck was bearing down on him. Catching the shocked man under the shoulder, Devin slammed him against the wall next to Martin.

Matt had been so intent on watching the attack behind he barely noticed what was happening in front of the truck. Gillian cried out. Matt swore, pulling hard on the wheel as three men ran out in front of them. The side of the truck scraped against the brick wall, crushing a metal trash can in its wake.

"Stop! Stop!" Gillian shouted, bouncing against the door. Matt slammed on the brakes, throwing Gillian forward against the dash.

"Careful!" she shouted.

"Sorry, I'm not really a truck guy." He looked her up and down, "and you should be wearing a seat belt." Matt pulled his angrily, showing her.

Pushing herself back up, Gillian frowned at Matt and his seat belt. Seeing her door blocked by a wall, she scrambled out of her seat through a sliding door to the back of the truck. There was already pounding on the doors when she reached them. She peaked through the small gun port at the man beating on the door. He looked terrified yet unhurt.

"Back up!" she shouted through the hole. "Not YOU!" she shouted at Matt. Throwing the door open, she reached out to help the first man in.

Devin jumped in next to the woman in a lab coat. Together they pulled in Trevor. Martin had hit the wall hard and was having a hard time catching his breath. It took Trevor, Devin and Gillian to pull him up into the truck.

The door Martin had slammed through burst open, sending chips of brick flying. All four turned to see the dead spilling out into the alley. Trevor fell back, kicking his way deeper into the truck, sending a bag of money tumbling out onto the street.

Devin grabbed one door, Gillian the other, and the steel clanged shut. Devin slammed the bar down, securing the doors. Three torn and bloody fingers poked through the gun port. Devin jumped back as pounding on the doors and sides filled the truck.

Matt peered over the back of the seat at the new arrivals. His eyes widened with recognition as Martin sat up. "Hey, you're the mayor! My dad worked for you."

Martin looked up at Matt and a sad smile crossed his face. "Yeah, you're Terry Schmidt's kid." Martin looked at the empty seat next to Matt. "Sorry."

Matt's face fell for a second. "Thanks," he muttered.

Trevor jumped up. "Get us out the hell out of here, kid!" he cried, pointing out the front window.

The alley was quickly filling with the undead. Matt checked the mirror. Behind them the dead continued to pour out of the city building. They were being joined by others coming from the street.

"Go!!!" came the collective shout from the back. Urged by the passengers, along with the fear swelling within him, Matt slammed down the accelerator. Metal screeched and then was replaced by heavy thuds as he freed the truck from the wall. Thick congealed blood painted the hood as body after body bounced off. Those in the back were thrown to and fro as they rumbled over the fallen dead.

Bursting out of the packed alley, they crossed Main Street, dragging corpses in their wake. They flew down the next alley. It was clear of the dead. Trash cans now took the full brunt of Matt's harried flight. Devin was at Matt's shoulder. "Turn left and head down Maple—left, man, left!" Devin shouted.

Slamming on the brakes, Matt turned the wheel with all his might. Devin flew forward. The truck skidded, and Matt stood on the gas. Devin was now upside down in the passenger seat. One of his feet collided with Matt's head. Dazed by the impact, Matt shook his head, attempting to clear it. His vision began to clear and the blur before his eyes became an oncoming car. Matt screamed, standing on the brakes. The tires protested loudly and the interior of the vehicle was filled with thudding bodies and cries of pain. He fought with the wheel but lost. Metal crunched against metal. With an earsplitting bang the heavy truck came to an abrupt stop.

Silence filled the truck for a moment. It was quickly replaced by grunts and moans from the back. Devin fought to extricate himself from under the dash. Martin was smashed against the passenger seat. His weight was not helping Devin. Gillian and Trevor were tangled in a couple of money bags. Matt's forehead was bleeding from hitting the steering wheel. Dazed, he looked over the hood of the truck. Steam was rising from the hood of a station wagon they had hit head on. Inside the car two people were moving slowly.

"Holy shit, I've only had my license for a month," Matt moaned.

"I'll give you a pass, kid," Martin grumbled, trying to help Devin up.

"We need to get them out of there," Gillian spoke, rising slowly with the help of Trevor. She pointed at the crowd of zombies who were moving toward the wreck. "We're not alone!"

Matt tried his door, but it was pinned against a wall. Devin, finally upright, threw his open. He was out, running to the car, Gillian following closely behind.

All Bill could see was white. His head felt like it was covered with a pillow, his hearing muffled. *It was just a horrid dream… Wait, I was driving. I've been in a crash.* Pushing the airbag out of his face, Bill looked at the smashed hood of his car. "Beth, Beth, you okay?" He placed a hand the girl's back. Her head rested on the dash.

Pain stabbed at Beth's head and neck as she slowly pushed away from the cracked dashboard. "I think I'm okay. You?"

Bill reached over, wiping some of the blood from her forehead. "I'm fine," he replied.

"What happened?"

Before Bill could answer, Beth's door was wrenched open. "Come on, we have to get out of here. They are coming," Gillian shouted, pointing down the street.

Devin opened Bill's door and helped him out of the totaled car. Grabbing Gillian's outstretched hand, Beth pulled herself free.

Standing unsteadily, she saw the way to the only open door on the truck was blocked by the wreck. Gillian began pulling her around the back of the car.

They made it halfway. "Wait, my bag!" Beth shouted, running back to the car. Reaching through the still-open door, she grabbed it, then hurtled back around car. The approaching mob at the end of the street caught her attention, causing her to stop at the back bumper. The zombies were shuffling closer, their moans rising as they approached. Beth studied their faces. She could see the hunger there. She saw their arms outstretched, reaching for her. Something in her memory, something about respect, hit her.

"Come on!" Gillian screamed from the open door of the truck.

Beth turned back to the truck, running for the door. Getting one foot on the running board she paused, gave the horde the finger, and then jumped in and slammed the door.

"We ready?" Trevor asked from the back, annoyance evident in his voice. Matt had gladly vacated the driver's seat so Devin could take over. A banging on the back door caught his attention so Matt went to one of the gun slots to investigate.

He peered out and quickly drew back. "Nobody we want with us," he stated as he turned around and sat on the floor. He looked up at Beth. "Hey, I'm Matt." He held out his hand.

Shaking it, Beth replied, "Hi, um, Beth."

Devin put the truck in reverse. Metal creaked and scraped as they pulled away from Bill's wrecked car. They were jostled as they ran over the thing at the back door.

"Now what?" Gillian asked.

In front of the truck was a crowd of the undead. Devin looked in the mirror. They were surrounded. The pounding on the back increased.

"Run them down. They are already dead," Martin stated flatly.

Devin looked back at him, saw the look on his face, put the truck in drive and drove into the crowd. "We have to get to the evacuation point." Devin exclaimed loudly, trying to mask the sound of bodies bouncing off the front and crunching under the wheels.

Matt looked over at Bill. "Hey, sorry about your car." Bill simply shook his head.

Haven

Steve didn't even swerve as the third zombie bounced off the hood. They drove in silence back toward the city. Wes barely flinched when the side view mirror was ripped off. Steve whipped around an abandoned bloody car, clipping a mailbox. Wes tried to call Beth again. Again, he was met with nothing but annoyance.

"No luck?" Steve asked, frowning as he took a sharp right to avoid several crashed burning cars.

Wes barely glanced up as the car veered around the corner. He shook his head. "Still saying all the circuits are busy. Not sure how that is possible." Wes followed the sight of several zombies standing over a decapitated corpse. "Looks like most people are too dead to make calls."

As if to further emphasize Wes' point, Steve turned the car around a corner and came to a quick stop. A crowd of zombies filled the road right in front of them.

"Better find an alternate route," Steve growled.

Wes pointed to the left. "That way. I think I saw a truck."

Steve quickly threw the car into reverse. He turned the wheel, heading in the direction Wes noted. This road was clear of debris and zombies. It was only a few seconds before they saw a red SUV speeding in the direction of the ballpark.

"Clear the way, brother!" Steve shouted.

For the next four blocks the SUV did just that. It smashed through rubble and zombies alike. Steve kept as close as he dared. Wes held tight to his seat belt. "Hang back a bit, will ya? Just in case, ya know, the driver gets in trouble. We don't need our plow to end up as our trap."

Halfway along the fifth block and still too many blocks from the evacuation point, the other driver made the mistake Wes feared. The SUV had been increasing speed the longer they followed it. Steve had just commented that the driver must have been standing on the accelerator as the speedometer registered seventy. Wes shouted a warning when the SUV smashed into an abandoned car that came rolling out of an alley. The SUV hit it dead center. The rear of the SUV flew into the air when the truck came to an instant stop.

Steve hit the brakes, stopping several feet behind the crashed truck. Wes and Steve looked at each other then back at the crashed car. "Do you think they are dead?" Steve asked.

Wes gave a shrug, Steve let out the clutch, allowing his car to cautiously approach the wreck. Stopping, he slipped the car into neutral and pulled the emergency brake. He reached over the seat, grabbing his rifle. Wes checked the chamber of his gun, gave Steve a nod, and opened his door.

Slowly they approached the crumpled wreck. Steam issued from under the hood. Steve took the driver's side and Wes took the passenger's. Keeping his gun ready, Wes looked in the backseat and saw a pack. He noticed the hilt of a gun sticking out of it and a rifle barrel against the seat.

He approached the front door. He jumped back. A woman was staring at him. Her mouth was moving, with her teeth scraping the window, trying to bite him. He stared back for a moment. He knew she was dead but couldn't stop staring. Looking at her he realized she had only been dead a very short time. It must have been the crash that killed her, he thought. Looking closer, he observed her head was at an impossible angle, her neck was broken. The zombie just bit at the window, glaring and chomping at him. Wes gave her the finger. He opened the back door to grab the pack. The creature in the front growled and clicked its teeth. Throwing the bag over his shoulder, he grabbed for the rifle. It was stuck. Wes was trying to free the weapon when Steve tapped on the window. Wes waved him off.

Approaching the driver's door cautiously, Steve looked in. The seat appeared empty. He looked in properly. That is when he saw him, half of him. Moving forward, he looked at the front of the truck. Sticking halfway out of the windshield was a man in his mid-forties. His graying hair was caked with blood and broken glass.

Steve shook his head. "Sorry...I wish you could have made... WHOA!" Jumping back, Steve raised his rifle. The man twisted to look at him, and his arm flopped uselessly next to him as he tried to turn grabbing at Steve.

"They're toast!" Steve yelled. "Come on, let's get to the Point!"

Wes was still struggling with the rifle when Steve ran around the truck to see what was keeping him. The zombie in the front seat growled and moaned.

"Forget it! Let's go!" Steve yelled to the younger man.

Wes gave a mighty tug, freeing the rifle. With a triumphant fist pump in the air he ran back to the beat-up Mustang with Steve. "Thanks for your help. Wish you didn't die." Wes shouted back to the crashed truck.

Steve backed up, turning down a side street. Finding a clear road, they turned back along it toward the ballpark. The silence in the car was deafening.

"You all right?" Steve asked.

Wes merely nodded. Steve turned back to the road and swore. A small orange tiger-striped cat darted out in front of the car. Steve pulled the wheel, and Wes let out a yelp of fright. The car went into a skid. Steve fought to regain control. The tires screamed. Wes was thrown back against the seat as the seat belt grabbed hold. The car jumped the curb, slamming into a pole.

Wes flailed. His head flew forward while his body was held tight to the seat. The impact sent his glasses flying. His vision blurred, and he tried to reach them, but was held fast by the seat belt. Next to him Steve was fighting to deflate the airbag. "BANG!" Wes' airbag inflated, too late. "Oh, that was helpful!" Wes growled, coughing on the powder released by the deployment.

Steve finally got his airbag down. Wes found his glasses. Turning the key, the engine protested. Steve tried again. The Mustang whined and sputtered but refused to turn over. The last few hours of abuse had been too much. The car refused to start.

"Grab your gear. We're on foot now," Steve said, turning to grab a pack. Wes followed suit. The air was thick with the smell of smoke and death. Wes had his gun out, scanning the street for trouble. Steve held both rifles, and then he tossed one to Wes. "Come on this way," he yelled.

Cut Off

Beth was surprised at how close to the ballpark they were. She had been so wrapped up in trying to call Steve and Wes that she completely missed most of the trip. She had given up trying to keep track of where they were. It seemed every street Devin drove down was blocked at some point either with crashed cars, burning debris, or just too many zombies. If something happened to the truck they would never survive. A trip that usually took no more than ten minutes had dragged on for nearly an hour. Now the end was in sight. A feeling of relief filled the truck as the Point Ball Park came into view.

"We are as good as out of here," Trevor sighed. A military helicopter cleared the top of the stands, heading east.

Devin swerved when out of nowhere a pickup truck flew into their path. It skidded, bounced off a parked car, jumped the sidewalk, and kept going. The driver barely slowed as he regained control and headed toward the ballpark. Accelerating, Devin followed. The truck stopped with a screeching halt in the crowded parking lot. Six people piled out of the pickup. Without a glance back they ran to the field. Devin was so preoccupied with what they were doing that he never saw the abandoned car. Letting out a yell, he hit the brakes. Tires squealed and metal screamed. Everyone in the back was thrown forward.

"Sorry, sorry!" Devin called over the muffled swears and exclamations. He put the truck into reverse, trying to free it from the crumpled trunk of what had once been a very shiny BMW.

"We aren't that far, maybe we should…" Gillian started.

"Oh shit!" Matt shouted, pointing.

A helicopter had come into view, rising above the stands. It pitched forward, then lurched sideways. Beth's hands covered her mouth. Martin was gripping the back of the passenger seat. Gillian gasped. The helicopter smashed into the bleachers. Rotor blades threw seats and debris from the top of the stands. The sky lit up as the machine pitched forward slamming into the bleachers. Fuel ignited, throwing a fireball twenty feet into the air.

"No! Oh no! Please, NO!" Trevor cried. Another helicopter began to struggle to get above the flames.

The group in the armored car watched as this aircraft also began to pitch violently. Beth cried out, pointing. The bottom of the helicopter became visible. Several people were hanging onto the runners. Two fell into the flames as the helicopter flew higher. The stands were now totally engulfed. As darkness fell, the flames lit the scene. They could see people in the helicopter trying to help the ones on the runners.

"Oh my God, what are they doing?" Gillian screamed. Then came the realization that the people weren't trying to help. They were trying to knock the others off. Beth swore as one of the people on the runner pulled a woman out of the helicopter as he tried to climb over her to get in. He was immediately pushed back out and off. Beth could imagine the scream as the man fell. She nodded at his fate, then cursed herself for thinking it.

"Oh my God, don't you do it, don't fucking do it, NO!" Beth yelled. A man in a uniform appeared at the door of the helicopter. He pulled his gun and fired at the people on the runners. Three bodies fell before he too was thrown from the helicopter. In a frantic grab, the soldier took another person with him.

"Let's get out of here," Matt whispered. Muttered affirmations followed.

Devin resumed his attempt to free the truck. Back and forth he rocked it until finally they were free. Beth watched the helicopter, now free of its extra weight fly off into the distance. Flames from the ballpark grew higher into the sky.

Backing up and turning the truck around, Devin turned to look at the passengers in the back. "Where should we try next?" he asked. He was shaking as he spoke.

Trevor stared out the window at the bright red flame billowing from the stands. "Great, just great. Now even the military can't help us, and they actually had a clue this time," he exclaimed, slamming his fist on the dash.

Devin turned to stare at Trevor, "The Army knew what was going on?"

Two small spider webs burst on the passenger window. A man had emerged from between several parked cars. He held a rifle up and fired again. The bullet bounced off the armor above the bullet-proof glass. "Get outta that truck!" the man screamed.

"Time to go!" Devin noted as three more people emerged. They were running toward the truck, all firing their weapons.

Not in the Plan

Abandoning the car, Steve followed Wes a few steps down the road. He paused. With an ache in his heart he turned back to his once prized possession. The fenders and doors were dented, the paint scraped and scratched. Sadness filled Steve for a moment— not just at the loss of his car, but for everything that he knew was lost. He allowed himself one shuddering sigh before turning to run after Wes, who had just disappeared from view.

Around the corner, Wes waited against the wall for Steve to catch up. Panting, Steve was at his side in seconds. "Sorry, I'm sorry," Steve gasped. "I shouldn't have swerved."

Wes grabbed him by the shoulders and looked up at him straight in the eye. "Don't be. You saved a life. No matter how small, it was still a life."

Steve held onto Wes' shoulders, gripping tightly. "I just hope I didn't kill us in the process." Steve pulled Wes into a rib-cracking hug, slapped him on the back, and let go. Steve started down the alley. Wes gave him a moment's head start. In that moment Wes knew—no matter what happened with Beth, he had a brother.

Two blocks down and no problems. They continued toward the Point, the sound of helicopters getting louder with every block. Looking up, they could see one of them pass overhead.

"Almost there," Steve smiled at Wes. Wes whooped. Up ahead was the parking lot, just visible between the buildings. Wes' heart was pounding. They were going to get out of this mess. They were going to find Beth and get out of the city. Picking up the pace, they covered the last block at a jog. At the end of the building the street opened up before them.

"There it is, there it is, look! Helicopters and cops and the Army! We are going to get out of here!" Wes shouted, punching Steve on the arm.

The parking lot was full of cars, all parked at odd angles. Several were smashed into each other. There were abandoned possession and luggage everywhere. Steve and Wes emerged from the darkness of an alley across the street from the lot. A cop saw them and raised his gun. Then he lowered it, waving them on. Steve stuttered to a stop when the gun came up, but Wes never slowed. The cop gave a hurried wave to an entrance that wasn't completely covered up with vehicles. Steve had to hurry to keep up with Wes.

"Run, boys, they might be right behind you. I don't think the Army is going to wait around much longer," the officer shouted as they ran by.

Steve nodded his thanks as they passed. The officer didn't seem to notice, as he was distracted by his radio. Steve heard the crackling static-distorted voice through the speaker. "Evacuate all areas. Repeat; evacuate all areas."

They are giving up on the city, Steve thought as he continued winding his way through the labyrinth of cars. Wes was still several feet in front of him. Steve kept a watch to the left and to the right. He marveled at the dexterity that Wes showed navigating the parking lot. He wondered why Wes never went out for football or track. This thought left him as he spied a barricade up ahead.

The blockade was manned by a couple of police and three military men. As Wes approached, the men grabbed at their radios. They looked at each other for a beat then turned, hurrying off into the ballpark. One of the soldiers paused, urging Steve and Wes to follow. Wes hesitated, waiting for Steve to catch up. "What's up with them?" Wes shouted as Steve neared.

Steve stopped short of Wes. He started to laugh. Hands on his knees, Steve tried to catch his breath. The heavy pack on his back shifted, forcing him to stand up straight. The look on Wes' face, combined with the stuffed bunny ears poking from his shirt, caused Steve to break out laughing even harder.

"What the hell is so funny?" Wes asked, perplexed. "Come on, we need to go find Beth."

The soldier shouted something at them, threw up his hands in anger, and was gone. Wes was about to follow when Steve's hand shot out to catch him. Both men halted, listening. Gunfire had erupted off to their left. They could see a crowd advancing on the gate in the fading light. The flashes from the gun barrels looked like flashbulbs going off.

"Let's move!" Steve shouted, pushing Wes forward. They returned to picking their way through the tightly bunched cars. The gunfire intensified, now from their right. Wes climbed up onto the roof of a car. He stopped. Steve ran past him. It took him a moment to realize Wes was no longer with him. Looking back, he saw Wes staring at the top of the stands. Steve turned just in time to see flames shoot high into the air. Fire and metal starting raining down around them.

"This way, this way, toward those tents," Wes screamed, pointing to a group of military tents set up close to the river. They were at the far end of the parking lot. Steve followed Wes, again marveling at his speed. Approaching the tents, they saw men running. All of them were armed. One of the tents burst into flames as parts of the stadium fell on it.

"Shit, the other way, the other way!" Steve yelled. They turned back toward the car.

Wes stopped dead. Steve slammed into the younger man. "No good! Zombies." Wes pointed at the shuffling crowd coming toward them.

Steve grabbed Wes's arm. "The river!"

They jumped over hoods and ran over roofs to get to the edge of the concrete flood prevention banks along the river. Skidding to a halt at the edge, both men stood in shock at what met their eyes. In the river below, just behind where the tents were set up, was a pile of bodies.

"Dear GOD!" Steve shouted, "They were killing people?!"

"Come on!" Wes cried, pulling Steve down the bank to a small ridge halfway down. He pointed to a ladder several hundred feet away in the opposite direction of the bodies and the now flaming stadium. "That should come up behind that group we saw."

"What if it comes up right in the middle of them?" Steve asked.

Wes didn't have time to answer. Several splashes from the river urged them forward. People were jumping into the water. Several were on fire.

Steve and Wes watched for a moment until a couple of zombies fell over the bank, their arms outstretched, still trying to reach the fleeing people. "Yep, time to move again," Steve said, pushing Wes forward.

Edging along the bank, they cautiously approached the ladder. Behind them they could hear screams from the water. The quick current, along with the undead, was making fast work of the jumpers. Finally reaching the bottom rung, Steve looked over at Wes. "I hope you're right."

"Yeah, me too," Wes whispered, beginning to climb.

Steve reached the top. He waved Wes to stop. Peeking over the edge he spied several zombies about fifty feet from them. "Come on, hurry!" he whispered. Scrambling over the bank, the two raced for the cover of an alley.

"Now what?" Wes questioned, breathing heavily with his hands on his knees. As if to answer his question, somewhere to their right they heard a church bell tolling.

Story to be Told

Devin accelerated over a small median. His passengers were thrown back and forth around the back of the truck again. Four men were all screaming and running after the armored car. Bullets pinged off the thick metal. Slamming through an old VW bus and taking a hard turn, Devin watched the group slow their run. They fired once more. A zombie rose up from between two cars behind the men. It was latched onto one of them before they even knew it was there. Devin lost sight of what happened as he turned the corner. Finding the road smoother, the passengers began to right themselves.

"What were you saying about the military knowing what was going on?" Beth demanded, throwing a heavy money bag against the wall to make a seat. They rumbled over a motorcycle lying across the road. Beth found herself under the bag. Angrily she pushed it off, crushing Matt in the process. Matt glared at Beth, who glared at Trevor, who did not speak up right away. After several seconds of pretending not to have heard Beth, the others began to press him for information.

"I was in the meeting; when did we talk to the military?" Devin asked while they scraped against a burning police car. Several people protested about the driving. Devin pulled down an alley that seemed clear of any movement. Parking the truck, he turned to Trevor, waiting for him to explain.

Matt pulled Martin back up into a seated position. Martin looked around at the others. He knew by the look Trevor was giving him that he wasn't going to speak anytime soon. Martin sighed. "Well, Devin, after you left, I contacted Colonial Miller. You know, the man in charge of the National Guard post." Devin nodded, while Trevor seemed to be trying to will the mayor to remain silent. Martin shook his head and continued. "Well, Miller said the military had found out a few things about the infected people. Basically, and most importantly, he said they were dead." This statement was met with a silence so loud it was almost painful.

Beth spoke up, startling Matt. "What do you mean? Dead? Are you talking like zombie dead?" She demanded.

Martin rubbed his hand over his face. "From what the military doctors could tell, the virus kills the host. But then it takes over the brain and nervous system."

Gillian shook her head, trying to grasp the details. "Is it really brain death and not just an infection?"

Martin shrugged. "I didn't ask. They said the victims were dead but the virus causes a reanimation of sorts. Colonial did say the victims came back with only the most basic brain functions actually working."

Again Gillian interrupted, "So they are brain dead but the heart is still going and they are walking around?"

The mayor looked frustrated but not angry with her. "No, both the brain and heart have stopped working. He told me this allows the virus to control the reanimated corpse without the need for oxygen or blood flow to the muscles. But they are still able to move around."

Gillian shook her head again like she was trying to clear it. "Without heart and lungs working, the muscle tissue is starved of oxygen and nutrients, so they tend to not function," she argued.

"Well that might explain why the zombies don't seem to run, but why are they attacking, and well… eating people?" Beth asked, as if this was simply something in a textbook that she couldn't quite get. Matt felt like he was back in class for a moment, just as confused as he was in algebra.

Martin thought for a moment, scratching his chin. He seemed to struggle with his answer. Taking a deep breath, he spoke again. "Well, according to Colonial Miller, the zombies, for lack of a better term, only seem to be driven by hunger for living flesh."

"So they stop eating as soon as you're dead," Matt perked up happily, "That is just like the movies." The smile fell from his face as he saw the looks of the others.

Martin frowned at him with raised eyebrows, then continued, "As soon as the blood of their victims stops pumping, they lose interest. When the heart stops, yes, the attack stops."

Beth spoke up, "That is why there are so many of them that only have a few bite marks or damage."

Martin nodded, "The infection spreads fast once someone has been bitten, so if they get away, they still die within an hour or so." Gillian looked over at Matt. She could see he was thinking the same thing she was about Jeremy. Martin continued, "When people are attacked, while they're still alive the zombies will keep eating them, but once their heart stops, like I said, the attack stops. But then the dead one...the one they just killed...well, they reanimate within seconds."

Devin shuddered. "That is what happened when Lacy died. She attacked Norm, then he died and came right back."

"Just like Jeremy," Matt interjected.

Beth sat with her hand clutching the straps of her backpack, her mind racing. "That means.... my dad might be attacking people right now?" She clamped her eyes shut, trying to drive out the mental image of her dead father eating Wes, or her brother. "Oh God, why is this happening?" she moaned.

Thump, thump, thump, on the side of the armored car made them all jump. Devin put the truck into gear. "We've stayed here too long."

The truck rumbled up the alley. They turned up the side street, getting farther away from the flames. When they gained the open road, Beth glanced out the window. What she saw only made her stomach squirm. She resolved not to look, so she sat with her back against the wall, her mind still trying to grasp what she just heard.

Matt spoke up, breaking into her thoughts. "Well I always knew zombies wouldn't eat brains. If they did, a lot more people I know would have been safe."

Martin tried to suppress a smile but nodded. A moment later he noted, "The brain does have something to do with it. The army guys contend that once the brain is destroyed the virus is also destroyed."

Matt pumped his fist. "Yeah, I knew it! Just like the movies! No running and no brain eating! I bet no Rage virus. either." He sat smiling triumphantly. Beth wanted to, but refrained from smacking him upside the head.

Welcome

The bells continued to toll, urging them on. Steve ran down the street with Wes close at his heels. Darkness was falling quickly. Panting, Steve paused. Leaning against the wall of the old drug store, he asked "Ok where's that coming from? Which church do you suppose?"

Wes looked back the way they had come. The flames from the ballfield's stands painted the sky a blood red. "Ok, so the mall is no good, and the ballpark is, hhmm let's see...fucked. Now we have church bells and no idea where they are coming from." Wes pounded the brick behind him in frustration. "So where the hell should we go from here?" Groping in his front pocket, he pulled out his phone. He tried Beth's number again. Steve stared hopefully at him. Wed pulled it from his ear, snarling, "No signal."

"Come to the church."

Steve and Wes stared at each other, shocked. "Did you hear that?" Steve asked.

"There is safety at the church. Saint Andrew's Catholic Church on Pine," proclaimed a faint voice.

"We are just a few blocks from there. Come on," exclaimed Steve, "This way." He pointed. Pausing at the corner, they readied their weapons. Steve swept around first, with Wes covering him. They kept close to the walls, one looking forward, the other behind them. Coming to the end of the block, they stopped. They were about three feet from the end of the building.

"Just about a block and a half a to go, past the park, then left on Pine," Steve whispered. Wes nodded then proceeded around the corner. At the end of another building they paused again. A chain link fence surrounded a small park. Steve started forward but then froze, holding up a hand to halt Wes.

Wes heard it too—cries for help coming from inside the park. Steve glanced around the building. Turning quickly back, he flattened himself against the wall, his eyes wide. Looking over at Wes, he shook his head. "We have to go into the park."

"What! Why?" Wes demanded.

"There are a bunch of kids trapped on the play fort."

Through his trepidation Wes nodded his assent. He knew they had to help. Taking a deep breath, they sprinted along the fence to the gate. Wes fumbled with the latch for a second before throwing the gate wide. He flew through it, Steve right on his heels. Ahead of them was a play fort. Wes saw in an instant there was no longer anything *play* about it.

The playground's usual cries of joy were replaced with the howls and moans of undead children mixed with screams of terror from the living. Ashen faced, bloody, and torn, the small ghouls were trying to reach five of their former friends and school mates. The living kids on the fort fought them off with makeshift weapons. A boy at the top of the slide was pushing the dead back down with a broom. One girl was throwing bricks, while another was using what looked to be a sling shot. Her aim was incredible. A blonde-haired boy was holding the swinging bridge. He looked like a knight with a bat for a sword and a trash can lid as a shield. They could see another boy swinging a shovel at ghouls that were clawing at the edge of platform that lead to the fireman's pole.

Wes fired at a zombie child who was advancing on the boy with the bat. Steve raised his rifle. He took out a girl who was almost at the top of the slide. Both men took aim carefully picking out targets. Wes was nearly knocked off his feet as a body flew past.

"That is not fast enough!" yelled a woman.

Another person ran past the stunned men. Wes stared as a grey-haired black woman rushed at the zombie children, swinging a crowbar. She was followed by a balding black man who was swinging a large metal bat. It clanged deadly across tiny skulls.

"Cover them!" Steve shouted.

Wes aimed and fired, and Steve's rifle blasted. Something caught Wes' attention. He glanced behind them. They were no longer alone on the street. A couple of adult zombies were about twenty feet away, shambling toward them.

Wes ejected his empty clip. He slapped a full mag in as he swung around, taking down one of the adult zombies. Steve watched the action at the fort. The children were being helped down by the older couple. Ten small corpses litter the playground.

"Help me!" Wes shouted.

Steve spun around, saw the incoming trouble and fired.

The woman appeared between Wes and Steve. "Good job, boys. We need to get to the church," she ordered.

Behind the woman the children were being herded toward Steve and Wes. A couple of them had started to cry. "We'll be okay. It's going to be okay," the man with the bat soothed.

Suddenly Steve recognized the woman."Mrs. Johnson?" he gasped.

"Hello, Steven. Let's get to the church. Clear the way if you would, please," she responded.

Wes noted that Mr. Johnson, he assumed, had broken the bat. Wes unsheathed the sword from his back. Without a word he tossed it to him. Mr. Johnson received it with a nod of thanks.

"Nice," he said, inspecting the shining blade. His broken weapon clanged to the ground.

They could see the bell tower of the church less than a half a block away, just diagonal to them around a short office building. Wes dropped the last zombie in the street. Together the group began to move. They made it to the end of the office building, where Steve stopped. Their way seemed blocked. Up ahead were three school buses set up like a fence in front of the steps that led up to the heavy oak doors. At the top of the steps between two flaming trash cans they could see a man. He spotted them.

"There is an opening between the buses at the left corner!" he shouted.

"THERE!" pointed one of the children.

"Come one, come on!" the man urged.

The group ran forward, led by the Johnsons. Reaching the corner, Mrs. Johnson ushered the children through the small gap between the buses. Just as Steve was about to move ahead a zombie lurched out of nowhere, grabbing his arm. He jerked away, trying to wrench free. Steve lost his footing and fell. The zombie tumbled down top of him. He heard the snap of the zombie's wrist. The pressure on his arm was relinquished, but the undead man's weight was still on him. He had no leverage to push it off. Growling, it chomped and bit at him. Steve struggled to push it off.

Its relentless attempts to bite him suddenly stopped when music erupted from Steve's jacket. *"Beth I hear you calling but I can't come home right now..."* The zombie and Steve both looked at the jacket, confused.

Up by the buses, Wes tried to aim his rifle. The zombie had lost interest in the noise. It returned to trying to rip Steve's face off. Steve, for his part, was able to force the barrel of his rifle sideways into the ghoul's mouth, which kept it from biting him. Turning his face from the stench, he watched Mr. and Mrs. Johnson disappear through the gap in the buses with the children.

Wes aimed, hesitated, and then started to move to aid Steve. A shout recalled him back to the bus. "Here!" Mr. Johnson yelled. Wes' sword slid under a bus just out of reach. He knelt down, reaching for the hilt. His fingers barely scraped the metal. "Aw, come on!" Wes growled, stretching further under the vehicle. His fingers closed over the cold steel. Scrambling out, he held the sword high. He ran back toward Steve. "Get its head up!" he cried.

Wide-eyed Steve grabbed the barrel and the butt of the rifle. The zombie's teeth began to crack on the metal. Steve forced the head up. It felt like bench pressing a Buick. Pain shot into his shoulder. The zombie was trying to claw through Steve's jacket. Slowly Steve forced the zombie's head up higher. Wes swung at it like a ball on tee. The head separated from the body, smacking with a thud against the wall. Dark, foul blood oozed over Steve's chest, and he threw the headless body off, scrambling to his feet. Wes helped him with shaking arms.

"Yeah asshole! Not so tough without a head, are you?" Steve swore, walking to the severed head. It lay on its side by a stoop. The eyes watched Steve approach and its mouth moved furiously. "Oh, you still want some, huh?" Steve ran up and kicked it as hard as he could. It flew down the street, bouncing off a trash can. "Damn it!" Steve yelped. "That bastard's head was like a frickin' rock."

Limping, he found Wes laughing at him. "Feel better? Come on, Beckham." Wes continued to laugh while watching the head roll lopsidedly to a stop. Steve punched Wes in the back of the shoulder then leaned heavily against it heading to the gap in the buses. The man at the top of the stairs waved them forward into the church. When they gained the top of the steps Steve noted the man was a priest.

"Thank you, Father," he said as he passed him.

"I'm glad you made it, my son," was his reply.

Steve nodded his thanks. Wes muttered so that only Steve could hear, "I guess we'll be-heading...inside." This earned him a slap on the back of the head.

New Friends

Beth glared at Matt for a moment. "How can you be so happy about being right about zombies?" she demanded. Matt merely shrugged. Shaking her head, she turned to look out the small back window. There were two zombies approaching. She watched them running after the truck. "Wait, didn't you just say that zombies don't run?" she asked, grabbing Matt by the shoulders.

Matt's eyes were huge as she shook him. "Yes, that's right, they don't," he squeaked.

Jumping up to her knees, Beth gripped the rubber gasket around the window. She watched the two figures fleeing and running. A zombie stumbled out of a doorway close to them. Beth saw a muzzle flash from the hand of the taller runner. The zombie crumpled.

"Stop! Stop the truck!" she yelled.

The two figures were waving frantically at the back windows.

"What's wrong?" Devin asked, applying the brakes.

"There are a couple of guys running after the truck. Stop!" Beth yelled, throwing the back door open.

"Wait! What if they are like those guys who tried to kill us at the ballpark? These could be more like them!" Trevor protested.

The smell of burning wood mixed with burnt meat assaulted Beth's nose. She was waving the two men on, ignoring the admonishments from the other passengers. Beth gave a small scream and ducked. One of the men raised his gun and fired. The bullet whizzed past the truck. Beth opened her eyes to see a zombie with a bullet hole through its head lying just at the back bumper.

"Move!" one of the men shouted, gesturing to Beth. She did not need telling twice. Flattening herself against the wall of the truck, the two men jumped in. One was in a police uniform, the other in military fatigues.

The police officer spun around, pulling the door shut. He yelled, "Go Go Go!" Devin did as he was told.

The man in the fatigues hit the wall next to Beth. He fell to sit with crossed legs, head cradled in his hands. Across from her the police officer slid down, knees held close to his chest. Both men sat in silence except for taking deep breaths. The police officer stared straight ahead while the military man clutched at a stitch in his side. Martin looked over at the cop and asked, "What is your name, officer?"

The officer looked up, and recognizing the mayor, he tried to compose himself. "Sorry sir, Officer Kline, Max Kline."

Martin nodded. "Welcome aboard. Glad you made it this far, Officer Kline. And you are?" Martin gestured to the military man.

"Corporal Hector Rodriguez, sir," was the man's reply between breaths.

"Corporal, are you with the National Guard post in Somerset?"

"Yes sir, we were ordered to town to evacuate the civilians." Hector shuddered. "It didn't go so well, sir."

Devin turned sharply down another alley. He put the truck in park and turned to address the two additions to their crowded vehicle. He opened his mouth, stopped, took a breath, opened his mouth again, shook his head, then lost all composure. "What the hell happened?" he blurted out.

Hector looked over Max. Max stared back. Hector sighed, "We lost control, we lost control of the situation."

Max spoke up. "I was sent to the ballpark to secure the area for the evacuation. The first couple of helicopters that came in were just dropping off soldiers. There was this Captain who kind of took control as soon as he landed."

"Captain Rhodes," Hector interrupted. "Complete asshole, didn't have a clue how to run an op."

Max looked at Hector and when he didn't continue, Max resumed his story. "I couldn't believe what was happening or what that Captain told us. The guy told us the people with the flu; the sick people were going crazy. It was like rabies or something, it made them attack and kill other people. He told us to shoot them on sight, but not just shoot them, but to shoot them in the head, only."

Hector interrupted again, "That is because he didn't tell you everything. They weren't sick anymore, they were already dead."

Max stared at him. "What do you mean they were already dead? You mean like zombies and shit?" At this Martin spoke up and filled in the story for the shocked officer. "Holy shit," Max muttered at the explanation.

"Well at least we know that zombies don't eat brains. I mean that would defeat the whole purpose of infecting the brain," Matt added. Everyone stared at him. "What?" he asked. "It is all about the brain. That is where the infection is and why you can only take them down by shooting them in the head. Destroy the brain, destroy the zombie." He looked around at all the faces staring at him. He gestured a "well, duh!". Beth shook her head while Martin pinched the bridge of his nose. Hector was looking right at Matt, who raised his shoulders.

"Yeahhh... okay. We had orders to take out anyone who was sick. None of them were to make it out of the city. So we had to break up families and tell people they couldn't leave. A buddy of mine in another unit told me they were going to the hospital to sterilize the infected," Hector stated. "Sterilize, nice way to say kill. We lost contact with them right before it all went to hell at our post." Hector sighed, rubbing his eyes.

Martin persisted, "So what happened, though? How did we lose control?"

Max took a moment to gather his thoughts. "Well, I took up my position behind my cruisers just in front of the concrete barricades that were set up at the entrance of the ballpark... I still don't believe it—really, zombies?" Max stared around the truck, waiting for someone to say it was a joke. Beth nodded at him. "Shit...Well, like I said, I was at the Point, there were two other places that were set up as evacuation sites. The park up on Eisenhower, and at the Richland Mall Movie Theater on top of the hill. We had just lost contact with the guys at the park and the guys at the theater were having a bad time of it. There was a lot of shooting going on up there, with people overrunning the barricades, panicking, trying to get to the helicopters."

Max shook his head. Hector decided to give him a break. "I was briefed at the camp and told all about the virus and to avoid anyone that was sick. If you got bit you were pretty much screwed." He paused, thinking back on the briefing. "I understand this started yesterday in New York. The Army guys there got over-run pretty damn quick. They blew up all the bridges and tunnels out of the city the last time we had contact with them."

"We lost New York?" Beth sat stunned.

"New York, Philly, Pittsburgh, we haven't been able to reach any of the big cities for hours. We got orders to come here and evacuate from Colonel Miller. No one is sure where he got orders from but he's in charge, so we loaded up and came here."

Martin gave a sad smile. "Well, at least he tried to help out the city."

Hector grunted at this. "By the time we got here the city was already lost. We just didn't know it." Martin raised his eyebrows at the corporal. Hector stared back. "My chopper landed. We fanned out to assist the local police with their barricades and to set up an orderly evac."

Max nodded. "They were armed to the fucking teeth. Oh, sorry," he said, noticing Beth and Matt.

"Please. I'm in high school; like that is the worst I've heard." Beth gave a laugh at the embarrassment on the officer's face. Hector gave an impatient snort.

"Go on," Martin encouraged.

"Well, like I said we landed and deployed around the ballpark. The police had things set up for like a concert or that kind of crowd control. We started closing the holes in their setup while moving the civilians through." Hector closed his eyes for a moment. "We had a special area set up for the sick to go to be…"

Max interrupted. "The tents along the river? What did you do?"

Hector looked down at the stock of his gun. "Those guys were to shoot the sick and dump them into the river."

Gillian gave a strangled cry. Matt grabbed her arm.

"Dear God," Devin exclaimed.

"We couldn't take the chance of one of them dying in the helicopter and attacking the others. We had already decontaminated our camp. We couldn't let any infected in."

Beth glared at the soldier. "Decontaminated? You mean killed."

Hector fired up at once. "We lost two of our doctors to some guys who turned. We couldn't lose anyone else! We had families coming in who needed us to keep them safe! We had our own people to look after!" He slammed the back of his head into the wall of the truck.

"Well, sorry for ruining your day! But it hasn't been a ray of sunshine for us here, in case you missed it," Beth threw back at him.

Max looked back and forth from the military man to the teenage girl like he was watching a tennis match of shouting. Hector glared at Beth for several seconds, but she did not look away. Hector's expression changed to exhaustion. "Sorry," he mumbled.

Trevor shouted out, exasperated, "We're all having a shitty day! What the hell happened and where should we go? I mean more of you guys are coming to get us, right?"

Hector glanced over at Max. Max shook his head. "No, I don't think they are."

Trevor stuttered, " Wh... what do you mean? No?"

Hector looked up. "We lost control of the city. They own it now."

"How? How did we lose control?" Trevor pleaded.

Max put his head into his hands and sighed, "What difference does it make?"

Martin straightened up and spoke with the authority and presence of a man used to being answered. "What the hell happened?"

Shocked, Hector looked around at the faces in the truck. He nodded to the mayor and spoke in a clear military tone. "Things were going all right, at first. We were separating the sick from the healthy."

"How" Gillian asked.

"We told them..." he faltered, "we told them we had a vaccine and to go to the tents."

Gillian looked down at her hands in her lap. Beth closed her eyes and turned her head from the men. She looked out the back window and listened to Hector return to his story.

"We had the people leave their stuff and go up into the stands. We took their guns so they couldn't cause trouble if they couldn't get out on the chopper they wanted."

"Or if they found out what was happening in the tents," Beth interjected.

Hector nodded. "We had heard that was what happened up at the theater. People didn't want to wait, combined with wanting to know what was going on in the tents."

Hector gathered his thoughts as Matt breathed..."Dude."

"Like I said, things were going OK until we saw a group of them heading toward the south entrance. These were not refugees. This was a whole group of infected. I don't know if it was the noise of the helicopters or the living or what, but they started coming out of the woodwork. The cops were shouting at them to stop but, well, that didn't work."

Max gave an angry grunt, "Like we knew what the hell was going on! No one told us they were already dead."

Hector continued. "Well, we knew they weren't going to stop so we opened fire. There were so many of them we had to fall back. Head shots aren't the easiest and grenades don't work if the person isn't going to notice shrapnel sticking out of them. These things don't exactly bleed. So we start to fall back. Then, well, I guess the people in the stands took notice of us losing ground and they start to panic."

Max spoke up, "What the hell did you expect? There they are in a place with barricades all around it, the army shooting and falling back, and all their weapons were confiscated when they came in!"

Hector gave a mirthless laugh, "Yeah that caused a lot of problems. Captain Moron is trying to keep those folks from getting their weapons, so the dumbass has some of the guys open fire on the crowd. On a crowd already in a panic. That turned it into a total cluster fuck," Hector sighed.

Disgusted, Beth snarled, "So he opens fire on the people he was told to come get?"

"Yep, and then he calls for a full retreat. The rest of the guys start heading for the choppers, and so do all the civilians. I grabbed this guy," Hector motioned to Max, "and I head in to try to get the fuck out of dodge, and that is when that chopper slams into the stands." Hector looked back down at his rifle.

Max spoke up. "It was total anarchy after that. Living, dead, army, everyone was attacking everyone. People were getting shot left and right and then getting right back up to try to chew your face off. That chopper sliced through the crowd, its blades dicing bodies as it slammed into the stands." Max sat there staring at nothing. He just kept talking. "People were jumping out of its belly as it careened into those stands. Then it burst into a fireball. The living and the dead were engulfed in the flames. The only difference was the dead were still walking." Max seemed to have lost the ability to continue. He covered his face.

Hector reached across the van and gave Max a pat on the knee, then continued their story. "Well, now the flaming dead were shuffling toward the barricades. It was a mess of screaming, those things making this howling noise, gunfire and explosions. The rest of the people who were trapped just started shooting at anything living or dead as we tried to evacuate and…"

"Left several hundred survivors to scatter and run from their fate," Beth finished for him.

"I don't see *me* safe at camp, do you? Me or half the guys that were outside the park. We were fighting for our lives on two fronts, and lost both," Hector said bitterly.

Devin turned around in his seat. He noticed their path was starting to become blocked with the undead. "Time to find another place to be," he said quietly. They pulled forward through the outstretched arms.

For the Moment

Stopping just inside the doors to the church, Steve rested his head against his arm. "That was too close," he muttered.

"You're not kidding. Don't do that crap to me again. You're supposed to be the big hero, not me." Wes slapped Steve on the back.

"I *am* a hero!" Steve straightened up to his full height. "Come on, ya loser." He pulled Wes into a headlock while dragging him through the second set of doors. Letting go, they pulled the heavy doors open.

Wes noticed, with relief, that the doors were several inches thick and sat on massive iron hinges. "It will take a lot to get through those." Wes nodded to both sets of doors.

"My guess is the windows aren't easily accessible." Steve nodded to one of the huge stained glass windows showing a scene from the bible of Noah's ark. Wes turned and gave him a quizzical look. "We had to climb stairs to get to the front door, right? Those windows start about waist level, so I guess they are about ten feet off the ground. Must be a level or basement below us."

Wes looked down at his feet as if he could see through the floor, "Let's hope there are no windows down there."

"They are very small and reinforced, as is the glass covering our stained glass," said a voice from behind them. "We had some trouble with vandals a few years ago." A small woman in her seventies explained as she hurried past them with a bottle of water and some paper towels. Steve watched her bustle up the center aisle of the church. Looking around, he noticed most of the pews were empty. The woman had reached the front of the church where several people were huddled together in small groups. They all looked like they had a rough time getting there.

Wes nudged Steve, pointing to a person lying on the floor covered in a blanket. They approached slowly, trying not to bring attention to themselves. They saw it was a man and he was moaning. The woman who had spoken to them was pouring water onto the paper towels and handing some to another woman sitting next to the injured man. She was speaking low and comforting him. A smell made its way to them as they approached. Wes looked over at Steve with raised eyebrows.

"Smells like barbeque," he whispered. Steve shushed him, pointing. Wes closed his eyes and groaned. He couldn't believe he had just said that when he realized the man on the floor had been burned badly. "Oh man, that is gonna linger," Wes muttered, covering his nose and turning away. He headed for a pew several rows behind them, slung off his pack, and slumped down in the empty pew.

Reaching into the pack he retrieved a box of ammo. Immediately he started reloading his empty clips. Steve noticed how intensely Wes was loading his weapon. He dropped down next to the young man.

Wes brushed at his eye with the back of his hand. "How many times am I gonna do this today?" he choked.

Steve sat next to him in silence for a moment. "As many as you need to, man," he whispered, and put a hand on Wes' back. Wes finished loading the bullets. He slipped one of the mags into his gun.

Steve jumped up. "BETH!" He yelled reaching into his jacket. "One missed call," his phone read.

"Beth?" Wes jumped up, looking around frantically. He saw Steve had his phone out. He bounced on the balls of his feet.

"Beth. I heard Beth's ring tone," Steve said, smiling down at the phone.

"She hates that song, you know," Wes said, his face glowing with excitement.

Steve checked the phone. His face fell. "No message." Disappointment crashed over them.

"She called though, so she must be okay," Wes stated, like this made it fact.

"I'm number one on her speed dial...something could have hit the button and called me...it's happened before," Steve noted, miserably staring at the phone.

"Call her back. Call her back now," Wes ordered.

Steve hit his speed dial for Beth.

"Well?" Wes asked anxiously.

"No service. Damn it," Steve muttered. Sinking back down into the pew, he buried his face in his hands. Wes grabbed the phone and tried several times to call or send a text message, but nothing would go through.

After several minutes he stopped trying. "She's okay." He sighed. He looked at Steve who kept his head down. Wes could tell by the movement of his shoulders that Steve was now the one crying. Wes rested his hand on his friend's shoulder. "She's okay, she's okay, I know she is okay," he reassured them both. Steve nodded but never looked up.

No Place Like Home

Devin had driven through the streets of the city for a couple of hours. After picking up Max and Hector, they had agreed to help any other survivors they could. So far, they had not been able to help anyone else. The closest they came was a woman around Beth's age. She was almost to the door when they noticed the bite on her neck. Her cries for help still echoed in Beth's ears.

Now the truck was climbing slowly through one of the suburbs. Devin turned down the last street before the houses changed to woods. Trevor noticed Devin's grip on the wheel tighten. "Do you know this neighborhood?'

Devin grimaced, "Yeah, it's mine."

The truck lumbered to a halt in front of a brick two-story house. Devin stared out the front window. Taking a deep breath, he turned to look at the front of the house. Past the immaculately trimmed front lawn, the front door hung open. The glass storm door was smeared with bloody handprints. No one could tell if it was on the inside or outside. Devin saw the shattered front window and his blood froze.

"We'll go check it out." Beth spoke as she put her hand on Devin's shoulder.

He turned to her and gave a weak smile as he said, "No, that's okay." His voice cracked as he faced forward, putting the truck in gear. He pulled into his neighbor's driveway to turn around. "I'm sure they left for her mother's." Tears streamed down his face. The light was gone as they returned to the city. "Should we try anyone else's house?" Devin asked. The others either already knew the fate of loved ones, or had no one in town to check on. Silence filled the truck as they made their way back to town.

Beth pulled her cell phone from her pocket and hit her contacts. Steve's name came up, followed by Wes'. One of them had to be safe, she assured herself.

Nice Night for It

Jeremy sat on the roof of his house drinking a beer and watching the road. He was waiting for his wife to get home. If he was honest with himself, he knew she never would. He had been on the phone with her when he heard the shooting. The line had gone dead and he hadn't been able to reach her since. She had been at work at the hospital since this thing started.

He put the bottle to his lips, but then pulled it away, a look of disgust crossed his face. The bottle was empty. He watched the people in the street milling around. He knew what they were. He had heard the news reports, seen his neighbor die and get back up.

Jeremy stood up. His balance was a bit off from the drink and angle of the roof. He chose a target and threw the bottle. SMASH! It landed several feet from where he had intended. Even though he missed, the result made him laugh. The zombies in the street gathered at the bottle. They bumped into each other, and one fell down. The undead seemed completely confused by the noise.

Jeremy watched for a few moments, then fell back to a seated position. He reached over, flipping open the cooler next to him. Retrieving another beer, he twisted off the cap. He flipped it from the roof. It hit the ground with a small clink. Several zombies moved toward the sound. Jeremy pulled the revolver out of the back of his pants. He grabbed the box of ammunition he'd brought up with him. Loading six shells into the chamber, he thought, "Well, they are already dead, right?"

He fired off a shot. It pinged off the road. Somewhere to the left, glass shattered. Jeremy's ears rang but he stifled a laugh. The three noises caused the zombies to return to their slow spinning as they looked for the sources. Jeremy finished his beer. He took the empty to the edge of the roof for target practice. The gun bucked, the muzzle flashed, but the bottle remained intact. Another cap flew from the roof. Another shot, then another. The gun was reloaded. A bottle flew off the roof, followed by another cap. The noises helped the undead find Jeremy's house.

Standing on the edge of his roof, Jeremy relieved himself on the crowd below. He fired several shots into them as well. He heard the front window of his house shatter. "Nice night for it, isn't it boys?" he shouted. Weaving his way back to the cooler, he repeated, "Nice night for it." He reloaded the gun. Sighing at the empty ammo box, he threw it off the roof.

He reached into the cooler, searching through the cold water to find the last beer. He sipped it slowly, enjoying every drop that passed over his tongue. He aimed at the empty bottle still perched on the roof's edge. Thought about it, took another long drink, then walked back to the edge. Looking over, he saw in the glow of his dusk to dawn light that his house was completely surrounded. He could hear them in his house breaking furniture and glass.

The empty bottle dropped from his hand, shattering on the head of a neighbor girl. Five shots blasted in the night, three of his neighbors lay unmoving on his lawn. A single tear ran down his face. Jeremy tasted the warm steel and sulfur of the barrel. A shot rang out, and then Jeremy's lifeless body crashed down on the undead below. The zombies looked at the man. The top of his head was missing and his heart no longer pumped.

After an hour, the undead had almost completely dispersed. A lone zombie clawed at the window, trapped in the house. Jeremy lay among some of his neighbors, a picture of his wife still clutched in his lifeless hand.

Resupply

"We can't just keep driving around," Martin grumbled.

"That and we don't have the gas for it. If we run out, we are screwed. I, for one, would like the option to keep moving," Devin stated. He looked down at the fuel gauge. It was showing a quarter of a tank. "We really should consider trying to fill up and soon."

"Are we that low?" Gillian asked.

"No, but the power isn't going to last more than three days without people to take care of it." Devin's response left the truck in uneasy silence. Devin turned away from the suburbs, heading back to the edge of the city.

"Do you think this will last that long? I mean, for us to lose power? What if the gas stations are out of gas?" Matt questioned in a panic.

"Why would they be?" Gillian inquired.

"Well, if I were to try to get out of the city," Matt explained, "I would make damn sure I had the gas to get as far away as possible. Gassing up here would feel safer than trying to find a place when I'm on the highway."

"We'll have to make finding fuel the number one priority. I think there is a station up ahead," Devin said, trying to keep his tone light. Darkness had fallen around them. The lights of the gas station could be seen as they crested a hill. Devin surveyed the area as they approached. Nothing was moving, and the houses nearby were all dark.

Max and Hector began to discuss who was going to cover which end of the truck. Beth spoke up. "I know how to handle a gun," she said, pointing to the semi-automatic Hector had holstered. "I notice that you have an extra sidearm." Hector looked at the young woman, then at the sidearm. Max made an impatient noise in his throat. Hector ignored him and looked back at Beth.

"A cheerleader with weapons training?" The soldier scoffed.

"I was the drum major, actually," Beth replied dryly.

"I knew it! For the Yellow Jackets, right?" Matt interrupted. Beth nodded. "Oh man, you guys do not have a good football team.

But... um... the band is good," he finished lamely, taking in the look she gave him.

Beth turned slowly from glaring at Matt to look at Hector. "And yes, I have. My father was in the army and he taught me and my brother."

Hector gave her an evaluating look.

"Come on man! She's just a kid." Max threw out, annoyed.

Hector pulled out his sidearm and handed it to Beth. She checked the safety and ejected the clip to count the bullets. She checked to be sure a round was chambered. "There are only three rounds. Do you have a spare mag?"

Hector laughed and reached in his pocket. He pulled out a full clip and handed it to Beth.

Devin pulled into a gas station lot. They could barely see outside the ring of light surrounding the pumps and small convenience store. It was a small station, only having four pumps. Devin pulled to a pump in the middle of the light.

He noticed one pump was missing its hose. The other's was on the ground. The store's glass door was broken and hanging open. The floor just inside was brownish red with dried blood. Turning in his seat, he addressed the others. "Doesn't look good, but let's give it a try."

Hector, Max and Beth jumped out of the back and took positions around the vehicle. Devin jumped out. He scooped up the nozzle from the ground. His sigh of relief at pulling in on the correct side for the gas tank turned to one of frustration. "Drat! I need the keys!" He hissed into the cab. Gillian crawled around the front seat, grabbing the keys. Jumping from the cab, she searched through the ring quickly, finding the one that opened the cap. Behind them they heard Trevor moaning about the engine being off.

Beth, Hector and Max scanned the area for any movement. Their guns swept side to side, ready to fire. A light breeze swept Beth's hair into her eyes but other than that, nothing moved. In the distance they heard glass breaking and several shots. "Well, let's get this done while they are distracted." Hector whispered. Max jumped at the sound of nozzle clattering in the gas tank. Devin flipped the pump to the on position. Nothing happened.

"We have to pay first!" Gillian hissed to Devin. Immediately Devin began frantically searching for his wallet.

"Here! The city will pay for this." Martin was waving his credit card from the cab.

Gillian grabbed it and swiped. "Yes, it's a credit card!" she muttered impatiently to the pump. "No, I don't need a receipt!" Finally, with the gas flowing, Devin motioned to Gillian. She got the message and hurried back into the truck.

Time seemed to be moving slower as the gas pumped into the tank. Something caught Beth's attention off to her right. It was a scraping sound, like metal on concrete. Training her weapon to the direction she thought it was coming from, Beth gave a short whistle to get the attention of her comrades.

Nervously looking around, Devin muttered at the pump, "Come on, come on, you have to be about full." He urged it to pump faster. "I've already put in 20 gallons, how much more do you need?"

Beth strained to see out of the pool of light into the darkness across the street. "Whatever we have is good enough!" she shouted over her shoulder. Out of the blackness surrounding the station, an old man was staggering toward them. A hunting rifle hung from his outstretched arm, the butt at his elbow and the barrel scraping along the street. Behind him Beth could make out several more figures moving in the shadows. She aimed between the old man's eyes and fired. He crumpled in the middle of the road. Max and Hector were at her side in a second.

"Should I try for the rifle?" she asked wide-eyed to Hector.

"What? Hell no!" Max stammered, motioning to the shambling dead in the distance.

"Ya know what? I can make it," she told the two shocked men. With a small hop she ran forward, barely noticing the tug on her jacket where Max tried to restrain her. Her footfalls seemed to thunder in her ears as she ran to the fallen corpse. Reaching the body, she began struggling with the sling. Freeing the weapon, she glanced over at the man's other hand. The red label of a box of ammo had caught her attention. Forcing it out of the death grip, she began to pat the pockets of the corpse, looking for more ammunition or another gun.

"Beth! Look out! Get back here now!" Hector ordered, pointing to the advancing crowd.

Looking behind her, Beth saw the other zombies were only about five feet from her. She could see the yearning in what was left of their faces. Straightening up, she looked them in the eye for a second. The nearest one raised its arm, letting out a low moan. That was all Beth needed. She sprinted back to the truck.

The handle of the pump clicked, denoting a full tank. Devin tapped the nozzle several times then put it back on the pump. He waited a moment for the receipt, then realized it wasn't coming and the situation he was in. He was in the truck in a moment with the engine running and in gear. "What is with men and shaking the gas nozzle?" Gillian asked, receiving a snorted laugh from Matt.

Beth was tucking her handgun into the back of her jeans with the rifle slung over her shoulder. She returned to the front of the truck. Max shook his head and then started to move to the back when Beth grabbed him. "Hold on. Hector, wait." Hector was opening one of the back doors. "Hector and I will l hold them off. You should check the store; get some water and anything else we might need."

"What the hell are you talking about?" Max shouted. "The truck is gassed up, the dead are coming and we need to be going!"

Beth raised her new rifle, checking to make sure it was loaded. She stuffed the ammo box into the pocket of her jacket and fired. Another of the undead dropped just inside the pool of light.

Hector looked at the panicked cop. "I'll go." Banging on the hood of the truck he yelled, "Devin, back up as close as you can up to the store."

Devin nodded. He reversed to the smashed glass door with Hector directing him from the open back door. Beth walked backward, keeping her back as close to the front grill as she could. Max's head was quickly moving from side to side. For every three shots he took, only one found its mark. Beth's aim was steady and spot on. They kept up a steady fire, dropping several zombies as they backed away toward the store.

Broken glass cracked under the dual rear tires. Hector yelled a halt, and jumping down, he hurried into the store with his gun raised. He checked the four aisles but found them empty of anyone, alive or dead. Gillian and Martin quickly joined him. Matt came scrambling after them. He looked left then right, and "Ah HA!" he yelped, and ran to a door marked "restroom."

"Ya know, he has the right idea, it may be a while before we see another one," Gillian noted. Hector, Martin and Gillian had formed a kind of fire bucket brigade, tossing food and water to each other and up to Trevor in the back of the truck. Hector yelled for Matt to take his place as he emerged from the bathroom. The line ended as the store was mostly cleared out of necessities. They quickly checked shelves and hit the restrooms.

Outside, Beth fired nine shots from the rifle before it clicked empty. She slung it on her shoulder, pulled the gun, and fired the last two rounds in that. She ejected the clip, stowing the empty one in her jacket and slapped the new one in as she surveyed the on-coming horde. They just kept coming out of the darkness. Hector was at her shoulder, "There is a bathroom in there; use it but make it quick." Beth gave him a look of disgust.

"May be the last one we see for a while." he shrugged, firing at an older man who wore nothing but a flannel shirt.

"We don't have enough time for everyone," Beth exclaimed as she backed into the store.

"Hey, we're men. We can go anywhere," he laughed.

"Men are nasty." Beth said, lowering her weapon while running into the store.

"You got that right sister." Gillian agreed as Beth passed. "But that ladies room isn't what you'd call clean." Beth groaned as she pushed the door open.

Hector and Max slowed their rate of fire to only take down the undead closest to them. Max muttered under his breath. "Why does it take them so long to pee?" Beth gave a shout as she jumped into the back of the truck.

Hector took a second to give the store a once-over. "That's it! Time to go! Everyone in the truck now, now, NOW!"

Max didn't need telling twice. He was in the back before Beth had even gotten settled. She jumped out of his way. Hector slammed the back doors. "We're all in, go man, go!" In the time it took everyone to get back into the truck, the dead had covered the distance of the lot. Hands were beating the hood and windows. Devin yelled at the dead while he slammed on the gas. Unable to see through the zombies, they drove over the end of the gas islands and several of the undead. The truck bounced hard over the concrete. Those in the back were thrown around, bouncing all over as they sped away from a mass of undead.

"Dude, I think I smashed the chip," Matt groaned, rubbing his head where he had banged it on the side of the truck. Several bags of chips had exploded when he landed on them, sending crumbs all over the floor.

Looking back at her chip-covered companions, Beth tried to stifle a snicker. Suddenly she was hit with a severe case of the shakes as the adrenaline left her body. She tried to busy herself by loading shells into the clip of the rifle. Her fingers were shaking too badly to get the bullets loaded. Noticing her trouble, Hector handed her a bottle of water. She smiled as she took it. She reached behind her, pulling out the handgun to give it back to him.

"That is yours," he said, taking the bullets and the clip of the rifle from her. "I think we should give the rifle to someone else, if that is okay. You know, spread the weapons around—or do you want to keep it?"

Beth only shook her head, not sure whether if she opened her mouth she would vomit. Slowly she took a drink of the water. To her surprise, it was still cold. It calmed her a little, but the sight of Matt eating a chocolate cream filled cake made her stomach do a flip. She had to look away.

Hector rummaged in his pockets for a couple of seconds, then looked into his pack. He emerged with a couple of boxes of nine-millimeter ammo and handed them to Beth. She opened them and then searched her pockets, retrieving her empty clips. Her hands were a little steadier and she began to load the bullets. Finishing one clip, she fished in her pocket for the second magazine. Her hand grasped her cell phone. She retrieved it, hitting the buttons to call her brother. Excitement filled her as the phone rang. Then it rang again, then again, then, "Your call is being routed to an automatic voice mailbox...Steve McDaniel is not available." Beth ended the call, drawing a heavy breath. Leaning forward, she returned to her shaky loading of bullets.

Hector's hand gripped her shoulder lightly and he whispered, "I'd take one of you over two of him." He jerked his head toward Max, who was muttering to himself again. Beth gave a weak laugh and leaned back against the steel wall. She was suddenly so tired.

Night

Wes was running ahead of her. Beth called out to him. He turned his head and laughed at her. He disappeared around a corner. She hurried after him, calling out as she spun around the corner. He was just up ahead, crouched down. She slowed her pace. Something was wrong, very wrong. She got closer and she could see Wes was leaning over someone on the ground. Holding her breath, she didn't want to see who it was, but she couldn't stop. Suddenly she was right behind Wes. The person on the ground was her brother, Steve.

Wes turned to look up at her. His face was covered in blood, torn flesh filled his mouth. In his hands he held intestines and other gore. Steve's body was ripped open. Beth staggered back while Wes returned to his hellish feast. Steve's eyes flew open. They locked onto Beth's. "You should have helped Dad," he said.

Beth's eyes flew open. Slowing her breathing, she realized she was still in the truck.

Devin swerved to miss a group of three undead as he headed deeper into town. "We have to find a place to stop for the night," Max called from the back as he pushed himself off Trevor for the fourth time in the last fifteen minutes.

"I think I know a place," Devin nodded. It took several more minutes and a very uncomfortable incident with Matt's hands and Gillian's body, something Matt was still apologizing for, when Devin finally found what he was looking for.

"There it is." He sighed, looking ahead at the tall parking structure. Devin pulled the truck into the parking garage, driving all the way to the top. From there they could see out over part of the city. The flames from the ballpark had died down but were replaced by those of several of the surrounding buildings. The streetlights had come on, but many parts of the city were dark except for the reddish glow of fires.

Devin pulled to the middle of the lot, not wanting to be seen from below. They were alone at the top. There was one other car up there, but it looked abandoned with its door hanging open. Putting the truck into park, Devin slowly released the wheel. Beth watched him. It looked like it hurt to let go. Flexing his fingers, Devin looked over at her. "I guess I was holding on a little tight."

"Do you think we are alone?" Matt asked, pointing out the front window to the lot's other occupant.

"Better check it out," Beth said, reaching for the door release.

"Hold on, we'll go together," Hector said as he stoop-walked to the back doors. He looked over at Max, who was suddenly preoccupied with something is his bag. Hector shook his head in disgust.

"I've got the door," Gillian reassured Hector, frowning at Max, who only ignored the three of them. Matt got up to help, manning the other door.

Hector nodded his thanks. "Ready, Major?"

"What? Oh, Drum Major, right." Beth smiled, took a deep breath, returned a nod to Hector. The doors opened. Hector sprang out, sweeping his weapon from side to side, Beth at his heels. The lot seemed empty. As quietly as possible they approached the car. Beth headed to the passenger side, Hector to the open driver's door.

Beth looked through the window. Nothing. Hector dropped down and checked under the car.

"Clear," he whispered.

"Oh, right, clear." Beth returned. Hector smiled and winked his approval. The car was empty. Nothing in the front seat or back. Hector reached in. He motioned for Beth to get ready at the trunk. He pulled the lever and the trunk clicked open. Joining Beth at the back, he nodded to her to open the trunk. It was also empty, except for some tools for the jack and a blanket. Hector grabbed the lug wrench and the blanket. Beth made a face at the filthy cloth.

Hector smiled. "You may change your mind if it gets cold."

"Doubt it. That is nasty."

As soon as the others saw Beth and Hector relax, they all piled out of the truck. Having been bounced around in the back of the armored vehicle for the last four or five hours had made everyone want a little space to themselves. Still embarrassed by the earlier incident, Matt moved far from Gillian. Beth noticed this and caught

Gillian's eye, and they both laughed. Bill and Martin met Beth and Hector halfway back across the lot.

"Anything useful in the car?" Martin asked, frowning at the stained cloth in Hector's hand.

"Just a tire tool and a dirty blanket," Hector reported.

Martin gave a silent nod, and then headed to edge of the structure to have a look around. The other three followed. Martin rested his hands on the thick concrete wall and looked over at the building across the street. It was one of the three hospitals in town.

"That dipshit captain sent some of our guys there to try to secure it," Hector whispered as they watched a steady stream of zombies stumble out of the front doors. "Don't think they fared very well." He pointed to the Humvee parked behind a news truck.

"Oh my," Bill gasped.

The lights were still on in the hospital. They could see many undead dressed in normal clothes, as doctors and as patients, in the windows. Some seemed trapped in their rooms, clawing at the doors, while others stared out the windows at them. Devin wandered up. He looked at the hospital windows. "I think we should stay here for the night," he said, without looking at the others.

Trevor looked over at him, terrified. "We are right next to the hospital and close to downtown. There could be hundreds of them down there."

"Right—they are down there, and they don't know we are up here. They don't climb so good, so the steep ramps will make it hard for them to get to us," Hector explained.

Devin nodded. "Exactly. We need a rest and this seems like the safest place at the moment."

"I don't know," Bill cut in, "they move pretty good when they see us."

"This will be OK for one night, right, sergeant?" Martin asked giving support to the military man. Hector saw the look the mayor gave him and agreed. It might not be the right decision, but they had made it and were going to stick to it. Hector hoped it was as safe as they thought.

Beth also saw the look and knew this wasn't the best place to be, but they needed the rest. She also silently agreed they needed to set up a kind of chain of command. She looked down at her phone and hit the speed dial for her brother. Frustrated, she pocketed it. There was no service here.

"Power must be out to the cell tower," Hector noted as he passed her.

Pulling her phone back out, she looked down at it. She felt betrayed by the technology. Stuffing the useless phone back in her pocket, she watched Matt who was peeking over the edge of the parking garage at the hospital. She missed Wes and Steve. She said a silent pray that they were ok. Matt rose up a little and spit over the edge.

"Got ya!" he yelped.

Beth *really* missed Wes. He would never do anything that immature, she thought, disgusted.

"Shhh...don't give away our position," Max hissed at Matt.

"Whatever, dude, they can't get up here," Matt shrugged.

Max glared as Matt wandered over to the truck. Beth followed, taking a bottle of water from the back. She walked over to Hector, Devin, and Gillian. "So what is the plan?" she asked.

"We need to get out of town, but I'll be damned if I can figure a way, other than trying to hike out," Hector responded.

"I'm not real keen on that plan," Devin sighed.

Gillian had noticed Beth trying the phone. "Were you able get a hold of anyone?" she asked. Beth shook her head. "Could I... could I borrow your phone?" Gillian asked.

Beth shrugged and handed it over. Gillian dialed a number, hung up, and tried another, then another. After several attempts she returned the phone to Beth. Tears ran down her face. Beth looked at the phone and then looked at the others in her group. "I still have a pretty good charge; anyone else want to try?" she asked. "Maybe on the other side of the garage or something?"

"No thanks," Matt said, not looking at her, "Everyone I know is dead." He shrugged, and wandering back over to the roof's edge, he sat down. Gillian followed, sitting next to him.

Hector took the phone. He made a few call attempts at different sections of the lot. Devin just sat on the back of the truck. Hector gave up, handing the phone to Martin, who took out his own, handing Beth's to Trevor. After several minutes Beth had her phone back, and no one had spoken to anyone.

"I guess we are alone," Beth said, staring at the phone in her hand.

Martin looked at his phone. "Damn it!" he shouted. He threw the phone as hard as he could. It flew over the edge toward the hospital. "Why? Why?" He sank to his knees, crying. "Why couldn't we get more out? What more could we have done?"

"We did everything we could." Trevor said, trying to comfort his boss.

"Hey, …Martin, right? We came here because of you. You convinced the Colonel to help out. You tried, man," Hector said sympathetically.

"Yeah, and that worked out well," Max grumbled from behind Beth.

She spared him a second for a dirty look. "You saved us," she said to the mayor, gesturing to Bill, Hector, and Max.

Martin slumped against the side of the truck his head in his hands. Everyone was quiet for a while.

"Let's get in the truck and try to get some sleep," Devin suggested several minutes later.

"Should we have someone stand guard?" Hector asked.

"I don't want to leave the truck open." Trevor quickly spoke up. "The truck is armored and it has places we can shoot from. Besides, they don't know we are here."

Hector shrugged but did not argue. It was a cramped arrangement but eventually they all found a place in the truck to be as comfortable as they could.

Sanctuary?

Steve woke with a start. Looking down at his watch in the candlelight, he noted he'd been able to sleep for three hours. Prior to that, he recalled that only two other people had joined their ranks. He hoped others had come while he slept. Looking around, he mentally counted the people. It didn't seem there had been any additions. He fought the disappointment.

Rubbing the sleep from his eyes and the stubble on his chin, he wondered why he had woken up. He listened for anything to explain it. The only sound was the gentle hiss of whispered conversation and the rhythmic breathing of someone asleep nearby. Steve looked over the side of the pew he was lying on. Wes was on the floor, snoring softly. Steve watched the young man sleep and smiled. He had known Wes for years. Ever since Wes and Beth had met in first grade, they had been fast friends. Steve chuckled, seeing Wes still had Beth's stuffed bunny with him. It was lying next to him, his arm over it. Then Steve saw that Wes' hand was on a gun. He frowned at this. Beth should have her bunny, and Wes should never have had to do the things he had done that day.

Candlelight danced across the ceiling. The glow of distant fires dimly illuminated the tall windows of the church. Steve rose to a sitting position, still trying to figure out what had woken him. Perplexed and somewhat disturbed, he got up, careful not to wake Wes, and stretched.

Steve looked to the front of the church. He saw the priest kneeling over the burned man. A woman was next the priest, clutching her hands tight to her mouth. Steve could tell she was sobbing. Next to her, a man was patting her on the shoulder. Steve looked away. It felt like he was intruding on them.

Suddenly his attention was again brought back to them as the woman wailed in despair. Steve leaned over the pew, slowly retrieving his rifle. When he stood back up, he saw the priest covering the burn victim with a blanket. The woman was being held and consoled by the man who had been patting her shoulder.

Steve checked his rifle, chambered a round. He got up quietly. As he began to head up the aisle the priest saw him coming. As the priest moved to intercept him, Steve's attention was on the clergyman.

"Wait my son, wait just a moment."

Back at the alter, the woman fell backward with a screech. Her arms and legs flailed as she tried to get away. The priest spun on the spot. All sound and movement stopped for Steve. The blanket slid slowly from the burned man's face. Blackened skin cracked and peeled as the face contorted, the lips peeled back over bloody teeth.

The zombie turned to attack the man who had given the woman a shoulder to cry on. That shoulder now turned crimson as teeth ripped into it. The man howled in pain. The burnt man chewed happily, until the left side of his head exploded into red and grey across the alter.

The gunshot finally broke Steve from his trance. Turning to look, he already knew what he would see. Still, it pulled at his heart. It was Wes. Steve shut his eyes. Poor Wes had to do it again.

Wes stood, his gun still aimed at the zombie. Steve saw Wes adjust his aim to the bitten man. "Wait, wait!" Steve called to Wes, bringing his own rifle to his shoulder, and he headed up to the wounded man. "GET BACK!" Steve ordered, taking aim. The man was holding one hand up in surrender, the other clutched at the free-flowing wound on his neck and shoulder.

"NO WAIT! NO—I'M NOT DEAD!" the man screamed at Steve. The wound on his neck was spewing blood. His shirt was now almost completely red. The woman moved to block Steve's shot.

"No no…." the man paled and lost consciousness.

"GET BACK!" Steve yelled again, shooing the woman away with his rifle. She stood her ground, anger and hatred etched in her features. Steve could see the man starting to stir behind her. The priest moved quickly to pull the woman away. He grabbed her around the waist, pulling her out of Steve's line of fire. She fought hard to keep her place.

She was screaming, "Dave, get up!" She demanded he show them he was OK. Dave did get up, but he was far from OK. Steve aimed. Blood splattered over the woman, adding more gore to the altar. Silence filled the church for several seconds. The woman slid from the priest's arms to the floor, sobbing. The priest followed, holding her by the shoulders, whispering reassurances into her ear.

Steve realized he hadn't fired. He looked over to see Wes lowering his weapon. Then Wes disappeared into the pew.

The woman pried herself from the priest and slowly got to her feet. She ran her hands over her face and looked down at them. They too were red with blood, like the floor and the two corpses. Suddenly she was screaming. She turned pointing from where Wes was to Steve and back again. "Murderer, MURDERERS!!"

"We just saved your..." Steve felt a tug on his shirt. Wes was there, pulling him back toward the rear of the church. The woman's venom followed them as they went. Several other people in the church stared at them as they walked back to their pew.

"You did what you had to," Mrs. Johnson said as they passed. She was comforting the children, a couple of whom drew back in fear as Wes walked by. The woman at the front of the church was still wailing as Steve slumped down into a pew.

"Are we heroes or cold-blooded killers?" Wes asked with a mirthless laugh. He curled up under his jacket. Steve knew that he did not go back to sleep. They lay there until the stained glass began to lighten as the sun rose. Only one more person came to the church that day. Steve counted fourteen people, including himself and Wes.

"Well, like Gandalf says, lucky 14," Wes tried to joke. Steve looked confused, so Wes just shook his head. He did not try to explain. He just asked, "Are you sure you're Beth's brother?"

New Day

Beth woke as the sun hit her eyes. For a second she was blind-ed. Shading her eyes, she tried to make sense of her surroundings. "Damn it," she mumbled, "it wasn't a nightmare."

"No, no it wasn't," Martin grimaced from beside her. He stretched and rubbed his back. Soon the back of the truck was full of groans, pops, stretching and restless people trying to wake and move.

Devin stirred in the driver's seat. He stretched, scratched the back of his head, opened his eyes and jumped back in his seat. "Ho-ly mother of pearl!" he shouted.

Trevor woke with start, and pressed himself as far back as pos-sible in the passenger seat. "Holy SHIT!" he cried.

Everyone was now fully awake, looking out the front window of the truck. Matt's hand froze on the handle to the back door. Zombies were everywhere. The once deserted parking lot was now full of the undead. The mass hadn't reached the truck yet, but they moved toward it, so there could be no mistake that it was their goal.

"Aw man! I really gotta pee," Matt whined.

"They must have wandered up the ramp all night," Beth postu-lated, ignoring Matt.

"Why do you think that?" Matt asked. The others turned with quizzical looks.

Moving up between the front seats, she pointed at the ap-proaching zombies. "Well, they don't move that fast, and the exit ramp is really steep. I doubt they'd take the harder route and..."

"Let's just get out of here! We can theorize about how and why they are here later," Trevor cried. "WHOA! Let's GO NOW. Go go go go go NOW!" he screamed, throwing himself away from the window. A grey torn hand slammed into it.

Devin turned the key. The truck roared to life. The advancing ghouls became more excited by the sound. Their moans urged the approaching shamblers to move faster toward the living. Devin aimed their mobile fortress. In seconds, they plowed into the oncoming horde. The undead slammed into the grill and bounced off the sides.

Cries of fear and pain mixed with the whine of the engine and the groans and thuds of the dead. "There, there!" Martin pointed to an area where the horde was thinner. The zombies clawed at the sides of the truck as it passed. Devin urged the vehicle forward as he made the turn down the spiral ramp to the exit. He glanced at the side view mirror. Dead faces blurred above the words, "objects in mirror are closer than they appear".

Beth gripped the dash, still on her knees between the two seats. She looked out the passenger window past a terrified Trevor to the other sideview mirror. A zombie's hand had torn free from its owner, becoming a grotesque addition to Beth's view under the mirror. It was only temporary. The mirror was torn off an instant later as it scrapped against the wall.

Devin took the ramp as fast as he dared. Those in the back were slammed to one side with the force of the turn. The tires squealed while metal scrapped. Around and around, down the circular ramp. Beth had to grab Trevor's seat to keep from being thrown across the cab. She closed her eyes to keep from getting dizzy, and instantly regretted it, so she decided to stare at the air conditioner controls.

The centrifugal force eased up. Devin let out a grunt, straightening the wheel at the end of the ramp. The truck bottomed out, and the crunch of metal met the thumps of bodies hitting the floor in the back. Beth instinctively covered her face with her arms as Devin flew through the gate at the exit and out into the street.

Bright morning sun filled the cab when they broke free of the garage. Devin pulled hard on the wheel, turning the lumbering vehicle toward the hospital. They weaved through empty ambulances, gurneys, and walking corpses. Swerving around the back of a crashed van, Devin swore while trying to alter their course. The attempt was too late, and they clipped the front of a wheelchair-bound zombie. Beth turned to the small windows in the back to watch the chair spin, throwing its occupant out into the street. It clawed at the road, trying to follow them.

Beth was so intent on watching the determination of the crippled ghoul that she had no time to brace herself as a little red Miata burst out of an alley to their left, right into the path of the truck.

Good Morning

Wes was back outside Beth's house. It was just starting to get dark. He looked back at the battered car he had driven here. He wasn't positive she would be here, but he had to start looking somewhere. Cautiously he pushed open the door, silently slipping into the shadowy house. It looked like he always remembered it looking; nothing seemed out of place. Closing the door with a soft click, he proceeded deeper into the familiar surroundings.

Easing his way down the hall, he entered the living room. He stopped abruptly as he spied a figure standing by the sliding glass door to the back yard. Familiar loose curls fell onto the bare shoulders of Beth. She was wearing a light yellow summer dress with little flowers on it. "Beth, oh thank god, I was so worried..." Wes sighed as he reached for her.

She slowly turned toward him. He gasped, stumbling back. Half her face was missing. Her right eye was gone and so was most of her cheek, as well as the flesh of her lower jaw. Her white teeth clicked at him through the angry red flesh. She reached for him with an arm that gleamed with congealed blood, the white bones of the forearm plainly visible.

"NO! NO! NO!" he screamed, backing away. She advanced toward him. Wes tripped over a body on the floor. Beth's father glared up at him. A seeping red hole stared at Wes between the man's eyes. Then Beth's nails scraped Wes' arm. He raised his gun. "No, Beth, please!" he pleaded. Her mouth opened wide, the lower jaw barely attached.

"BAM! BAM! BAM!" Wes sat bolt upright on the pew. He was sweating. Tears cascaded down his cheeks.

Steve whispered, "You're all right... and that wasn't her."

Wes tried to cover his face. "Not who?" he questioned, more scared than he wanted to let on.

Steve's hand gripped Wes's shoulder. "Beth," Steve stated simply. "I had that dream too, where she is..." Steve stopped.

Wes took a deep breath. "No, she is okay, I can feel it. I know it." Wes rolled back over, repeating to himself. "She's okay, she's okay...."

BAM! BAM! Wes sat back up and looked at Steve. "I thought I dreamt that."

"Nah, they are adding some wood over a lower window and some other stuff to the barricade." Steve stretched. "Remember that lady that called us murderers?"

Wes nodded grumpily.

"Well she got pissed, didn't want to stay here, so she tried to leave. Well, then she met some zombies that changed her mind. Problem is, she led them back here."

"Did she make it?" Wes questioned, but he didn't care. Then he felt terrible that he didn't.

"No, they got her. But she at least let us know where our defenses were weak."

"Well, that is good, I guess." Wes tried to make her death mean something, but he couldn't, and he shrugged it off. Daylight filled the room, letting them see the others they shared the church with clearly. "You'd think, with the end of the world, there would have been more people here," Wes yawned.

Steve turned to him, shocked.

"What? I'm just saying."

Shaking his head, Steve turned from his friend. A familiar smell wafted to his nose. "Coffee.... mmmm," Steve moaned.

As if on cue, the older woman from the night before came bustling into the church pushing a large cart. On the cart were two large coffee decanters and a stack of cups. Next to the coffee was... "Sweet! Danish!" Wes pushed past Steve.

Steve also started forward toward the already crowded cart, only to pause. He saw the movement at the front of the church and headed away from what he now knew was a diversion.

"Can I be of some help, as it really is...um, my mess?" Steve asked the priest. As soon as the question had been made, Steve realized how callous it sounded. Looking down, Steve watched as the other man swirled the mop over the blood-stained marble in front of the altar.

The mop entered the deep red water of the bucket then slopped back to the floor. "This was not your mess... I don't know who is to blame." The words hung in the air between the two men.

"Steve McDaniel." Steve held out his hand.

Taking it, "Michael Lewis, and if it helps...he was already gone; you just destroyed an empty shell."

Father Michael returned to his mopping. Steve watched for a moment, then asked the question without meaning to. "Are they evil?"

The mop stopped but Father Michael did not look up. "I don't know. I don't know if this is the rapture or judgment day or we were left behind or something else entirely. I just don't know." The silence that followed was only cut by the sloshing of water and the swirling of the mop. Steve wandered off, wondering if the Father had been asked this several times, or if it was what he had been thinking since it all began.

"Black with one sugar, right? What were you and the priest talking about?" Wes asked, passing Steve a cup of coffee.

"Nothing, really." Steve looked at Wes and saw the same face he had known for years, but he noticed the new look behind the eyes. He wondered— if he ever saw Beth again, would she have the same look? The look of someone who has seen and done things that they never should have. He wondered if Wes saw the same thing when he looked at him.

"Dude! What?"

Steve realized he had been staring. "What? Nothing." He quickly looked past Wes. "So, did you meet anyone we know?"

"No, just your old teacher and her husband. A couple of the kids we ran into yesterday were pretty cool to me. They said you were awesome." Steve choked a little on his coffee and laughed. Wes continued, "A couple from Westmont, a family from Altoona that was visiting friends and a few people who just seemed too freaked to talk. Mrs. Jones, the lady with the cart, was cool. She called us heroes for what we did last night." Wes suddenly lost interest in the cherry Danish he was eating.

Steve glanced up at the altar where Father Michael was pushing the mop and bucket away. Several people were looking in Steve and Wes' direction. "Come on." Steve grabbed Wes by the collar, pulling him to the door.

"What's up?"

"I dunno. I just need to not be the center of attention right now." Pushing open the heavy front door, Steve shielded his eyes from the bright morning sun. The smell of the fires and the sickening odor of death accosted his nostrils.

"Whoa—is that them?" Wes whispered.

"You get used to it after a while. It is a good warning though, as they get closer. That and the moan," said a balding man who was holding a rifle. He barely glanced over at them as they emerged from the church.

Wes' attention was drawn from the man to the dark red stain on the ground near the small space between the buses. A light wind blew his long hair across his face. Wes pushed it away as he turned to talk to Steve. Steve held up a hand. Wes heard it. It was the sound of metal scraping concrete. The noise grew louder as if coming down from a height.

"Where is the closest parking garage?" Wes asked, excited.

"Over by the hospital," the gunman replied, pointing to a building hidden from view by other structures. The scraping stopped and the men strained to listen. All cringed at the sound of a collision.

More

Devin screamed, and yanked the wheel with both feet thrust on the brakes as hard as he could. Bodies flew forward, slamming hard into each other in the back of the truck. Beth's head slammed into the dash. Even standing on the breaks, Devin couldn't stop in time. The little car was smashed. Stars swam before Beth's eyes and a warm trickle of blood seeped over her forehead from just under her hair. Several people groaned from the back. "Is everyone okay?" Devin asked, rubbing his own forehead. He reached over to brush Beth's hair back, inspecting her injury.

"I'm okay. Better than them, I bet." Beth pointed at the wreck of the little red convertible. Devin looked stricken. Beth knew he was thinking he had just killed a fellow survivor. "We should check…" Beth began, placing a hand on Devin's arm.

"Look!" Matt pointed from between them.

To everyone's amazement, the hard top of the convertible was thrown off and three people clamored out. A blonde middle-aged woman wearing a red fancy dress ran as fast as she could in high heels toward the truck. A second woman with dark hair was helping a younger man out of the wreck. They followed, although much slower, as the man appeared injured.

The blonde was already pounding on Devin's door. The other two had barely made it half the distance to the truck. The woman helping the injured man was also dressed in evening clothes. She appeared to be of Asian descent. The man was in his twenties. He was also dressed nicely but looked more like a waiter than a party attendee.

The blonde never looked back at the other two as she continued to pound on the door. Devin was trying frantically to get her to go around to the back door.

"Are they alive? They're not zombies are they?" Trevor asked, terrified from behind Beth.

"No, they appear to be okay. Well, hurt from the crash, but alive," Beth announced.

Hector jumped up, throwing open the back door. He jumped out and surveyed the street. Several zombies were closing in. He ran around the side of the truck, yelling for the crash victims. The blonde pushed past him, throwing herself into the back of the truck. She landed painfully on Matt's legs. Without any apology she was up, pressing herself against the wall and screaming, "Go, let's get out of here!"

"Your friends aren't in yet," Devin shouted from the front.

"Come on!" Hector encouraged, glancing back at the approaching undead.

When the two had reached the side of the truck, Hector grabbed the injured man. The woman hurried around the corner. She was helped in by Martin. Gillian jumped out to help Hector. The man groaned as they piled him into the back. The doors slammed. "All right, Devin, get us the hell out of here!" Hector yelled.

Throwing the truck into reverse, Devin floored it. Three loud thumps echoed through the back as the truck slammed into the advancing group of zombies. Clearing the wreck, Devin put the truck into drive and sped from the scene. The woman in red was taking deep angry breaths, her hair covering her face. The other woman was thanking Hector and Devin.

"Oh, shut up, Linda! If it wasn't for them, we wouldn't have needed their help. Did you forget, they hit US!" The blonde glared from her companion to the others in the truck. Beth was shocked at her hostility.

"Settle down, Stancy. We are safer in this than in your little sports car," Linda explained, exasperated.

"You got that right! Nice driving, by the way," Stancy spat out.

"Hey! Enough with the yelling! Who the hell are you people?" Hector demanded. Stancy spared him a sneer before ignoring him to stare out the front window.

"Sorry about her. My name is Linda Vu. This is Seth Carpenter, and that lovely even-tempered woman is Stancy Greene."

"Were any of you bitten or scratched by any of them?" Hector asked, his hand on the hilt of his sidearm.

"No, no one was bitten or anything. Seth was hurt in the crash," Linda spoke uneasily, her eyes on Hector's hand. Seth moaned from the floor of the truck as it hit a bump.

"Oh, suck it up," Stancy grumbled.

Gillian gave her a look of loathing as she tried to determine the extent of Seth's injuries. "He's banged up pretty good," she explained to Hector. "This bumpy ride isn't going to do him any good. I can feel several broken ribs."

"Devin, we're gonna need a place to hold up." Hector leaned over between Beth and Devin. He looked over Beth's bloody face. "You okay, kid?"

She gave him a weak reassuring smile. "Yeah, just a knock on the head. Glad we picked up such charming company for it."

Stancy snorted, "We were doing fine until you smashed into us."

"We were smashed in there like sardines! Seth was crammed on top of me; we were not fine!" Linda shouted.

"No one asked him to come along!"

"He would have been killed if we didn't bring him."

Stancy raised herself slightly, pointing at Linda. She looked as if she were a gathering storm about to release a tirade to fill the entire truck.

"That is enough! I will stop this truck and take you right back to your car and leave you there!" Devin shouted from the front. He looked over to see Beth desperately trying to stifle a laugh.

"Damn! Sounded just like my dad on vacation," Matt said from the back, a note of awe in his voice.

That was all Beth needed. The giggle fit broke over her. Her laughter was joined by Matt and Gillian. Hector shook his head, smiling. Devin wore an amused look as he slowed the truck, trying to ease the bumpy ride for the injured man. Stancy glared murderously around at her new companions. Seth groaned, and Gillian returned to his aid. Beth got herself under control, but she kept looking over at Devin, amused.

Martin watched both Stancy and Gillian as they stared daggers at each other. "So, what is your story?" he asked, waving his hands at the evening dresses the two women were wearing.

"We were at a dinner party..." Linda began but Stancy cut her off.

My brilliant husband," she started sarcastically, "decided to raise everyone's spirits by throwing an *everything is going to be all right* party. The idiot, like he had a clue." She wore an ugly expression. "So we set up this expensive-ass party and invite all of his clients and golf club friends. Oh what fun."

"You seemed to enjoy yourself just fine," Linda cut in, giving a significant nod to Seth.

"Huh! He didn't last long enough for me to enjoy myself," Stancy sneered.

"What?... ohhhhhh. Hey, you said your husband had the party. You mean you were..." Matt was slow to catch on.

"Oh please, like he ever noticed or cared."

"Well, it was lucky you were in the backyard screwing Seth when the zombies came in the front door. He probably saved you life!" Linda angrily threw at Stancy.

Seth moaned a little and held his stomach. "Devin, we really need to find a place. This guy is in really bad shape," Gillian called.

"So, you were having a party when the zombies broke in?" Matt asked.

"Yeah, but they didn't really break in," Linda began. She took a deep steadying breath. "We were in the living room. I was by the front door when we heard a knocking. Ray just opened the door." She closed her eyes. When she opened them she continued, "They were on him as soon as the door was cracked. Biting and grabbing. There were so many of them. So much blood."

"Well, that was just like the idiot. I'm sure he was thinking the more the merrier. Just let the bastards in. If he had been more intelligent he would have known better. So there we were, with zombies killing everyone at the party. Serious downer," Stancy said with a harsh laugh.

Seth gave another moan as Devin took a sharp turn to avoid another wrecked car.

"I ran out of the house into the bac yard as these two were finishing up," Linda motioned between Seth and Stancy, "I told them what was going on and we ran for my car. Trouble was, it was only a two-seater. Stancy took my keys and Seth jumped in on top of me."

Seth coughed, and blood appeared on his lips. "Damn it, this guy definitely has internal injuries," Gillian called out. "Devin, if you see an ambulance... or maybe go by my office..." She started when Seth grabbed her hand. He sat up slightly, eyes wide. He coughed, then groaned as he slumped onto the floor.

"Oh shit." Matt breathed, pushing himself as far from Seth as he could. Gillian began checking for a pulse. Beth pulled her gun and nodded at Hector, who was also getting ready.

"What the hell?" He just pissed all over the floor," Stancy cried, trying to get away from the liquid.

"He's gone," Gillian stated in a fear-laden voice, edging away from the corpse. Linda stared down at Seth's lifeless body.

"He's gotta go. He's gotta go, gotta go now." Matt began panicking.

"What? We can't..." But what they couldn't do never was spoken as Linda's argument was silenced by Seth sitting up. She screamed as Seth's teeth ripped into her arm. Stancy's screams joined Linda's, and chaos filled the truck. Stancy pushed Matt toward Seth as she tried to crawl over him to get as far away as possible. Linda was screaming in pain and terror as Seth was happily chewing, her arm still clutched in his hands. Hector tried to pull him from her. Martin punched Seth repeatedly in the face. Trevor was cowering in fear against the passenger door, curling up as tight as he could.

"Max! Open the door!" Beth shouted, pulling her gun and aiming it at Seth. Max turned to find the door handle, wrenching it open. He threw the back doors wide. Devin hit the accelerator. Hector tore Seth away from Linda as Beth fired. The corpse's jaw exploded sending broken teeth and jaw clattering against the metal shell of the truck.

Linda's screams increased, a tooth sticking out of her face. Seth's hand grabbed her hair, pulling her toward his useless shattered mouth. She fought to get away, but Seth's grip was too tight. Beth fired again, and the sound reverberated around the truck. Devin was dazed and swerved, trying to clear his vision. Beth blinked the pain away, her ears ringing.

Seth's corpse swayed, falling backward out of the truck. Martin grabbed at Linda's hand, but she was pulled out with the corpse. Her screams ended as she hit the pavement with a sickening crunch. Beth couldn't help but watch her roll for several feet. Hector joined Max and together they pulled the doors shut.

With the doors finally closed, Max flung himself against the wall, breathing as if he had run a mile. Beth sat on her knees in the front, facing toward the back of the truck, her gun still at eye level. She shuddered as she turned around, letting the gun fall to her lap. She opened and closed her mouth several times, trying to clear her ears. Hector handed her a bottle of water and gave her shoulder a squeeze. Beth took a drink and closed her eyes.

"Great. Now the floor is piss *and* blood covered," Stancy whined.

"Then why don't you clean it up?" Beth yelled from the front. She threw the water bottle into Stancy's lap.

Stancy began to say something, but quailed under Hector's glare. She settled for mumbling something about, "Think you're something 'cause you have a gun, little girl."

Sounds of the Morning

Wes and Steve listened hard. There was a loud smash. "Damn, they hit something," Wes moaned. Several moments passed. "Nothing! No gunfire, nothing. They've had it." He shook his head as he began to slump away.

"Wait!" Steve held up a hand. Wes listened. The truck's engine could be heard accelerating. The two men smiled at each other. Both were thinking the same thing, "There are others out there. Beth could be okay." They instinctively high-fived.

The moment ended with the reverberating crash of a trash can being knocked over. The man at the top of the church stairs tensed, raising his weapon. Steve and Wes followed suit. The three swept the area back and forth, trying to locate the source of the sound. "Psst." The bald man pointed at his eyes, then to the bus to the boy's left. Wes spotted a shadow moving under the vehicle.

Being the smallest, Wes quickly and quietly edged down the stairs. He cautiously approached the bus. Steve made a sound behind him. Wes turned to Steve. Who was cautioning him not to get too close. He waved back that he understood.

Readying his weapon, Wes crouched down. Peering under, he could see two legs slowly dragging along the side of the bus. They were heading for the gap that was the entrance to the makeshift courtyard. He followed the legs with his gun. Steve spied the head of the zombie through the school bus windows. It was a man with dark, messed-up hair. He seemed to know where he was going, but the bus was an unexpected barrier. The zombie kept bumping into the side and bouncing off to stumble several feet, then bumping into the bus again.

Wes moved to the front tire, ready to take the undead creature down. Steve spotted in his scope to the gap in the buses. The other man kept glancing over, but he was also keeping watch over the rest of the compound. The zombie appeared in the gap. He did not appear to be injured in any way, but he was definitely one of the walking dead. The creature bounced off the front of the bus. It stumbled forward for a pace or two, then paused. Steve's finger tensed on the trigger. The ghoul looked around. It sniffed at the air, groaned slightly, then continued past the gap. Steve followed its progress through the next buses windows until he lost sight of it.

Wes came hurrying back up the stairs. "Why did it keep going? I swear that it could tell we were here. Not that I'm complaining, mind you."

"I've seen a few of 'em do that," the sentry said.

"Do you want a break?" Steve asked the man.

"Thank you, no. I just got on point recently."

"Former military," Steve whispered to Wes, "a good person to have."

"I wouldn't say no to a coffee though," the man commented as Steve and Wes turned to re-enter the church.

"Black?"

"Yes, please."

Wes nodded, continuing through the door. Steve took a moment to look up at the bright blue sky. He said a quick prayer for his father, and one for his missing sister.

Searching

Disgusted, Matt threw the filthy, blood-soaked, empty money bag he had used to clean the floor out the side door. He couldn't help but laugh as it smacked into the face of a zombie wandering down the road. The truck's surfaces were clean, but the smell lingered. Stancy had refused to help out in any way, so Matt ended up doing what he could. Shaking his hands and rubbing them on his jeans, he shuddered. Hector pulled the door closed. The sound told Devin he could speed up a bit.

The mid-morning sun was already high in the sky. Devin had already tried several routes out of town, only to find all of them blocked. He was aware of the increasing grumbling from the back. Gillian was now seated in the passenger seat while Trevor was crammed in the back with the others. Beth did her best to keep upbeat. Devin and Gillian put on a brave face, but Matt seemed to be the only one who stayed truly positive.

At each blocked road, zombie packed route, or obstacle of flaming debris, Matt would just sigh and say, "Well, that was obviously not the way to go."

After the third time they turned around to head back toward the dead city, Stancy had had enough. "Oh, shut up! What are you, one of those 'God opens a window' types?" she demanded.

"No!" Matt shouted back, his façade failing. "I just don't see the need to be negative all the time! Like *you*." From there it started to spiral out of control, until Hector put a stop to it. In the tense silence that followed, Beth grudgingly couldn't help agree with Stancy. Matt's constant reassurance was kind of annoying. She also agreed with Matt; Stancy's negativity was doing nothing to help. In the end she decided she would rather have Matt's overly optimistic view even if it led to constant disappointment.

After a while Devin attempted to roll the stress from his shoulders. He flexed his fingers and cracked his neck. He had been driving for hours. He had suggested someone else could drive. The trouble was that no one else knew the town as well as he did. On top of that no one wanted the truck to actually stop for a driver switch. So Devin remained in the driver's seat.

"Ok, this is no-go. We'll try to get to the bridge to Tire Hill." Devin put the truck into reverse. He had tried to push a couple of cars out of their way to get to the open road just beyond a three-car pileup. The cars did not budge. He was beginning to feel the frustration from the others as well as the feeling of being trapped.

"We could try to make it out on foot." Gillian suggested half halfheartedly, "maybe find another vehicle?" This idea was not met with enthusiasm. Devin pulled forward. He headed around the block toward another two-lane bridge a couple of miles away. This one, he hoped, was still open. If it was, they could finally get out of the city. Where they were going to go he didn't know; he just needed to get out. He needed to be anywhere except this familiar but dead city.

Glumly Gillian stared out the side window. The side streets slowly slid by. Her mind wandered to her friends and family. Then suddenly something caught her attention as they passed a burnt-out car buried in the blackened front of a house. "Stop! Stop!" Go back, back up," she cried.

Devin slammed on the breaks and immediately apologized to everyone in the back. Gillian was jumping up and down in her seat. Devin backed the truck up to be even with the side street. Several feet down the alley they saw an ambulance. Its rear doors hung open; a stretcher lay on its side a little way away from the doors. "There might be something we can use in there." Gillian slapped her hands on the side of the door. Hector and Beth had both pressed their way up front to see what the commotion was about.

"What do you think? Worth the risk?" Devin asked.

Beth and Hector looked at each other. "Definitely," they both confirmed.

Devin hesitated, and then eased forward, shifting into reverse and swinging the wheel to backe down the side road toward the ambulance. Matt directed them by looked out the small window in the back door. It took a few scrapes on fences and garages for him to get the lefts and rights straight. Beth and Hector picked their way to the back doors, with Hector taking over the navigation from a grumpy Matt. Beth stood ready, bracing herself against the door, waiting for Devin to get close enough. Gillian appeared at her side. Her face was anxious, but she seemed ready.

"Max! Come on, we need you," Hector growled, while the police officer tried not to be noticed.

Giving up on his attempt to stay in the safety of the heavy vehicle, Max got to his feet, reading his weapon. Matt was also ready to leave the truck. Gillian noticed. "Sit down. We have more than enough already."

"Why can't I go? How come she gets to go and I don't? Matt protested, pointing at Beth. "I think she is only a year older than me."

"That may be true, but she is much more mature," Hector shrugged.

Matt began to protest, but Max interrupted, offering to give Matt his weapon, "If the kid is crazy enough to want to go out there, let him. Hell, the girl wants to get herself killed, why not him?" Gillian immediately shouted him down, followed with protests from everyone except Stancy. In the end, Hector made sure Matt stayed in the truck, making it clear what type of person he thought Max was. Max simply grunted at that affirmation and Beth's disgusted look.

Gillian didn't care if Matt was pissed or Max was annoyed; she only cared that Matt should not leave the safety of the truck. Matt, on the other hand, was less than thrilled. "I'm a year behind her," he said again, pointing at Beth. "I should be allowed to go."

"Don't whine; it doesn't help your cause," Beth advised.

"I'm not whining," Matt whined. Gillian gave him a look that caused him to immediately shut up. Hector fought the urge to laugh. Beth, on the other hand, couldn't contain her smile until the four of them were laughing.

The truck stopped, and so did all levity. The doors opened to the smell of burned wood and death. It filled the back of the truck. "I can't get used to that smell," Beth hissed, covering her nose.

Gillian rushed forward, anxious to get to the ambulance and back to the truck's safety. Max stayed at the back doors, nervously sweeping the area. Hector jogged backward, keeping the other side of the truck in view. Beth tried to keep up with Gillian.

"Slow down! I can't cover you if you are moving too fast," Beth hissed. Gillian nodded, but fear was evident throughout her body. The distance was minimal but felt like miles. Beth glanced at the overturned gurney. It was, as she knew it would be, covered in blood. Feet and lower legs were visible under one of the open rear doors. They were clad in what appeared to be a paramedic's uniform. Beth waved, getting Hector's attention, and she pointed to the legs. Hector nodded but waved her on. She raised her eyebrows in question, shaking her head and pointing at the legs.

"Top of his head is gone. Pretty sure the brain is also gone." Hector whispered, waving her on.

Gillian clamored loudly into the back of the ambulance. Beth cringed at the noise, moving up to the side to make sure they were not surprised.

"Should we take the whole thing?" Gillian poked her head around the side.

"See if the keys are in it."

"Not in the ignition."

"Hector, see if your guy over there has the keys," Beth suggested.

"No joy. I wonder where his partner is. He might have them." Hector began looking around.

"Let's just hope he doesn't come back. Or if he does, he can use them," Gillian noted from the inside. She was stuffing almost everything in reach into a bag she had found. Beth saw movement in the window of the building across from them. The curtains in the window swung as if someone had just passed by them.

"I think we are going to have company soon," Beth growled.

"Over here too." Hector warned.

Gillian was out of the ambulance, heading back to the armored car. She threw the bag in and turned to return to the ambulance.

She took a step before she was caught by Beth and Hector. Max brushed past, jumping into the back without a word.

"Dear God," Gillian gasped.

The road in front of the ambulance was filling fast with the undead. From the building, Beth had noticed, came the other paramedic and an older woman dressed in a housecoat. Both showed bites to their face and arms. "It's like a block party in hell," Beth cried.

Gillian was pushed into the back of the truck, Hector and Beth close behind. The doors snapped shut and Devin was off again. The moans of the dead followed them as they sped off down the street. Gillian sat looking through the bag she had acquired, bemoaning her inability to have retrieved more. She had been able to salvage bandages, antibiotics, pain killers, and several other useful first aid items. Matt tried to reassure her she had done all she could.

"It would have been better if you had gone back for more. Then the zombies could have eaten you. Then I would have more room and the peace and quiet of not having to listen to you bitch," Stancy interjected.

The uproar in the back was deafening, with Stancy giving as good as she got in the way of shouting and name-calling. The crowded conditions had worn them to the last raw nerve. When it had calmed to a muttering of vicious names and threats, Beth crawled up into the empty passenger seat. "We need to find a place to rest and stretch our legs."

"No shit, really? We're only packed in here like sardines." Stancy sneered.

Hector rose, his face contorted in rage. Beth decided to end this before it returned to chaos and something happened that they would all regret. She turned in her seat and replied cheerfully, "You can always get out and walk." Devin stifled a laugh, which earned him a glare from Stancy. Beth noticed Gillian covertly give Stancy the finger as well. "I never thought I would meet someone more horrible than the living dead," Beth muttered. She truly disliked the woman.

"Well? Any ideas where to go, little missy?" Stancy retorted in a false happy tone.

This did nothing to improve Beth's opinion. She thought about several places she wanted to tell Stancy to go and was about to make a suggestion.

"We need to find a place where there weren't too many people, ya know, before." Max commented.

"How about the old bra factory down by the river? That has been closed for years. There wouldn't be anyone there," Trevor suggested.

Devin thought for a second and nodded. He eased the truck down a side road that didn't seem too badly blocked off.

What Was This Place?

Steve returned to the darkness of the church, but he felt considerably less comfortable than he did outside. Several people stopped whispering to stare at him as he passed. He knew they were thinking he and Wes had acted too quickly the night before. He wasn't even positive if they weren't right. But he had seen too many of those "people" with bites that couldn't have been fatal. He felt sure that if a person was bitten, they would turn. The problem with his theory was that waiting to *prove* it could be fatal. Deep in his own thoughts, he caught Wes as he was on his way to take coffee to the man still on guard outside.

Hey," Steve muttered, looking around at the others in the room, "hurry back. I want to take a look around, OK?" Wes, who also had taken in the demeanor of their fellow occupants, nodded, and was gone. Steve slowly made his was way to a door he had seen the older woman come out of. He felt the eyes of the others follow him. Light burst into the room for a moment, then the darkness resumed. Steve knew Wes had returned. He didn't need to look as he felt the presence next to him.

"Not liking us much, are they?" Wes murmured as they passed a man who pulled his children closer as they got near.

Approaching the door, the duo stopped quickly as it abruptly opened, revealing Father Michael. "Whoa! You scared me," he hissed, hand over his heart.

"Yeah, we seem to have that affect on people around here," Wes grumbled. Steve swatted him, but the priest laughed.

"Yes, it seems that they don't have enough to fear. So they decide to worry about someone who is trying to keep them safe." He said this loudly enough for everyone in the church to hear. This was met with indistinguishable muttering. Wes gave a weak smile, while Steve began to feel a little better. He knew the Johnsons were on his side, but it was nice to know the Father was in his corner as well.

Father Michael ushered them through the door into a well-lit hallway. It was more modern than the stonework of the church. The floor was tiled and the walls were painted cinderblock. Several doors led off the hall. They were very institutional with little windows in them above the handles.

"This is the school, isn't it?" It was a statement more than a question that Wes made. He stepped up to one of the small windows; looking around inside.

"Yes, but more than that, we have some truly excellent resources here," Father Michael smiled.

"What would those be, Father Micha…"

"Father, or better yet, Mike is fine." The priest interrupted with a smile.

"Um, right… Mike…what other resources?" Steve continued. He felt uncomfortable calling the priest by his first name, having been raised, if only barely, in the Catholic Church. Mike smiled, beckoning them down the hall to the first door. The door had a radiation symbol on it and a sign that read "Fallout Shelter."

"Well, that is good if they bomb us. I think the zombies want to eat us, not nuke us," Wes said before he could stop himself. Steve swatted him again. He glared at Wes as he shook his head, about to apologize. Mike waved off the comment.

"Right. I also think bombings are the least of our worries." He laughed. "But if our hungry friends get into the church, we can fall back here and be safe. More than that, we have plenty of food, water, medicine, and even fuel for cooking," Mike said, bouncing on his feet.

"That is great!" Steve tried to sound enthused.

"I can see you want to explain, so, I'll bite. Why do you have so much stuff?" Wes asked.

Mike's smile burst through. "Glad you asked. The previous pastor… well, he was a bit paranoid. He believed in God, but he also believed in being prepared."

"Did he see signs of a coming apocalypse?" Wes asked, a little frightened. "I mean, is this, you know," his voice dropped to a whisper, "Revelations? With the resurrection of the dead and all that?"

Mike's smile faltered. "I don't know. If this is the end of days, then can you explain why you were left behind?" He looked from Steve to Wes.

Steve felt he knew why he would be, but Wes looked confused, as if searching his memory for a transgression great enough.

"Didn't think so," Mike stated. "No, this is something we did, something man-made."

"Or nature just got sick of us destroying the world, and decided to show us who was boss," Wes suggested.

"Yes—or that." Mike shrugged. "Anyway, come down a take a look." He took a key from his pocket to unlock the door.

"You keep this locked?" Steve asked.

"Yes, the door locks on its own. That way, we could keep the kids out." He paused for a second, then shook off a thought. "Now, I guess it is just to make sure no one decides they need it more than the rest of the group."

"Good plan," Wes noted with a nod.

Steve was uneasy with the door being locked. "Is there another key?"

"Yes." The tone of suspicion could not have been clearer in Mike's voice. "It is in my office in the church. Mrs. Miller knows where."

"Hey, I just want to make sure *someone* knows where it is, in case something happens to you," Steve exclaimed, holding up his hands. An awkward silence hung in the air for a few moments.

"Right then, well, maybe Steve and I will just have a look around the rest of the school, then," Wes suggested, trying to ease the tension.

"No, no nonsense. You're right. It is good to know who would have access if… something… happened."

Wes knew that Steve meant "something" was being killed by zombies, but he had a feeling Father Mike thought the danger might be something closer and living.

The key clicked in the lock and the door squeaked open. Mike reached in and flipped a switch, bathing the descending stairway in light. "After you," he gestured.

Wes looked over at Steve. It was clear that he was as uneasy as Wes. Since the conversation had turned a little odd, Wes couldn't help but think the priest was about to lock them in. He knew they scared the other survivors in the church, so maybe this is what Mike thought was a good solution. Get rid of the troublemakers. Wes was about to suggest they just leave when his fears were calmed. Mike entered the stairwell. "Look at this, will you? This is all reinforced concrete." Mike motioned to the walls. "Usually the stairs aren't built this tough in these old shelters but this one…well, they did this one right." He patted the wall as the three men continued down the stairs.

Reaching the bottom, Wes stood face to face with a heavy steel door. "Excuse me." Mike's former cheerfulness had returned as he turned the metal wheel unlocking the door. Wes relaxed, a little, nodding to Steve as he slipped a hand onto his gun. He noticed Steve doing the same. They knew each was ready to do what they had to, and they had each other's back. Mike didn't seem to notice.

"First it was the cold war. That is why this was built. After that it was Three Mile Island. Then there was Y2K. After that was Bird Flu, Swine Flu, and Terrorism. It didn't matter what the current threat was, Father Dan took it seriously. He kept this place well stocked and always ready. He renamed it the 'fallback' shelter instead of fallout." Mike smiled, flipping on the lights.

Steve and Wes marveled at the supplies. Food, bottled water, medical supplies, several rows of cots, chairs and even a library. At the other end of the room was another door.

"What's in there?" Wes asked, pointing to the portal.

"That is the generator room. There are hundreds of gallons of fuel in there. I estimate we could run on the generator for a couple of months if we had to," Mike responded. "I guess to answer your previous question, yes, we did see this coming…in a way."

"I'm thankful you did," Steve said, patting Mike on the back.

Steve and Wes spent several minutes looking through all the supplies. Wes spent a long time looking over the well stocked shelves of the bookcases. "Not a lot of new stuff, but a decent selection."

"Did you want to borrow one?" Mike asked, smiling around at the supplies.

"No. That's okay, thanks. I have one with me," Wes explained, thinking back to the latest wizard chronicle he had in his pack. The one he hoped to loan to Beth soon. He turned around, taking in the whole room. It was spacious and clean. The cots looked comfortable and the seating area open and inviting. "Why aren't we down here right now?" Wes asked. "I mean, we could take it in turns to call people to the church, but wouldn't it be safer, ya know, down here?"

Mike looked pensive. "I guess it just feels too final." He gazed around room. "I keep hoping to hear something. Keep hoping there is an end in sight. We tried to get out of town. We loaded up a couple of the buses." Mike paused, staring at a spot on the wall. "We made it to the hospital, where we tried to pick up some friends and relatives. We got there just after the army lost control. They were on us before we knew what was happening. I was in the bus we were going to use to transport them...They swarmed the other bus. I could see the blood, hear the screams. I saw friends running from the back door get tackled and killed. The other bus didn't wait. He was gone...I don't know what happened to them. We got away." Mike turned his attention to Wes and Steve. "We picked up anyone we could on the way back here. Built the barricade and called to anyone to come to safety."

"We were all over this town," Steve whispered, "and we never saw a bus. I think they got away."

Mike smiled his thanks, but the look he wore told Steve he didn't believe that outcome. He followed them out through the thick steel door to the stairs. "I keep listening to the static on the radio. I just pray I will hear they have solved this. I...just can't believe this can happen." They climbed the stairs back to the hallway.

Back above ground, Mike smiled sadly at Steve and Wes. "I have to get back to the others. Feel free to look around, and if you see something we need to fix, please let me know." He waved to them as he headed back toward the heavy oak doors leading into the church.

"What do you think?" Steve muttered to Wes.

"I don't know. Better in here than out there. All the same, I don't like the idea of that door being locked." The pair walked down the hall in silence, away from the church and further into the school. Through the high steel mesh-reinforced windows, they could see a few of the undead wandering down the street. Wes stopped to watch what had once been a young man around his age. He moved toward the window to see if he could recognize the unfortunate soul. The face was too torn and caked with gore. Wes stepped back, frowning.

"Um, gentlemen?" Father Mike called from the end of the hall. Steve and Wes turned, watching him approach. He looked grim as he walked up to them. He glanced out the window at the small group of undead. "I'm sorry for the way I acted a moment ago." He sighed.

"We understand. You don't know us and you were trusting us, then thought better about it, then thought better about it again. Hey, this is a really messed up thing going on out there. I get it," Wes stated.

Steve agreed, but just wished his friend was a bit more articulate. "Seriously? I don't know what my sister sees in you."

Mike blew out a sigh of relief and then continued. "I... I was wondering if you two might... um, might help us," he stuttered. His gaze moved from Wes and Steve to the zombies as they wandered further down the road. Wes didn't see why the priest was so unnerved. The small group didn't seem to notice the church or its inhabitants.

"How can we help?" Steve asked.

"Well, I was hoping... you seem to be a good shot. I was hoping you would continue to help keep us safe.... and help call others to us."

Steve could sense there was something Mike was not saying.

"Could you perhaps go to the bell tower to keep a watch?" he asked.

"Is this to help keep the church safe or is it to keep the others from worrying about us?" Wes asked. Steve slapped Wes on the shoulder, giving him a stern look. Mike looked slightly embarrassed. Steve caught on quickly. The others in the church were scared of them after the incident the night before.

"Honesty is always the best policy, I guess." Mike nodded to Wes. "Yes, the others are a bit uneasy. I was hoping you would take a shift in the bell tower, perhaps thin these devils out."

"How long do you want us gone?" Wes asked.

"Just until this evening if you don't mind. I'm sorry to have to ask."

"We understand," Steve grumbled.

"Hanging out in a drafty bell tower is better than just hanging out here," Wes noted. "Come on, let's check it out."

Slow Travels

"Damn it!" Trevor shouted, banging a fist on the dashboard.

"We had to expect this," Devin tried to sooth. They had tried several routes to get across town, to no avail. They were currently idling on the main road through town. It was blocked with several wrecked and burning cars.

"What's that?" Beth pointed over Devin's shoulder.

"That looks like one of our tactical trucks," Max stated, with the first note of enthusiasm they had heard from him. His face got too close to Beth's for comfort as he pushed in to get a look.

"Your what?" Matt now crowded in against Beth. Annoyance grew in her as she was jostled around so the others could see. What they were looking at was a deep blue truck, buried halfway into a storefront. One of the back doors was shut, the other was halfway open. The group couldn't see the inside from their vantage point.

"Is that like a SWAT squad?" Beth asked, pushing Matt off her arm.

"Why would we have that?" Matt laughed. "Nothing ever happens here. Well, it didn't," his smile faltered quickly.

Annoyed, Max looked over at Matt, "That annual biker rally we have," he stated, as if this explained everything.

"And did we ever have a problem?" Beth scoffed.

"Does it matter? There should be plenty of guns, ammo, riot suppression gear and…."

"I knew that was a giant waste of money," Martin sighed. "The bikers were generally really well behaved. A few arrests for fighting and alcohol-related stuff."

"The riot gear isn't gonna help much. I don't think those things will respond to tear gas," Beth thought out loud.

"You were quick enough to go for the ambulance. That, and the riot gear is made to protect the officer. I doubt they could bite through it," Max grumbled.

It was Gillian who took up the conversation now. "The ambulance had medicine we *needed*, and it was out of the way. Here we are much closer to… them." She pointed to a group of the undead wandering around a car. "I think we can all agree the weapons are important, but we are downtown now, and they are thicker here."

"Which is weird, because I never saw anyone down here when everyone was alive," Matt commented.

"Come on, if we are going to do this, we should do it sooner than later. The noise of the truck is only going to bring them out," Beth stated.

"Right, let's do this then." Devin said as he backed the truck up the police vehicle.

Hector called out directions until they were close enough. Matt moped at not being trusted to help. Beth picked her way over the others until she was at the back doors with Hector. Max was there as well, without the usual urging from Hector. Hector raised an eyebrow at Max as he readied his weapon.

"What? This is my idea, in a way. I better be part of it," Max explained trying to sound confident. Beth noticed his hands shook almost too much for him to chamber a round in his weapon.

The doors swung open. Beth again found herself out in the smoky air of her once-peaceful hometown. Her white sneakers kicked rubble from the smashed building when her feet hit the pavement. An eerie quiet pressed against their ears as only the sound of the truck's engine could be heard.

In a flash Max was at the doors of the police van, while Beth and Hector rushed to cover him. Max cringed when the metal banged at his arrival. He stood still with his back against the closed van door. Waiting. Nothing. Beth and Hector exhaled. Max pushed forward on the opened door with his rifle barrel and it creaked it protest. Taking a calming breath, he stepped forward, instantly jumping back as the door began to open on its own.

A tattered deep blue sleeve appeared, followed by two white hands. The face of the dead officer was contorted and white like the hands. A dark stain covered half of the uniform shirt. The ghoul stumbled, falling out of the van. It hit the ground hard. Max ran to it, slamming his knee into the creature's back. He swung his rifle high, bringing the butt down again and again on the zombie's head until it stopped struggling.

Beth watched, stunned by the brutality of Max's assault, until movement in the van caught her attention. Another figure was stumbling toward the back. Beth raised her weapon. Max spun on the zombie's back, his knee pulling at the uniform, revealing a deep tear in the former officer's side. The bloody face of an old woman appeared out of the shadows.

Beth guessed the policeman had tried to help the old woman and was repaid by her attacking him. The woman's face bore the signs of the officer's battle to fend her off. Max grabbed a large brick from the ground. He was on his feet, ready to meet the woman at the back of the van. She reached for him while he brought the brick down hard on the top of her head.

The woman barely paused at the impact. Her hands reached for Max's throat. The courage he had shown in the last few minutes evaporated in an instant with the woman's advance. It was Hector's knife, thrust through the woman's eye socket, that ended the fight.

Max sat next to the zombie officer he had ended. The terror was still etched on his face. Beth held out a hand to help him to his feet. He accepted it with a nod. "Come on," he shakily said, "let's get this done and get out of here." He stood for a second, holding onto Beth's arm for support. "Thanks," he said to her. Moving forward, he slapped Hector on the back.

Returning to the door, Max pulled a flashlight from his belt, clicked it on, and gasped. The inside of the van was covered in bloody handprints and smears. In the front driver's seat, arms swung violently, trying to reach behind the seat. Max raised his weapon as he mounted the bumper. Beth followed him; Hector stood guard. The pair inched forward. Clicks of the zombie's teeth and grunts filled the empty space.

Max avoided the flailing arms, weapon raised but relaxed. The zombie was pinned against the seat by the steering column. "Must have happened when they hit the building," Beth surmised from behind Max.

Max just stared at the face. It was smashed and cut with bricks and broken glass. Its teeth clicked at him from its mutilated mouth. Max had known the man. He had been very popular with the women on the force, a very attractive, nice guy. Max had not liked him but hadn't really disliked him either. Now he wished the other officer had made it. "Come on. Like you said, let's get this done," Beth reminded gently. Max nodded, raised the butt of his rifle and caved in the zombie's once handsome face.

Several minutes later found the three back in the armored car, rumbling down the road. They had recovered a bag full of ammunition, three nine-millimeter handguns, four semi-automatic rifles, and two shotguns.

Beth made her way up front, handing Devin one of the handguns while Max and Hector began to give a quick lesson on gun safety and aiming to several of the other members of the truck.

The Tower

Looking out from the bell tower, Steve and Wes were stunned by the damage around them, as well as to the building they were in. They could see several fires burning out of control in the distance. The few streets they could see were either completely deserted or had several wrecked or abandoned cars in them. Around these cars were always signs of violence, dark stains on the ground or streaks leading away.

Wes looked through the scope of his rifle. He could see movement in one of the closer cars. Judging by the repetitious movement and the fact that the occupant never left the car, he assumed it was not someone they could help. He checked the other cars and windows of surrounding buildings. Nothing else moved.

Steve tapped Wes' shoulder, pointing to the church and school. Smiling, they saw a ten-foot-high fence surrounding the school and playground. Steve remembered the high windows in the church itself. "Man, this place was a fortress before they added the buses as a barricade. Why do you think that was?" Wes asked.

Steve shrugged. "Even though we aren't that big of a city, we still had problems down here."

"Mix that with the paranoid old priest and well, I guess you see what you get." Wes couldn't stop smiling at the fence.

Steve nodded. "Looks like we might be safe here for a bit." Concern creased his brow. Pointing at the fence, he said, "I don't think that fence will hold out if we get too many of those things."

Wes leaned out slightly over the railing to get a better look at the fenced courtyard. "Looks like they bricked up several windows, but I think they only painted over a few of those near the end of the building. That could be trouble."

Steve leaned over to see what Wes was looking at. "Maybe, but it is in the fenced area, so we should be okay." Then he added, "For now."

They spent the next few hours up in the tower watching the streets below. Occasionally an undead would wander close by, but for the most part nothing moved. Wes would pull out his phone every now and then to check for a signal, but to no avail. Steve would mirror this every time Wes tried it.

"Where do you think Beth is hiding?" Wes muttered, sliding down to lean his back against the wall.

Steve leaned on his elbows, watching a piece of newspaper blow down the street. "I hope she got out of town. Did you notice if the car was still in the garage?"

Wes thought back to the house. Several terrible jumbled memories fought for dominance in his mind's eye. Shaking the thoughts, he said, "I don't think I went to the garage."

Steve frowned down at the paper that was now caught in the fence. Wes stood up, crossing to the other side of the tower, looking toward the front of the church.

Steve watched as another piece of paper blew down the street. He wondered where all the paper was coming from. "Why do you always see paper flying around when the streets are deserted in movies? I never noticed paper flying around any other time," he asked. Wes did not answer. Steve turned to ask again.

Wes stood still and rigid. He turned his head slightly to Steve then pointed at another church, caddy-corner to theirs. The front doors were slowly opening. A man dressed as a reverend stumbled out. One of his arms was missing from the tattered sleeve of his vestments. Following the reverend were several bloody children dressed in what appeared to be choir robes. Following the children were a few zombie adults. "Oh man, no way," Wes moaned.

Steve handed Wes his rifle. The two men fired several rounds at the group until nothing was moving on the street except Steve's tumbling papers.

They stood staring down at the scene. The image of a small head exploding still burned into Wes' vision every time he closed his eyes. After sweeping the scene several times to make sure nothing was getting back up, Wes slumped down against the wall, checking his ammo.

"God, how many times am I going to have to kill dead kids?" he asked angrily, refilling his clip and slapping it into his gun.

Steve gripped his own gun, shaking his head. Is this what life is going to be now? How many times will we have to do this? What is our alternative? How do we get out of here? One thought chased the other through his head.

Rest Please

Darkness had begun to fall fast. Devin pulled on the headlights. The instrument panel illuminated, showing they had used almost a half a tank of gas as they wandered through the city. Many of the streetlights had lit but no lights came from any shops or windows. It gave the impression of driving down an endless tunnel, broken only here and there with small fires and wreckage.

There was no sound in the truck except for the engine. It had been many hours since the emergency broadcast had ended in static on the truck's radio.

Beth looked around at the other passengers. Hector was checking ammo and loading weapons with Max's help. Gillian was talking quietly to Matt, who kept looking down at the shotgun in his hands. Bill and Martin had found a pack of cards somewhere and were playing poker. Stancy held her arms tight to her and glared at no one in particular. Trevor sat in the passenger seat, trying to help Devin navigate.

"We could try Elm over to Menoher," he suggested.

"Elm was closed with sewer work. The whole street is torn up. There is no way we would get through." Devin sighed. "You never read my memos."

"How much further to the factory?" Hector asked, finishing the last of the loading. He put the remaining ammo boxes back into the bag they had taken from the van.

"I think if the road stays clear we should be there in ten minutes." Devin replied.

"We'd be there in five if you'd pick up the pace," Stancy grumbled. "It's not like there is a speed limit, and besides you've got a cop and the stinking Mayor with you for crying out loud."

Devin chose to ignore her keeping the vehicle moving at a slow pace.

"Seriously, what is the hold up? You've got a seat; we're crammed in here."

"If someone is alive and hears the truck, I want to give them every opportunity to get to us," Devin replied calmly.

"Well, there have been plenty of things hearing us. The problem is none of them have been alive."

Devin continued to ignore her, keeping the same pace.

"I don't want to agree with the unpleasant one, but it is a bit cramped back here," Bill spoke up.

Devin sighed, "I want to give anyone around here a chance to get to us."

"Why? Because this is a black neighborhood?" Stancy grumbled.

Again Devin ignored her, but Beth noticed from his profile that his jaw tightened as did his grip on the wheel. She also noticed they had gained a little speed. Beth knelt down next to Devin's seat. She placed a hand on his arm, "You okay?"

Gillian appeared over Beth's shoulder. "I think Bill is right, we all need a little space from her and each other."

Devin nodded, increasing their speed up a bit more as they reached the end of some row homes. The outline of the old factory was barely visible in the fading light against the mountains. It was still a way off, but it felt like relief from the cramped conditions was close at hand.

Reaching the fenced front gate, Devin pushed through slowly with the truck. The rusty chain holding the gate shut gave out, and with a squeal the gate opened.

Once through the fence, Hector jumped out. He closed the gate, holding it in place with some zip ties they had found in the bag from the police van.

Other than one security light in the lot there were no other lights on in the building. Devin made sure to stay out of the light as he drove up to the front of the building. They couldn't see any movement inside. The front and all the windows were either boarded up or too dark to see into.

"This should be perfect!" Max exclaimed.

Was that Yesterday or the Day Before?

Wes looked over the side of the pew he was using as a bed at the remnants of the sandwich he had been eating. He hadn't been able to finish it. It, like his day, wasn't sitting well. He still could see the faces of the zombie children from the other church. Turning over, he lay on his back staring at the ceiling. He was so tired, but sleep eluded him. Rubbing his eyes, another memory flashed into his mind. Steve had left the tower to grab them something to eat. Wes had been watching the street when he saw a zombie round a corner. It had been a girl. When she was alive, Wes guessed she would have been around his age. He didn't know her.

"She must have gone to another school." he mumbled to no one. The thought of school struck him as odd suddenly. He doubted he would ever be going back. He shivered slightly. It was cold in the church. It hadn't been a particularly warm past few days. That is what had struck him about the dead girl he had seen. She was wearing a t-shirt, gym shorts and flip flops. He guessed she might have been a cheerleader or some other athlete coming back from practice. This was the type of girl that would never have talked to him.

This thought made him laugh. Would she want to talk to him now? He felt the handgun, heavy and cold in his jacket pocket. Now that he shot zombies in the face. The image still hovered in his mind when he closed his eyes. No, she would want to talk to Steve. But at least Beth liked him. Thinking back to the girl again. He guessed she would have been pretty if not for the fact that she was dead.

Staring up at the ceiling he imagined how it happened. She was leaving the gym after cheer practice. She was probably cheer captain, he mused. She had her gym bag over her shoulder. Someone grabbed it. "Hey! What is your problem?" She would say in that superior tone.

She would then see the living corpse that had grabbed her bag. He would be staring at her, dead eyes bloodshot and bulging. His filthy hands clawing at her while a torn mouth would try to bite her. She'd let go of the bag when she started to run. The zombie would stand for a moment stupidly holding the bag before it dropped it to pursue her. As she ran, she'd have lost a flip flop and hurt her foot. She couldn't get away fast enough.

He'd never liked flip flops. That is when those stupid shoes let you down, he thought. That is why you should always wear appropriate footwear. In case you need to make a speedy getaway. The picture of her filled his mind. One flip flop, blue gym shorts, a blood-stained t-shirt, and one arm missing.

Wes shook the image from his head. He spent the next two hours trying to remember a time over the summer with Beth. They were hanging out at the pool. Every time he started to fall asleep, the girl in the blue shorts would show up. She would come out of the pool or be in the picnic area. Finally, he fell into a restless sleep filled with classes with the girl in the blue shorts, and a zombie choir singing KISS' "Beth".

Best Form of Sleep

Devin turned off the headlights as they crept along the front of the building. The large windows were mostly covered with newspaper. A few boards were still held in place, and several lay on the ground, but most had found new homes long ago. The paper hid the giant windows of a former showroom in the middle of the building. At one time it had held all the latest fashions; now it was dark, holding only mystery.

In several places the paper had fallen away. This caused some excitement when Trevor saw a figure standing in the window. Devin stopped the truck and waited. All the occupants collectively held their breath.

"Where else should we go?" whispered Matt.

They waited. the figure didn't move. Devin squinted into the darkness. "I think it is a mannequin."

"You sure? I really don't want to get inside to find the place crawling with those guys," Max shuddered.

"Well they seem to get pretty excited when they see us, and this guy hasn't moved."

"Maybe it is a survivor," Beth stated hopefully.

"Or maybe it is someone who wants to take our guns," Stancy grumbled.

Beth turned to retort but was cut off by Hector. "Fair point. Thing is, they haven't moved...at all...So I am leaning toward the dummy idea. I am ready to fight for a place to stretch my legs." To emphasize the point, one of his knees popped loudly as he shifted on them.

"I wouldn't say no to a bathroom with walls. That last pit stop was...nerve-wracking. I've never wanted to do my business outside, and that was *before* someone wanted to eat me," Gillian said.

Devin did not say a word but slowly drove along the building, turning at the corner. They continued the length of the building. Everyone tensely looking for signs of life, or death. Nothing moved in the wooded area just past the pavement. Devin reached the end of the wall. Slowly, he turned the truck along the back.

"The loading dock doors are too high for us to get into easily," Hector noted, pointing at the closed doors.

"That looks good!" Trevor exclaimed, pointing at a door at the top of a small staircase halfway along the building.

"Why are we parking in the back?" Beth asked. "Don't you think it would be better to be seen? You know, in case there are people alive around here."

"We can get some rest and not really worry about someone trying to steal our vehicle," Max spoke up.

Beth turned to him, a confused look on her face.

"Well," stated the officer, "if you were in need of a safe vehicle to try to make it out of the city, this is the best one, and if you saw it sitting with no one in it... why wouldn't you try to take it?" He shrugged.

"Don't you think they would try to find out who was here first?" Beth argued.

"You've got a lot to learn about people, little girl," Stancy said mockingly.

"Just what is that supposed to mean?" Matt defended.

"People only look out for themselves," Stancy answered matter-of-factly, as if this closed the matter.

"If that were true, your ass would still be downtown," Bill noted.

Trying to head off the building tension, Devin spoke up. "That should be just above the back bumper."

"Huh?" Matt questioned.

"The door." Devin pointed out the front window. "That should make it easy to get in and out, and we can use the doors as a kind of shield if we get surrounded."

"Surrounded by whom? Come on, let's just get out of this damn truck. Seriously, I think we are safe. When was the last time anyone came near this dump?" Stancy urged.

Nobody answered her, so she crossed her arms and glared at Matt. He stared back, made a silly face, then looked out the back window. Devin eased the truck up to the staircase.

Hector opened one of the back doors. Bill grabbed the back of his belt. Hector looked back at Bill, a slight look of discomfort on his face. "Don't flatter yourself." Bill stated, noting the look on the other man's face.

Hector looked Bill in the eye and laughed, "Sorry, but I am a damn good-looking man, ya know."

This earned a laugh from Bill and a derisive snort from Stancy.

"Okay, Devin, back it up," Hector yelled.

Devin slowly positioned the truck against the stairs. Metal on metal screeched as Devin backed as far as he could against the building. There was only about six inches from the edge of the truck's back door to the wall of the old factory. All but one of the metal grate stairs sat under the rear of the truck. The handrail was bent by the force of the engine pushing back against it.

"Did you make enough noise?" Stancy commented.

"What do you care? Remember, you said no one has been here in forever," Matt shot back.

Again, Stancy glared at him.

"Oh, give it a rest, you haggard old vulture," Matt sighed.

"How dare..." she fired up at once.

"Matt, help me with this door," Hector called.

Matt climbed over Beth to help Hector and Bill with the door. Beth took in a quick breath of pain as Matt tripped over her leg. He fell onto Stancy, who pushed him hard away. Beth glared at her until Matt stepped on her knee again, falling into Gillian's lap.

"It opens toward us," Bill pointed to the hinges on their side of the door.

Hector grabbed Matt, pulling him away from the three annoyed women. "I don't know if you're a klutz or you planned that." He smirked at the red-faced boy.

"We need something to wrench the door open." Beth observed, joining the others at the back. She rubbed her knee, not looking at Matt.

Matt tried to distance himself from her. He was looking anywhere but in her direction when he noticed a strip of metal that had broken off the stairs. Pulling one of the truck's doors forward a little he squeezed around it and jumped down to retrieve the shard, accidentally kicking it several feet away.

The piece was only a short distance from the back doors but once clear of the truck he froze. Carried on the light fall breeze he could hear a distant moaning. "Matt, hurry up!" Beth called. Looking all over he couldn't make out any movement near him. Gathering his courage, Matt grabbed the metal bar. He ran flat out back to the safety of the armored car.

"Man, there is some really creepy moaning going on out there," he told the others as soon he was helped up.

"Well it can stay out there," Hector replied, taking the piece of thick metal from Matt and inspecting it. It was of a good thickness, tapering to a flat edge. "Great eye, this is perfect."

Matt beamed at the compliment. Beth got the feeling he rarely received much praise.

Hector worked the flat end of the bar into the crease between the doorknob and the frame. Hector and Max applied pressure while Bill pulled the door and Beth pulled Bill. The frame gave a loud crack. Bill and Beth fell back into a protesting Stancy.

With the door open, Hector snapped on the flashlight on the end of his rifle. Beth clambered to her feet, pulling her own gun out. Max cut her off, moving into a cover position behind Hector. Matt moved to get his gun but Gillian stopped him.

Beth waited at the back of the truck, holding her breath. She watched Hector's light dance over the walls and floor.

"Looks clear," Max hissed to the others.

The group spilled out into the open area of an empty loading dock. They all spread out, stretching and groaning, but stayed within an arm's length of each other. Standing in the dark they listened for any noise, any hint they were not alone.

"This is great; cold, dark, and empty," Stancy's voice whined, making Matt jump.

"Give it a rest," Gillian griped from her left.

As her eyes grew accustomed to the dark, Beth could make out some boxes and debris ahead. A light suddenly came on from behind her. "I found a flashlight in the truck." Devin explained unnecessarily to her. She hadn't even realized he hadn't been with them. Beth decided from then on to always do a mental headcount every time they left the vehicle. "It is always good to know," she muttered to herself.

Devin shut the back doors to the truck. He then closed the door into the building. "Please tell me you have the keys." Hector joked. Devin hit his pockets in mock panic. Matt started to freak out until Devin held up the jingling keys.

"Don't upset the kid. He's annoying enough." It was Stancy again.

"Pot," Beth held out a hand, then pointed with the other, "Kettle." She shrugged. This received an annoyed look from both Matt and Stancy.

As a group they moved closer to the center of the open warehouse. The pile Beth had noticed turned out to be several broken pallets, empty boxes, and various packing materials. Looking through the boxes, they found two contained rolls of padding for bras and a box of under wires.

Stancy picked up the padding. She glared at Beth. "With this stuff you might actually attract a man."

"I have one, thank you."

"I doubt that now," Stancy sneered.

Beth looked stricken for a moment. Anger boiled up inside her.

Seeing what was about to explode, Matt quickly picked up one of the long wires. "If we only had some hot dogs."

Distracted, Beth sighed and shook her head at Matt. Passing by him she squeezed his upper arm in thanks.

Devin swept the flashlight around the dock. There were several doors on either side of them and a glass door toward the front. He cautiously made his way to the glass door. He turned off the flashlight as he looked through it. "It's the showroom." He whispered. "And...oh thank god, it is just a mannequin. I thought it had to be since they didn't..." He stopped. Looking back at the others, they smiled at his relief.

"Yeah, the factory is on either side of the dock. The one side made the everyday underwear and the other side made the sexy stuff," Matt explained. Everyone turned to stare at him. "What? My mom used to work here. She brought me and my brother with her when we couldn't afford a babysitter," he explained as he started rooting through the boxes again.

"Where are the bathrooms?" Gillian asked.

Matt pointed toward the front of the building. Gillian started to head in the direction he pointed. "Wait, wait, no one should wander off alone." Beth immediately moved to catch up. "I know it sounds lame, but we have to use the buddy system." Gillian laughed but readily agreed. Beth borrowed the flashlight from Devin then led the way to the door marked "Women".

"So who gets to be Stancy's buddy?" Gillian asked from a stall. Beth just laughed.

Returning, they saw a busy, but spread out group. Trevor was building a fire out of several of the broken pallets and cardboard. Matt was busy dividing up the left-over padding, Martin was breaking down some of the larger boxes. Hector and Max were discussing who would take the first watch.

The decision was made that Hector would take the watch. Devin, Max and Bill took some of the larger pallet pieces to furnish barricades to the doors leading to the other parts of the factory while the others began to make beds out of the padding and cardboard.

"That should hold 'em," Max stated proudly when he returned to build his own bed.

This Is the Way It Is

As quietly as he could, Steve sat down next to Wes, watching his fitful sleep. Steve rubbed his eyes. "What do you think?" Wes asked, making Steve look over.

"Huh?" Steve replied

"What do you think about staying here? I don't know if I can handle too much more of this."

"What?" Steve questioned.

"I appreciate the food and the shelter, don't get me wrong. I don't really think I want to be their armed guard." Wes jabbed a thumb over his shoulder.

"Listen, I know what we had to do today is shit but I..." Steve tried to explain. "I mean we probably freak them out a little."

"I don't care what they think of us. I don't like what they expect us to do," Wes grumbled.

Steve searched for a way to discuss things without bringing up shooting kids.

Several long seconds passed before Wes spoke up. "It's not that...entirely. Yeah, we had to do some seriously crappy stuff today. I understand that. That is the way it is for now, but they don't appreciate it. We come back from keeping this place safe and they recoil like they're next."

Steve sat for a moment. "I know what you mean. Mike is happy with us, but the rest? I don't trust 'em. I know they don't trust us."

Neither of them spoke for a while. "I noticed that guy we talked to, the one with that bad beard, is missing. When you talked to Mike, did he tell you what happened to him?" Wes asked, changing the subject.

"Oh yeah. Mike said he decided to try to make it out of town. His phone rang, it was his wife, she was safe somewhere close to Bradford. He said they moved slower there." Steve explained.

"Must be the cold," Wes noted.

"What?"

"The cold, it makes it hard to move and well, if they are dead, I don't think the heart is pumping, so I guess they would maybe freeze or something. Listen, the body is mostly water, right? It stands to reason if regular water freezes then the water in the body would also freeze."

Steve sat thinking this idea over. "I hope he makes it." He sighed, reaching down to grab the unfinished sandwich Wes had left.

They sat in silence for awhile. Wes watched Mike wandering through the pews. "I don't know, man," Wes muttered. "If he suggests we all go down to the shelter, I think we might want to follow that bearded dude's lead."

"What do you mean?"

"I don't know. I just don't think hanging out in the shelter is a good idea. There is something Heaven's Gate/Jonestown about it."

"Well if Mike goes that route, at least he has something those other guys didn't."

Wes just raised an eyebrow at this.

"The world really does seem to have ended. If ever there was a time for a doomsday cult..." Steve shrugged. "I think he wants to live as much as we do," he concluded, noticing his joke fell flat.

"All the same, I think I'd rather try to make it to Bradford."

Steve laughed. "You sure? Not much difference if you ask me. Still the end of the world there, plus it is always ten degrees colder there than anywhere else in the state."

"Yeah, but the summers will be nicer," Wes suggested.

Steve smacked the back of Wes' head. Wes sat up, throwing his arms over his head. For a moment they smiled. The moment faded. Steve returned to eating as Wes began going through his pack. He pulled out the stuffed bunny. He looked it over running his hand over its ears. "I always joked with Beth about moving to Bradford. I asked her if she would go with me. She always said 'no way.'"

"She might change her mind about it now." Steve shrugged. "If it is true they freeze. Then it would be a safer place."

Wes replied with a grunt. "We'll just have to ask her when we find her."

Interruption

Beth was exhausted but she couldn't find sleep. Every creak, every thud screamed in her ears. Shadows lumbered toward her. Every time she closed her eyes she was surrounded. She was aware that Gillian was still awake. The others seemed to have drifted into uneasy sleep. Soft snores mixed with uncomfortable grunts told her as much.

Matt woke with a start in a panic. Gillian immediately reassured that he was okay. He looked around at the dark warehouse and his companions. The realization of where he was sank in. It didn't really help him to relax. "Really hoped it was just a nightmare." He whispered glumly before dozing off again.

Beth's heart hurt for him. She wondered if Wes was dealing with the same fears, waking from the same nightmare only to find it was still going on. She watched Matt's profile in the low fire light. Her thoughts were soon consumed with her brother and best friend. Silently she prayed they were okay and had found a way out of town.

An idea hit her. She quickly searched her pockets. Her hand hit the hard lump in the inside pocket. A brief smile flashed across her face. She brought out the phone and hit a button. The glow of its face made her smile again. A picture filled the little screen. It was of her and her brother, Steve smiling back at her. She stared at the picture for a few seconds, and shaking her head slightly, she tried to call him. The phone beeped at her. She pulled the phone from her ear and stared at it. Above Steve's smiling face read the words, "No Service".

"Damn it," she whispered. Sitting up, she looked toward the front of the building. Thinking she might have better luck in the glassed front, she slowly got to her feet. Stepping lightly, she tried not to disturb the others. Something caught her attention and she paused. There was something... something not right. That sound? Holding very still, she strained her ears. There is was again, a thumping from somewhere. Lowering her head against her chest, she closed her eyes, listening hard.

Beth's head snapped up as she heard the breaking glass. The motion around her told her the others were now awake and alert. Everyone's attention was pinned to the direction of the store front.

Hector burst through the door. His eyes were clearly terrified even in the dim light of the fire. "They're here, they're getting in!" he cried.

The chaos was instantaneous. Everyone was on their feet, but no one seemed to know where to go. The room was cloaked in black. The fire went out for a second as someone's cardboard blanket fell on it. Next moment the entire room was full of light as it burst into flames. Their shadows danced on the walls, causing more panic.

"They're everywhere!"

"No, that's just us!"

"Where's the door?"

"Which way? Devin, where are the keys?!"

Voices called over each other. Someone knocked painfully into Beth. She staggered, trying to regain balance. Her right side ached from the contact. Stuffing the phone back into her pocket Beth hastily grabbed the rest of her things and drew her gun.

"Everyone stick together," Beth shouted.

"This way to the truck," Devin called. Beth shoved someone toward the waving arm she hoped was Devin.

"Let's move, people." Beth was joined by Hector. Together they tried to herd the others toward a door. It took only a second for Matt to realize the mistake.

"NO! This is the way to the sexy factory. Turn around, turn around!" He was in front of everyone, waving them back.

"This way!" someone yelled.

Beth felt the collar of her jacket being tugged. Hector was now leading them. The door they had been heading toward burst open, sending several boards skidding toward them.

"Yeah, that'll hold 'em," Stancy sneered at Max.

"Come on!"

The group bumped and pushed each other toward the back door, Beth walking backward, keeping the zombies in view. The sound of more shattering glass told them the front was now open and full of the undead.

Suddenly Beth was off balance again as the group came to a sudden stop. Matt's elbow jabbed at her already sore ribs. They were only about fifteen feet from the door when they stopped. Beth pushed Matt as she turned to see the issue. Ten zombies advanced toward them, blocking their route.

"We have to get out another way, come on!" Beth called. She pulled Matt along with her toward some windows near the exit. They skidded to a halt as three more ghouls appeared around some crates. "Other way!" she called.

The group moved in the other direction. The door to the daily garments side of the factory remained closed. Hector took a step away from the group toward the closed door. The door rattled in its frame as several fists pounded against it.

"No good...back up. Back up!"

"What the hell? They're everywhere. How did they all get in?" Beth asked as she looked back toward the front of the warehouse. The door to the store was open. The dead were streaming in one after the other. Frantically she looked for any way out. Max and Hector began shooting the closest undead. Finally, she saw it. She opened her mouth to call out when she was suddenly dazed.

Her ears rang and her head throbbed from the explosion of Matt firing a shotgun. His shot did little, as he aimed too low. The zombie that had been shuffling toward them now crawled. One of its legs had been blown off. Matt kept pulling the trigger with no effect. He had forgotten to use the pump to load another shell.

Where was it, where? Beth shook her head to clear the ringing and the double vision. She looked up again, scanning the row of windows set high near the ceiling. "There!" She pointed to a window above the door to the truck. "There! There!" she shouted.

Hector followed her hand. He saw the walkway above them. "We need to get up there!" he yelled, pointing.

Max searched the area frantically. "There!" he called, pointing at a large elevator. "Come on, we have to get to the second floor. We know they have a hard time with stairs, come on!" Beth fired at a couple of the zombies that were close to the elevator doors. The group ran for the lift.

"They have a hard time with stairs?" Matt questioned as they ran.

"Why the hell didn't we make our camp on the second floor to begin with?" Trevor asked angrily.

They reached the elevator. It was an old cage type with a metal grate gate as a door. The group crushed inside. Hector slammed the gate shut and pressed the up button. The group waited and waited. All the guns were pointed at the approaching zombies. Hector hit the button again.

"Why aren't we moving?" Trevor screamed.

"Because there is no power in an abandoned factory!" Beth exclaimed, slapping herself in the head.

"Aw, come on man!" Max responded.

Hector let off a burst of gun fire into the approaching ghouls, to no avail.

"In the head, man, in the head!" Max yelled.

Hector shook his head angrily and adjusted fire, and several zombies fell. The gate was thrown open. The group ran out.

"This way!" Trevor yelled, spotting the stairs at the far end of the dock.

Beth ran for them, followed closely by Matt and Gillian. A zombie lurched at Gillian. She dodged its grip but slipped and fell. Matt spun around, dropped the shotgun and began to pull her up. Beth slid up to them. She heaved Gillian to her feet. The others ran past and had already gained the stairs.

Devin called, "Come on, MOVE IT!"

Beth pushed Gillian ahead of her as the three tried to catch up with the others. She felt her long hair pull through ragged fingernails as she mounted the second stair. Turning on the fourth step she kicked a zombie in the face as it tried to navigate the first step. It fell, knocking two others over with it.

Max was running full speed to the window above the door, his footfalls clanging on the metal grating as he ran. Skidding to a halt at the window, he looked out. "It is only a couple feet to the truck's roof. We can jump. There aren't any of those things around!"

He backed up and ran at the window as fast as he could. *SLAM, Crunch*! Max lay on his back, staring at the ceiling. The window remained unbroken. He was completely dazed. Devin stepped over him. He began using the heavy flashlight from the truck as a club to smash the window.

"Back up!" Max called from the floor of the walkway.

Devin moved aside, and Max fired several shots into the thick glass. It shattered. Devin helped him up. They cleared the jagged edges of glass with the flashlight. Devin handed it to Max, then jumped to the top of the truck.

He was barely out when Stancy pushed her way through and jumped down. Devin was on the stairs behind the truck, unlocking the back doors, when Martin hit the roof. Devin clambered inside, Trevor was now out of the window.

Trevor jumped to the stairs and held out his arms to help Stancy. She shook her head. With the grace of a gymnast she swung from the roof, through the back door into the truck. Trevor looked back at the roof to Martin, who wore the same look of surprise. Max landed heavily next to Martin with a thud. Hector called from the window, "Get ready."

Matt came flying out. He hit the roof and rolled to the edge, his legs sliding off the end. Martin and Max grabbed his arms, pulling him up. Gillian was hanging out the window. She let herself drop down to the stairs with a clang.

Hector jumped down next, and Max steadied him as he slipped on the roof of the truck. Beth and Bill were the only ones left in the building. Beth could hear the zombies falling over themselves on the stairs behind them. They were relentless in their attempts to reach them. She could see several had fallen on the stairs. The other zombies were using the fallen as a ramp.

"Come on Beth, time to go," Bill stated, squeezing her arm.

Bill braced himself in the window frame. Beth could tell he was scared to jump. He adjusted his grip to push himself as he jumped. Hector and Max stood below, encouraging him to hurry. Beth crouched behind him, silently urging him to move as the zombie ramp continued to build, getting ever closer to the top.

Bill leaned forward, his knees bent, and he finally pushed off. His foot slipped on the broken glass. He fell, hitting the side of the building and bouncing onto the roof of the truck, where he crumpled. Max and Hector pulled him up. They began handing him down to Martin and Trevor.

They were no longer alone in the lot. Three undead had wandered out of the woods and were starting to beat on the hood of the truck. Beth heard the panic below. She could make out Stancy demanding that they get moving. She heard Hector argue that they all weren't there. She frowned at Stancy's response. "No great loss."

"Bitch," she muttered, then looked back at the warehouse. The dead were still streaming in. She took a deep breath and jumped onto the truck, tucking and rolling to a stop. She grabbed the side. "I'm on," she yelled.

"Great, get your ass in here!" Max called from the back as Hector jumped down.

Scurrying to the back of the truck, Beth hung her legs over the edge, ready to jump. Hector was still on the stairs. Something heavy fell past them, hitting the door. A pair of legs barely missed Beth's face as she flung herself backward against the roof of the truck.

Looking up, she saw several zombies crammed in the window frame. One was working its way free. She knew it would fall right on top of her. Praying Hector was still there, she flung herself forward off the roof.

Thick arms caught her. Beth kept her eyes shut, waiting to feel teeth rip into her. Instead, without her feet hitting the ground, she was in the back of the truck. The doors slammed shut and her feet touched the floor.

"You can let go now," Hector laughed hoarsely.

Quickly letting go, she smiled at the soldier. "Thanks." She steadied herself against the back doors. She looked out the window to the back door to the factory. It burst open as they pulled away. Beth jumped back a little, then laughed as two zombies got stuck trying to make it through the door at the same time. "Too slow," she taunted as the truck drove away.

Sanctuary?

"I'm serious. I think we should start thinking about another place to stay," Wes whispered to Steve.

"I really don't see what you do," Steve replied.

"I can't put my finger on it, but there is something not right about..." Wes broke off as a woman tiptoed by them in the darkened church.

Steve and Wes watched her move quietly to a pew a few rows up and to the left of them. A child coughed. They watched as the woman raised its head to give it a drink. Wes continued to stare until Steve hit him on the arm.

"Something not right?" Steve questioned.

"Yeah, about the Father."

"Such as?"

"Why are we up here?"

Steve pulled a face. "What do you mean?"

"Why are we up here in the exposed church?" Steve made to protest, but Wes held up a hand and continued, "I mean, I know the windows are high and the doors are thick, but the school isn't so protected, and it is attached right through those doors."

"There is a ten-foot-high fence and the area that isn't exposed has bricked-up windows. Remember, he said they had trouble down here."

"That is fine for a few vandals and thieves, but you get ten, twenty, thirty, a hundred of those things and that fence is coming down. You know it and I know it."

"I prefer to be up here with several exits than sitting down in that shelter. If this place is overrun, I don't like the idea of the dead walking around up here when the lights go out down there," Steve explained. "Plus, you were the one who didn't want to be all Heaven's Gate down there. Dude, you need to make up your mind."

Wes sat silently digesting what Steve had just explained. Steve fought to get comfortable on a mat that was pulled in from the gym to sleep on. "This thing smells funny."

"I remember a girl in kindergarten that peed on one of those." Wes snickered at the look on Steve's face.

"Was it Beth?" Steve asked, smirking.

"No," Wes laughed, "and she is going to kick your ass when I tell her you said that."

The woman a few pews over shushed them. Wes stifled his laugh, then his face turned serious again. "Okay, so why keep it locked, then?"

"What locked... oh the shelter? I guess like he said. It locks on its own and so no one runs off with stuff that would benefit the whole group."

"If he decides we need to pool our weapons, I am not going to give up my guns," Wes stated.

"You sound like one of those militia guys," Steve laughed.

"Wish I was one of those guys right now. I bet they are safe out in their compounds in the woods. They have guns, food, mines..."

"Craziness."

"Just because they thought it would be the government and not the undead...well the government was brain dead."

"Go to sleep, dude."

"Seriously Steve, let's think about getting out of here."

"I am, I am."

Wes was quiet for a while then he whispered, "We need to find Beth. I don't think she is coming here."

Now Where?

"How did they find us?" Beth gasped. The adrenaline was still pounding through her veins, making it hard to sit still.

"They must have followed us," Bill replied, grimacing and rubbing his ankle.

Gillian moved over to him to take a look. She pulled up the pant leg and frowned. His leg was already swollen and black and blue.

"How?" How did they follow us? We didn't see any of them on our way there," Beth demanded.

"Because he drove so damn slow! You let them know where we were. We could have stayed there for days but you led them right to us," Stancy cried, pointing at Devin.

Devin silently drove away from the factory.

"Listen, stupid! We couldn't have stayed there for days; we had no damn food," Beth shouted. Her annoyance reached its breaking point with the older woman as she remembered the comments Stancy had made about her. "They found us! So now we know we have to find a more secure place. One without so many ways in," Beth finished, glaring at Stancy.

"Next place needs to be defendable. I think someplace on a second floor or higher," Hector mused.

"I don't know if that is good enough. I saw what happened back at the factory. Yeah, they don't do stairs well, but they will crawl over each other to get at us. They ended up making a ramp out of each other. The best thing might be to tear up the stairs once we're up," Beth offered.

"Oh, that sounds brilliant. Let's trap ourselves. Stupid little girl," Stancy fired.

"I've had just about enough out of you," Hector shouted, "She is right."

Stancy furiously sputtered. Martin slammed his fist against the side of the truck. Everyone turned at the noise. The former Mayor was furious. "We have been forced out of every place we have tried so far. It is damn early in the morning. Our first order of business is to get some damn food and water. Then we need to locate someplace where we can hold up for a while until we can figure a way out of this deep shit we're in." He finished by glaring around at everyone as if daring them to contradict him.

"Feels like I just got yelled at by my dad," Matt whispered to Beth. She nodded, also feeling like she had just been caught doing something wrong. Silence filled the truck for several long minutes. Devin drove at a slow pace, but not as slow as when they had first passed through this neighborhood.

Finally, as the quiet was starting to become unbearable, Devin spoke up. "I'm sorry about the warehouse. I agree that we need a new place. I just have no idea where I am going now, so any suggestions would be great."

Gillian wrapped a cold pack she had salvaged from the ambulance around Bill's ankle and gave him some pain killers. She sat back on her heels for a moment, thinking. "I had a friend that lived downtown above a store. There was only one door in and a fire escape."

Martin's hand hit the side of the truck again, causing everyone to jump. This time though he smiled at her as he spoke. "So, we can use the truck to climb up the fire escape and barricade the stairs up to the apartments. Now we're thinking!"

Hector thought for a moment. "Sounds like it could work. Be better if we could block the door with the truck...but that doesn't seem likely. We'll have to check the logistics when we get there."

"Sounds like we have a plan," Bill said, wincing as Gillian tied off the wrap a little too forcefully.

"Sorry," she said, noticing the look of pain.

"Oh, brilliant plan; where the hell are we going?' Stancy challenged.

Gillian sat for a moment thinking. Max and Hector exchanged questioning looks.

"Okay, it was down on Locust near Park, if I remember correctly," Gillian finally spoke. "I don't remember the number, but I think I'll know it when I see it."

Trevor, who occupied the passenger seat, reached over and gave Devin a slug on the arm. In a would-be chipper voice he exclaimed, "Well, my friend, back to town, then."

Stancy sat in the back, mumbling several derogatory things aimed at both Devin and Beth. Beth tried to ignore the more questionable slings against her morals as she moved up behind the driver's seat.

"You okay?" she asked Devin.

Devin looked over Beth. He rolled his eyes and shook his head. "I'm not going to worry about someone that ignorant," Devin said as he looked out the windshield.

Beth patted his shoulder, but couldn't help feel that Devin was extremely bothered. She understood his annoyance. The world seemed to be ending. They might be the only ones left alive, and he still had to deal with the ignorance of a bigot. Her thoughts were interrupted by a suggestion from Martin.

"We should get some supplies before we try to hole up someplace. We won't know what is at this place until we get there, and I don't want to have to leave for a while."

"Any suggestions on where to stop?" Devin asked.

"Where are we?" Max asked.

"The Pine Ridge area.".

"Perfect. The Cost Club is just a little way away. We can pick up bulk stuff that will last for a while." Matt grinned as he joined the others to look out the front window.

"Sounds good," Devin agreed, and sped up a little. He didn't even try to swerve as a zombie stumbled off the sidewalk in front of them. Its arms flung out in the air as it flew off the front of the truck.

First Light

Distracted by a motorcycle embedded in a van, Devin took the turn late, going in through the out lane. Matt was about to comment but shut his mouth at the look on Gillian's face. Devin continued through the parking lot of the huge warehouse store. The sun had just begun to break over the mountains. Several zombies shuffled around the lot. They all seemed to be heading to the front of the store.

"What the hell?" Hector asked as they watched the zombies march to the doors.

"The gates are down. Looks like it was closed up when everything went to hell." Max pointed excitedly.

"There are too many of them out here. Head around the back." Trevor suggested. Devin nodded, pulling the truck around the corner of the building.

"How do we get in?" Matt asked.

"We open a door, just like we did at the factory," Max replied.

"Glad we have a cop to help us break in," Beth laughed. Max turned to her, an actual smile on his face. Devin located a delivery door and backed the truck up close to it. He put the truck in park but left the engine running. Getting up from the driver's seat, he stretched. "Trevor. Take over driving for a bit, will you?"

Trevor nodded, moving from the passenger seat to the driver's side. Devin looked around the back of the truck for a moment. Kneeling down, he shifted Matt and Gillian to pull up a panel in the floor. Inside was a spare tire, a jack and a tire tool with a wedge-shaped end.

Matt gawked. "Sure, now you think of that. Why couldn't you have found that before I jumped out of the truck at the bra place?"

Devin gave Matt an apologetic smile. "Found it when I found the flashlight." He then moved to the back doors of the truck. Readying himself, he looked at Hector, Beth and Max in turn.

"Ok I guess Devin's going, who else?" Hector asked.

Beth leaned close to Devin and whispered, "No one blames you. You don't have to do this."

He nodded at her and patted her arm reassuringly. Beth smiled at him, placing her hand over his. She returned to getting ready when Hector spoke. "Okay, we need someone to stay out here and guard the truck. Beth, that'll be you and Max. Martin, Matt, the doc and I will go in."

Beth began to protest, but Hector held up his hand to quiet her. "You're a better shot than any of these guys, and god willing, there will be more zombies out here than in there."

The ones going into the store began to gather the guns they had. Max took the shotgun away from Matt, giving him a 22 instead. Matt frowned at the gun. Max gave a revolver to Martin. Stancy had already moved to the passenger seat, making it obvious that she was going nowhere.

"You know I can push a cart and use it as a walker." Bill protested.

"Come on Bill, what if we run into problems? There is no way you will be able to outrun trouble if we get into it. What if there are a bunch of them?" Gillian put a hand on Bill's shoulder to keep him from rising.

"Seriously, Mr. Reager, You're better off here, for now. I'll be just outside," Beth comforted him.

Bill lay back wearily against the side of the truck. He gave Beth a weak smile. Gillian nodded a silent thanks.

"Great. Stuck out here with Annie Oakley and a gimp," Stancy muttered.

"Well you could get off your ass and help out," Max commented.

Stancy turned her back on them with a huff. Trevor glanced at her sideways from the driver's seat. The others spared the back of her head a look of annoyance before readying their assault on the huge package store.

The next few minutes held a flurry of activity. Devin and Hector worked to force the store's rear door open. Beth took up a position at the rear of the truck while Max ran to the front. Matt, Gillian, and Martin nervously waited behind Devin and Hector.

"Hang close to me, kid," Martin winked at Matt.

Matt looked over to Gillian, and she nodded for him to go with the Mayor. Gillian hung close to Devin as he worked on the door. Hector, it was decided, would sweep the store front. If he saw trouble, he would alert the others to get out quick.

The rear door of the store popped open. Instantly alarms began to blare. Beth instinctively covered her ears. The cold of the handgun she was holding against her ear reminded her to ignore the sound. This is going to bring them, she thought. She immediately began to check around for the most probable places the undead would come from.

Hector had already entered the building. The others waited a couple of seconds then rushed into the blackness through the door. The alarm stopped. Beth stepped behind the truck, looking toward the front. Max was sweeping his rifle back and forth across the area. Beth returned to her position. Looking at the nine-millimeter handgun, she wished for something with more kick.

Movement at the far corner of the building captured her attention. Two of the undead rounded the edge of the structure. Beth watched them for a moment. From this distance they looked perfectly normal. Beth gave a hesitant wave to show she was alive; she quickly lowered her arm adjusting the aim on her weapon.

The two responded, but it was the response of the undead, a low longing moan followed by outstretched arms and a quicker shuffle toward her. Beth's heart ached with disappointment. She raised her weapon, sighting on the head of the ghoul in a light windbreaker. Using the team emblem on the dead man's ballcap, she readied to fire.

The shots she heard did not come from her gun nor from Max's. Max appeared at the front of the truck, a questioning look in his eyes. Beth shook her head to say she hadn't fired. They looked at each other, then at the open door to the store.

Answering their question, Gillian burst through the opening. Terror was etched deep onto the features of the young veterinarian. Devin followed closely on Gillian's heels. "Start the truck," he screamed from the back door. Stancy shrieked, flailed and pounded the dash. Trevor turned the key, making the starter scream against the already running engine.

Beth saw that neither Gillian nor Devin had any supplies. More gunfire erupted from inside the building. Devin paled, turning to look behind him. He took a step back, stumbled, turned and fell right over the threshold. Running blindly, Hector tripped over him as he came out next. Devin was clawing his way to the truck. Hector heaved him to his feet, pushing him into the back of the rumbling vehicle.

Beth was moving toward the door. "Where are Matt and Martin?" As if to answer her question, several small pops followed by three really loud bangs sounded from inside. Beth spun as one of the back doors to the truck was slammed shut by Max.

"MATT! MARTY! WE HAVE TO GO!" Hector was yelling from the still-open door. He pointed to either side of the store. Zombies were streaming around both sides. He grabbed Beth's hand, pulling her in. Trevor began to pull forward.

"Wait! WAIT! They are coming!" Beth screamed over her shoulder at him.

In the dark of the doorway she could see the flashes of guns firing. Then Matt flew out the door as if he had been thrown. He hit the pavement and didn't get up right away. Beth started to move when Hector pushed past her. He jumped out and in one fluid motion scooped Matt up, turned and was back in the truck in a flash.

Martin appeared at the back door covered in blood. His face was a mask of sorrow and terror as his eyes locked with Beth's. They stared at each other. Beth took a step forward. Her hand found the door handle as she readied to jump out. Martin held up his hand, wearing a look that begged her to understand.

"NO!" Beth screamed. Martin reached over, then slammed the door shut. Hector's strong arms strained to hold Beth as she fought to get out.

"Trevor, go! Max, get the door! Beth, there is nothing you can do," Hector yelled.

Beth fought against him. She stared at the closed portal through the open truck door. Max pulled the door shut just as Beth broke free, and she scrambled around Max to the window. She watched the receding closed store door, the image of Martin's face seared into her brain.

Trevor sped through the oncoming crowd of undead. Soon she could no longer see the door through the sea of zombies. Slowly she turned to see the faces of those that had been inside. They all held a look of horror and pain. "What...what happened?" she gasped.

Matt lay on the floor with his eyes half-closed. He propped himself up slightly on his elbows, and looking past Beth he slurred, "I thought that place was crowded when everyone was alive." His eyes rolled back and his head thudded against the steel as he promptly passed out. Gillian checked his pulse.

Trevor's voice came cracked and strained from the front. "I knew him for fifteen years. Fifteen. Since he was a city councilman."

Gillian looked from Max to Beth then to the floor. In a shaky voice she spoke, "God, there were so many in there. So many. It was like they went there for a hiding place or something. It was packed...and so many." With that she dissolved into tears.

Hector just sat and shook. He was trying to load his weapon, but his fingers wouldn't work right. Beth found a bottle of water and handed it to him. He looked up at her, tears streaming down his face. "Children, so many children," he breathed. Only the sound of the engine was heard for the journey back into town.

Hungry

Britney stumbled out of the house to the front lawn. The bright sun blinded her momentarily after the dark of the house. The grass needed to be cut, but this had never been her job. That had fallen to her brother. Her brother had been missing since the outbreak had started. She wandered down the empty streets toward the downtown. She was so hungry, and something told her she could find food this way.

She found her way blocked many times. It took a long time to get around the burned-out cars and fallen ruble. She had left the house hours ago, but time didn't really matter anymore. What was time when no one was around to meet you, with no appointments needing to be kept?

Many times she saw several zombies shambling off in the distance. They took no notice of her, so she kept moving forward. The life she had known was over. The things she had cared so much for no longer mattered. She just needed to find food. Her reflection showed a torn t-shirt with the logo of her favorite book and movie. She didn't care about any of that now.

She stumbled out of the alley, tripping over a half-full trash can. It rattled loudly along the empty street. Moving forward, she slipped on the rotting corpses of several children all dressed in choir robes. She took no notice of the smell or the tragedy of the little lives lost. She tripped over more debris and headed for the fence. It was inside, the food was inside.

Steve was at his post in the bell tower of Saint Andrew's downtown church. He looked through the scope of his rifle down to the barricade of buses and whatever else they could pile up. Something moved to the right of an overturned car. Steve sighted in the rifle and waited. It had been a while since he had seen one of them wander this close. He wondered if it knew they were here or if it just chanced upon them. If they knew we were here, this place would be covered with them, Steve reassured himself. It seemed strange that in a city this size they had seen so few of the undead around. Especially after seeing so many at the ballpark, it made him wonder if they might be safe. Maybe the zombies had moved out of the city. His thoughts were interrupted by the sound of metal clanging down the street.

Steve returned to his scope, searching for the source of the sound. Sweeping the street, he discovered a girl stumbling out of the shadows. At least that was what he concluded, judging by what was left of the thing's clothes. She was a teenager, he thought. He noticed the "Twilight" t-shirt and had to laugh at the irony.

"Well, you loved the undead," he mused, "and now you are the undead." He thought of Beth and how much she hated those books. "I guess you and Beth wouldn't have been friends. I wonder if she knew you." He thought back to the last time he had talked to his sister. Hadn't he given her a hard time about that stuff? He smiled. it was just an older brother messing with his sister. A frown crossed his face. She knew that. Right?

Steve looked back through the scope, but he had lost sight of the zombie. He scanned the area, Beth was too cool for that vampire soap opera crowd. *Is* too cool, he corrected himself angrily.

Looking over the scope, he spotted her at the fence. She was clawing at the interlocking metal rings, trying to get through. He returned to the eyepiece, adjusting the crosshairs on her face. He flipped off the safety, exhaled, and squeezed the trigger.

Britney crumpled, now completely lifeless. Her broken body lay at the bottom of the fence outside the church.

"Beth, you had better be safe," Steve grunted.

Apartment

The truck rolled on in a deep silence, the quiet only broken by the huffing of Stancy or her whine of discomfort. Finally returning to the downtown area, Trevor broke the spell. "Hey Doc. Where do we go from here?" They sat idling at an intersection.

Startled, Gillian looked up from Matt. She gave him the cold compress to hold against the knot on his head, then struggled to move up to the front. Looking out the window, it took a moment to get her bearings. The downtown area was littered with debris, crashed cars, and signs of violence. Gillian knelt down next to Trevor. Stancy had refused to give up the passenger seat. She was staring out the window, not looking at anyone but silently daring them to make her move.

It was uncomfortable for Gillian to sit on her knees giving directions. She heard grumbling and turned around. Max gave a disgusted look at Stancy. He was about to say something, but Gillian shook her head. It took a while for her to find her way back to the apartment. It had been several years and the way she remembered had been blocked by a fire. It looked as if an entire block of the city was burning out of control. Fear boiled up: what if that had been the building they needed? What if this was another wasted trip, another disappointment, or worse... what if she got them trapped?

After a the third backtrack, Stancy wasn't the only one grumbling. Finally, Gillian breathed a sigh of relief. There it was, the place she was looking for. They were idling in front of a hardware store with two stories of windows above it. "There is a dance studio on the second floor and three or four apartments on the third." She smiled, pointing to the building. "Down the alley is the door to the stairs. You had to either be buzzed in or have a key."

"No way!" Max exclaimed as he slapped the back of the driver's seat happily.

Gillian looked at him, perplexed. "What?"

He pointed at the fire escape hanging out into the alley. "Perfect. It is perfect. We don't have to force the door, we just have to climb up on the truck and up the fire escape." He grinned at her, pulling her up into a one-armed hug.

Beth interrupted, "That is, if we are the only ones here." She pointed out the windshield to the open door just below the fire escape. Max's face fell. "Damn it. Now what?"

"Maybe it got left open when the residents left?" Trevor asked hopefully. Beth felt that the way their luck had been, he was being grossly optimistic.

Hector slapped a full clip into his rifle "It looks like we need to check this out." Beth pulled her gun. The look she gave Hector told him she refused to be left behind this time. He nodded. "The rest of you stay here. Beth and I will check it out." She gave a quick nod and clicked off the safety.

Trevor pulled up to the door. Beth and Hector jumped out. As soon as they cleared the bumper the doors slammed shut. It sounded louder than a cannon being fired to Beth. Standing in the deserted alley, she was suddenly aware of how fast and loud her heart was beating. She followed close to the military man. The gun in her hand felt light, too small, like a toy.

What are you doing out here? her brain screamed. Shaking the thoughts away, she charged forward. The door into the building swung a little in the light breeze. Beth hesitated. The breeze brought with it the smell of smoke and old garbage from down the alley. Hector signaled her to wait and keep watch. He took a deep breath. Swinging around the door he aimed his weapon up a flight of stairs. He clicked on the flashlight attached to the barrel. Seeing nothing, he reached into his pocket pulling out a second flashlight. Beth glanced over her shoulder as he flashed the light around the stairwell. The streaks of blood on the walls caused her stomach to tighten.

"This is not going to be good," she whispered.

Hector nodded, handing Beth the flashlight. He motioned her to keep quiet and watch behind them as they ascended the stairs. Gaining the second floor landing, they had a choice between a door to the dance studio and another that led to more stairs. Beth wanted to go up, but Hector indicated the door to the studio. They spent several seconds having a silent argument with furious hand motions, pointing from door to door. Finally, Beth threw up her hands in frustration. She moved closer to Hector and the closed dance studio door. She really didn't want to see what was in there.

Carefully and quietly Hector pushed the door with his foot. It opened into a huge open room. Their lights flashed through the empty space. Beth's light fell on a large pool of drying blood on the floor. There were no streaks to show a body being drug. Moving closer they checked the floor for signs of the blood's owner. Only one set of bloody footprints led toward the stairs, disappearing before reaching the door. Scanning the rest of the room, they saw no sign of the living or dead, just a couple of doors at the far end of the room.

Moving further in, Beth jumped with a squeak. She swung around to aim at the person who appeared directly across from her. She gave a small stifled laugh and sigh of relief as she saw only herself in the wall-length mirror. Behind her she could see Hector trying to cover his amusement. She gave him the finger in the mirror. This did nothing to stem his mirth. She motioned him to move. He saluted, took a breath to regain focus, and moved on, gun at the ready. She took a moment to calm herself as well. She followed, keeping an eye on their backs as they snaked around the support columns.

Hector headed to a door in the middle of the opposite wall. He kicked it open, shining his light around. "Clear," he whispered. Beth was at his side. They were looking in at an office. The desk was messy but clear of any sign of violence. Hector pointed to another door. Together they eased silently toward it. Hector held up a hand. He showed three fingers then two then one. Beth nodded. Three fingers…two… one… he reached out, turned the knob, then threw the door open and stood back.

Beth held her flashlight next to the barrel of her gun, breath held. The light weakly illuminated the next room. Hector peeked around the corner, then went in. Beth followed him into a locker room. Again, there was no one there. He motioned for them to head out and up to the next floor.

"Where did they go? Beth whispered when they returned to the stairway to the third floor.

"I'm hoping out the front door and far, far away." Hector replied quietly. Reaching the top of the flight, they came to yet another door. Hector looked at it, then at Beth. She shrugged and raised an eyebrow. "How many doors do they need?" Hector grumbled. There was a small window on one side just above the handle. Beth mused this must be so people could see who was coming up. Hector reached out slowly and tried the knob. It was locked.

"What do we do?" Beth hissed.

Hector looked at her, then at the small window. He raised the butt of his rifle and smashed the window. Beth's ears rang. She frowned at Hector. He stood listening for a moment, pointing both his flashlight and the rifle through the opening. He motioned for Beth to open the door. She stared at him questioningly; he urged her forward. She shook her head. He motioned for her to put her arm through and unlock the door. She pointed at him. He pointed to his rifle, she to her gun. In the end their grunting and motioning led to Beth edging up to the door. Frowning, she ducked as Hector pointed his rifle over her head.

"You so owe me for this." Beth slowly snaked her hand through the broken glass. Hector moved close to her, continuing to aim down the hall. She noted with some satisfaction that if anything touched her hand, she would jerk it back through, causing some severe discomfort to Hector. Fumbling for a second, she quickly found the knob on the other side, unlocking the door. Every hair on her hand felt the tiniest movement of air. Quickly as she could, she pulled her arm back through. She made sure to give Hector a soft elbow to the gut, earning an "oomf" from him.

Smiling, she turned the knob. Her smile faded as she saw the blood on her hand, tacky and congealing. She quickly started rubbing it off against the wall. A panic began to swell. She wanted it off her hand Now! Hector quickly handed her a rag. She couldn't suppress a shudder as she wiped her hand clean. Hector moved around her through the opening. The hall was empty. Beth followed. Hector looked at the back of the door. Cautiously Beth peered around him. The knob was covered in blood, but the rest of the door was clean. Still shuddering and rubbing her hand raw with the rag Beth turned away from the sight.

Hector gave her hand a squeeze as he took the cloth away. Shaking her head to clear it she observed the rest of their surroundings. Three doors stood on the right; light came in from two windows on the left. Looking out the window Beth could see a balcony that ran the length of the building. It also led to the fire escape.

Returning her attention to the doors, she saw the third door down the hall was open. Hector eased to the first door. He tried the knob. It was locked. He edged down along the wall to the second door. Pressing himself flat against the wall, he motioned for Beth to do the same. Reaching out he tried the knob. It turned. With a soft click the door moved slightly. Hector let go and held up a hand. Beth readied herself. Hector pointed to her and she understood. She was to kick open the door and he was to go through it. He moved out of her way. She took a step back lowered her weapon, built up the energy rocking back and forth ready to kick in the door. She stumbled and fell back as Hector waved frantically.

"What the hell!?" Beth hissed angrily. He hushed her. He was listening. She moved closer and heard it too. A soft mournful type of cry emanated through the slight crack in the door. Hector motioned Beth behind him. Slowly he pushed the door open with the muzzle of his rifle. Beth gasped but held her aim. Standing in the middle of the apartment with her back to them stood a small woman. Beth thought she couldn't be more than five one or two at the most. The floor creaked under Hector's boot. Slowly the woman turned toward the sound.

Her face, while pale, was framed with unnaturally deep red hair. Her mouth and chin were covered in dark dry blood. Hector flipped his rifle up and charged the ghoul. She advanced toward him, oblivious of what he intended. Beth flinched at the crack of rifle butt against skull. The small girl crumpled, but still clawed at Hector's boot. He brought the stock down again and again. Beth looked away as the head came apart all over a tan and blue area rug.

Covering her mouth and nose from the stench Beth closed her eyes to the gore. The cracking of bone still rang in her ears. *No that wasn't it!* Her eyes flew open as a pale hand missing two fingers appeared around a door frame to her right. The door slowly opened, revealing a young man soaked in blood from his chin all down the front of his shirt. He gurgled at her from a torn throat. He slowly shuffled out of the bedroom toward her. She raised her weapon, pointing right between the eyes.

"No, don't shoot!" Hector gasped, "You'll let them know where we are." Beth looked over at Hector. He motioned for her to smash the zombie on the head. Beth backed away. The zombie wasn't much taller than she was; he was thin, deceptively so. She knew the type from the wrestling team. She had one shot at this. She turned the gun like a hammer and rushed forward, smashing it on his face. The ghoul took a step back but came at her again. She smashed it harder in the nose. She heard the crack.

"Hit it again!" Hector yelped, rushing to her aid. Gathering her strength, she smashed the metal of the gun to the broken nose. The zombie faltered, then dropped. Hector was at her side. She looked away, covering her ears, but she couldn't completely block out the crunch. Hector stomped on the boy's face. Beth felt Hector's hand on her shoulder.

Shaking slightly, they checked the rest of the apartment. Thankfully they found it empty. Moving back into the hall they moved toward the third apartment. The door was unlocked, and to Beth's relief it was empty although it was a terrible mess. It looked like the occupants had left in a hurry. Drawers stood open and their content spilled out on the floor. "Maid must be off this week." Hector commented.

They swept through the rest of the empty rooms and then returned to the hall. Beth followed as they returned to the first apartment. Hector gave a quick rap on the door and waited. No sound came from inside. Beth pressed herself against the wall. Hector moved into the hall, braced himself, then kicked the door open. He pointed his rifle ahead and rushed in, Beth following. The

apartment was completely empty. It apparently had not been rent-
ed.

Wiping a cold sweat from his brow, Hector returned to the
hallway. Beth followed, her breathing and heart rate slowly returning to normal. Hector moved to the middle apartment. He paused
at the door for a second then closed it.

"No need for the rest to see that." He said, "Do you want to
wait in the other one?" Hector motioned to the furthest door.

Beth thought for a moment, torn between not wanting to be
alone, and with really not wanting to go back outside. She pulled
the clip from her gun, checking her ammo and stalling for time. Finally, she spoke. "I'll, um, what do you guys call it? Secure the
area."

Hector laughed, gave her a salute, then headed down the stairs
to get the others. His footsteps disappeared, leaving Beth alone in
the hallway. Every sound in the building became suddenly amplified. Every creak was a zombie wandering closer. The slightest
draft was the hands of the undead about to grab her.

Backing slowly away from the stairs, Beth found the wall. She
stood in the corner of the hall with her back firmly against the plaster, gun at the ready. Nervously she kept watch, eyes darting from
the doors to the stairs and then back again. Wooden floorboards
creaked. Her ears detected the labored climbing on the stairs.
THUMP, THUMP, THUMP. Closer and closer the footfalls came.
With each slow step Beth's anxiety grew. After an eternity of watching, Matt's bandaged head appeared at the top of the stairs
followed by Gillian helping a badly limping Bill.

Lowering her weapon, she exhaled in great relief. Beth hurried
forward to help them into the apartment. As soon as they made it
through the door Bill collapsed on the couch, breathing as if the
climb had cost him his last bit of strength. Matt altered between
very pale and tinged with green. He crumpled into a chair as soon
as he could. He put his head between his knees, taking deep
breaths.

Beth eased slowly away from Matt, concerned he was about to
be sick. She was just getting ready to see if the others needed help

when Stancy and Trevor came in. Stancy pushed past Beth with an irritated grunt. With the couch and chair were already occupied she was left with only one of the hard kitchen chairs. She made her displeasure known. Everyone ignored her.

"The guys will be here in a second; they are hiding the truck," Trevor explained to Beth, who was looking expectantly into the hall.

"Hiding?" Beth questioned.

"Yeah, the kid fell down and yelled, attracting a few of those...Things," Stancy snarled.

"He moaned...slightly." Gillian explained, patting Matt on the shoulder. This had the effect of making Matt hold up a hand and close his eyes tightly. The slight movement made his stomach go on a roller coaster ride. He had to lean forward again, willing himself not to throw up.

"Should I go help them?" Beth made a movement toward the door.

"Relax, Commando Barbie, I'm sure the *men* can take care of themselves," Stancy said over her shoulder as she sneered at the apartment. "How can people live like this?" she asked, wiping a hand over a dusty cupboard.

Anger rose up in Beth. The snide comments followed by the pretentious attitude made her want to slap the older woman. Beth's hand flew up behind Stancy, a string of insults and obscenities forming and tumbling over themselves in her mind. Gillian saw the lighted fuse heading toward the powder keg and moved to diffuse the explosion, raising her own hands up defensively.

"Well, the dead kept moving, looks like we are also... what's going on?" Hector's smile slipped off his face as he entered the apartment.

Stancy turned to the soldier and saw Beth and Gillian's posture. Her eyebrows rose. "What do you think you..."

"ENOUGH! I HAVE HAD ENOUGH!" Max shouted, slamming the butt of his rifle against the floor.

Hector immediately shushed him. Matt had fallen from the chair in shock and was now a disturbing shade of green. Gillian quickly moved to his side. Beth immediately retreated. The look in Max's eyes was one she did not want to trifle with. Bill looked anxious; Trevor was downright scared.

Max's attention was fixed on Stancy. Hector moved slowly behind the cop, tense and ready. Beth sucked in a breath and cringed as Stancy defiantly threw out hip, put her hand on it and opened her mouth.

In a deadly calm voice Max spoke. "Don't," he unclipped the clasp on his holster, "say," he slowly drew his side arm, "one," he pulled back the hammer, "fucking," he aimed the weapon at Stancy, "word." The pompous sneer died on her face, and her arm fell loosely to her side. She took a staggering step backward. Hector stood behind Max, readying to grab his arm. Beth could see the fight coming, and the outcome looked bad.

"Hey, hey—it's all good, no problems, everything is cool." Beth moved between Max and Stancy. "There is no problem here. Our only problem is outside, you know—bad zombies and all."

Max's hand shook, and the fire left his glare. He shook his head slightly and lowered his weapon. "Don't test me, woman," he growled.

Beth knew she wasn't the "woman" he was speaking to. Behind her she heard Stancy mumble.

"I don't need your help."

"Oh, shut up already! You're lucky she didn't let him shoot you," Gillian hissed.

Hector put an arm around Max and led him to the apartment door. He looked back at Beth for a moment. The look he gave was full of thanks and concern.

It was several minutes before Max and Hector returned to the apartment. In that time Gillian had taken Bill and Matt into the single bedroom. She made them both lay down. Matt lay on his side, still looking as if he might be ill. Bill lay on his back with his injured leg elevated on a couple of pillows.

While Gillian was helping the injured, Beth and Trevor were taking stock of the kitchen. The former occupants had been more interested in taking their possessions than thinking of survival, it seemed. The fridge and cupboards were still relatively stocked. They had some fruit, bread, lunchmeat and various canned items.

"We should be good for a few days." Beth smiled as Hector and Max returned.

Stancy was seated at the kitchen table. She turned her back on Max as he walked in the room. The look in his eye was murderous.

"Hey Max, want an apple?" Beth held up a shiny red apple.

"Yeah, sure," Max replied distractedly, never taking his eyes off Stancy.

Nice Shot

"Wow, you really had a bad time of it, didn't you?" Steve asked the magnified view of the zombie through the scope on the hunting rifle. Its walk was nothing more than a slow limping shuffle. The knee of one pant leg was torn and black with dried blood, the foot at the bottom was turned sideways. A trail of thick blood, tissue, and shoe pieces led back into the alley. One arm hung lower than the other. It swung as if the only thing holding it on was the torn sleeve of the jacket it was in. As Steve looked over the top of the scope the arm fell free. The sight made Steve laugh, but he admonished himself immediately. Damn it, that used to be somebody. The zombie didn't even pause or look down at the lost limb.

Steve returned to the magnified view. Half of the creature's scalp flopped on the side of its head, the ear bouncing off the ghoul's shoulder. "Did someone take a machete to you?" Steve pulled the bolt back on the rifle, locked a round into the chamber and took a deep breath. He moved the cross hairs to the thing's forehead. His finger twitched on the trigger.

The dead eyes looked up as Steve looked down. Steve paused. The thing seemed to be looking right at him. It stopped shuffling and stared. Steve studied the face. Was it sadness, remorse? "Aw crap!" Steve hissed as the zombie's teeth bared and its head leaned back.

The rifle report cracked loud in the tower. Steve knew this could attract others to the area but convinced himself that it was okay. Thinking it over, he decided the height, mixed with the sound bouncing off the buildings would make it hard for the zombies to find the place. The howl from the zombie would have brought them straight here. Still the feeling in the pit of his stomach nagged at him. He couldn't shake the feeling he had just made a mistake.

Every time one of those creatures let out that moan, several more would arrive. If they shot one, then only one or two would show up...eventually. This is what Steve told himself. "I don't care how bad you had it. You aren't going to bring your friends to the party," he said to the corpse. It lay in the street, the top of its head completely missing now, torn away by Steve's bullet. "Sorry, dude."

"Nice shot, Steve," came a voice from behind, causing Steve to jump. Turning quickly, he lowered his weapon. Relaxing slightly, he recognized the woman.

"Uh, thanks, Mrs. Johnson," he replied sheepishly. He was embarrassed about the conversation he had been having with the former undead corpse. He hoped she had not heard him.

"You still see them as people, don't you?" she asked, looking over the railing to the street below.

Drat, he thought, she had heard him. The road in front of the church and even the side roads leading to it now contained several corpses. Some of these lay over each other, some were just lone figures rotting in the street. Most of them had been put down by either Steve or Wes.

Steve shrugged. "Yeah, kinda. I mean they didn't choose to be the way they are now. Ya know."

"No, I don't guess they did," Sarah sighed. "But I don't think there is anything left of them. Anything that was human anyway." Her face grew dark. "I've seen them claw over each other to get at a child."

"I saw that for an iPod or a new phone when they were alive," Steve replied bitterly.

"Maybe, but when they got to the iPod they didn't rip it apart and try to eat it, did they?"

"Not sure, maybe a few of them," Steve tried to joke. He turned away, staring out of the bell tower. He could see the road below, but he really wasn't looking at it.

"I'm sorry, Steve. I know it bothers you…"

"Yeah, it does," he interrupted, "but you know what bothers me more?" Sarah stood quietly waiting. Years as a teacher had taught her when someone just wanted to talk, not to have her solve the problem.

"It's Wes. I've known that guy since he was like five years old. He's been through some pretty bad stuff, ya know." Once Steve started talking, he couldn't seem to stop. Sarah just stood listening and encouraging when needed.

"Even through all the crap, he has been a nice guy. He has always been there for Beth; hell, all he wants to do is go find her." Steve looked down at his hands. "He still thinks there is hope she is...not dead. The thing is... this isn't easy for him. I mean it isn't easy for any of us but he takes this hard. It seems like every time the undead show up for him to put down," Steve took a deep breath, "it seems like they are always kids. Why is it that he always has to kill the kids?" Steve rubbed his eyes. "It isn't fair. I mean, of course none of this is fair. The thing is, every time I have to take down an adult one, I feel like I am less of who I used to be." He turned back to the road. "I wonder if Beth will recognize us if... I mean *when*, we find her."

Sarah waited. When Steve did not continue, she took her cue. "Is that why you talk to them? You think you are losing your humanity? You think Wes is losing his?" She turned Steve to look at her. "Listen. There are things that we have to do now that we never thought we would. I'm not saying we can't feel, we just can't dwell."

Steve shrugged his reply. A low moan reached the tower, carried on the musty wind. Steve scanned the area for movement. A cat darted out from behind some debris. Steve followed its movements, then checked the opposite direction from where the frightened animal ran.

There she was. An older woman in a pale green housecoat was shuffling into view on torn and dirty slippers. "Oh man, she's carrying an arm. Oh, that just isn't right," Steve groaned.

"Looks like someone gave her a hand," Sarah noted. Silence rang loudly between them. Steve stared at his old teacher. She stared back, shock on her face from what she had just said. Fighting it until it hurt, Steve burst out laughing. Sarah joined in and they couldn't stop for several seconds.

Wiping tears from his eyes, Steve shook his head at his old instructor. "That was wrong on so many levels."

"I know and I'm sorry," Sarah replied, trying to keep from giggling, "sometimes it's either laugh or go crazy." They stood in easy silence for a moment until Steve began to aim his rifle at the approaching zombie. Sarah placed a hand on Steve's arm, "I'll get this one. You go down and check on Wes. He seemed rather anxious when I passed by. I think you should try to embrace his hope."

Steve looked up from the scope, "What do you mean?"

"I've seen a lot of young people go through my classrooms over the years." Sarah took over the shooter position. "Sometimes you just know." She took the rifle from Steve, checked the safety and the chamber. Steve stood waiting for her to finish. As she took aim he was reminded of her actions in the park. He wondered how she did it. He had always seen her as a very kind and caring instructor.

Desperate times, he thought. He jumped when the shot rang out. The shuffling dead woman dropped the severed arm. Her crumpled body joined it on the ground.

"Those two," Sarah said, bringing Steve back to the conversation as if nothing had happened. "Beth and Wes; you could tell. There was always something more between them." Sarah ran the bolt through its paces, loading another shell.

"What do you mean?" Steve asked.

"I mean they have been a couple forever; they just didn't know it." She turned, smiling, with that knowing look he remembered. It was the smile that encouraged him. It said you know the answer when he had a tough question.

Steve smiled back and then frowned. He shook his head, "They figured it out, right before all of this. Better late than never, I guess. I just hope it wasn't a little too late."

Sarah smiled and reassured him, "She'll recognize both of you. If I remember her correctly…She is kicking zombie ass somewhere and is wondering the same of the two of you."

"Thanks." Steve smiled. "You know," he said opening the hatch to the ladder, "If I knew you were such a badass, I don't think I would have acted up so much in class."

"Get out of here!" Sarah laughed, shaking her head, taking up the vigil in the tower. Steve returned to the lower levels. He was thinking of Beth and almost laughed as visions of her kung fu fighting zombies played out in his head. The smile evaporated from his face the moment he walked into the church and came face to face with Wes.

"How much longer are we going to hang out here?" Wes demanded.

"Listen, maybe a little while longer. There seems to be more of those things moving around today."

The look Wes gave Steve told him this was not welcome news. Looking over Wes' shoulder Steve could see their belongings were packed and ready to go. "I've been thinking about it," Wes regained Steve's attention, "and I think Beth would go to the distribution center looking for you. That is where we should start looking." He looked into Steve's eyes expectantly.

Steve's shoulders slumped. Wes had made it very clear he wanted to start looking for Beth and a way out of town. He also thought staying in the downtown area was a bad idea. Steve had countered with the fact that very few people actually lived downtown prior to the dead rising so it seemed safe enough to him. Steve also wanted to find Beth, but he also feared finding her dead or not finding her at all.

"We are going to find her," Wes stated as if he were reading Steve's mind. "We'll try the distribution center first, then your house, then mine, then school... the library...You know all the places she would go."

"All right, but not today. We need a plan." He hurried on as Wes started to argue. "A better plan than go here, then here. Let's go about this logically. Let's pick the most likely places. Then we'll figure out a way to get there and get back if we have to." The look on Wes' face was mutinous. Steve continued. "I don't think we'll easily get around, search the place, and be safe for a night. We know this place is safe, so let's use it as a base," Steve suggested.

Wes looked as if he wanted to argue. Instead he sat down and took out a notebook from his pack. "All right, where do we go first?"

Too Long

"Hey, whatcha doing?" Matt asked, looking over Beth's shoulder. She had taken a grocery list from the fridge and was making a new list on the back of it.

"I'm just trying to think where to start looking for my brother and… my boyfriend." The thought of Wes as her boyfriend was still so new and yet so right to her. Having a moment to breath had made her start to think about where they might be and if they were looking for her.

"Makes you wish you had a rendezvous place, huh?" Matt asked, sliding into the chair closest to her.

"A rendezvous place?"

"Yeah. Remember when they taught us fire safety?" The quizzical look on Beth's face told that she did not. "You know, when we were in like second grade or something?" Matt smiled. "You were supposed to talk to your family about escape routes out of the house. When everyone was safe you would meet at a tree or something."

Beth thought for a second. She remembered the poster on fire safety from years ago. "I remember, yeah. I wonder what the poster for this would look like."

"I don't even want to imagine," Matt said, although he got excited at the thought. "Hey! Maybe we should have a place. Just in case we go out and get separated," Matt suggested.

"Any ideas?" Gillian asked as she sat down across from Matt.

He shook his head solemnly, the excitement fading from his face. "I don't even know where I am."

"There was a paint store a couple of buildings down. How about we make that the place." Gillian suggested as she looked over at Beth's list. Beth chewed on the end of the pen, looking at the short list.

"Dude, that is gross. You have no idea what the people who lived here were like," Matt said, pointing at the pen.

"Hmm, you said you went to school in Ferndale. That is a pretty long way from here, but the distribution center isn't too far away," Gillian interrupted noting the look on Beth's face as she took the pen from her mouth. She looked slightly sickened. "When we go for food, we might be able to swing by and see what it looks like."

A derisive snort came from a bundle of afghans covering Stancy. Devin, on the other hand, seized the idea. "That is a perfect place to go. There will be all kinds of things there we could use. Plus we might be able to find some equipment to help clear some of the blocked roads." He spoke as he began to pace, "We should see what Hector thinks."

"How long does it take to loot a tiny apartment?" Stancy grumbled.

"It's not looting. It's called salvaging," Hector answered, coming through the door. He carried a box that was overflowing with blankets. Max follow close behind with another box full of food. He also dragged a duffel bag behind him.

"There was not much that could be salvaged over there. The bed was covered in blood, so the quilt was no good. We got some clean blankets, so everyone will be able to have their own," Max stated as he began to hand them out.

"All that time and we get a few blankets and some kiddie breakfast cereal." Stancy whined.

"We did find something for you to change into," Hector said as he threw a pair of sweatpants and a sweatshirt at her.

She gave the garments a scornful look. "Not exactly what I am used to."

Beth quickly brought the list she was making up to her face to hide her smile. She was sure there was something better available, but Max had picked out the most horrendous and stained garments available. The sweatshirt truly was awful. It was pink with a faded flower print on the front. Beth remembered her grandmother had had a similar one years ago. Stancy pulled the sweatshirt over her head, grumbling the whole time. Beth and Gillian took the time to smirk at one another.

"What's this about a list and moving vehicles?" Hector asked.

Stancy had emerged for the horrible pink collar and noticed the looks being shared around the room. She regained her smugness almost immediately. "At least I am used to finer things, unlike most," she commented. Beth allowed herself to roll her eyes before completely ignoring Stancy.

"Beth here was trying to think where her brother might be holding up. One of the places is the distribution center, you know, the one close to the highway. I was thinking maybe we could get something to move some of the blockages and get out of town," Devin stated.

"I know they have forklifts. That might do the trick; one of the bigger ones might be better. Like a wheel loader. There are a lot of them down at the distribution center. They are actually pretty easy to run." All eyes were on Beth. She beamed. "My brother works at the center. He got me a job in the office during the summers, but I liked running the forklifts. He taught me."

"Great! How far is the center from the highway?" Hector asked, excitement in his voice. Beth could see the plan coming together in his eyes.

"Not too far, about a mile or two," Devin smiled, but then the smile faltered and died.

"What?" Matt asked.

"That is a mile or two with slow moving, loud forklifts calling out to those things," Gillian noted.

"What if we loaded it on a truck and drove it there?" Matt wondered.

"You must have been top of your freaking class at stupid school," Stancy scoffed.

Beth bristled, "Wow, now that was brilliant. Someone makes a suggestion, a suggestion that has merit, and you come back with 'stupid school'? Wow, I mean, wow, you really are a wretched bit...."

"Okay, that is enough," Hector interrupted. "Matt, that was a good suggestion, plus another vehicle wouldn't go unwanted. Stancy shut up, Beth let it go." Taken aback, Beth shut her mouth. "Now tell me if there is anything there that will haul a forklift," Hector demanded.

Stancy sputtered her anger while Beth, turning slightly pink, thought about the distribution center lot. "Nothing I can think of, mostly just trucks delivering stuff. They have the bigger loaders for the trailers that are shipping containers. I don't remember anything there to haul them."

"Why can't we use the smaller ones? Ya know just load em in the back of one of the trailers," Matt inquired quietly.

Hector stood in the middle of the room, arms crossed, occasionally scratching the stubble on his cheek. Stancy sat up, about to say something, when Hector held up a hand. "I think that is a decent plan."

The room was silent as everyone looked at each other. Trevor finally asked the question on everyone's mind. "What plan?"

Beth sat up straight in her chair. "Yes, that might work. We just have to get a couple of them into the back of a trailer and take it to the highway. Oh, but how do we unload them? I mean, we'd drive them onto the truck off the loading dock, right?"

"We'd need to have a ramp of some kind with us. There has to be something there," Devin added.

Trevor looked around the room, confused. Gillian looked like she was also trying to work out what was going on. This made him feel a little better until she inquired, "That is all well and good, but does anyone here know how to drive a big rig?"

Stancy immediately looked at Beth. Eyebrows raised, she waited for the confirmation. Beth just looked back at her. She then noticed several others in the group were also waiting for her to say something. "What?" Beth shrugged, raising her hands.

"Well it is just…" Matt started. Beth looked over at him expectantly. He blushed. "Well, you seem to be able to do everything else. I guess we just expected you to be able to drive a truck as well."

"I can," came Bill's weak voice from the bedroom. "I drove a truck before I became a teacher."

Max walked over to the bedroom door. "You can barely move."

"Can't walk easily and no I can't run, but I think I can push down an accelerator."

"Well, before the whole group goes out on the mission, I think we need to do a little recon," Hector said, walking over to Max and slapping him on the shoulder. "Before that happens, Max and I have something we need to do."

What they had to do made Beth and Matt happy they weren't asked to help. They watched from the window as the two men took out the bodies from the other room, wrapped in a rug and a quilt. Beth gasped when the men reached the street. They grabbed the side of the rug and pulled, flinging the body of the girl out onto the pavement. They did the same with the quilt's occupant. The two bodies lay close to each other, their hands almost touching.

Beth met Hector at the top of the stairs, a look of confused anger on her face. "What? I'm thinking most creatures don't like the smell of their own dead. Maybe that will keep them away." He shrugged.

"Glad it's not summer," Matt said over Beth's shoulder, "then we'd be not liking the smell of their dead either."

A map of the city lay out on the coffee table. Several red Xs covered a small area around the downtown section. These were small convenience stores and a few specialty shops. All the food that had been found in the apartments was sitting on the counter behind the group in the kitchen. Several members sat at the kitchen table, playing cards. Beth looked around at the scene. If she didn't know better, she would have sworn this had the makings of a party. People playing cards and a counter full of soft drinks and snack foods. However, after living off nothing but corn chips and snack cakes, Beth was coming to the conclusion that this party sucked. Matt, on the other hand, didn't seemed fazed by the lack of choice. It made Gillian wonder if this was already his diet.

Beth lay on the lumpy old couch, watching the shadows grow longer across the ceiling. She was barely listening to the conversation that was going on around her. Matt was engaged in a debate with Trevor over what movies were better than others. Beth covered her eyes with her arm and thought, What is the point? The electricity went out two days ago, so we can't watch anything anyway. A frown creased her lips as she remembered how disappointing the apartment's books had been. She rolled onto her side, facing the back of the couch, and grumbled about the former residents' lack of literacy.

Matt had pointed out the e-reader when she had voiced her discouragement. The reader had been a godsend—until the battery died. Again, with no power, she had no escape. With a huff that no one noticed, she rolled back over to watch the room. Matt and Trevor continued to shuffle through the collected movies, making stacks of good versus bad, and a stack of what they could agree on. Over in the kitchen, Gillian was playing cards with Devin, Max, and Hector. Stancy was sleeping noisily in a chair across the room, and Bill was still recuperating in the bedroom.

Beth had been in to see him earlier and it wasn't good. His leg was swollen and hot to the touch. He had been running a fever for a couple of days now. Since the power had gone out the apartment got very cold at night, which Beth felt could not help matters. Bill continued to put on a brave face, but she could tell he was scared.

She stared at the door frame for a few more minutes, then shook her head and got up. Gillian lit a candle while Devin shuffled the cards. Matt and Trevor didn't look up as they intently discussed the merits of a science fiction movie Beth had never heard of. That was saying a lot, since Wes seemed to have seen them all and forced her to watch most of them. Wes. She wondered what he was doing right at that moment.

"I'm going out," she announced. Hector slowly put his cards down on the table and studied her. "Just to the hall and maybe down the stairs. Don't worry, I won't leave the building and I won't be seen," she defended. Hector gave her a demanding look. Beth reached behind her, pulling her gun from the waist of her jeans and waved it at him. He held his mouth as if he didn't approve, but he didn't say anything.

"You want some company?" Matt asked eagerly.

Beth tried to smile, but it came out more like a grimace. "Um no, sorry I …just need a few minutes alone."

Matt's face fell a bit, then he shrugged and grabbed a truly awful movie from the pile. "Now this is a classic." Trevor groaned.

Stancy gave a snorting grunt when Beth turned the deadbolt. Passing through the door, Beth pulled it closed slowly and quietly. She didn't want to wake Stancy, which would annoy everyone else. The silence in the hall pressed in on her ears. Beth stood for a long moment listening to nothing, enjoying the solitude. Moving quietly down the hall, she thought about how long it had been since she had been alone. She loved being with Wes and hanging out with her brother, but she treasured the time she could just listen to the quiet and enjoy a good book.

Her feet carried her to the end of the hall without her even noticing. Standing at the door that led to the staircase, she realized her need to leave the apartment was now fighting with her desire to return to it. The stairwell was already dark; the fading sunlight coming from the window behind her blazed deep orange. Slowly she pushed the door open and stood listening. Nothing, not a sound, save for her own breathing.

Stop being scared of your own shadow, she berated herself, yet did not take a single step forward. Fine—go forward or listen to Matt discuss the finer plot points of *Squirm* again." She shuddered, yet a slight smile played on her lips. Beth carefully made her way down the flight of stairs to the dance studio.

Pushing the door open, her eyes immediately found the brownish red stain on the floor. Skirting the spot, she moved toward the doors in the back of the room. Beth knew she had seen some books back there. She just hoped they were not all dance books. The door opened with a quiet squeak, revealing little of the space inside to the fading light. She moved into the door frame and stopped, her body blocking what little light she had. This wasn't going to work. Making her way back to the middle of the room, she slid down the mirrored wall.

How long had they been here already? Was it just a week? Had it been more? She tried to remember what day it was. It all started on a Sunday, right? She counted off the days. It had been about two weeks; they had been in that cramped apartment for about two weeks. Why did they all have to be in that one, single bedroom apartment? She really didn't see how it was safer. There was more danger of them killing each other at this point than the undead getting in.

They would need to leave soon anyway. The food was running out. Maybe they could finally start looking for Steve and Wes. She punched the floor. It thudded satisfyingly. She drummed out a familiar beat for a few seconds. Smiling, she applauded her performance in her head.

A creak outside the door caught her attention. She slipped a hand around her back, pulling her gun. Pulling back the slide, she made sure the weapon was ready to fire. We would have heard them break in, her mind reassured her. Then another voice in her head that sounded a lot like Wes' countered, Unless they were already here, and we didn't find them.

"But we have been here, what was it? Two weeks," she replied out loud. Could have found a way in we missed or been stuck in a closet, the Wes voice countered.

"Stop it," she muttered.

The door to the studio slowly opened. Beth did not raise the gun, thinking it had to be Matt or Hector coming to look for her. Matt, most likely, she thought.

The hand that came around the door to grasp the side was not Matt's or Hector's. Beth used the wall for leverage to push herself to a standing position, raising the gun to eye level as she did. The noise was sure to attract others. If this one found a way in, what would stop them? The greenish-grey hand held the door with a torn-away finger next to a whole one with a brilliant diamond ring. Beth did not move, holding her breath, waiting for a clear shot. The hand did not move.

Anger began to rise up. "If this is someone's idea of a joke, I might still shoot you," she hissed. The sound of her voice, as hushed as it was, caused the hand to move. It curled around the edge, followed by a sleeveless grey arm. A leg clad in a ballet slipper and tights came into view. The light was fading fast as the head appeared around the door.

The woman would have been middle-aged. Her long graying hair was falling out of the tight bun that was held loosely now on the back of the creature's head. What Beth noticed was the hair had literally fallen out of the bun and hung with a part of the scalp still attached.

The creature spotted Beth. The lips withdrew in an angry sneer revealing brown broken teeth. It groaned as it raised its wasted thin arms. It would have been comical as the zombie lurched across the room. Its arms outstretched, it screeched as it moved. Beth pulled the hammer back on the gun. She hesitated then let it return. Quickly she flipped the safety back on. Decision made, she turned the weapon around, holding it by the barrel. The room seemed to dissolve around her as Beth quickly closed the distance between herself and the ghoul. She was barely aware of more movement at the door. She would deal with that after she took care of this one.

Beth swatted the arms away. With all the strength she could muster she brought the butt of the gun down on the zombie's head. It staggered for a moment. Several of Beth's hairs parted from her head, caught in the prongs of the diamond ring. Beth lunged sideways, but her legs were caught in the dead woman's. Crashing to the floor, Beth was stunned. Pain swirled through the side of her head. She felt nausea swell as she blinked repeatedly, trying to clear the stars from her vision.

She was aware, through her pain, that the ghoul couldn't be far away. Her vision swam before her. Unstable and dizzy, Beth tried to regain her feet. Falling over again, she scrambled along the floor, trying to get a little distance between her and the dancer of death. Several confused and muted grunts and thumps met her ears. Through the pain and darkness, she made out at least three pairs of legs. It was then she realized she had lost track of her gun. Something heavy fell close by her.

A pair of strong hands grabbed Beth's shoulders. She kicked at the legs in front of her. She opened her mouth to scream for help. A rough hand covered it, "Shh, shh, it's ok!" Devin grunted through Beth's impacts with his shins. She could make out Hector's shoulders silhouetted against the door frame. His foot was raised for a second. A heavy thump and crunch announced the end of the zombie's skull.

"What the hell were you thinking?" Hector demanded, "Why didn't you just shoot her?"

"I thought it would draw more... oh God, I'm gonna puke." Beth had risen to her feet with Devin's help. The pain in her head became overwhelming, and mixed with the stench of the corpse, her lunch threatened to escape. Black tunnels appeared on the outside of her vision, getting steadily larger. "I think... I... might..." Beth staggered, and Devin caught her.

Hector stared at the unconscious young woman. "She will either be the best asset we have or die trying." He grabbed her feet, and Devin grunted his agreement. The two men carried her up the stairs.

"We better do another search of this place," Devin said when they reached the top. Gillian was hurrying down the hall. "Any ideas where it came from?" he asked.

Beth stirred and her eyes fluttered. The world spun as she tried to see, so she decided not to. Gillian was looking at the bruise on the side of Beth's head. Beth kept her eyes closed but was able to answer Gillian's questions as Hector watched.

"We missed something. Let's barricade the top of the stairs and search this place top to bottom tomorrow," he whispered, and Beth nodded, immediately regretting it.

Hope

"We've been here for two freaking weeks, man! Beth is out there! We need to get out of this place and find her!" Wes punched his pack.

"Yeah, I know. I keep waiting for her to come busting through that door and give me an earful," Steve muttered, burying his face in his hands. He rubbed his eyes with his palms. He knew what was coming. They'd had this conversation at least three times in the last two days. Steve had lost count on the times in the last week.

"So, what are you saying; we should continue to hang out and just wait to see if she finds us? Dude, I can't do that. I, we—*we* seriously need to get out there and find her."

"Wes, I know!" Steve yelled. Looking around, he saw several people staring at them. "We need to get out of here, I know this." He lowered his voice. "The thing is, we need a plan. We need a base of operations, so we need this place."

"Yes, we do, but I... you're gonna be pissed." Wes lowered his voice. Steve turned questioningly to him. "I found a way out. I've been out a few times. I...found a few things. I have them hidden in one of the classrooms at the far end of the hall." Wes was speaking so low he was almost just moving his lips without sound by the end. He glanced around nervously as he spoke.

Steve gaped him. Millions of thoughts fought for dominance: anger, pride in his friend, disbelief that he would sneak out without telling him. "What the fu...."

Wes cut in. "Listen! I don't trust this place. I want to be able to get away if we have to, and I don't want to be unprepared. "I know you and Mike think this place is safe, protected, but I don't see it. I spend time in that tower too. I see how many more of them show up every day. Like I said, we need to be prepared."

"I don't remember you being a Boy Scout."

"Not a Boy Scout, but I did go to camp two years in a row." Wes smiled. "You learn to be resourceful."

"Yeah, I remember. You called Beth every day," Steve shot back, taking the smile from Wes' face.

"I just wanted to make sure she was okay. You know, without me," Wes grumbled.

"Happiest two weeks of her life, as I remember it," Steve shrugged. Noting the look on Wes' face he quickly amended, "Dude, I'm kidding, she waited for your calls. She was bored out of her mind without you around."

"She's...I need to find her."

"We have to. She's my sister, you know."

"I know." Wes nodded to Steve. "It's just, we need to start thinking of where to look. I can cover a few blocks in each direction every day. You just need to cover for me," Wes suggested.

"We're not prisoners here. We can both..." Steve stopped as a man slowly walked by their pew.

"Yeah, I don't know. When we first got here, I would have believed you. Now... not so much." Wes followed the shuffling man with his eyes. "I think the sooner we leave, the better off we are going to be."

Steve raised his eyebrows to this statement. "Seriously, a city of the undead is safer than here?"

"I know what they are capable of; "the dead you know." I know what they want from me. People? Not so much." Wes shrugged. "It's just the people *here*. They fear us, but they..."

"They also expect us to be their protectors. Yeah, I know. I don't want to be responsible for them, but I also can't just leave them."

"Um...have you met our old teacher?" Wes asked.

"Yeah, glad she never had a club in class." Steve laughed, pulling Wes into a headlock.

"Get off, you dumb jock." Wes pushed Steve's arm off. "Come on, let's figure out how to find her."

***

A cold wind blew through Steve's hair as he stood in the tower. The planning he and Wes had done earlier that day filled him with a small burning idea. They had put together some of the most likely places Beth might have gone. He had relieved Wes a few hours ago. Now armed with a notebook, a flashlight, and his rifle, Steve leaned against the rail, going over the notes they had come up with. The first place they were going to look was their houses. Now all they had to do was find a working car, navigate a city of zombies, get back home, search, and make it back before they were missed if they didn't find her. Easy. right? Steve looked up and down the street, hoping to see a usable vehicle. He was sure the buses surrounding the front were still in working order. He also knew that was not an option. There were a few cars up the road, not far away. One was half buried in the front of a building. Let's not take that one, he thought, there's the one with the zombie in it. No, that ran out of gas, stupid. He smacked himself in the forehead. Looking past the wreck in the building, he noticed a powder blue VW Beetle just beyond it. Checking through the rifle scope, he studied the car. In the reddish yellow glow of the streetlight it looked to be in decent shape.

Movement just past the bug grabbed his attention. He adjusted his gaze. Nothing moved. Maybe it was an animal, or some more of that damn paper blowing around. He returned his attention to the car. Suddenly two figures emerged from the darkness, heading straight to the Beetle. Steve held his breath. They were moving too fast to be zombies. Their heads looked too big as they turned this way and that, searching the area. Steve couldn't understand what he was seeing. Their heads were huge. They kept turning, looking in all directions as they sprinted to the car. Steve noticed that one sprinted while the other lumbered. The faster of the two was short and slight, the other much larger and taller. The larger of the two tried the door. It didn't open. The man, Steve assumed by the large build, raised a crowbar to smash the window, but was stopped by the smaller one. There was something in the way they moved that made Steve think this was a woman. She shook her head, pointing down the road.

She was pointing to the church and the barricade. They were alive, that was for sure. Moving further into the light, Steve saw they both were dressed in all black and were wearing what looked like full motorcycle helmets.

That explained the heads. Last thing they needed was aliens *and* zombies. He laughed. Steve adjusted the sights on the scope. Now he could tell they were dressed in leather. Leather from head to foot: Boots, gloves, pants, and jackets. Good protection, Steve thought. Not the most comfortable, but still He shrugged, glad for them it wasn't any warmer.

A thought struck him, causing hope to balloon in his chest. This might be Beth! He watched the pair for a few seconds. He was sure it was a guy and a girl. The way the big one moved, that was defiantly a dude, a really, really big dude. How many cows died to make that jacket? Looking over the scope, he watched the figure running down the street. Returning to the scope, he focused on the big man's companion. This was a girl, Steve was sure of it, a girl about Beth's size. Beth is smart, she'd think about ways to keep from getting bit, Steve told himself.

Then another thought made his blood run cold. What if one of them were bit? If Steve let them in and they infected anyone, it would be his fault. It would also be up to him to "take care of them" if something did happen.

The two cautiously looked up and down the empty street. The girl moved forward, but the man stopped her. He pointed at the front of the church, then up at the tower.

"Yeah, dude, we're here. So, what do you want to do about it?" Steve murmured. He watched the silent argument going on several feet below. The girl wanted to get to the church, the man wanted to keep moving. Steve could almost hear the frustration between the two in their violent gestures toward the church and up the street.

Steve laughed as the big man's shoulders slumped in defeat. The girl had won the fight and they were heading slowly to the front doors. Steve took out his flashlight. He signaled the guard at the front. Light hit the tower, letting Steve know the other guard had been watching this transpire from his vantage point. The guard below used his light to illuminate the small gap between the buses. The two froze for a moment. "Come on, come on, move." Steve hissed.

The girl grabbed the man, pulling him toward the gap. He moved, but then he slipped off the curb. He grabbed at a street sign to steady himself. Unfortunately, this sign had been hit by the car they were hiding behind. The post gave out, crashing loudly to the ground. The man stood with his gloved hands on his helmet. The girl grabbed his arm, pulling him. She suddenly froze.

The low moan started. This moan was joined by another, then another. Like wolves across the mountains the howl of the dead began to echo through the city. Steve's blood ran cold. He could see the pair in the street, heads swiveling this way and that, trying to see where the sound was coming from.

From his vantage point in the tower Steve could see the source. It was everywhere. Zombies were flooding down every street. They seemed endless. "Don't stop! Move! They are coming…the zombies are coming," he shouted down. Steve waved his light all over the gap.

The girl could have easily outstripped the large man, but she stayed close, urging him forward. A zombie lunged out of a doorway. The girl swung her weapon, smashing the attacker's skull. She pushed on the back of the big man.

Reaching the buses, it was the man's turn to push the girl. He grabbed her by the shoulders nearly throwing her through. She was through easily. The man, on the other hand, had a little more trouble.

"Oh crap! He's stuck!" Steve targeted the closest undead. The big man struggled.

A crack of a rifle and a shambler fell motionless. The one behind it stumbled over and onto the corpse. Steve fired another round. Below him the girl was pulling on the increasingly panicked man. The bald front door guard ran to help. He tried to pull on the big man with one hand as he fired past him with his rifle in the other, using the stuck man's shoulder to steady it.

The gun was thrust into the hands of the girl, whose crowbar clattered to the ground. The two men struggled to get into the compound. Steve fired shot after shot until his rifle clicked empty. He reached down for more ammo.

Another figure had joined the tug of war between the buses and the large biker, it was Wes. This did not surprise Steve in the least. What did was the rifle report next to him. He hadn't noticed when Sarah joined him in the tower. Quickly Steve reloaded. His fire joined hers, trying to thin the crowd.

"There's no end to them!" Sarah cried, adding another body to the growing wall between the mass of undead and the stuck man.

In his mind Steve heard a sound like a cork flying free from a champagne bottle. The big man stumbled free from the passage. He collapsed to the ground, half-crawling, half-dragged by several of the church survivors who had finally come out to help.

A pew was thrown over the opening, then another followed. Steve and Sarah continued to fire into the throng. After several minutes Sarah put her hand out to stop Steve's volleys. The group below had retreated into the church. The door guard had hidden himself beside the stairs. "Give it some time. Let them forget why they are here," Sarah muttered. Steve became aware of the sweet on his face and the ringing in his ears.

Several zombies tried to look into the windows of the buses. Their hands clawed and grabbed at the glass. Angry groans and pounding met Steve's ears even through the ringing. Several of the large vehicles rocked a little as the undead beat against them.

"Shhhh. If they can't hear or see us, they might go away," Sarah whispered, more to herself than to Steve. He watched. It did seem to him that many of the zombies had already lost interest in the area. They were no longer pouring into the street, but they weren't in a huge hurry to leave it either. The ones closest to the busses, the ones that had seen the living, were still very agitated. They were pacing back and forth or banging on the buses. Steve knew they were trying to see where their prey had disappeared to.

"Wonder where they were holed up, and why they left," Steve whispered.

"Why don't you go and ask?"

"Um..."

Sarah studied him for a moment. "What if it is Beth?" she finally asked.

"Yeah, and what if it isn't?" Steve muttered.

"Go!" Sarah ordered.

Steve smiled. Leaning over, he gave her a peck on the cheek, then headed for the ladder. He had already made his way down when he started to get excited. That was definitely a girl with the big guy, definitely. She was about Beth's size. He shook the thought, trying not to get his hopes up. No, it couldn't be her. Beth wouldn't carry a crowbar; she would get something stronger. Dad had taught them to shoot. Then again—he burst into the hall at a jog—she was definitely leading the guy and taking charge, which was just like her.

Hope swelled in his chest, carrying him, forcing his feet to move him faster down the hall. Stopping at the door into the church, he tried to calm himself. He steeled his nerves, pushed the door open, and walked into the open room. He made his way to the small group of people surrounding the two newcomers.

The large biker couldn't be missed, with his long hair and beard, braided and graying. His face was shining with sweat and relief. Beside him was a girl. She had her back to him, but Steve's heart sank. She had reddish-brown straight hair. He knew it wasn't Beth's brown curls. She turned to face him. She was immediately taken aback by the look on his face.

Trying to recover from the disappointment, Steve tried to smile at the pair saying, "Hey." Steve grimaced, thinking to himself, what, you see a pretty girl around your age and you turn into a dork?

"Um, hi, thanks for your help." The girl held out her gloved hand. Her face was shining from the run, but her green eyes were bright and alert, taking in her surroundings. She looked at Steve with mild dislike, a look that increased as her hand stayed extended and empty.

Out of the corner of his eye Steve could see Wes cover his eyes with one hand, shaking his head. Steve silently questioned him with a raise of his eyebrows. The gesture wasn't missed by the new girl.

"I'm Kate, and this is Bear." She gestured to the biker.

"Hello Kate, Mr. Bear, my name is We,s and this is Steve. He was covering you from the bell tower." Wes spoke up, gesturing to Steve while shaking Kate's extended hand.

"Steve…you the guy shooting? Man, thank you. You rock. And there's no reason for that Mister stuff. Bear is just fine," Bear responded, grabbing Steve's hand and shaking it vigorously.

"Bear, huh?" Steve smiled, taking in the man in front of him. The name definitely fit. Bear was about 6'4, barrel-chested and hairy as a Wookie.

"My name is Marvin Steeks, but the guys in the club just started callin' me Bear. Well, her dad mostly," he motioned to Kate.

"Bear is a mechanic and he and my Dad just got along. Mostly because Dad liked to work on cars in his spare time and Bear liked to help. Weird for an accountant, but so was the bike." She smiled. "Dad was weird like that."

"Helluva guy." Bear's arm was around Kate now. He eyed Steve like a father whose daughter was about to go out on a date.

"Have you run across anyone else?" Wes asked hopefully.

Bear and Kate exchanged a look. "We…we were with a couple of other people until yesterday. Met them up at the library. They didn't make it out of that place." Bear muttered.

Wes slumped into the pew next to him. "Was one a girl about my age, with brown hair?" Wes asked into his hands.

"No. A middle-aged man, an older woman, and," Kate's voice cracked, "a little boy." Relief and sorrow crashed over both Steve and Wes.

Plan

"What the hell was that?" Beth asked as the noise of the howl began to die down.

"Keep it down, and stay away from the windows," Hector hissed, tiptoeing into the room. "The street is filled with them. They are all heading into town."

Matt eased his way over to the window to peek over the sill. The road was covered with the undead, moving slowly, but with a kind of propose. Beth glanced out the window and thought it looked like a sea of people—a parade, in a way. Then she made out the state of them. Bloody, broken and horrid. She closed her eyes, but she could still see them.

Turning away, she looked around for anything to clear the vision from her mind. On the table was a magazine with a beautiful ship on the cover. She scooped it up and began flipping through the pictures of gorgeous places and happy people. After several minutes Beth began to get lost in an article about Mexican pyramids.

"Seriously?" Matt whistled as he pressed both hands against the grimy window.

Beth glanced up at Matt, closing the magazine. She looked at the cover and wondered if the cruise ship sailing the beautiful clear blue waters might still be out there. The idea appealed to her: a huge floating palace with food, medicine, and a means to stay away from land for a prolonged period of time. For a moment she closed her eyes and felt the warmth of the sun on her face. She was on the deck of the cruise ship. Wes was laying on the deck chair next to her, and Steve was calling them from the diving board, about to do a belly flop into the pool. A smile broke over her face. Her thoughts were again interrupted by Matt.

"Are there really that many? I mean, yeah, I know they are with a circus and all, but why do they always appear?"

Matt now had Devin and Gillian's attention. Opening her eyes to reveal the dirty small apartment, Beth sighed, "Matt what are you talking about?"

"Come take a look."

Beth joined Matt at the window. "So? What's the deal?" she asked.

Matt pointed to a lone figure wandering slowly down the now-deserted street. The grease paint was cracked and streaked, the baggy pants stained with blood. The big red floppy shoes made the already uncoordinated corpse even more unsteady. Behind the clown trailed several strings holding the remnants of red, yellow, green and blue balloons, long since popped.

"I mean, in every zombie movie there is a clown, but I just thought that was because clowns were creepy enough to begin with," Matt explained.

"Yeah, Wes liked...likes...well, I don't know if he still...anyway—" Beth shook her head, frustrated, "like you said, why is there always a clown? Who would get one for a party? It'd scare kids."

"Well I think people fear clowns because they are a representation of death." Matt shrugged, still watching the slow progression of the undead clown down the street. Turning from the window, he noticed all the confused faces staring at him.

Beth broke the silence, "What the hell are you talking about?"

Matt looked around the room, waiting for someone to back him up. When none of the expressions changed Matt took a deep breath and began to explain, in a tone as if explaining that two times two equaled four.

"Well let's look at the general appearance of the clown. First is the white pallor. The lips are generally red and larger than normal. The nose also is bulbous and red. Generally, they have a look of bloat and the hair is wild. Sometimes they wear gloves that make their hands look huge."

"You had a bad experience at the circus when you were a kid, didn't you?" Beth asked, pinching the bridge of her nose and shaking her head.

"Yeah, but that isn't it. Popcorn and too much cotton candy; it wasn't pretty. Anyway, the white face is very corpselike. The lips start to recede as the corpse starts to decompose. Gases build up in the body, causing the torso to distend until it eventually ruptures."

Beth wore an expression of disgust.

"What?" Matt asked her, confused. "The gases created by decomposition have been known to raise a body that has been weighed down with a 200lb weight from the bottom of a lake."

"Why do you know this?"

"Anyway, the hair and nails are rumored to keep growing after death, but it actually is the skin of the scalp and hands receding from decomposition. That is why the clown's hair and hands look the way they do."

"So why do people have them at the circus and parties to make them laugh? And seriously, why do you know this?' Beth asked, torn between amusement and slight concern at his mental state.

"I think people came up with the clown as a way to deal with death. To make it less scary. People feared death and a corpse. So they came up with the clown. A walking corpse that couldn't hurt them but would make them laugh."

"Well I don't find these walking corpses funny and they sure don't make me laugh," Beth grumbled.

Matt turned back to the window. The clown corpse was almost even with the window. It stopped turning its head to look up at Matt. He backed away, hoping he had not been seen. "Yeah I know what you mean."

Beth looked back down at the gleaming white ship on the magazine cover. She wondered if she would ever see the ocean again.

"Right, after that, um informative and truly disturbing exercise, lets discuss this plan to get the hell out of dodge," Hector said.

"First thing on our list needs to be provisions. There isn't much here and we have no idea when we will find someplace to restock." Devin explained.

Beth put down her magazine and picked up the hand-drawn map she had made from memory of the distribution center. "There is a grocery store on the way to the center. We could stop on our way back," she said hopefully.

"Sorry, but I think food has to be our first priority." Devin smiled apologetically at her.

Beth sat frustrated. She had wanted to leave to search for Steve and Wes hours ago. She knew Devin was right, they needed food, but that didn't make her feel any better. If they went to the grocery first, they may not have time to go to the center. If they didn't make it there soon Steve might not be there. Beth opened her mouth to protest but Hector held up a hand to stop her.

"Beth, I know you want to look for your brother and your friend, I understand that. But we have to plan as if we aren't going to find them. We need to have food. If we get there and the place is too dangerous, we will have to make other plans to get out of town." Beth began to speak, but Hector talked over her. "No matter what, we will need to eat. Look at it this way. Your brother is a football player, right?" Beth nodded. "He will be happy if we have something to eat when we find him."

"He is always hungry," Beth conceded.

Hector took this as her agreement to go to the grocery first and put off the center for later. "Okay, then tomorrow I'll take Beth, Devin and…" Matt hopped in his seat, hand in the air, "…Matt to go and check out the grocery store. Max, I need you to stay here to keep this place secure."

"What about me? I can help," Gillian demanded.

"Wait! What do you mean, tomorrow?" Beth stood up, shouting.

"Calm down. It is too late and too dangerous to go out there right now." Beth protested but Hector continued, "I don't want to be out and about when it gets dark. We will plan this out and leave early in the morning."

"Fine! Then we might have time to go to the center afterwards then," Beth shot at Hector.

Gillian slowly stood in between them. "I think that is fair. So tomorrow morning, Beth, Hector, Devin, Matt and I will head out to the store and, time permitting, check out the distribution center." Hector did not look pleased by this compromise.

Matt did a quick count in his head and noted a problem. Beth seemed to come to the realization at the same time because they both began to talk at the same time.

"Not good, not good."

"No, we need another."

"Seriously, that is uncool."

"Trevor or Max needs to come."

Holding up his hands, trying to calm the two teens, Hector loudly asked, "What? Wait, what is the issue?"

"Go on, tell him!" Matt urged Beth.

Beth spoke up. "We have to do this in teams. Two people to a team, and we stick together. Nobody goes off by themselves."

Hector looked at Beth, amused. "Good plan. Seems like you are pretty sure of this."

"Seriously, dude? You haven't watched too many movies, have you?" Matt questioned.

Beth looked back at the man. "Common sense. If we go off by ourselves and then one of us gets bit— we don't tell the others because we don't want to be killed or left behind, so we hide it."

Matt took up the explanation, "Of course, no one notices that we keep getting sicker and sicker until we inevitably attack the others..."

"So we stick together, and that way no one gets jumped and no one gets bit, right?" The others stared at Beth. "That is what happens in all the movies," she shrugged.

"All right, that makes sense to me," Gillian agreed.

"I'm with the smart one," Matt smiled, putting an arm around Beth's shoulder.

"No, you are with me," Hector stated.

Matt's arm dropped from Beth's shoulder.

"Beth, you are with Gillian, Devin with Trevor." Hector continued.

"What is with the splitting it up girls and boys?" Gillian asked, offended.

"Fine. Beth can go with Trevor and you and Devin can stay in the truck."

Devin and Gillian began to protest loudly, until Hector offered to leave everyone behind. "Listen! I want two people in the truck. One driving, one acting as a lookout. I want one person to push the cart and the other to cover them. Beth and I have some weapons training. Matt, Gillian, Devin and Trevor have no training. So that is why I chose who I chose. Questions?"

"No. I think I would rather go with Beth than a grump like you," Gillian teased. Matt still looked slightly disappointed.

"Um, why isn't Max going?" Trevor ventured.

"Max needs to stay here to keep our home base safe. No offence to Bill or Stancy," he gave a derisive sniff, "but I want someone here who knows how to handle a gun."

Frustrated by the delay in leaving, Beth spent the rest of the evening rummaging through various household items. She was trying to determine what would make a decent weapon by testing their weight and durability. So far, a brass lamp and a table leg were the most promising. When questioned why she was bothering, Beth replied that clubs didn't run out of ammo and never needed reloading. That fact no one argued with, as Beth swung another sturdy item with ferocity.

Explanations

Steve watched Kate cross the room. She had changed out of her leathers and was now wearing a blue polo shirt and jeans. Steve thought the jeans fit her very well. He let his eyes wander over her, from her dark hair to her white sneakers. He wondered where she had found the shoes until he saw her swing a pack off her shoulder, dropping it next to her boots. Now he remembered that pack. He realized he was staring and looked away quickly as she turned around. She had caught him.

"What?" she demanded.

"Huh?" was his reply.

"What? You were watching me!" She eyed him suspiciously.

"What? No I wasn't." His voice cracked with guilt. "I mean, I was, but it wasn't…well, I mean…"

She fixed him with a glare. "What were you looking at?" Her hands were on her hips and she was looking straight into his eyes. He noticed that her eyes were as blue as her shirt. He lost himself in her eyes for a moment, then he noticed she was talking.

"You're doing it again!" she growled.

"Sorry, what?" Steve cringed at her tone. He looked at her knitted brows, her eyes flashed dangerously at him, her straight nose flared with anger and her perfect lips in a frown. He stared at those lips, wondering what they would feel like to kiss.

"Damn it! Knock it off," she yelled.

"Oh God, I'm sorry. I just…I was just…," he stumbled.

"What! What were you just doing? Ever since I got here you have been watching me. Every time I turn around you're hovering, watching everything I do. It's like you are keeping an eye on me. You think I got bit out there?" She became, if possible, even madder. "Or you think I'm going to steal something?" She advanced on him, finishing her point by poking him in the chest.

"Ow! Jeez, relax! That is not what I think," he shot back, firing up to match her anger.

"Then, what? What the hell is so wrong with what I am doing that you have to keep such a close eye on me?" Kate spat.

"Paranoid, much?" Steve sarcastically responded.

"I've been here for three like hours and every time I turn around, you're spying on me. No one else seems to have a problem with me. Your buddy barely even looks my way, so what the hell is your problem?" She was right up in his face now. "What? So what is it?" she demanded. "Why are you always watching me?"

Steve was starting to get angry at her by this point. Pretty or not, she was yelling at him, poking him, and accusing him of spying on her. "Now wait just a damn minute," he shot back. "I am not spying on you!"

"So what is it? You just checking me out?" she scoffed.

Steve's head swam. She didn't think he was... "Well, as a matter of fact I was, but now that I see you up close, you're really not that attractive," Steve threw back at her.

She stepped back, looking stunned. "Wait, what?"

Steve was really pissed now. "What the hell did you think?" It was his turn to growl.

Kate backed up further and quietly responded, "I thought, well, you are always with that younger guy, and you aren't related and he's kinda feminine, so, well, I thought..."

Now it was Steve's turn to be stunned. "Yeah I'm always with Wes. I grew up with him around. He may look frail but he is tough, and for your information, little miss perceptive," he put extra sarcasm on that last part, "Wes happens to be completely in love with my sister." Steve was breathing hard, like he had run a mile. Never had he been thought of as anything but the football hero, but here this girl is accusing him of being gay and on top of that... she had the nerve not to be his sister, when he so wanted her to be Beth. He let out a shout and punched the top of the pew.

"Oh, I'm... oh." Kate continued to back away, her face was glowing red. "I'm gonna go," she mumbled, heading toward the door. Reaching for the handle Kate jumped back in surprise as the door swung open. Wes nearly collided with her.

"You two done shouting?" he asked.

Kate closed her eyes and groaned, "Oh, could you hear us?"

"You were loud enough to wake the dead. Oh, wait, too late," Wes laughed.

She stared at him, and behind her, Steve laughed. Kate excused herself and hurried past Wes. As soon as she was gone Steve exploded. "You won't believe what she thought!"

"Thought we were gay, huh?" Wes replied. Steve gawked at him. "Hey, it isn't the first time someone thought that of me." Wes shrugged.

Steve closed his eyes, shaking his head. This had never occurred to him, as he knew Wes always had feelings for Beth. Opening his eyes, he looked at Wes and a smirk crossed his face, "Might be the pretty hair...you stinky hippy."

Wes spun around, anger boiling up inside him, until he saw the grin on Steve's face. He tried to hold onto angry tone. "I may have pretty hair, but I never put my hands under another dude's ass."

Steve was confused, then it hit him. "He is the center, and I am waiting to grab the ball."

Wes smirked. "Not helping your cause, dude." They stared at each other until they both burst out laughing.

"I've been talking with Bear," Wes explained, trying to catch his breath. "You should cut Kate a break, man. They have had it really rough. She saw her Dad get killed, she almost died like three times. If she is a little paranoid...well, they have had a few problems with other survivors."

Steve suddenly understood what Wes meant. Kate was very pretty. Seriously? he thought. With everything going on, all the people dying, why do the sickos get to live? Steve looked up at the cross above the door. "Don't we have enough to worry about?" he asked. Wes followed Steve's gaze, and agreed.

Execution

Morning broke to find Beth up and ready to move. She had snuck into the one bathroom before anyone else was even awake. She decided to get a quick shower since she was the first one up. She hoped to finally get some hot water, a luxury she had not had since they had arrived. There were so many other people in the apartment, it seemed she was always waiting to get clean. Hot water didn't last even if you were the second person in. She then remembered that the lack of power made any hot water impossible. Taking a deep breath, she jumped into the frigid water.

After hurrying through the icy shower, Beth quickly toweled off and frowned at her clothes. She had been wearing the same thing for days. It seemed counterproductive to put them back on after a shower. The raised voices in the other room changed her mind, urging her to dress quickly. Beth was determined to head off any more delays. Today was the day she was going to find Steve and hopefully Wes.

"You think I am leaving here to go run around out there with all those... Those *things*. Oh, hell no. That is not happening," Stancy screamed.

"It has already been established that you are to stay here with Bill and Max," Hector replied calmly rubbing his temples.

Beth could see by the look on Max's face. She knew he would rather be facing an army of undead than stay behind with Stancy. Nervously Beth watched as he flipped the safety on and off his rifle.

"You know, maybe I should stay behind instead," Trevor offered.

Beth's wet hair slapped across her face as her head snapped around to glare at Trevor. They had a plan. This was all agreed upon last night. Her frustration was building quickly. She was positive Steve and Wes were waiting for her right now and these people were keeping her from finding them. She moved quickly through the room, collecting her things.

"No, I don't think that is the best idea," Devin commented. "I would like you to drive. You have shown you know how to get around town, and we may need to find some alternate routes back here."

Beth was angrily stuffing her hand-drawn maps and lists into her bag when a hand lightly touched her shoulder. She turned quickly to face whoever was about to stop her. Gillian took a step back, seeing the determination and anger in the younger woman's eyes. "We are going. I promise. This is a minor delay. Hector will get it straightened out."

"I am tired of waiting. Steve is at the center, I know it. I need to find my brother!" Beth grabbed Gillian by the shoulders. She stared into her eyes, trying to make her understand.

Gillian calmly pulled Beth's hands from her, taking them in hers. "We need you. Give it ten minutes, and if we are not heading out the door," Gillian took a deep breath, "then you and I will go."

"Hey, you aren't leaving me," Matt piped up from beside Beth. Beth smiled her thanks at the two of them. Beth liked Gillian; she felt they were becoming friends. Matt on the other hand, was annoying, immature, and goofy, qualities that endeared him to her and made her want to protect him. It was something she had seen Gillian doing time and again. No, she couldn't leave her friends behind. She knew she needed them. Forcing herself to calm down, Beth listened to the argument that continued behind her.

"Oh, so I get stuck with the gimp? I want a gun. I am not going to stay here undefended, and that fairy can't walk, and I doubt he knows how to shoot. The only thing he knows how to do…"

"You will have a gun, and you will watch your mouth," Hector stated with finality that even Stancy could not argue with. "As I have told you, Max will be here as well. You and Bill will be fine."

"Great left behind with a gimp and a crazy man." Stancy grumbled as she took the gun from Hector. He held onto the butt of the gun for a second. She pulled the barrel, then stopped to look at him with a confused yet defiant glare.

"You are not well liked. You may want to check some of that attitude," he responded to her gaze.

A brief second of fear crossed Stancy's face, but it was quickly replaced by her normal arrogance. "A lot of people resent their *superiors*."

Hector shook his head, walking toward the door.

"I would much rather come with you guys than stay here." Bill's voice called from the bedroom.

"Sorry Bill, we need you to rest that leg." Turning to the others, Hector called. "Okay, people. We are leaving in ten minutes. Stancy, Max, you will stay here with Bill. Everyone else will have a weapon assigned to them, a firearm and a club-type weapon. I want to thank Beth for finding several suitable options." Hector gave a nod to Beth.

Suddenly the apartment was alive with movement as everyone got ready to leave. Matt and Gillian had a disagreement about the types and size of the weapons he would be using. Trevor made several more attempts to stay behind while Max remained silent. Hector stepped closer to the policeman. "I'm sorry, trooper. I would rather have you on this mission, but you are our best hope to hold this place if trouble breaks out." Max nodded his understanding.

Beth stood next to Hector, getting more anxious to leave by the second. She checked in on Bill, double-checked her weapons and pack, then bounced on the balls of her feet near the door. Fifteen minutes later found those who were going piled into the armored car. Beth had never been so excited to be going to a grocery store in her life. She couldn't help but smile as they headed down the alley. Trevor was behind the wheel, with Devin navigating. She knew she was going to see her brother soon.

Finding several roads blocked by debris and abandoned vehicles, some of her excitement began to wear off. It took about a half hour to go the four blocks to the store. The roads were eerily devoid of the undead. Her anxiety grew by the minute. Where were the dead? They saw no sign of them or any activity at all as they continued on their journey.

Trevor slowed the truck as they approached the parking lot. The lack of any undead seemed to be unnerving him more than an encounter might have, a fact he pointed out to the rest of the group.

"I know they are all in there waiting for us. Oh man, let's just go back to the apartment," he whined.

"Let's be thankful we haven't found any. We'll worry about where they went when we are safely done with our errands," Devin tried to reassure him.

Easing the armored car into the lot, Trevor continued to whimper under his breath. Beth poked her head between the seats to survey the area. Several cars scattered the area. The windows of a minivan were smeared with blood. Another car had smashed through the front of the building, shattering the huge windows that ran the length of it.

"That looks like a good place to enter." Hector pointed over Beth's shoulder.

"Yeah, that will make it easy to get in and out. The hole is huge." Matt remarked, trying to feel as if he added to the conversation.

Trevor continued to slow as they approached. Suddenly he cried out. "Whoa! What do we do about him?" A zombie had appeared from behind an overturned car. It was pushing a couple of shopping carts in no particular direction. "No good, man. We should get out of here."

"There is only one. We can avoid him easy. If we have to, we can put him down," Hector reassured him.

"It's like it remembers!" Beth gasped, pointing to the store logo on the vest of the undead.

Trevor gave the shambler a wide berth. Matt peered out the back window as they passed. "I remember that guy. I think he was, um… challenged in life. Deaf, too."

The zombie never looked up from its carts as the truck rumbled past. "So we do nothing as long as he stays away," Devin replied to Trevor's original question. Frowning, Trevor angled the truck so the back was close to the gaping opening in the front of the store. The power was out here too, but the morning sun shone deep into the building. Hector moved Beth so he could be centered between the two seats to address everyone at once.

"Trevor, you stay in the truck with the engine running, Devin, you'll be loo out." Hector turned his head to explain to the front. Devin and Trevor nodded. Turning back to the rest of the group, "Matt, you and I are a team. We'll start at the left side of the store. We grab whatever won't spoil. One person loads the cart, the other covers them. Right?" Matt nodded his affirmation. "Gillian and Beth, start at the right side. Head toward the pharmacy first; I think it is on that side of the store." Hector finished by checking the chamber of his rifle.

Beth peered out the back window. "Well at least we won't have trouble getting a cart," she joked.

Hector moved next to her and put his hand on the door handle. Everyone readied their weapons. "Remember, one fills the cart, the other covers them," Hector stated again before throwing the doors open and jumping out. Sweeping the area with his weapon, he motioned to the others. Devin took up his post behind the truck as Trevor stared nervously out the front.

"Cover or cart?" Beth asked Gillian.

Gillian looked at the younger woman. "You know your way around the gun. I know my way around the pharmacy."

"Sounds like a plan," Beth replied, readying her weapon. She watched as Hector and Matt headed to the far end of the store, Matt pushing the cart with Hector aiming the rifle all over. Beth's heart beat faster the longer they were in the store. The deeper in, the darker it was. The air was thick with the sickly smell of spoiled meat and vegetables. She was surprised at the amount of stuff on the shelves. "It's as if nobody even tried to stock up."

"Most people were home sick or taking care of the sick. We didn't think we needed to," Gillian whispered. Beth nodded, throwing a few more items in the cart. After several minutes they took one full cart to the truck, where Beth moved to the lookout spot. Devin ran to the registers to get bags and unload the cart. When he returned, Hector and Matt had dropped off their first cart.

Beth and Gillian returned to the store, filling another cart. Each step Beth took in the store, the more tense she became. Nothing was happening. They had already been there for about forty-five minutes and so far not one zombie had appeared. Beth screamed as they turned a corner at the end of an aisle. She had run right into Matt's cart. Laughing nervously, she and Hector lowered their guns.

"Ok, that should be it. Let's get the hell out of here. It is too damn quiet for my tastes," Hector stated. Beth was only too happy to follow him out. The quiet was starting to play on her senses. Loading the last of the bags into the truck, she watched the zombie at the end of the parking lot still pushing his carts around. He seemed completely unaware of the living. This seemed to bother Hector as well. "Why doesn't he come after us?" he asked.

Beth looked across the lot. "I guess we should be thankful."

"Yeah, maybe," he replied, getting into the truck. Hector kept watching the zombie as he slowly closed the door.

Trevor headed toward the exit. As they passed the cart pusher Beth watched him. His gaze never left his carts. The truck lumbered by, but instead of going after the vehicle he seemed confused. She felt sorry for the creature. His head was moving back and forth as if trying to figure out which way to go.

Trevor began to retrace the route they had taken to get to the store. Beth took immediate notice. "Wait! Wait, I thought we were going to the distribution center after the store."

"Listen, I hope you find your brother, but I want to get back. We'll unload, then you and whoever else can go wherever, but I want to... WHOA!" Trevor shouted, slamming on the brakes. The road ahead was completely choked with zombies. A few of the undead near the back turned their attention to the truck. Slowly they began to approach. The rest seemed to have not noticed anything yet. They moved together as if they had an agreed-upon a destination.

"God it's like a frickin' herd." Matt pointed to the mass.

Trevor threw the truck into reverse, and Beth was thrown off balance. She was really beginning to hate the back of this truck. "We so need to find an additional vehicle!" she grumbled, rubbing her arm. Matt readily agreed.

Suddenly they were both slammed against the side of the truck. Gillian cried out, hit by several heavy bags of canned goods. "Careful what you're doing up there!" Hector called from the midst of the bags.

Devin was trying to calm Trevor. "Ok, let's try another one. Relax, they can't get us."

"I know. I know, but everywhere I go is blocked. How am I supposed to get through this?" Trevor demanded hysterically. Trevor's panic was being felt by everyone in the armored car, as road after road was blocked with either zombies or debris.

"We need to get through this. I want to get to the distribution center!" Beth called, pulling herself up for the fourth time.

"Are you INSANE? That is the direction they are all going!" Trevor screamed.

"We are going back to the apartment first. We'll hide out there to let this group go by. THEN we'll go to the center," Hector called to Beth.

Beth began to argue but was drowned out by a frantic Trevor. "I can't go anywhere, nowhere! It's all blocked, nowhere to go... I can't... they... too many!"

"Go through them," Hector called from under several bags that had fallen over him for what felt like the hundredth time. Trevor stared wide-eyed at the road in front of them. There were several zombies in it, but less than on the other roads. He was muttering while looking in all directions.

"GO!" Devin screamed as he rose to take over driving. He was slammed back into his seat. Beth flew into Matt, who bounced off Gillian, who grunted in pain. Trevor had floored the massive vehicle. Walking corpses bounced off the front and crunched horribly under the wheels. Beth shut her eyes tight, trying not to hear the sounds. The thuds died away and the road became smooth. Beth opened her eyes to the familiar street leading to the apartment. Devin tried to get Trevor to slow down.

"The road is clear. They are not heading this way yet. Slow down so they don't hear the engine and follow." Beth gave Hector a look that he immediately understood. The silently agreed never to let Trevor drive again.

Trevor pulled up to the apartment building. Beth and Hector jumped out with Matt and Gillian at their heels. Beth shook her head as Trevor flew from the cab to the door. Hector whistled to call him back, giving him several bags to carry. Everyone loaded up on supplies and hurried inside. Reaching the second floor they were met by Max coming out of the dance studio?

"What are you doing down here?" Hector asked.

"Stancy thought she heard something down here and… well, it was nice to get away from her bitching." He looked over the bags. "Looks like it went well."

A loud thump from above them made everyone look up. Then a shot rang out. Everyone looked at each other. Bags hit the ground and feet flew up the stairs.

Understanding

Wes shook his head as he watched Steve and Kate do their absolute best not to talk to or interact with each other. "I thought that stopped after third grade," he told Steve.

"What are you talking about?"

"Oh, nothing. Why don't you put gum in her hair, already?"

"Seriously, Wes, what the hell are you talking about?"

"Dude, you like her."

"You are out of your mind, and besides, she thinks we're a couple, remember?" Steve motioned between him and Wes. "Besides, I think she really wants nothing to do with us."

"You yelled at her. She might also be a bit embarrassed about the assumption," Wes explained.

"I think it is best if she and I just ignore each other for the moment," Steve stated, as if this was an obvious plan of attack.

"Yes, that ought to work. There are so many places to go where the two of you will not run into each other."

"The sarcasm does not help your chances of continuing to date my sister."

"First we have to find her again for me to date her. Speaking of which, when are we planning on doing that?" Wes asked politely, putting his fingertips together in front of his lips. Steve turned his back on Wes, not wanting to see the disappointment and annoyance there. "Steve I'm serious, I do not want to stay here. Beth is out there and I, we, need to find her." Wes was suddenly hit with a thought. "I think we should talk to Kate. See if she saw anything that might give us an idea."

"No!" Steve replied in a panic. "We will find Beth, I swear, but we don't need Kate's help."

"Fine! Ask that bear guy. Just do something. I am leaving here tomorrow with or without you!" Wes added angrily. Steve turned to face Wes. They stared at each other for a moment before Wes shook his head in disgust and stormed out of the church. In the hall he ran into Kate, literally, as she was leaving the bathroom.

"Oh, hi... um, I'm sorry, are you ok?" she asked.

"As Steve said, I'm tougher than I look."

"Look, I shouldn't have jumped to conclusions, and I'm really not judgmental, and, well..." she rambled.

"Listen, it's fine," Wes said. He noticed the look on her face and explained, "You're not the first... well maybe you are, to think *Steve* is. He was a big-time jock in high school. That was probably a huge blow to his ego, you know, to have an attractive girl think he is gay."

Kate blushed but smiled. "You know those jocks need to be taken down a peg every once in a while." Wes laughed, and she was noticeably relieved.

"Steve has always been more down to earth. He has always been really great to me. Either he or Beth have always stuck up for me." Wes brushed the hair out of his eyes. "He really is a good guy."

Wes continued down the hall. Kate walked beside him. She smiled as she looked at him sideways. "Are you trying to get me to like him?"

"Hey, I'm just saying, he's a good guy. As far as I can tell you're the first girl he has shown interest in since his girlfriend dumped him in college." Wes grimaced.

"Where does he go college?" She inquired.

"Oh... he kinda doesn't go anymore... even before all of this," Wes muttered.

"Oh? Really, what happened?" Kate asked, walking over to one of several chairs in the hall. Wes followed her, not sure if he should be telling this story to someone who, earlier, seemed to seriously dislike Steve.

"You know, maybe I shouldn't say anything."

"No, please tell me," Kate asked sincerely, grabbing Wes by the arm and pulling him into the chair next to her. "Seriously, I feel really bad about earlier and I......overreacted. We had some....trouble, you know, before. I guess I just thought...the way he was looking at me. I just want to talk about anything that feels kinda *normal*. Does that make sense?"

"Bear not much of a conversationalist?" Wes grimaced as he said it, hoping he didn't offend her.

Kate laughed. "I love him, but no, not really. If it doesn't involve an engine, he really couldn't care less about it." Her smile faded. "He is great and protective, but I can't talk to him. After what happened…" She went quiet.

"Hey, it's okay. We've all seen things we shouldn't have. Hell, none of this should be happening." Wes tried to comfort her.

"Sorry, it is just that these guys… They had me alone and they were going to…" She stopped. "Bear burst in. You have to understand he is a real gentle guy normally." She swallowed. "It is fine to kill the ones that are already dead but…they…I don't know."

"They deserved it. What good is having survivors with no souls?" The look on Wes' face was one of pure hatred. "Beth dated a bastard that thought like those assholes. He would be someone I would…" Wes held up his hands, making air quotes, "'accidentally mistake' for a zombie."

They sat quietly for a few moments. "So, tell me about Steve and college."

"I feel like I'm back in school," Wes looked up and down the hall at the classroom doors, "Like I am gossiping."

"No, you're just telling me a little bit about my new friends. Okay, tell me about *you* then."

Wes looked her straight in the eye and without flinching said, "I'm a loser geek, a stereotypical loser geek. You know my story."

"Steve said you had a girlfriend. His sister in fact. Is she a geek?"

"What? No! Beth is awesome. She is strong, smart, courageous. She is not afraid to tell people what she thinks. She is the drum major—well, that might be geeky, but that is because she is the only one that can take charge and get people to do what needs to be done."

"And she is dating you. Doesn't sound like she would date a loser. Besides, there is nothing wrong with being a geek. I love Star Trek *and* Harry Potter," Kate said, as if this were common. It took Wes a few seconds to process this statement, but after he did, he knew he liked Kate. The conversation flowed easily after that. They were talking about where Kate was going to college and where Wes wanted to go after graduation when Kate asked, "So where was Steve going to school?"

"Oh, he was going to State before all that crap happened with his girlfriend," Wes said, and immediately regretted it.

"He left school over a girl?" She frowned at Wes.

"No, no, Steve isn't like that. He was there on a football scholarship, and the girl he was dating cheated on him at this party," Wes quickly explained. The look on Kate's face told him he wasn't doing a very good job. "He caught her and got, you know, mad, and left. He was hanging out with his friends and well, they started drinking. Steve didn't want to go out but the guys dragged him to this other party on campus. Thing is, she showed up with the guy."

Kate covered her mouth and gasped. "That had to be awkward."

Wes nodded. "Oh yeah. She was all drunk and belligerent. She started yelling at Steve. He tried to walk out, but she grabbed him and tried to hit him. The guy she was with stepped in and tried to pull her off of Steve."

Kate was shocked. "He didn't hit the guy, did he? What was she all pissed about?"

"No! The dude was cool about it, apologizing. Steve was just like, whatever, and that is why she was pissed. She wanted him to fight for her or something stupid. That is what Beth said, anyway." Kate thought Beth had a point. "Anyway, the girl was screaming and kicking and just losing her mind. The cops showed up and she claimed Steve hit her and the guy. Since the guy had a bloody lip, from the girl, the cops believed it."

"That is total crap!" Kate stammered indignantly.

"Yeah, the guy backed Steve up, saying he didn't do anything wrong. He said he didn't even know the girl had a boyfriend. I mean, Steve and him were pretty cool by that point. She was still all crazy with the cops. People at the party even said Steve and this guy didn't do anything, but they both got arrested."

"No way!" What for?"

"Underage drinking, but then the local paper got a hold of it and it made the school look bad. You know, football player accused of hitting a girl and getting into a fight—so the school booted him."

Kate looked furious. "That sucks! Why didn't he fight it?"

Before Wes could answer, they heard several shots from the bell tower. "I guess it doesn't matter now." He got up and wandered over to one of the windows.

"You know, for just a second, it felt like normal life," Kate said. Wes nodded and they walked back into the church, Kate by his side. She stopped as they approached where Steve was cleaning his rifle. He hadn't noticed Wes or Kate yet.

"I'll talk to you late,." Kate mumbled to Wes as she started to edge away from Steve

Wes looked over at her and smirked. He caught hold of her arm and pulled her over to Steve. "Hey dude, have you met my friend Kate?" he asked.

Steve looked up at Kate and she gave a shy smile. "Hey." Steve gave a non- committal nod. "Wes tells me you were a football player," Kate ventured.

"Does he?" Steve gave Wes a look. Wes shrugged and became interested in one of the pews.

Kate said, "Listen, I'm really sorry about yesterday. I don't know why I acted that way." Steve looked up at Kate. Her eyes told him of her sincerity.

"Couldn't have anything to do with zombies, could it?" Steve asked, smiling at her.

She relaxed and replied, "No, that isn't stressful at all."

"Oh, hey—I've got that thing… in that other place; I gotta go." Wes looked at his arm where a watch should have been, pointed over his shoulder, and left them.

"Subtle, isn't he?" Kate laughed.

"Yeah, except when it came to my sister. It took him forever to say anything." Steve shrugged.

Kate looked around and tentatively asked, "Where is, Beth, is it?"

Steve said, "Not here, but I know she is safe. We both do." Kate didn't ask any more about Beth. She stared at him for a few moments. It became his turn to get nervous.

"What?" he asked, looking around. Then he looked back into her eyes. He realized he knew them.

"Mustang!" She pointed at him.

"Bike!" He pointed back.

"And football." She smiled, shaking her head. "McDaniel, right?"

Steve, shocked, nodded. "You screwed up our season. We had the championship in our sights, and you threw for like a thousand yards or something."

"City High. You were the statistician," Steve laughed.

"Wait, what? How did you know that?" Now it was Kate's turn to be shocked.

"Um... remember that fumble in the third quarter? That was when I noticed you."

Death

Reaching the landing, another shot rang out. "That's three," Hector hissed to his companions.

"Too many to be an accident," Max commented over Beth's shoulder.

Hector pushed the door to the hall open. Beth moved quickly into the passage, Hector covering her. The door to the apartment at the end of the hall stood open slightly. Hector motioned for Max to head to the end of the corridor, Beth to go low at the door; he'd stay high. Matt made a move to join them, but Gillian held him back.

Reaching the door, Beth crouched low, while Hector stayed against the wall. They readied themselves, then Max nodded that he was set. Hector pushed the door open, Beth cried out and flattened herself against the floor. A bullet smashed into the frame next to her head. Wood shattered and splintered off the molding, scratching her face and sticking into the back of her hand.

"Whoa, whoa! It's us!" Max yelled.

Hector moved into the room, taking a gun from Stancy. Shaking with anger, Beth slowly got to her feet. She pulled a long piece of wood from her hand. Blood poured from the wound, running over her hand. "What in the hell are you doing!? Be sure you know what you are shooting at before you pull the trigger, you idiot!" Beth shouted.

"Oh, you're fine, those scratches won't hurt your pretty little face," Stancy shot back hysterically.

Beth wiped the blood from her face and fought to keep herself from hitting Stancy. The wound on her hand was bleeding quite badly. Gillian was at her side, inspecting the damage. She grabbed a towel from the kitchen to wrap it.

"What were you shooting at?" Hector demanded.

"Zombies!" Stancy was shaking and wide-eyed.

"There aren't any in the building. I checked," Max jumped in.

"In there, in there!" Stancy pointed.

Beth followed the end of Stancy's finger to where it pointed; the bedroom where they had left Bill. It felt as if someone had poured ice directly into her chest. How did a zombie get in? "Is Bill okay?"

"OKAY? HE'S THE ZOMBIE!" Stancy shouted. Trevor moved her to the couch, where she collapsed staring at the bedroom door.

Beth started toward the closed door. Hector held out a hand to stop her. Gillian held her lightly by her shoulders. "Don't," she whispered into Beth's ear. Beth hesitated while the door was pushed open by Hector. Max hung back, still holding his weapon at the ready. Beth could see Bill's feet and legs sticking out from beside the bed. He was lying on the far side, between the bed and the wall. Red glistened, vibrant over the plain white paint. The bed was soaked in blood. A pillow laying on the floor was covered in it.

Hector walked around the bed. Bill lay face down on the floor. He carefully turned him over. The front of Bill's shirt was drenched from a chest wound; Hector looked troubled. He next inspected the wound to the man's head. Beth broke free from Gillian's grip and rushed to look over Hector's shoulder. He stood up quickly, not realizing Beth was there, and slammed into her. She hardly noticed. All she saw the gaping wound in the front of Bill's head. "What happened?" Hector shouted at Stancy. He grabbed Beth by the upper arms, forcing her out of the room.

Max slipped into the room past Beth, who was handed off to Gillian and Devin. Both looked confused but understood the look that Hector gave them. Then knew they had to keep Beth under control. "What happened?" Hector repeated more loudly.

"He died and tried to kill me," Stancy replied shakily.

"Really?" Max asked. "So, what side of the bed were you on when he attacked you with the club?"

"What?" Stancy asked. "No. No! He died and came back just like all the others," she shouted, panicked. "I heard him moaning so I grabbed the gun to check."

"You said he had a club?" Gillian asked Max.

Max looked over into the bedroom. "Yeah, here it is." He ducked into the room, returning with a long pole that Beth had fashioned with duct tape over the ends.

"He had that! He was coming after me," Stancy shouted, pointing.

"You idiot!" Beth made that as a cane for him. Could he simply have been trying to get up to use the bathroom or something? Maybe he was moaning from the pain?" Gillian asked.

"You murdered him!" Beth cried. Gillian was not prepared, but Devin had a tight grip on Beth's waist. "Didn't you? You hated him! You thought he was holding us up, so you murdered him," Beth screamed, trying to fight free from Devin.

"No! He was already dead! I know it." Stancy looked terrified.

"She murdered him, and she tried to shoot me!" Beth shouted.

"No, he was moaning and shuffling."

"He had an injured leg!" Matt screamed, joining the fray.

Beth forced herself free from Devin. Stancy jumped back in fear. Beth turned, not knowing where to go. She returned to the bedroom door, too many thoughts crashing through her head to pick one to hold onto. All she could do was stare at the lifeless corpse of the man who had been her teacher and her savior. She was stuck with the woman who had, in all likelihood, killed him needlessly.

"He died!" Stancy shouted trying to convince the others in the room as much as herself. Max took her gun.

"Bill was in bad shape, but it sure looks suspicious," Max muttered to Hector. "Maybe Beth's right. What if she killed him on purpose? She's nothing but dead weight, so why are we putting up with her?"

"Because she is alive, and until we have proof, we aren't going to leave her to die." Hector stated.

Beth shook her head. "You know she killed him."

Hector was in front of her in a second, holding Beth back from Stancy. "No, I don't. Neither do you. She is a raging bitch, but a murderer? I just don't know. She could have just panicked, so until we have a better idea…" he whispered to her.

"Let's hope she doesn't think one of us is dead next," Gillian muttered.

Beth needed space. She had to get away from Stancy. Checking the chamber of her gun, she made several people in the apartment nervous. Beth shook her head, disgusted, as she left the room. Walking to the window that led to the fire escape, Beth leaned her head against the glass. Anger coursed through her. She threw open the window. Her feet clanged too loudly on the metal platform. She walked to the end that looked out into the alley, where she sat down and cried hot angry tears.

Overstayed

Kate and Steve had spent the last few hours getting to know one another better. The more time Steve spent with her, the more he liked her. He found that he had many things in common with her, but also, she shared many interests with Beth and Wes. They talked movies, TV, music, even video games. That was a conversation that Wes had joined in with; he spoke with a distinct longing.

"Seriously, what I wouldn't give to lose myself in a movie or a video game," he sighed.

"Looks like you'll have to go back to playing D & D with graph paper and a dungeon manual," Steve laughed.

"Great, I'll be the DM," Kate laughed, "Oh and by the way, knowing how to play with the graph paper just makes you a geek like us." She put an arm around a smiling Wes.

"You want to know one of Steve's secrets?" Wes asked. Kate nodded enthusiastically.

"Wesley!" Steve warned.

"Steve used to make the dungeon maps for me and Beth."

"Only because the ones you guys came up with were incredibly lame."

Their conversation was interrupted by Father Michael. "Can you join us in the church? We need to meet," Father Michael called to them from the door leading back to the church.

Wes looked over at Steve, a distinct look of concern on his face. Steve tried to reassure him.

"What is it?" Kate whispered as the three of them hung close to the back of the small group.

Bear joined them. rubbing a paper towel over his wet hair and beard. "Sorry, trying to wash up a bit. What've I missed?"

"Nothing yet, my son," the priest responded. "We have been safe so far. We have plenty of food and water. I have heard that some of you want to leave the safety of the sanctuary to search for family and friends. I don't believe this is a wise course of action."

Steve and Wes exchanged glances. "Try to stop me," Wes muttered, so that only Steve and Kate heard him.

"That being said, I want to make it clear that this church will be open to anyone, to come and go as they please. If someone from our group decides to leave us, that is, of course, their decision. If they decide to return, we will welcome them. But leaving and coming back multiple times could lead the dead to follow them back to us. I simply have to forbid it."

"That seems a reasonable request," Kate spoke.

"I don't disagree in principal, but I also don't like the feeling I just got of being a prisoner," Steve noted.

"I will look for Beth, no matter how many trips I have to make. If that means he won't let me back in then he can explain it to God, or to the Devil when he meets him," Wes stated hotly, "and if you want to stay here while your sister is out there hiding, then I'll tell her you say hi when I find her."

"Wes—shhh, listen. That is not what I am saying. Come here." Steve pulled an angry Wes further back into the church. Kate followed, checking over her shoulder as they went. Bear trailed them with a look of confusion on his face. "What I am saying is we need to look like we agree, and we need to plan this out."

Wes looked rebellious. Kate blocked him from the view of the front of the church. "Wes, relax. Steve has told me about your plans to find Beth. I'm in. I also agree with you that something feels off here."

"Katie, what are we talking about?" Bear looked from face to face.

"Nothing, big guy," Steve answered. "Wes and I are planning a trip to find my sister. You and Kate will stay here and make sure that guy lets us back in."

Kate grabbed Steve by the arm. "Hold up there. You will not play that game with me. I've started to like you, so don't mess that up with the whole 'you're a girl so you need to stay behind' thing."

Steve looked into her eyes, then motioned with his eyes and a tilt of his head to Bear.

"No, no, the dude's right. You're staying here," Bear grunted.

Steve gave her a look that said, "I have no intentions of leaving you."

Kate caught on, knowing Bear would never quietly let her go. "Fine, but *I* might not agree to letting you return." She stormed from the church.

Wes caught the exchange, which had clearly done its job on Bear. Steve waited a moment before following after Kate. A few moments later, he was sitting with her at the end of a dark hall. "Thanks for offering to help."

"Well, before you thank me you might want to teach me how to shoot a gun. I've never shot one before."

"You've played video games, though. It's not too different from that—except the weight, noise, and aiming is a bit different, and of course you don't respawn if you get killed."

"So, not at all like a video game," Kate laughed. Steve shrugged but smiled. Kate, still grinning, shook her head. "Besides, I always played the ones where I wield a sword so big it breaks the laws of physics."

Steve looked at her in the long shadows. "I mean, you should think of the zombies as the same as the video game enemies. Soulless and never-ending." He looked away. She seemed disappointed. Steve got to his feet and held out his hand. "Let's head up to the tower and I'll show you the basics, okay?"

Kate took his hand and allowed him to pull her to her feet. "That sounds like a plan."

Mayhem

The night passed quietly in the apartment. The bedroom was closed and everyone was camping in the living room. Hector and Max had wrapped Bill's body in the comforter and taken him outside.

Beth had followed to say goodbye. "If it wasn't for him, I would have been killed...when was that? How many days ago did this all start?" Max patted her on the shoulder as he passed. Hector turned her away from the body to face the building. He then gave her a little push. She allowed herself to be steered away. When they returned to the apartment, Hector had informed the group that they, all of them, would be going to the distribution center in the morning. They would leave at first light. All eyes turned to Stancy, who for once quietly consented.

Morning broke and the apartment was again alive with action. Devin and Trevor were moving supplies to the door just inside the truck. Stancy questioned this, without lending a hand.

"Just in case we can't get back here, we want to have supplies," Matt explained coming down the stairs behind Devin.

Max, Hector, and Beth double-checked and triple-checked weapons. Gillian put together a medical bag in case they came a across anyone who was injured. Then she changed the bandage on Beth's hand. First light had already seen the sun up, and was heading to mid-morning by the time the last person crammed themselves into the back of the truck. Beth felt edgy and excited.

Stancy was the last one in, and she sorely wanted her gun to be returned. Everyone had already agreed she would have an old brass lamp body, and not a gun. As they passed the blood-stained quilt that contained their fallen friend, she seemed less eager to pursue the return of the firearm.

The trip to the distribution center was quiet and empty. "I wonder where they all are today," Hector muttered. He thought back to the previous day's movements. "They came from the ballpark area."

Beth was next to him. "After they finished there, they were at the hospital, and it looked like they were heading to the retirement community. They must have run out of...food...and are now on the move." She shuddered.

Hector thought her theory was probably a very good one. The buildings changed from shops and apartments to amore industrial neighborhood. Thick smoke hung over the streets. Finally, the distribution center came into view. A building close by had collapsed. It was still smoldering. One of the warehouses had heavy smoke coming from several windows, and another building was burning freely.

Beth stuck her head between the front seats. She surveyed the parking lot and was torn between relief and disappointment. The lot was almost completely empty; only three cars remained. Two sat idle and untouched, the third, a van, sat with its driver's door hanging open. As the truck passed, they could see the interior was stained with blood and various parts of a human's vital organs. What wasn't in the lot was a beautiful well-kept Ford Mustang.

"If Steve is here, it looks like he'll be in the office," Beth pointed to building with several broken windows.

"Okay—Beth, you, Matt, and Gillian check that out, then meet us by the heavy equipment. Max, Devin, and I will secure some forklifts. Trevor, you and Stancy stay with the truck."

"Is that the best idea?" Devin questioned Hector in an undertone. "They've both panicked on us, to our extreme detriment."

"Better they stay here than panic out there," Hector jerked his thumb over his shoulder. They pulled to a stop in front of the office. The back doors opened, and their shoes crunched on the gravel. The air was cold and Beth shivered, but not due to the temperature.

What if Steve was here but...? Shaking the thought, she said, "Keys to the lifts are in a case just inside the door to warehouse number 3." Beth pointed to the only building behind the office that wasn't on fire or already destroyed.

"Well, that's lucky." Hector started jogging toward the warehouse, Devin and Max following quickly.

Beth ran to the front door of the office. Gillian had to grab her hand to keep her from running right in. "Take it slow, just in case," she whispered.

Moving into the shadowy reception area, Beth took in the scene. She had worked here for two summers but she hardly recognized the place. Chairs were overturned, as were several tables. Papers covered the floor along with a dark brownish red stain that ran up one of the walls.

"Steve?" Beth hissed. Matt and Gillian joined her in the open room. They listened for any reply but only heard the papers underfoot and their own loud breathing. "This way," Beth motioned.

They slowly made their way down the hall. Every door they looked through caused Beth to become increasingly frightened and hopeless. Room after room was covered in horror. Blood, and pieces of victims, mixed with broken furniture and papers. Reaching the back office, Beth could only gasp and turn her back on it. On the floor lay half of a woman that Beth was sure she had once worked for. Through the broken window they could hear one of the forklifts firing up in the yard.

"I don't think Steve was here," Beth sighed, leaning heavily against the wall. "His car was not in the lot."

"That thing is making a lot of noise," Matt anxiously noticed. The truck's horn blared out a warning. Matt ran to the window. He could see the zombies, now visible down the road. "Not good! They know we are here," he called to the others.

Gillian joined Matt at the window, but Beth couldn't bring herself to enter the room. "Beth, we're in trouble! Where is the back door?"

"This way," Beth called. They barreled halfway down the hall. Beth hit the panic bar on the heavy door and they burst out into the yard. Beth sucked in the cold air. It stank of death and smoke, but it felt less oppressive than the building they'd just left.

Devin was pulling a forklift to the gate. He waved to them. His wave faltered when he noticed their expressions and panicked movements. He pointed to the still-standing warehouse. Gillian nodded, pulling the others with her. They could see Hector and Max as they approached the building.

Beth and Matt skirted a pile of burning pallets. Gillian went the opposite way around, but reaching the building's threshold, Gillian tripped and fell over a concrete block. Looking behind her, she screamed. The undead were pouring through the doors from the office.

Matt cried out, pulling Gillian to her feet. Beth leveled her weapon, firing several shots. Hector tugged on her collar, urging her to follow. The first of the zombies had reached the fire. Beth was stunned to see it walk right through the flames. She ran through the door. Spinning around, she tried to shut it. A piece of wood was blocking the door.

"I thought these things were afraid of fire!" she yelled, giving up on the door and running from the now-flaming ghoul.

Matt ran next to her, speaking in between gasps for breath. "That is actually a common...misconception...whoa!" A zombie lunged for them. Matt dodged as Beth smashed it with the butt of her gun. She grabbed his sleeve, swung him around, and pushed him ahead of her.

"You see, people fear fire because of getting burned..." Matt clutched at his side. "A zombie doesn't feel pain, so why would it fear fire?"

The flaming zombie was now stumbling around, setting several other undead on fire. "So why is it still moving? I thought fire would kill it," Beth shouted as she put down two of its comrades.

"Well, the body is something like 90% water, so it doesn't burn all that well." Matt weaved around some crates. "To get a body to burn. you need a large amount of accelerant, or a very hot flame." Matt grabbed Beth's shoulders, spinning her to face a too-close-for-comfort zombie.

She fired. The gun's chamber locked back, showing the magazine was empty. Matt pulled one from her back pocket. Beth slapped it into the gun and fired again. "I seriously want to know...why do you know this shit?" she shouted.

"People think bodies are easy to burn because people used to use mummies for firewood. If the body was all dried out..."

"Seriously? There is something wrong with you." Beth pushed Matt toward a door near back of the warehouse.

"Yeah, I've heard that a lot."

"Didn't date much, did you?" Hector asked as he joined them. Three rounds left his rifle, covering his laugh.

Matt, Hector and Beth pushed through the heavy steel door into an office. The three waited as Gillian rushed through, turned, and slammed it shut. The crunch of several zombie fingers was immediately drowned out by the rhythmic pounding of undead fists.

"Why in the world do you know this? I mean, really? Why?" Beth asked again.

"I don't know; weird hobby, I guess. I thought about becoming a mortician for a little while. I guess *those* guys are out of a job...if they haven't been eaten by their work, that is." Matt rested his back against the door. "This would be kinda nice, like a back rub, if the ones on the other side of the door didn't want to kill and eat me, that is."

Beth just stared at him. She really couldn't understand him. A smile played at the corners of her mouth. "You and my boyfriend will get along really well."

"I look forward to meeting him." Matt smiled, even though he doubted introductions would ever be made.

Beth could sense what he was thinking. "You'll see—you guys will be playing Dungeons and Dragons and whatever..." The door lurched forward, and Hector and Beth slammed against it.

"We'll work on character sheets later. Let's get out of here," Hector shouted.

Beth and Matt looked over at him.

"What?" he asked.

"Nerd," Beth and Matt said in unison.

"Bite me."

"That might be what they are thinking. Where is Max?" Gillian asked.

Several shots sounded, answering her question. The horn of the truck blared. It was joined by a second horn. "That's a forklift's horn. He must be with the truck," Beth informed the others.

Gillian was on a desk in the small office, looking out a window set high in the wall. "It looks clear back here. I can see the truck; I think we can make it. Oh! Max is heading for the forklift; Devin is coming to meet...Oh! Oh my God!" Beth and Hector ran to the desk. Beth jumped up, her hands pressed against the glass.

Max stumbled, and a zombie crawled after him. He clutched at his neck, and even from a distance they could see his hand was covered in glistening red. He turned and fired at the undead, and its head exploded. Max waved Devin away. He turned to the group in the warehouse, motioning for them to come out. He then headed away from both the warehouse and the vehicles.

"Damn it! Come on!" Hector banged his head on the window, then threw it open. Matt scrambled up on the desk. Gillian was through and running for the truck. Beth was out next, followed by Matt, with help from Hector. The door to the office burst open and a hand clawed at Hector's boot as it slipped over the sill. Hector landed in a heap next to Matt, who helped him up. Beth was running toward Max. Max was screaming at her to get away, while calling for the undead to come get him.

"BETH! Get over HERE!"

The truck crashed through the gate with a wild-eyed Trevor at the wheel, Stancy screaming and pointing behind them in the passenger seat. Matt jumped up onto the forklift. Devin had chosen one with an enclosed cab. Beth knew this glass was meant to be heavy duty in case anything fell on it. It should hold off the fists of the dead. Matt slipped in beside Devin.

Good thing he is so small, she thought. Hector appeared by her side. Her arm nearly separated from her shoulder as he yanked her to the back of the truck.

Max fired three more shots, then threw his rifle at the zombies. He pulled his sidearm, turned, gave Beth a wave, and ran at the oncoming horde. Beth tried to pull free from Hector but his grip held firm. He was barely able to keep her in the back of the truck and shut the doors.

"He's a hero. He saved us. Don't mess that up by getting killed now," Hector yelled as he pushed Beth against the wall of the truck. She pushed him off, scrambling to look out the back window. The forklift pulled in behind them, blocking her view.

"We are out of time. Let's get what we need and get out of here," Hector stated shakily as he looked from Beth to Trevor. Trevor nodded, terror evident from his face to his white knuckles.

Heading down the road, they noticed the zombies were flooding in from only one direction. Unfortunately, it was the direction they had come from that morning. "I don't think we can get back the apartment," Trevor whimpered.

"It looks as if they have massed in one place and are now moving as one through the city." Hector pointed at the huge group. "Maybe it is like you thought." he looked over at Beth, "Like they are following the food."

"Now where do we go?" Stancy angrily hit the dashboard.

"We need a new place to hide until we can figure a way out of here," Trevor exclaimed.

"It will need to be someplace defendable if they are coming at us in mass now," Hector noted.

"Why wait? Let's get the hell out of this town," Beth cried.

"What about your precious brother?" Stancy shouted.

"He's smart enough to get out of this insanity. There is no place safe here. Did you see them? No matter where we go, it will never hold up to their assault."

"Do you think we can clear the bridge with one forklift and a truck?" Trevor asked.

"Damn, I wish we had some two-way radios." Hector grumbled.

"I think there is an electronics store on the way to the bridge. We could try there," Trevor noted.

"Is it worth the risk?" Beth asked, tears streaming down her face.

"It would be good to be in communication. We can watch each other's back a little better."

"I don't give a damn about talking to any of you—I want to be somewhere safe! We should never have left the apartment. This was a stupid waste of time." Stancy finally had an opinion. No one answered her.

Thin Blue Line

Max fired into the crowd as he ran further away from the safety of the truck and forklift. Beth had tried to follow him. Silly girl, he thought. Didn't she understand it was too late? He blinked away the dizziness that threatened to overtake him. He knew he was bleeding out, and quickly, but he had to give them time. Climbing up on a pile of pallets, he threw the empty rifle at an undead woman. She barely noticed the butt ripping away half of her scalp. Max pulled out his service weapon and counted the shots.

One. The head of a man in a bathrobe exploded. Reminds me of my neighbor; that bastard never seemed to work.

Two. She may have been pretty when she was alive, but the gaping hole in the middle of her forehead and the way her skin hung sagging from several tears in her side made her undateable. Not that she would have gone out with me if I ever asked, Max thought, kicking away a dead hand that grabbed his ankle.

Three. "Damn it." It tore through another man's shoulder with not so much as a stagger backward.

Four. Yeah, take that! The back of the ghoul's head exploded, showering the zombie behind it with blood and chunks of brain and skull.

Five. You look like my father. He never liked me. The old zombie fell.

Six. A zombie that reminded him of a teacher. Seven. His captain at the precinct. Eight. His high school girlfriend. He chose his targets well. Each one that fell became someone in his life that he had never had a chance to tell how he really felt about them. With each round the bitterness in his life seemed to ease. He was getting tired and cold. The deep stain on his uniform shirt had reached his belt. The gun in his hand was getting very heavy. He staggered, barely able to keep standing.

Nine. That will help them… kept you bastards…occupied…but I will not join you."

Ten. Black. Max's body slumped down on the pallet. The zombies stood, arms outstretched, reaching for him. A second ticked by, and then a moan grew from the crowd as they turned to follow where the truck had gone.

Clearing the Way

"Up there. Turn left up there. OK, now go up, about a block. The electronics store is just ahead," Beth instructed Trevor. He did as he was told, pulling up to the smashed glass window of the small store.

"Huh, even with everything that happened, people still looted," Trevor grumbled.

"Cover me!" Hector called as he threw open the back door. He hurried to the smashed window. He was about to step over the low wall into the interior when he stopped, looking down. Beth watched him wondering why he stopped. She was about to ask when she was distracted by Matt waving frantically from the forklift. He had his hands raised in a questioning manner. Beth put her hand to her ear to mimic a phone then pointed at Hector. Matt didn't seem to get it until he saw what Hector was holding, a package holding a pair of two-way radios. Beth gave him a thumbs up. He looked at the package and frowned, then looked into the darkened store then back to the ground.

"What are you doing?" Beth hissed, but Hector either didn't hear her or ignored her. He kicked a few pieces of broken glass and an empty box aside. Then with a start, he saw what he was looking for. He held up a package of batteries. Pulling his knife from the sheath at his shoulder, he cut the packaging off the two ways. He tossed the batteries to Beth who opened them quickly.

It took a few seconds to get the batteries in right and the radios to communicate with each other. Hector ran one back to the forklift, Matt hung out the door to grab it. Hector ran back to the truck and keyed his radio. "You guys hear me okay?"

"Yep, loud and clear, what is going on?"

Hector explained that the way to the apartment was blocked and they were going to try to get the way to the highway cleared. Devin agreed to the plan relayed through Matt. "Did Max get away?" Matt asked. The silence that followed answered his question.

Devin took the radio from Matt. "Trevor."

"Yes, Devin?" Hector held the radio close to Trevor so he could drive.

"Head up to Vine, then take Ridgeview up to Cambira. We'll come to the interchange from the north."

"Ridgeway?"

"Yeah, it's a block south of the churches."

"Oh yeah, right." The truck rumbled up the road.

Beth sat across from Gillian. Gillian could feel Beth's pain. She watched the other woman for a moment before she asked, "You okay?"

"We've lost two friends in the last two days. I'm just…"

"We're going to get out of this. I promise."

Several minutes later found them idling several yards from a mass of cars. The bridge was empty beyond the five or so cars that were blackened by fire. All that remained of the huge RV was its metal frame and engine.

"This might not be as difficult as we thought." Devin clicked into park. "Beth, I think it is time you took over."

"Um, copy that," Beth replied. "You and Matt will switch places with…" Hector pointed to himself, "Me and Hector. Give us like a minute." Hector made sure Gillian was ready with a gun before he checked his ammo and his weapon. Beth did the same, then threw open the back door. Hector handed the radio to Gillian.

"They're on their way. Leave the radio in the cab…thingy," they heard Gillian say as they jumped from the back of the truck.

The smell of burnt rubber and meat was overpowering. Beth faltered as Devin ran past her to the truck. Several creatures were moving in the burned-out cars. Then she noticed that many of the cars that hadn't burned also had moving occupants. Corpses still strapped into seat belts flung fists against glass or struggled to try to free themselves through broken windows. Strips of flesh peeled off as they raked across shattered glass.

"Come on!" Hector pulled her sleeve. It took just a second for Beth to remember how all the controls worked. A zombie crawled up onto one of the burnt cars' hood. Its head snapped back, and it fell off the car. Hector checked his weapon. He sighted on the next closest zombie.

Devin's voice came through the two-way. "There are a lot of them out there, so we need to move fast. I'm going to try to push some with the truck. I'm handing the mic off to Jill." In the background they could hear Stancy starting to panic.

Gillian now spoke through the small speaker. "Beth you take out the barriers…."

Stancy's voice could be heard clearly. "The road is clear! We can just go, run for it. They don't move fast, but if we sit here, moving cars, they are going to swarm us."

Gillian again, "If you take out that one…yes…then you have a clear shot at the thing that is the big holdup." She was referencing what was left of the RV.

"Look at them all, they are everywhere!" Stancy's voice was higher this time.

"For all her bluster and arrogance, she really is a wuss," Beth grumbled.

"She's not wrong, though. We need to get this done, and quick." Hector pointed to a growing crowd on the other side of the barrier. Another group was forming on the far side of the line of cars. Beth positioned the lift forks under a small half-burned compact car.

When the driver's window was even with the cab, Beth gave a cry. The blackened thing inside was fighting against the steering wheel. It looked as if the hands had become part of the melted plastic. As it fought the arms broke free at the elbows. It began beating its stubs against the door. Beth moved the car to the edge of the bridge, dumping it into the swollen river below.

They heard a crash from where Devin had slammed into the tangled mess, breaking a few cars free. Hector clicked the radio. "Be careful, we need to be able to drive that thing out of here." Beth and Hector glanced at each other when they received no reply.

Hector opened the door of the crowded cab and shot three zombies that had made their way too close. The undead at the barrier were starting to fall over it, one by one. The far side of the cars couldn't be seen because the horde was now on top of the cars. Beth cleared another vehicle from the bridge.

The entire forklift was rocked as the armored car hit the huge rear wheel. Hector fell forward, slamming Beth into the steering column. The truck she had just lifted fell off the forks as she pushed the controllers forward. "What the hell?" Beth coughed rubbing her chest.

In the front window of the truck they could see why they had been hit. Stancy was holding onto the wheel. Gillian and Trevor were trying to pull her off from the back of the truck. Devin's lip was bleeding freely.

"Stancy, stop it! You're going to get us all killed," Hector yelled into the radio.

Stancy was pulled away, her foot connecting with the side of Devin's head. Beth cringed watching it. What happened next in the truck she didn't know, as the pounding fists on the side of the cab drew her and Hector's full attention. Hector pushed the door open to dispatch the zombies. "Get the bridge cleared," he ordered.

Shot after shot rang out. Beth had two cars to move before a clear getaway was open to them. The pickup truck strained the forklift. It was fused with the burned body of the RV. "Just move it enough for us to get around," Devin's voice instructed. "I think that If you just…What the…Jill, grab her! Stancy!"

The back door to the armored car had sprung open. Matt fell to the ground, and Stancy jumped down, looking in all directions. Hector fired at the closest zombies, but more had already breached the barrier. More fell over, pushed by those who had made it over the cars. "Get back in the TRUCK!" Hector called out. Gillian was pulling Matt back through the doors and then pulling them shut behind her as Stancy ran this way, then that. "Get over here!" Hector yelled, waving her over.

Beth worked the pickup truck free, pulling it out of the burned RV. When it finally broke free, it had also pulled the RV out of the travel lane. "They're clear! They're clear," Beth called. Jumping to the door of the forklift she poked her head around Hector. "Stancy, get back to the truck!" Beth pointed. "The road is open."

Stancy had not heard what Beth said, but she saw where she was pointing. She began to run. She skidded to a stop when she saw a few zombies blocking her path. She turned and ran in the opposite direction, then turned again. She was now running away from the open road. Beth pushed past Hector, who called out, "What the hell are you doing?"

"She may be insufferable, but I will not let her die!" Hector started to follow but was cut off when Devin pulled between him and Beth. She was now running to where Stancy was scrambling around, trying to avoid the ever-increasing mass of undead.

The back doors of the truck swung open, and Gillian hit the ground running. She caught Beth in a second, painfully tackling her to the ground. Beth's knees connected with the pavement. Matt and Hector joined Gillian. Beth was lifted from the ground and pulled backward. Hector fired round after round into the horde. Stancy was everywhere. Hector called and called for her.

"HELP ME! HELP ME!" Stancy screamed, but never seemed to figure out where she was going.

"We have to help her. We can't leave anyone else." Beth's screams added to Stancy's.

"This way!" Come back to the truck!"

Zombies surrounded her. The truck was the only way out. Devin threw it in reverse. Beth was thrown around in the back, where she was still being held by Gillian and Matt. Blood blossomed on Stancy's arm. More spread from her neck. Her screams grew higher and higher in pitch. Hector flung himself into the back of the truck. Stancy's left arm separated from her body. She called them horrid names until her throat was torn out. The doors slammed shut. Beth stared at the blood soaking through the knees of her jeans. Devin pushed the accelerator down as far as it would go. The supports of the bridge flew, by barely visible.

Almost

"Wow, did you see that?" Steve turned to Kate. Her stunned expression told him she had. A truck and a forklift had just rumbled down the road on the other side of the block.

"Where do you think they are going?" Kate asked.

Steve made a quick map in his head and turned a few times to get his bearings. "The highway, they are going to try to clear the bridge to the highway!"

"Then we'll have a way out of town. We can get to the countryside, get away from densely populated areas and have a shot. What is it?" Kate asked, noting the look on Steve's face.

His expression turned from excitement to concern to elation. "That was Beth! I bet anything that my little sister is with them!" Steve yelped and swung Kate around in a hug.

"How can you tell?" she laughed.

Still holding Kate in his arms, he looked into her eyes. "I just know. Beth would come up with a plan and she would have gone to the distribution center to find me. That was one of our loaders. I just know it was her."

Kate tried to keep the doubt from her face but didn't accomplish it completely. Steve saw this and loosened his grip. "Trust me. She's with them. You'll meet her soon." His arms fell from her completely.

Kate took Steve's hands in hers. "I'm sure you're right. Let's go tell Wes." Together they hurried down from the bell tower. Kate tripped on the last step, and Steve grabbed her arm to steady her. She took his hand and did not let it go as they jogged down the hall. Between the feeling Steve had that he had just seen his sister go by and the fact he was holding hands with Kate, spread a huge smile across his face. Bursting through the door to the church he was about to call out to Wes. To his surprise, Wes was at the doors. He slapped Steve hard on the arm, pulling him into the shadows. The room was abuzz with voices.

"What's up." Kate asked. Wes shushed her, pointing to the knot of people by the front doors.

"Settle down, settle down." Father Michael called. "I know what you think you saw or heard, but it is not a way out." Several people grumbled, including Steve. Wes hushed him again.

Father Michael called for quiet. "We are safest here. No one, NO ONE should try to leave. Not right now." Gunfire erupted in the distance. "No, please listen. I pray they make it. I pray they clear the way. But right now, they are calling all the undead to them. We need to stay here until it calms down. Then we'll send someone to check it out. Please, please, just calm down."

"I do not like the way this is going," Wes muttered. "You know who that someone will be."

"We will stay here, and we will wait. We have all that we need. There is no reason to go out there to lead them right back to us, to our sanctuary." The priest continued.

"Who would want to lead them back here? Who?" A woman cried from the back of the group.

"Imagine if you go out there. You find the way blocked, and you can hear how much trouble they are having—then you'll try to get back here." Father Mike was almost in tears. "Please, just wait a little while, let it calm down." Several people protested loudly.

"I *really* don't like where this is going," Wes said, pulling Steve toward the pew containing their belongings.

"Kate, get your stuff, quietly, and have Bear meet us in the hall to the school," Steve whispered.

Wes and Steve walked quietly to their area. Wes began to pack up everything as nonchalantly as possible. Steve had just finished getting all of his gear together when Kate dropped her bag next to his. "I think you are right," she said a little loudly, causing Wes to jump. "It will be safer if we were closer together. Bear said he'd get us a new spot with more space for all of us." She pointed to where Bear had staked out a claim closer to the doors into the school. Steve looked confused, but Wes noticed a couple of the armed men who usual kept watch were looking in their direction. Hearing Kate, they changed direction, advancing on the ever-increasingly vocal crowd.

"I don't know what you are planning or who you pissed off, but you need to chill out," Bear muttered to the three of them.

"We haven't done anything yet," Wes hissed back.

"Well I heard some of those new guys saying they needed to keep you two in line." Bear pointed between Wes and Steve, who exchanged shocked looks.

"What did we do, other than save their asses?" Wes demanded.

"It ain't the regular folks we're talkin' about." Bear grunted. He nodded to the group of three guys who had arrived a couple of days ago. "I know their type. The one percenter kind. You know, dirt bag bikers." Wes smirked as he looked at Bear's long hair and tangled beard. The smirk vanished under Bear's imposing glare. "Listen guys, I like you, I do. The thing is, whatever you are planning, you need to leave Kate out of it. She is safe here," Bear stated. He glanced back at the other bikers, a look of concern crossed his face. "For the moment." He pulled Kate a little closer.

"Thanks, but I can make my own decisions, and I don't think I want to stay here." She patted the big man on the shoulder. "I didn't want to say anything, but so far this place makes me uncomfortable."

"I thought you got over that once you realized this guy was okay." Bear slapped Steve on the shoulder.

"Funny." Kate grimaced. "Seriously, I think there might be too many people here. I like the Father, but he seems to be losing control. Those guys have been muttering a lot lately," Kate whispered to the others.

Wes looked nervously toward the door. "I know what you mean. This place has really gone downhill since we got here. At first everyone was really grateful, but now many of them think—I don't know what they think, but Mike is the only one other than Sarah and her husband that like us."

Bear nodded and in hushed tones told them of his experience. "Yeah, those two cornered me." He motioned vaguely. "They said something to me about, ya know, if I'm not being with them then I'm against them. Whatever that means, but then they started looking over at Kate." Bear ran his hand over his beard. "You know, I think us getting out of here is starting to sound like a good plan. Now that I think on it," Bear grumbled as he glanced sideways at Kate.

"I'm starting to wonder if their intentions are not on the up and up." Steve added but quickly stopped as footsteps approached. The crowd near the front had dispersed among a lot of grumbling and dirty looks.

"I was wondering if I might have a word." It was Father Michael and he was looking right at Steve.

"Uh sure. Be right back, guys." Steve followed the priest back to the rectory, through the doors and into an office.

"I am losing these people," Michael said as he took his seat behind a large wooden desk. "I can see what is going on and I am worried about your safety."

"Oh?" Steve asked, trying to keep his voice even.

"This will not last. One hundred and fifty days, I think."

"Seriously? We're Catholic, and we don't believe in that." Steve started, but Father held up his hand.

"Sorry, bad joke." Mike rubbed his eyes. "I don't know what to do. They are not happy about the provisions. Some want to be down in the shelter, some want to leave. Some think you are a threat and others think I will use you to keep them locked up."

Steve was stunned. "What do you think we should do?" he asked.

"I don't know, I just want you to be careful. I know Wes has been going out, but the problem is I'm not the only one, and people think he is going to—I don't know, get bit, or bring them back." Mike sat with his head in his hands. "I will not make you leave. I will not ask you to stay, but at the first sign of trouble, please run. I think we made a mistake by letting certain people in." He ran his fingers through his hair. "I just wanted to help..." Steve started to speak, but Mike spoke over him. "I am prepared, one way or the other, so please don't think you need to protect me." He looked up. "Steve, thank Wes for his help, and if there is a God, may He look out for you."

Steve took the priest's hand. "May He protect us both."

Returning to the group, he looked from questioning face to questioning face. He took a deep breath and explained everything he had just been told.

"Are you serious?" Kate stammered. "That is… that is…."

"Freakin' insane," Wes offered. "He should go hide in the shelter. Lock 'em all out. That would teach them."

"Let's wait until almost everyone is asleep and then let's get out of here," Kate whispered.

"I'm going to talk to Sarah. Be right back," Steve muttered. Wes watched him go. He saw Sarah and her husband talking to Steve. She covered her mouth, and her husband looked shocked. He watched the gestures. Wes frowned as he watched the hug between Steve and Sarah and the handshake between the men. She waved at Wes, who sadly waved back. Steve sat down next to Wes. He had tears in his eyes, and Kate took his hand. "Sarah wants to stay for the children. She is going to see if Mike will sneak them all into the shelter."

The night passed slowly. All around them they heard the murmuring of the other survivors. Steve watched shadows dance from the candlelight and listened to the growing silence of the room. Finally he grew too restless to stay put. He eased out of the church down the hall of the school. Passing the door to the shelter he noted the addition of a guard to the locked door. The man watched him the entire way down the hall.

Steve turned the corner and peeked back around it. The guard was looking right at him. His attention was distracted by the door to the church opening. Kate was coming down the hall. She stopped and whispered something to the guard. Steve saw the man noticeably relax. He pointed down the hall, motioning around the corner. Kate patted the man's arm and hurried down the hall. Turning the corner, she nearly collided with Steve.

"What was that all about?" Steve hissed.

"That guy was way too paranoid, so I told him I was looking for my boyfriend. We wanted to talk alone," Kate whispered as they continued down the hall. "What should we do about him?"

"I don't know, but I think this is as good as it is going to get in the way of getting out quietly. We should collect Wes and Bear."

"So where is Wes?" Kate asked. Steve immediately stopped, grabbed Kate's arms and turned her to face him.

"Wes wasn't in the church? I swear he was sleeping when I left."

Kate reached up and pulled his hands to hers, "He wasn't there when I left. Bear was sleeping but Wes was gone. I thought you were meeting with him."

"This isn't good," Steve muttered.

"Just wait. We don't know what is going on. He might have gone to the bathroom or taken a walk or something. He might be looking for a way to sneak out of this place," Kate reassured him.

Steve thought for a moment. It was true, he had no reason to think that Wes had been taken or was even in trouble. He had been eager to leave and could be doing just as Kate said, looking for a way out. Relaxing slightly, he became aware that he was still holding her hands. He looked again into her bright blue eyes, and then kept staring into their depths. The space between them began to shorten. Unconsciously he licked his lips and glanced at hers. Kate's eyes slid shut, and Steve inched ever closer. Then Kate's eyes flew open and Steve spun on the spot as gunfire echoed down the hall.

Now Where?

They had left town hours ago, yet they were only about forty miles away. After clearing the bridge, it seemed like smooth sailing. They were traveling outbound in the inbound lanes, without any other vehicles in sight. Over on the other side of the road it was just mile after mile of abandoned, burned, and wrecked vehicles. As the highway wound through the mountains the lanes got closer together, and people had attempted to cross the median. Now both lanes were scattered with discarded vehicles, luggage, and occasionally a body. All too soon the road had become blocked.

Devin had made an attempt to go around the jumble of wreckage. Crossing into the median, the heavy trucks tires sank into the soft earth. They were stuck.

"At least we have a moment to stretch our legs," Matt exclaimed, trying to put a happy spin on their predicament.

An hour later they were all sore from pushing and pulling. Several undead now lay crumpled across hoods or seeping thick blood onto the pavement. Matt wiped the sweat from his brow while Devin groaned, stretching his back. The vehicle was finally extricated from the mud.

"I think I will deal with cramped legs, next time," Beth commented as she wiped mud from her hands.

Later Beth drifted in and out of a fitful sleep. The faces of Max and Stancy kept swimming into view, causing her to wake with a start and stare around in the near-blackness. Devin had pulled over on the shoulder just a few minutes after they had freed the truck. Everyone inside was too tired to continue on. No one spoke about the ones they'd had to leave behind, but their absence weighed heavily. Max's did, anyway.

Dawn was finally breaking. Pale light began to filter through the front window. Beth blinked a few times while quietly struggling to her feet. Her back was stiff and her legs were sore. She had pushed at the back of the truck when they had gotten stuck, and combined with being tackled earlier, she was surprised she could even walk. Easing her way through the others, she made her way to the front of the truck. Devin snored softly from the driver's seat. Gillian was curled up on the passenger's side.

Sitting with her back against the center console, Beth watched the others sleep. She cocked her head to the side. She was sure she heard something. It was a muffled thumping; she was sure she heard it. Looking out of the front window on the lowly illuminated highway, she tried to make out where the sound might be coming from. There were several cars further up the road, but they all seemed empty. They had discussed taking one or two earlier in the trip, but ruled it out, as no one wanted to get stuck with so many windows.

Beth strained her ears. There it was again, rhythmic yet distant, as if brought to her on the breeze. The sun was breaking over the horizon. Devin stirred and mumbled in his sleep. Gillian's eyes were open and questioning what Beth was doing. Beth held a finger to her lips, then cupped her ear. Gillian turned her head to listen. "Thump… thump, thump, thump… thump."

"Did you hear that?" Beth hissed. Gillian nodded. They both looked out the window, aware that Devin was now awake and also scanning for the source.

"There!" Beth whispered, pointing at a large white panel van way up the road. Devin watched the back of the truck, trying to discern why Beth had chosen it.

"Thump… thump, thump, thump." The back doors shuddered, and a chain dangling from one of the handles jumped with each sound. Devin sat up straighter in the seat, stretched his back and reached for the key. "Bang!" The back door to the van flew open, slamming against the taillight, shattering it from the impact.

Torn clothes and torn flesh emerged, falling out of the blackness of the interior. Devin turned the key, firing up the engine. Five of the undead caught the sound and began moving toward them. Questions and grunts filled the air as the truck lurched forward. Devin swerved and dodged around the refuse of the road, clipping one car and a zombie. Beth fell back when the truck accelerated. She lay in pain, watching the ceiling and listening to the crunch of metal and bone. Matt helped pull her to a seated position against the wall.

"Good morning," he muttered.

The sun was now blinding them with early morning light. Devin slowed. The zombies were far in the rearview. The truck fishtailed a few times in mud when they had to take to the median. They began to be more cautious as they weaved their path along the littered highway. The number of abandoned vehicles thinned out dramatically. They were back to smooth, unimpeded travel, for a little while.

The road disappeared around a bend as the engine whined under the strain of pulling the heavy vehicle up the steep slope of a mountain. It was fortunate that the armored car was so heavy and the travel slower than Devin would normally have driven. Cresting the mountain and following the curve, the road ahead was littered with more crashed and burned out cars, almost blocking their path.

They had reached a set of tunnels through the mountain. Now they had a choice.

Eviction

Steve grabbed Kate, pulling her to the wall next to him. He raised a hand as he peeked around the corner back toward the church. Farther down their hall, a set of double doors burst open. Wes came flying out at them, wide-eyed and pale.

"Steve! Kate! They're here, they're here!!! They broke through the windows in the cafeteria and they are getting in! I tried moving some stuff in front of the window, but it won't hold!" Wes shouted.

"Come on! We have to get back to the church and warn them!" Kate called, running ahead of Steve.

Turning the corner, the sight that met them made Wes' blood run cold. Bear was thundering down the hall straight at them. Behind the huge biker they could see the priest shepherding the other survivors into the fallout shelter. Sarah's pained face disappeared as she herded a child forward. Steve motioned for Bear to turn around. "Get to the shelter!" he cried.

Bear slid to a stop, turned, took one step, and stopped again. Father Michael was arguing with the man who had been on guard. The guard pushed him, raising his rifle. Steve yelled, distracting the man. They aimed at each other, but Father Mike punched the guard.

"RUN!" he cried, with one last desperate look at Steve. Father Mike pulled the heavy door shut. Regaining his feet, the guard began pounding on the door, screaming. He stepped back and began firing at it. Bear had been running full-tilt to the door. He skidded and slipped, nearly falling. His boots squeaked on the floor, trying to regain traction. He covered his head and ran back toward Kate. He caught her by the shoulders.

"Come on, we have to get out of here!" He thundered down the hall with her in his wake. Glass shattered behind them. They could hear the tables tumbling down.

"How many are in the church?" Steve shouted as he stopped Bear's progress. Bear looked straight through Steve as if he hadn't heard the question.

"Bear, how many?" Kate asked again.

"Not many—they came from the back. I don't know how many." Bear trembled.

"We have to chance it; all our stuff's in there. It's close to the door. If there aren't too many we might be able to outrun 'em," Wes said. Ignoring the guard, who was too panicked to notice them as he pounded on the door to the shelter, they ran toward the church. Wes skidded up to the door, kicking it open.

The heavy oak door collided with something on the other side. Wes kicked it again, and the door swung open. A zombie was on the floor struggling to regain its footing. Wes ran up to it and stomped on its neck. A sickening crunch filled Steve's ears. Wes kept stomping on the head until he was pulled off by Kate. Bear and Steve were already at the pew, throwing packs on and grabbing guns. The bald man they knew from the front steps lay in a pool of blood. He was already twitching, coming back to life. One of the bikers sat on a pew, a bullet hole in his head.

Several zombies were shuffling through the church toward them. They were coming through a door at the very back of the church, the door that led to the priest's office. Steve knew that the key to the shelter was in there, but he could do nothing to get to it. His attention turned to the door they had just passed through. Undead after undead were streaming through it.

"Front door!" Wes called as he ran, with Bear at his heels, Steve and Kate close behind.

Moans filled the church with the steady stream of undead pouring through the doors. "How did they get in?" Kate asked, slamming through the doors to the entrance.

"I found a broken window as I was looking for a way to escape. It looked like someone threw a chair through it...UMPH." Wes pushed the huge door open leading to the outside. "I don't think we were the only ones who wanted to get out. I don't—over there!" he pointed to the gap in the buses, "—think they made it too far; they ran right into them by the look of the pieces."

The four headed to the gap. Bear slipped on the bottom stair step and faltered. Steve and Kate slipped through the gap quickly, followed by Wes. Bear recovered and hit the gap. Again, his girth caught him. The metal belt buckle of his jacket caught on the grill of the bus. Wes stopped crying out to the others. Steve was already firing his rifle at several oncoming undead.

Wes and Kate pulled on the struggling man. His head kept turning to the front doors. Zombies were already spilling out and down the stairs. Several had fallen all the way down to the bottom. Strips of flesh hung off them as they regained their feet, staggering toward the buses and Bear.

A tear leaked out of Bear's eye when he looked at Kate. "I have a great way to keep them from coming after you through here." He laughed. Kate began to sob and pull harder on Bear's sleeve. He held up a huge hand and pushed Kate away, "Here, get off, you two." Kate stumbled back, tears flowing freely. Wes grabbed at the lapel of the leather jacket as Bear pulled the gun from Wes' waist.

Kate screamed "No!" but it was too late. With one last look at the oncoming zombies, Bear shot himself in the head. His body immediately went limp, yet was still hopelessly wedged between the buses. He completely blocked the zombies from getting through after Kate.

Wes shook his head and picked up his gun. "Thanks," he said to the dead man, "I wish you could have come with us." Wes ran after Kate and Steve. Steve was half-pulling, half-carrying Kate down the empty street, listening for any sounds of pursuit and watching for movement. Huddling in a doorway, Wes clutched at a stitch in his side. He looked at the other two. Kate was crying onto Steve's shoulder.

"We're never going to make it out of here on foot," he breathed.

"There are abandoned cars all over the place. We need to find one with keys," Kate said between sobs. She looked sideways at the two men, "Unless one of you knows how to hotwire one."

Wes and Steve looked at each other, then at Kate. "No, do you?"

"No," was her choked reply. "Damn it Bear, we needed you."

Steve pointed up the street. "There is a garage. Let's hope they had some business."

"And they finished it," Kate said. If the car is still broken down it won't do us much good." With nerves on end, they cautiously approached the garage.

They were a block away, half a block, and still no zombies. They began to run. Then all three skidded to a stop. In their path was a lone figure. It slowly made its way around the corner of the building. "We can just outrun it," Wes suggested.

"What if the garage is locked?" Steve asked.

Kate raised the gun Steve had handed her when they left the church in her shaking hand. "If we shoot it, we might alert more to where we are," she whispered.

Steve stepped behind Kate and steadied her arm. "Just like a video game, remember?" he whispered to her. Wes stepped back. Kate exhaled and aimed at the zombie's head. Steve released her arms and also stepped back. She squeezed the trigger. Part of the zombie's ear flew off, but it continued forward. She turned and gave Steve a panicked look. He just nodded to her to try again. Wes had his weapon readied.

"Hey Kate, in the video games you might get something good if you get a head shot. Sometimes they drop ammo, or health," Wes smiled while taking aim at the ghoul.

"You can do this," Steve reassured her. Kate took aim again. Her next shot was true, and the zombie crumpled. As it fell something dropped from its hand. Wes walked up to the corpse, reached down and held up a box.

"Holy shit! Ammo!" he exclaimed. All three looked at each other. "Um, let's get to the garage," Wes said, looking down at the red box of bullets in his hand.

"Seriously?" Steve responded and the three ran to the garage. They weaved their way through a couple of cars parked in the front lot. Steve assessed them approvingly. They were all classics in various stages of restoration. Standing between the wall of the garage and 1962 Corvette that was missing its interior Steve turned to look at Kate. She was watching Wes checking the door.

"You okay?" Steve asked

"Yeah, I guess so," she replied, but jumped at the sound of Wes smashing a window. Steve edged closer to her, putting a hand on the side of her face. He looked into her eyes and inched closer to her. She closed her eyes and tilted her face toward his. A gun blast made them quickly cover their ears and jump apart. Something heavy hit the Corvette behind them, making them jump again. Kate spun and looked as Steve grabbed her and pulled her away from the back of the car. The zombie slid off the back of the classic car. Steve swung around and saw Wes standing in the doorway with his gun still aimed.

"Come on guys, I need your help finding the keys," Wes called, ducking back into the garage. Steve turned and looked at Kate. He was shaking slightly.

"Um, Kate I really like you. I also really want to kiss you, but I don't think I will try again until we are a very long way from here."

Shaking, Kate nodded and said, "I'll hold you to that."

He held out his hand and she took it, following him into the garage. Wes was in the office rummaging through the desk. Kate walked over to the workbench. Steve joined Wes in the office. Wes did not look up when Steve joined his search.

"You might want to calm your raging hormones until we are a bit safer," Wes grumbled.

"Thanks for saving us." Steve muttered. "I have already told her we are on hold until we get out of this."

"Yeah? You just don't want me saving your ass again," Wes laughed, "It might start to look like I'm the better catch."

Steve grabbed a pen from the desk and threw it at Wes, who tried to catch it, but went through his hands and smacked him in the face. "Nice hands," Steve smirked.

Wes gave him the finger and replied, "Twice. I saved your ass twice."

"Hey guys," Kate's voice called from the garage area. "I found the keys, so if you want to quit goofing off, we can get out of here."

Wes moved to the door, but Steve grabbed him and pushed him out of the way. Kate shook her head as the two men tried to make it through the door at the same time. "You know, right now neither of you is quite the catch."

"What've you got?" Steve asked, shouldering Wes out of the way. Wes punched Steve in the arm.

Kate shook her head again. "Looks like a Chevy key." She grinned, pointing to the Impala while holding up a key ring.

"Sweeeet," Wes moaned in appreciation, admiring the '65 Chevy Impala Super Sport. All three made their way over to the car. The interior was immaculate. Kate opened the door and slid in behind the wheel.

"Let's hope they were done and waiting for the owner to pick it up." She grimaced while putting the key into the ignition. Crossing her fingers, she turned the key. The engine roared into life. Wes gave Steve a high-five and ran to the passenger side. Kate leaned over, unlocking the door. Wes jumped into the back. Steve stared into the front window of the car and crossed his arms.

Kate glared at him and put her head out of the window. "You aren't going to pull some macho bullshit on me about women and driving, are you?"

Steve glared back. "No. I want someone to help me with the friggin' garage door!" Wes gave a guilty laugh and climbed back out of the car. Steve pulled the chain, raising the door about a foot. Wes dropped down to the floor to look under.

"Looks clear," he called. Slowly the door inched upward. Wes kept watch over the empty street in front of the building. He stood up as Steve got the door open enough for Kate to pull the car through.

She pulled level with them, "How's this for luck? Full tank!" Pulling out of the garage slowly, Beth kept the engine at a purr. Steve motioned Wes forward, and then ran out behind him, letting go of the chain. The door rattled down , hitting the ground with an almighty crash. Wes had thrown the passenger door open and was clambering over the seat into the back. Steve sprinted to the car as the street before them suddenly began to fill with the undead. He was barely in when Kate hit the accelerator. The door slammed shut as the 305 V8 roared and the tires squealed. Kate pulled the wheel hard right and tore down the road past the grasping hands of the zombie horde. They bounced down the road, took another hard right, and headed for the bridge out of town.

Choices

Devin slowed as they approached the tunnels. Hector checked the breech of the shotgun he was holding and looked over at Devin. Gillian leaned forward on the dash, looking between the tunnels on either side of the highway. "What do you think?" she asked.

Devin leaned forward on the wheel. "Looks like there was a nasty fire." He pointed to the top of the mouth of a tunnel that was black with soot.

"Well, we can hope they all burned up. There doesn't seem to be any around," Hector suggested hopefully from between the seats.

"Do you think it's safe to discuss this outside?" Trevor asked.

"Looks relatively safe," Devin replied.

"Thank god, I really have to pee," Beth whimpered. She smiled at the look on Matt's face. "Girls pee too, ya know." She clicked her gun's safety off, checked out the rear window, and opened the door.

Matt watched her jump down, "Yeah but I never heard one say that...except my sister."

Gillian was out at the front, stretching her legs and walking stiffly. "Ladies room on this side of the car," she hissed to Matt, who had just bounded out the door. He nodded, pointing to the far side of the armored car, indicating that the mens room was over there.

Beth was already taking care of business when Gillian pulled her weapon to stand guard. "We need to find someplace with plumbing soon," Beth grumbled, adjusting her jeans and pulling her own gun. She cocked her head to the side and listened intently. "Need to go?" Beth asked, trying to convince herself she hadn't heard anything.

Gillian shook her head, "Not right now, but wait until we get back on the road, then I'll need..."

"Shhhh," Beth hissed. She had heard it again. She turned toward the tunnel.

Matt was backing slowly toward them. "You guys done?" he whispered.

"Yeah, Devin figured out a plan yet?" Gillian asked.

"Nah, wants to know what you think."

Gillian swatted Beth's arm. "They can never make a decision without a woman's input." Beth smiled halfheartedly. She was still listening to a soft tinkling noise.

Matt rolled his eyes. "Come on, *mom.*" Gillian ran at him. He sprinted back to Devin, laughing as he ran. Beth started to follow, but the sound caught her attention more clearly.

"There are two options here; left and right," Hector stated.

Devin thought for a second. "If we cross back over to the inbound lanes we might not run into as much. I don't see the same soot over that tunnel, and I doubt people would be heading toward town."

"Yeah, maybe, but since there isn't any smoke there might be intact zombies down that tunnel," Hector responded.

"What do you think, Jill?" Devin asked.

Beth was sure she heard the tinkling sound. What she wasn't sure she heard was the *other* sound. It sounded almost like a dog whimpering. She slowly made her way to the mouth of the tunnel. She heard it again.

"What if we took that semi over there through first? That should have enough power to smash through most blockages, right?" Gillian suggested, pointing to a large truck a few feet behind them in the other lane.

"That assumes it runs, we can figure out how to drive it, and we can get it out of that mess," Hector grunted.

Beth heard the conversation behind her, but her attention was on the tunnel. It was definitely a dog whimpering. She couldn't see too far into the darkness. She could make out the shapes of several cars in it. Looking further down she could barely see light at the other end. The tunnel looked to be blocked.

"Could just be we have to weave through," she thought. "Better check it out." She was about to get a flashlight out of the truck when a small dog stepped out of the darkness. Beth stared at the dog and it stared back at her. Neither moved for a second. The tone of the conversation behind her was starting to take on that of an argument as the group tried to make a decision.

Beth crouched down, trying to coax the dog out of the tunnel. It moved forward slowly, straining on the leash that Beth hadn't noticed. She stood up slowly as a young girl stumbled forward. The end of the leash was twisted around her left wrist—most of her left hand was missing. Her white dress was covered in dried blood, her jaw was hanging on by a few strips of flesh, her tongue hanging out of her cheek. It looked like it had been half bitten off. Her eyes rolled in her head, then fixed on Beth.

Beth backed away while raising her gun. As she did, several more dead shuffled into the light. She could hear the group behind her.

"Guys!" she yelled, but no one responded to her. "Guys!" she yelled again.

"We should stay on this path! I bet the accident happened further into the tunnel and if the fire was that intense, we should have a clear path through."

"Guys! This is not the road to stay on!" Beth yelled as she backed toward them.

"Why?" was the angry question back to her. Beth replied by shooting the dead girl in the head.

"Oh hell! Beth, get back here!" Hector yelled, quickly firing into the oncoming group. Beth ran up to him. She pulled his knife from its sheath on his shoulder and took a hop-step to reach the dog. It whimpered and jumped at her. She cut through the leash and swept up the little dog. A dead hand grabbed at her shoulder, then another had her hair. Two cracks from behind her sounded, the bullets whizzing right over her head. The hands let go.

She ran toward to the truck. Trevor was already inside, Matt at his heels. Hector was at the passenger side door, rifle aimed. He fired and motioned for Beth to go around back. She ran to the rear, where Matt had the door open. She handed the dog to Matt as Trevor pulled her, in slamming the door.

"Dude! What the hell?" Matt looked at Beth, astonished.

"I couldn't leave him." The dog jumped up on Beth's lap. It yipped at her trying to lick her face. She reached into her jacket, pulling out a little beef jerky. The dog greedily ate the food.

"At least we know he wasn't eating them," Matt stated.

Devin crossed the yellow lines to the other tunnel as more and more undead crept out of the darkness. "Must have been full of tour buses or something," Matt speculated. The headlights broke through the blackness as they entered the tunnel.

Hector punched the wall, and Gillian glanced at him. "What the hell was she thinking?" he shouted.

Gillian took a deep breath. "She is the only one of us that paid attention to the tunnel."

"Lot of good that will do us if she gets herself killed over a dog," he shouted as he hit the wall again.

"I'm fine and I'm in the truck." Beth replied calmly, holding the dog as they swerved, clipping a small SUV that was half-blocking their lane.

"Only because we are good shots and took out the zombies that had you." He responded angrily.

"How's it looking up ahead?" Matt asked over Hector's yelling.

"What the hell were you thinking?" Hector demanded of Beth.

Silence filled the back of the truck for a moment, then Beth looked directly at the soldier and replied as if it was obvious. "Well, you were too busy trying to figure out which tunnel to take, so I had to find out which one was full of zombies."

This was not the response Hector wanted. He looked at Gillian, exasperated. She glanced back at him. "She is right," Gillian shrugged. Hector glared at Gillian. She hastily added, "We weren't paying attention."

"Still!" He turned back to Beth. "You...you can't go off on your own; we all need to stick together," Hector ordered, using his authoritative voice. Gillian flinched as a zombie bounced off the front of the truck.

"Right, thanks, I'll keep that in mind and let them eat us next time," Beth grumbled.

Hector glared, bracing himself as the truck slammed through several crashed cars and out of the tunnel and into the sunlight. Beth began to pet the dog, curled up next to Matt.

Devin spoke from the driver's seat, "He's right, we need to stick together."

Beth looked at the dog. "I know, but I just couldn't leave him to die."

Devin was silent for a moment. "No, but we don't want to lose *you* either."

"I appreciate that, but I can take care of myself pretty well," Beth muttered.

"Not if you keep running after strays," Matt laughed, "but I'm sure Romero here is happy you rescued him."

Beth questioned, "Romero?"

Matt smirked, "As in George Romero." Beth was still confused.

Trevor spoke up. "Night of the Living Dead, Dawn of the Dead." Beth looked from Matt to Trevor. "He was a director." They both stared at her.

"Potter fan," Matt snorted.

"Yeah, and?" she demanded.

"Nothing, nothing at all," Matt laughed, throwing up his hands. Then his face fell, "Ya know, those movies were much cooler before we were living them." He reached over and rubbed a very happy Romero's belly.

Speeding

Wes braced himself, marveling at Kate's driving. She swerved around abandoned vehicles to the bridge and across the lanes. Several zombies wandered nearby but didn't get close to the car as Kate stormed through the area, crossing the bridge in a blur.

The road opened up, and Kate urged more speed from the powerful V8 engine. Wes stared out the side window, watching the countryside getting lighter as it flew by. Steve was looking, but not seeing, out the front window. Kate slowed the car drastically and he threw his hands against the dash. Wes was thrown into the back of Kate's seat. "What?" Steve cried.

On the side of the road was a state trooper's car. "I seriously don't think you're getting a ticket," Steve laughed.

"Sorry, habit." Kate sheepishly replied.

"Habit?"

"Wait, pull over!" Wes cried, "there might be something useful."

Kate eased the car to the shoulder and backed up. She watched as the patrol car grew in the rearview mirror. "I don't know about this, guys. Why would that be sitting there?" Kate eyed the cruiser apprehensively.

"You think this might be some kind of a trap?" Steve asked. He surveyed the area, searching for hiding places. He opened the door to the car and stepped out cautiously.

"Okay— Kate, stay here and keep the engine running. Steve, cover me. I'll check it out." Wes crawled out of the backseat. "I mean it, pay attention to me! Keep your hands to yourselves."

"Just hurry up." Steve reached to smack Wes on the back of the head. Laughing, Wes ducked out of the car. The smile slid from his face as the feeling of dread grew in the pit of his stomach. Slowly, Wes approached the police cruiser. Glancing over his shoulder, he was reassured by Kate's watchful eyes in the rearview mirror. Steve turned around with his arm over the back of the seat and gave Wes an encouraging wave forward. Steve sighted the rifle in on the back seat of the cruiser.

Easing closer with his weapon ready, Wes watched for any movement from the vehicle. Looking up, he scanned the area behind the car. A few feet from the side, Wes dropped down to check under it. The space was clear. He turned and signaled to Steve that everything was clear.

"Come on, what is taking so long?" Kate anxiously asked, "I really don't like this."

"He's at the car," Steve reassured her, never taking his eyes off Wes.

Wes crept up to the driver's door. He peered through the dirty window at the front seat. It was empty. He checked the back. There were several boxes on the seat. Cautiously he tried the back door handle. It was locked. Moving back to the front door, he pulled at the handle. The door clicked open. The front seat was stained with dried blood. A brownish red trail lead to the passenger side door, which was open slightly.

The keys hung in the ignition. Wes leaned in and tried them, but nothing happened. It looked like the car might be out of gas and the battery was completely dead. Reaching over to the door he tried the automatic lock to open the back door. "Duh, the battery is dead," he muttered to himself.

"What's the deal?" Steve shouted.

"Car's dead, the cop must have died here with the engine running and crawled off somewhere. The front seat is all bloody. There is something in the back I want to check out," Wes called out, pointing to the back of the cruiser.

He turned back to the car and circled around the front to check the passenger side back door. Clearing the front bumper, he froze, then stumbled back a step. Leaning against the car was the corpse of a state trooper. His gun was in his hand. The splatter against the door told Wes all he needed to know. The officer had shot himself in the head.

He must have known he was done for and didn't want to keep walking around, Wes sighed. "Sorry, dude." He moved past the dead trooper and tried the door, but it was also locked.

"Come on, Wes." Kate shouted out the window.

Moving back around to the driver's side again, Wes smashed the rear window with the butt of his gun. Carefully reaching through the broken glass, he pulled the door lock. The door swung open, and Wes hastily stuffed his gun into the waist of his jeans and reached into the car to open the box.

"Jackpot!" he yelled. "Back up!" he excitedly waved.

Steve turned around, closing his door while Kate reversed to the back of the cruiser. Her eyes darted all over the landscape. "Hurry up, I still don't like this," she told Steve as he jumped out to help Wes. They unloaded three boxes from the back of the cruiser. The first contained canned foods, the second bottled water, the third a smaller box full of nine-millimeter bullets.

"This is great, except we don't have a nine-mil." Steve shrugged at the box of ammo in his hand.

"Hold on," Wes held up a hand, then ran around the car and dropped out of view. When he popped back up, he held a nine millimeter semi-automatic. Looking down, he smiled sadly. "Thanks, Officer... Miller," he said, reading the name on the badge.

Kate reluctantly handed Steve the keys so he could open the trunk. She had the car running as soon as the keys were returned. Steve and Wes hurriedly transferred the boxes to the trunk, then jumped into their seats. With everyone back in the car, Kate quickly eased back onto the highway and gained speed.

Someplace to Rest

"Static, static, and more static!" Trevor clicked off the radio with disgust. Devin had resumed their meander through abandoned vehicles, but upon reaching an open stretch had not sped up. At an area with a wide flat field on either side of the road and a small median, he rolled to a stop.

"What's up?" Beth asked, moving to Devin's shoulder.

"Where do we go?" he asked, turning to look at the others. The question hung in the air unanswered. No one knew the answer. Beth looked out across the field. An old car sat rusting in the middle of it. Further out, along the fence line, she could see them wandering back and forth, trying to find a way through.

"Where are we?" she asked. "I remember Amish farms out this way."

Matt spoke up, excited. "Hey, hey, I just came this way a couple of weeks ago. I remember that car. I thought it might be cool to try to fix it up." He faltered at the look on Beth's face that told him to make a point. "I...well, I remember that it took forever to get here from Harrisburg because of all the construction."

"So? There is always construction on this road. Steve, Wes and I go to the lake every summer and there is always one lane or the other closed," Beth noted.

"Yeah, but when we were stuck behind this cattle hauler— wow, that stunk— I noticed a huge farmhouse in the construction zone. I'm pretty sure it was Amish."

"If it was, that would be great." Beth smiled.

"If we can get to it, we might be able to use the construction barricades to build a kinda fort. I just hope it is a more progressive Amish house," Devin remarked.

Hector scratched his chin. "Why is it a good thing if it is an Amish house? Wouldn't any farmhouse be good if we can fortify it?"

"Well," Beth explained, "Any farmhouse would be good, but if is an Amish house it would be better suited for our current circumstance."

"Did the Amish have a plan for the living dead?" Hector asked with raised eyebrows.

Matt laughed. "No, not that I am aware of. What Beth means is they didn't have electricity prior to now. So the thing is, they would have things like oil lamps and candles, and maybe if they are more progressive they could have propane-powered refrigerators and ovens. If not, they will have wood for fires for cooking and heating."

"Never thought I would hope to end up in an Amish house," Hector mused.

Putting the truck back into drive, Devin asked Matt, "So how far do you think it is?" Matt couldn't remember if it was a half hour or longer to the construction zone. Beth watched the rusty car as Devin pulled away. Several zombies had found a hole in the fence and were now even with the old hulk. The field and the undead disappeared as they passed under a bridge.

After forty-five minutes the air in the armored car was becoming tense. Several signs had warned of the upcoming construction zone. The number of discarded automobiles and belongings had begun to increase. The trail of luggage told a tale of the change in priorities, from ownership to survival. The frequency of stains on the asphalt made it clear that survival hadn't always been obtained.

They passed a sign that informed them "Road Construction One Mile." Gillian called out from one of the small windows in the back, "Hey! Slow down! What is that over there?" She was pointing to something off the highway.

Devin slowed the truck and found himself crowded as everyone tried to find a larger window to look out. Not too far from the highway was a large white building. In the parking lot were several cars and a few tour buses. They were parked haphazardly all over the lot. "It looks like it was a rendezvous spot," Hector commented.

Trevor nearly bounced in his seat. "What do you think? Should we check it out? It might be an evacuation point. There might be information on where we should go."

New Friends

Ryan sat on the roof eating a cold microwave meal with a plastic spork. His legs dangled over the edge. He watched the undead below him milling about. Somewhere in there was his last companion. Ryan searched the crowd for the familiar hideous red jacket embroidered with a dragon.

He really loved that damn jacket, Ryan thought. He smiled and shook his head.

Finishing the last of the cold spaghetti, he wiped his mouth and surveyed the throng. He cleaned the spork and put it into his pocket. He returned his gaze down to the zombies. He needed to find the perfect one among the graying skin and torn clothes. 'Yes. There she was. If it weren't for the fact that she was dead, she looked almost normal.

Ryan watched her for a few moments and wondered how she died. Many of the zombies around her showed obvious wounds. Torn throats, ripped limbs; some even looked as if they had been disemboweled, but she looked untouched. Her business suit was a little dirty and wrinkled. Ryan attributed this to the recent rain. He kept watching her as he turned the food container over in his hand to empty any remaining sauce. Her face was clean—grey and sunken, but clean. He wondered if she had ever killed anyone. He knew for certain that many of the others below had. As he thought of this he saw the familiar red jacket. A smile crept over his face.

Returning his attention to the dead businesswoman, he wished her could see her hands. Would they also be clean, or had she ripped someone apart? They would be covered in blood then. As if to answer his question, the ghouls around her moved out of his view and there it was.

He could almost picture now how she had died. He told himself the story: she was working late at the office. Her husband or boyfriend called her to tell her what was happening. "Hurry home so we can escape." "In a little bit, I have some work to finish." She hung up the phone and finished filing the report that no one would ever read. Gathering her keys and briefcase, she headed to the door.

There was someone there—a janitor perhaps? She would have opened the door and come face to face with a zombie or two. Throwing up a hand in self-defense she would have tried to close the door. The zombie grabbed her hand and either ripped it off himself or had help. She would have been able to shut the door. She would have been leaning against the door while she bled to death, trying to keep them out.

It would only have taken a few minutes, by the look of the wound. Shrugging, Ryan took aim. When he hit her with this they would start to howl. They would moan and wail for hours while he hid inside, waiting for them to forget why they were there. It had become his daily entertainment.

He drew back. This was going to be a good one. Ryan froze. The sound of a large truck engine and then the chink of the gate opening on the other side of the building met his ears.

"We have new friends!" He smiled at the zombies below. "I'd better go and make them welcome." He dropped the empty container onto the roof and headed for the hatch that led back down into the massive warehouse.

Harrowdale

The closer they approached, the deeper the feeling of dread filled Beth. Several cars and a few larger trucks sat haphazardly in the lot. A moving truck with bright orange logos on its sides had its back door up and open. Devin paused at the closed gate. The chain holding the gates together was held with a padlock. "We could just push through the gates," he suggested.

"Why? The lock is open. We can just jump out and open the gate." Beth pointed to the lock that hung on the chain. Devin stared at the huge lock; it was indeed open.

"Who gets the honors of going out there?" Matt asked with raised eyebrows and a scrunched mouth. Everyone turned to look at him. "What? No, I did the factory."

"Oh, for goodness sake, seriously?" Beth huffed and climbed over Trevor. She wrenched open the door and hopped down to the pavement. The air was cold, with a hint of impending rain. A light breeze brought with it faint moans of the undead. Nervously looking around, she hurried to remove the lock with shaking hands. The chain fell free with a clatter. Beth jumped aside so Devin could push the gates open with the front bumper. The truck rumbled through. Hector jumped out of the back to get the other gate, catching up to Beth, who almost had hers closed. Several frantic seconds later they had the lock hooking the chains together, leaving it unlocked.

Breathing heavily, Beth regained the warmth of the interior. She looked over at Matt. "Okay, I see your point; that was no fun." He laughed while Romero forced his head under her hand, begging to be petted.

Devin slowly approached the first car near the back of the lot. The back window was dirty as if it had been sitting for a while. Through the grime they could see several boxes and luggage. The doors were closed and the windows were rolled up. Devin continued past several more cars on his way through the lot. He slowed to a halt near the back of the moving truck. Here again they spied boxes and luggage, but no signs of death.

"Okay, so where did they go?" Beth asked, barely able to keep the quavering fear from her voice.

"I don't know. Man, I really don't like this," Matt grumbled, staring out the back window at the lot and the empty vehicles. "I mean, it looks like there should be a lot of people here."

"Maybe they are holed up inside. You know, safe. This might be a great place. It looks like it might have been a distribution center," Trevor added hopefully.

Beth grimaced, "I heard them when I was out there. Sounded like a lot of them and they weren't too far away."

Instead of discouraging Trevor this seemed to bolster him, "Great! That means there must be people in there. I mean, the dead wouldn't be interested if there wasn't someone here, right?"

"Or they are all inside already," Hector offered. Trevor's face fell.

"Well, we're here, so we might as well check it out. Trevor is right. There might be something useful in there," Devin noted, pulling the truck ever closer to the front doors of the building. The front of the building looked as if it was just closed for the weekend. There was no sign of forced entry or of any attacks. The engine rumbled under the hood, the springs of the suspension creaked as a couple of people shifted to get a better look, but no one uttered a sound.

A sign hung above the doors, "Harrowdale Distribution." "Looks like this way in is closed," Matt commented, then shouted, "Look!" He needn't have shouted, as everyone in the truck had already seen the door open. A man peeked out. He looked around quickly, then beckoned them in. The group sat stunned for a moment. The door opened again. The man stood staring at them, then looked frantically around. He waved for them to hurry in. He let the door shut as he disappeared back inside.

"I'm starting to think Matt is right; I don't like this," Beth breathed.

"Come on, look at all the other vehicles. I bet there are a bunch of survivors in there. If there are a bunch of us, then we have a shot at the government coming to help us," Trevor exclaimed excitedly, and reached for the door handle.

"Wait! This could be a trap," Hector cautioned, grabbing Trevor's shoulder.

"No way, look at all the cars! There has to be a ton of people in there."

"Yeah, and how many might be infected?"

"I'm going!" Trevor yelled angrily as he wrenched his shoulder free of Hector's grip and threw open the door. Gillian moved into his seat, pulling the door closed as she did. Trevor paused for a second at the front door. He looked back to the truck, raised his hands questioningly. Then, with a wave of disgust, he pulled the door open and disappeared inside.

"Well, we can't let him go by himself," Gillian sighed. Devin grudgingly turned the key. Silence filled the cab as the engine died.

"I really don't like this," Matt grumbled. Gillian patted him on the back as she opened the door. Devin sighed, Hector grimaced and hiked his rifle onto his shoulder. Beth shook her head and checked her gun.

"I'm sorry, Romero you need to stay here," Beth sighed to the whimpering dog. She opened a window a crack, then joined Gillian and the others at the front entrance. Gillian reached out, opening the door. Hector aimed his rifle into the opening. Beth kept an eye out behind the group. Hector crossed into the building, followed by Gillian, then Devin. Matt and Beth, still outside, glanced at each other. Matt grabbed Beth's sleeve and whispered, "This isn't going to end well, I know it."

Beth saw in Matt's eyes that he was terrified. "This isn't like the factory. We're going to be fine," she tried to reassure him, even though she felt Matt was right. He shrugged and shook his head. She gave him a little push through the door. She was pulling the door shut behind her when she stopped to wave at the little dog. He was standing with his front paws on the dash. Romero yipped at her.

Field to Dream

"Where should we go?" Wes asked. Steve and Kate held a map down against the breeze. Steve looked left, then right, down the highway and back to the map. Kate leaned against the fender, staring off at three crosses in a field. "There is a church up ahead," Wes noted with a laugh that lacked any real mirth, "I think we'll pass on that."

"We should avoid towns altogether," Steve commented.

"So, we just drive around avoiding towns, and then what? Hope we run across more dead cops that just happen to have cars full of supplies? We need a place to hide until this all dies down," Kate said in frustration.

"Dies down... ha," Wes shot back.

Kate glared at him. "Oh, shut up," she said, rolling her eyes.

"Okay, how about this? There is a small, and I mean small, town about ten miles from here. Why don't we check it out? We might find a place to rest for the night." Steve pointed to a spot on the map with the name "Wellsboro". Kate and Wes looked at each other, then shrugged. Steve took this as an affirmation. He opened the driver's door. Kate headed around to the passenger side.

Climbing into the back of the car, she reached over the seat to pat Steve on the shoulder. "Any sign of trouble, we just turn around and head out. I don't want to get stuck in some building again, either." Steve put his hand over hers. Wes slammed the door, looked over at Steve and Kate holding hands, and made a gagging noise. Kate said, "Watch it, Wesley, or I will kiss him right in front of you."

Wes threw his hands up in surrender. "No, please, no one wants to see that." Steve turned to Wes. Wes opened his mouth to say something but found himself in a headlock. "Alright, alright, leggo!" Wes cried, pushing Steve's arm off.

Twenty minutes later found Steve slowing the powerful engine to a crawl on Main Street of Wellsboro. The street contained maybe fifteen or twenty buildings and houses. Boxes, paper, clothes and debris were strewn across the street. Several windows were broken, with signs of attacks. One window was covered in blood that ran down the wall and pooled into a dried stain on the sidewalk.

"We are not staying here," Steve whispered. No one protested. It took only a minute to creep through the empty town, but the silence would stay with them for a long while after. "Where did they all go?" Wes asked, without expecting a response.

Steve pulled off the road toward a baseball field. A chain link fence surrounded the field. The fence rose ten feet into the air behind home plate. Steve stopped in front of a gate that led into the diamond. Wes jumped out of the car, opening the gate. The car barely squeezed through. Wes closed the fence and jumped back into the car. Steve pulled right up to home plate, pointing the hood toward first base and the gate. Wes rolled up his window when Steve turned off the engine.

"Not what I had in mind," Kate mumbled, curling up in the back seat. Steve checked the gun in his hand and nodded to Wes, who eased his seat back and rolled onto his side as best he could.

"Wake me up in a couple of hours?" Wes asked. Steve nodded, then watched the light fade.

Hell Oh

Beth walked in to find the rest of the group standing with a tall unshaven man who was smiling at them. "Welcome, welcome, my name is Ryan. I'm so glad you found your way."

"You've been expecting us?" Beth asked, disbelieving.

The smile faltered a little on Ryan's face, but he replied quickly, "Well, not you specifically, but I have been waiting for all the survivors." Something in the way he said this caused Beth to shiver.

"So where are the others?" Beth asked in a tone she hoped was more pleasant than she felt toward the man.

Still smiling widely, Ryan answered, "Oh they're here, you'll get to meet them soon. First, I am sure you are hungry and tired. It has been a very trying time, hasn't it?"

"I guess this place is pretty safe? Looks like a lot of cars and a few trucks full of people made it here," Gillian stated, looking over her shoulder at the full lot. She caught Beth's eye and silently told her she wasn't comfortable with this either. Beth looked over at Hector, whose thumb was running along the safety of his rifle.

Trevor seemed to be beside himself with relief at finding another living human. "This looks like a distribution center of some kind. We stopped at one on the way out of town, but we didn't have time to pick up any supplies. We just had enough time to get a forklift and get out of town."

"We have plenty of supplies back in the warehouse. You had a forklift?" Ryan was trying to look past Devin into the lot now.

"Oh, we couldn't keep it, too slow." From here Trevor began to explain how they had all got together and their adventure up to that moment.

Ryan listened to the tale intently. When Trevor had finished, he asked, "So when you got back to the apartment Bill was dead and he had attacked... Stancy, was it? and she defended herself?"

Beth responded, "When we got back Bill was dead on the floor. Stancy said he died, but more likely she panicked when he got up to go to the bathroom and moaned. She was not what you would have called stable." Ryan considered her for a moment.

Hector interrupted, "That is our story. What is yours?"

Ryan seemed startled by the question. "How did I get here? It seems like I've always been here," he mused, rubbing the thick stubble on his chin. "Well, I had been at home trying to avoid getting sick, like everyone else. Then I just sat for a while watching everything fall apart. When the dead started walking, I barricaded myself in the house, like everyone else, it seemed. And like everyone else, I didn't know enough to be dark and quiet when they came around." Ryan shuddered at the memory.

"I had a couple of guns I used to go target shooting with. When the dead figured out I was there they wouldn't leave, no matter how quiet I was. They started breaking in, so I shot a few of them, then ran to the garage, got in the car, and drove as far and as fast as I could." Ryan seemed lost in the memory.

"How long were you able to stay in the house?" Devin asked, surprised.

"Only a couple of days. It seemed like the whole area was completely overrun. I stayed in the car for a while, but that only works as long as it runs and has gas." Ryan smiled, and Trevor laughed, turning to the others.

"So, I just drove around for several hours. It was strange that in this area there were very few of the zombies." Ryan paused, thinking back on that day. "I was getting pretty tired and I wrecked the car. Fortunately, I was only unconscious for a little while."

"Were you attacked in the car?" Trevor asked in a hushed tone.

"No, when I woke up there was only one on the passenger side, so I ran from the wreck and ended up on the roof of a building. After a day or so I was joined by a couple of other survivors. We sat up there shooting the dead with some rifles they brought. It was like a game for them." Ryan grimaced, remembering how they would make bets on who could make certain shots. "I don't know if we thought we would run out of dead before we ran out of bullets. Turns out we didn't. One of the guys knew about this place." Ryan motioned around at the room.

"We were a couple of miles away, so we decided to go for it. It was getting damn cold on that roof. There were five of us who left.

After the first day, we were down to three." Ryan watched the others as he spoke. He had Gillian's attention, and to his surprise, Matt's. Relishing the attention, he continued. "We were in luck on the second day and picked up some food and guns. After we lost another one of our party, we found this camping stuff. It was just lying in the middle of an alley. Right after we picked it all up, we got attacked. These three guys showed up and they were acting all scared and friendly. Then all of a sudden we were shooting at each other."

"Do you think it was a trap?" Trevor asked.

You mean people left the stuff so they could attack *people*?" Matt asked, "Why?"

"To get your guns and supplies," Beth explained.

"Damn, that's messed up," Matt replied.

"Well, it almost worked," Ryan said. "They killed Tim, the other guy I was with, then they ran off with some of his gear and the tent. So now it was just two of us. Me and this woman, I forget her name. We made it about three blocks from the alley when the guys who attacked us showed up again. I just figured they were back for the rest our stuff. So..." Ryan paused, and he seemed to be picking his words carefully.

He looked at Gillian and Matt "Well, you can understand; I shot one of the guys. Just shot him, right in the face. His buddy started screaming that they were sorry, they made a mistake. He started going on about how we needed to stick together. I thought I had made a mistake, so I lowered my gun. Well he didn't mean it. As soon as my gun wasn't aimed at him, he shot and killed the woman I was with. So I shot him."

Gillian nodded in understanding. Ryan nodded back to her. "The sound of the guns had alerted some of the dead. I looked up and saw I was in trouble. They were coming down the alley, so I grabbed as much as I could and started running. Then I just headed here. I went out a few times and found some more weapons and some other survivors—they're in the back—and we have food and water, so we just hide. We haven't seen anyone in a couple of days." Ryan had deliberately left out a lot of details in his story to the new arrivals. They didn't need to know what he had seen and done, and he didn't feel the need to share everything.

Devin spoke up, "We have plenty of food, water and weapons. We just need a place to rest up and not be bounced around for a while. Can we stay here, for a little while?"

Ryan smiled and opened his arms wide. "You are very welcome here. Let's go and meet the others."

Bottom of the Ninth

Steve's head snapped up; he rubbed his eyes and shook the sleep from his skull. Wes was curled up in the seat next to him. He turned and smirked at Kate, because she was almost short enough to stretch out completely. Steve rubbed his eyes again and adjusted in the seat. Sitting up straight he cracked his neck and tried to focus. It was really black outside. Clouds passed over the thin light of the moon. Steve held his hand in front of his face to see if the old adage held up. It did.

Kate mumbled and rolled over in the back, causing the car to bounce a little and the suspension to creak. Wes jumped, wild-eyed and tense. "Relax, it was just Kate moving around," Steve whispered. A breeze blew through the window. He had opened it a crack to keep himself awake, and because they had not bathed in several days. With the breeze came not fresh air but the sickly smell of the undead.

The sky was already slipping from inky black to a deep purple. Dawn was approaching slowly. "You smell that?" Wes' voice whispered anxiously from beside Steve. The horizon continued to lighten. The dark shadow of the tree line became more defined and pronounced. Dark shapes were milling around the outfield fence. "Oh man," Wes breathed.

"It's okay, there aren't too many, and they are all the way out there." Even as he spoke Steve was surveying the close-by fence, especially the break through which they had driven.

"Dude, look again—I think the whole town is out there." Wes pointed, and Kate stirred in the back. Sitting up, she rubbed the sleep from her eyes, looked out the front window, and swore.

The sky was now a beautiful light blue and golden sunlight was streaming through the trees, silhouetting full pines and leafless oaks. High fluffy white clouds were sliding across the sky, clearing out as the sun rose in earnest. All of this was lost on the three passengers of the car, parked on home plate of the overgrown infield. They watched as more and more of the previous residents of the nearby town came out, as if a game was being played at that very moment. Even from their distance they could see the outfield fence straining as the bodies pressed against it. Finally, the right side gave way and zombies spilled onto the field. They stumbled and fell over each other, then plodded on toward the car. The voice of reason questioned the two transfixed men in the front seat. "Why the hell are we still sitting here?!"

The engine roared to life and the tires spit dirt and grass as the first ghoul's feet hit second base. "I think the home team just won," Wes spoke shakily, after the diamond had disappeared from view.

Separation

Ryan turned toward a door with a sign that read "employees only" and pushed his way through. Just past the door was another set of swinging doors and several offices. The others followed. Beth looked around the area for any sign of other people. She found it odd that no one was out in this area. No one other than Ryan came to meet them. Ryan was almost at the double doors when he stopped and turned to face them.

"There is something here that might interest you," Ryan touched Hector on the shoulder, pointing to an office, then he gestured toward the doors. "You can go ahead, just through those doors." He smiled. Hector looked into the office and noticed a grenade launcher and several high-powered assault rifles just inside the door. He smiled and disappeared into the office.

The others pushed through into a large open area. Beth gazed around. There were several areas set up as sleeping spots. Personal belongings were littered around the sleeping bags and piled blankets and clothes. There were toys and a baby's car seat. Further in were piles of boxes. What was lacking was people. "Hello?" Beth called. They heard something at the far end among the boxes. Beth looked over her shoulder as she followed the others. "Where is Hector?" she asked. Gillian turned to look back as well and shrugged.

Devin, Trevor and Matt were already looking through the stacks of boxes that littered the loading dock when Beth and Gillian joined them. Beth kept checking over her shoulder for Hector. There were plenty of boxes, but still no sign of any people. Trevor kept saying how wonderful the places was. "Look at all this stuff! What is it, food? Clothes? What do we have?" He kept smiling nervously at everyone. "This place is great, isn't it?"

"Come on, there is nothing here." Gillian said angrily as she read the contents of the closest box. Devin looked over the labels as well, then up at the others.

Matt wandered over to the loading dock door. He stood on tiptoe to see through the small oval window. "Oh shit!" He jumped away from the glass. "The whole parking lot is full of them.," he cried, pointing at the closed door.

Ryan appeared behind them. He walked over to the window and peered through it. He watched the zombies stumbling around for a moment. He turned to the others with an amused look on his face. He calmly walked over to the chain that opened the door and began pulling it.

"What the hell are you doing?" Matt screamed as he ran to stop him.

Ryan threw Matt off and continued to open the door. "I want you to meet everyone. They are just *dying*…well, they died to meet you." Trevor panicked and threw himself at Ryan to stop him, and it worked for a moment. That moment was over when Ryan pulled a gun and fired three rounds into a stunned Trevor's chest.

"NOOOOOO!!!" Matt cried, running at Ryan again. Gillian ran to Trevor. Beth and Devin reached for their weapons, but Ryan grabbed Matt pointing the gun to his temple.

"I don't think we will have any of that." Ryan smiled, motioning for them to put down their weapons.

Beth' heart raced as she surveyed the scene. Trevor lay on the floor, blood flowing freely from his wounds. He held a look of terror as he tried to stem the flow. Gillian was trying to hold a cloth against his chest. Devin stood still, his hands out to his sides. Ryan had a hold of Matt, who struggled to free himself. Ryan was able to hold the gun under Matt's chin and still open the door with his free hand. Little by little, the loading dock door opened on about thirty of the living dead, who struggled and clawed to get at the living.

Devin lowered his gun and held out a hand. "Just relax, it's cool. We don't want anything—we'll just go."

"Where is Hector?" Beth demanded.

Ryan smiled. "Oh, your big friend is admiring my gun collection. Or he would, if he was conscious. I couldn't have him overpowering me, and no, I don't wish for you to go."

"Well, you don't want us to stay. You obviously didn't want them to. What do you want from us?" Gillian asked, never taking her eyes off Matt.

"It is time to embrace that which is your great gift. It is time to let go and enter my kingdom." Ryan spoke as if from a pulpit, "Look out upon the beauty of the new world."

"All I see is a living hell," Beth spoke, shaking with anger and fear, "and right now I am looking at the devil." Devin shushed her.

Ryan smiled, "This may be hell to you, but it is true heaven for them. Their cares and worries are gone." He surveyed the horde, clawing at the, inches from his feet. "Look, look there!" he said, pointing to the middle of the teaming mass of reaching arms. "See how they are all now equal. A rich businessman side by side with a poor man, racist next to black. They are all equal. Color, status, it means nothing. This is truly paradise. As God willed it to be."

"Paradise?" Beth spat, "They are mindless zombies bent on killing! How is this God's will?"

"Free will was always the devil's playland. This..." Ryan stretched his arms wide, throwing Matt to the end of the dock. "This is a return to purity. God has shown the sinners the way."

"You're insane!" Gillian screamed from Trevor's side. He was growing paler by the second. His life was flowing away across the floor from the bullet wounds in his chest.

Ryan turned to stare at Gillian. His eyes were as lifeless and cold as any zombie's. "Soon he will be cleansed of all sin and join his brothers and sisters. He will wake to judge you," Ryan whispered.

Devin moved to tackle Ryan but froze in his tracks, hands raised, as the gun barrel pointed in his direction. "I don't want to be the one to take you. It is their job now. You will become one with them."

Dazed from being thrown, Matt tried to regain his footing. He lost his balance and was again in Ryan's grip. Ryan twisted Matt's arm behind him, forcing the young man close to the edge. Fingers grabbed at the tips of his sneakers. Gillian screamed as Ryan pushed Matt further out over the horde. They grabbed at his feet and legs. Matt screamed in terror.

"Come on now, let him go," Devin soothed. Devin realized too late that Ryan was going to comply, just not in the way he wanted. "NOOOOOOOOOOOOOOOOO!"

Beth watched as if in slow motion as Ryan pushed Matt into the mass of ghouls. For a moment it looked like he was at a concert, being borne away on the hands of the crowd. Then they began to tear at his flesh. She couldn't stop watching as they tore away his limbs, ripped his head from the torso and flung bloody pieces into the air. His cries mingled with that of Gillian and Devin and the joyful shouts of Ryan.

Hatred and rage boiled over Beth's mind. She took a step toward Ryan, who instantly aimed one gun at her and pulled another to aim back at Devin and Gillian, who had advanced toward him. They stopped as the weapons trained in on them.

"Matt was torn to pieces! He can't join them; how do you explain that?" Beth screamed, anger swelling within her.

"His sins were too great. He could not be… reborn." Ryan turned his dead gaze to her.

"To hell with this," she heard Devin whisper, then he was a blur as Gillian ran one direction, he another. Beth took the clue and ran at him as well. Devin reached him first, slamming into his ribs. Ryan was flung sideways into the other door, His hand slammed into the metal track. A flash from the muzzle and a loud pop was barely noticed amongst the angry shouts and cries of pain. Beth fell back as something burned white hot into her left arm. The undead jumped and moaned and howled. From the corner of her eye Beth saw Trevor stumble to his feet.

"Get them, my child! Get them!" Ryan screamed.

Devin realized Ryan was pointing behind him. He ducked and rolled quickly out of Trevor's grasp. Beth raised her right arm to aim her gun and found that she couldn't raise her left, as she was half blinded with pain. Trevor moaned and advanced toward her. Beth, nauseous with pain, lifted her gun and fired. The bullet flew wide, showering Gillian with shards of splintered concrete. Ryan laughed and called for Trevor to destroy the sinners. Beth, clutching her arm, ran behind some boxes. There was an angry banging on the door leading back out to the armored car. She prayed it was Hector. Blood dripped off her fingers and black tunnels were forming on the edges of her vision. She knew she was seconds from passing out.

"Forget the little bitch!" Ryan yelled. Beth could hear Devin cry out and boxes tumble to the ground. "Help me, my child, help your master, help your king!"

Gillian cried out a warning. Beth crouched down, fighting through the dizziness. She snuck a peek around the edge of the pallet she was hidden behind. Gillian was backed against another tower of boxes. Devin was scrambling out of the way, and Ryan was getting to his feet. In the middle was Trevor—his face pasty white, his eyes lifeless and staring. He staggered with his arms outstretched. Angry frustrated growls escaped his grey lips at the movements of his prey. The incessant pounding from the door caused him to spin slowly in circles, trying to get at the closest of the living.

"Yes! Take them; free them," Ryan called, firing at Devin, who had taken shelter behind several crates to avoid Trevor. He next fired at the door that Hector was trying to break through. This did nothing to deter the pounding. "Get them!" Ryan yelled at Trevor, pointing between Gillian and Devin.

Beth's vision blurred and her head swam. A red puddle had formed next to her. It had to be a trick of the light or her slipping consciousness. Trevor looked from Devin, who was moving further from him around his boxes, to Gillian who was trapped against a wall, to Ryan. Ryan held a gun and had several escape routes. Zombie Trevor ignored the command. He moved straight at Ryan.

"What are you doing? Get them! This is my will as your king! As God willed it...Stop! No! No! NOOOOOOO!" Disbelief filled Ryan's eyes as Trevor advanced on him. "You will do as I say, and I say—AARRRGGHHHH." Ryan's words were drowned in his own blood as Trevor's teeth tore into his throat.

Falling backward, Ryan pushed Trevor off him. Taking aim, he shot him through the skull. Clutching at his throat, he mouthed futilely at Devin, his eyes wide as blood began to fill his lungs. The door finally crashed open, and Hector ran to Beth, raising his rifle and sighting it in on Ryan.

Ryan tried feebly to raise his own weapon at Hector. Gillian walked right up to Ryan, who then tried to aim at her. She slapped the gun aside. "You will not find your paradise," she said as she pulled the gun from his hand. There was a second's terrible pause when Ryan knew it was the end. Gillian shot him between the eyes. His dying expression was of shock.

Devin and Gillian pushed him to the edge of the dock. Ryan's body fell out the open door among the clawing and reaching dead. They held him for a second, then let his lifeless body fall to the ground to be trampled.

Hector looked down at the body until it was covered by the dead. He slammed the garage door back down, severing a zombie arm in the process. "Let's get the fuck out of here," he breathed.

Gillian stood staring at the closed door. Tears streamed down her face. "We had made it so far. From the office, through town, and he never, never lost his sense of humor!" She wiped furiously at her cheeks. "How? How could this happen? How could one of us, the *living*, do that to him?"

"Gillian, come on—Jill! Hey, Beth needs you," Devin whispered, taking her by the arm. She seemed to come to herself.

"Beth? Is she okay?"

"I think she got shot."

Gillian grabbed Devin's hand, squeezed it in thanks, and then rushed to Hector, who was crouched next to Beth. She helped her to pull off her jacket. Beth tried again to move her arm as Gillian inspected the damage. "Stop. Stop, we need to get that bandaged and into a sling," Gillian said, cradling Beth's injured limb.

Hector smiled at Beth. "Doesn't look too bad, sister."

Beth cried out, grabbing the sleeve of Hector's shirt. Gillian pressed Beth's arm and turned it. Beth turned greenish white. "Oh I may puke on you. OOOHHH."

"You are lucky. It looks like it was a small bullet..."

"Probably a 22," Hector suggested.

"It seems to have passed right between the ulna and radius. Might have nicked one or the other, but neither seems broken."

"Hurts like hell," Beth said through gritted teeth.

Hector and Devin searched through the warehouse, coming up with a first aid kit and several clean-looking sheets and towels. While they searched they ignored the banging on the loading dock doors, but avoided getting too near them. Devin eyed the rollers and rails with apprehension. Hector helped to fashion a sling for Beth's injured arm. "This totally sucks," she said, inspecting her bandaged limb, cringing as she tried to move her fingers. Gillian wrapped a new jacket over Beth's shoulders.

"Let's see if there is anything useful here, and then get the hell out," Devin said.

Devin, Hector and Gillian searched through all the sleeping areas. They found some clean clothes and toiletries. Gillian walked up to Beth, who was trying to help by sorting some of the items the others had found. She was filling several bags and boxes. She looked at some of the things people had thought to save. She thought about what was in her own bag. She thought about the book she had grabbed on her flight from the house. It felt like a thousand years had passed since Steve had given her a hard time about it.

"You doing okay?" Gillian asked.

"I'm okay. I will be better when I find Steve and Wes." She sighed, not looking up. "How are you?" She raised her eyes to meet Gillian's.

"I miss Matt. He...I just...he was like the annoying little brother I never wanted, but God I miss him already." Gillian smiled as a tear ran down her face. "I found this for you." She held out a couple of books and a new jacket "And this is for Matt." In her other hand was a bunch of silk flowers.

"Thanks. Can I come with you?"

Gillian held out a hand and Beth grabbed it, needing the help to her feet. They slowly walked to the closed door. Gillian put down the flowers, Devin and Hector joined them. Hector had made a cross out of some broken pallets and a scarf. He'd scratched

"Matt" onto it. "I didn't know his last name," he muttered. Beth blinked the tears out of her eyes. After a few moments they turned to the blanket that covered the body of Trevor. Devin said a few words, and Hector placed another cross on the blanket.

"I hope your brother and friend are safe," Gillian said, and squeezed Beth's uninjured arm.

"I'm sure they made it out of town," Beth said. She knew Jill didn't believe they were alive, but she *knew*. She knew they were okay. She laughed at herself as she imagined her brother and her best friend running around like Rambos through the city.

The group left their friends' gravesite. Hector found a can of paint and added a "do not open" sign to the loading dock door. Devin hurried the others through the door as an ominous clang of a falling door roller sounded behind them through the pounding.

They returned to the parking lot, where they did a search of the cars, collecting as many useful items as they could. Romero jumped and yipped at their heels. He kept stopping and looking expectantly at the door to the warehouse. Beth leaned over to the dog, who licked her face. "I'm sorry, he's not coming." Romero whimpered.

She helped the little dog into the truck, then tried to help load several boxes of supplies into the back of the armored car. She took a moment to stare at the building. She whispered a goodbye, then climbed into their mobile fortress. They left in search of a new, safe place that did not hold the death of two more of their friends.

A Few Hours

"I don't like the look of this.," Steve stated, looking out the front window. Wes stirred from the back seat. Kate stared over the steering wheel at the open gate. Several cars and trucks littered the lot in front of them. She turned to look at Steve, and he shrugged. Checking the rear view, Wes held up his hands to show he also did not know the best course of action. Frowning, she pulled forward into the lot. Steve rolled his window down as they proceeded. The moans of the dead filtered through the opening. Even over the powerful V8 engine they could be heard. "They're near. I don't think this is a good idea."

Kate slowed the car so they could look into the empty vehicles they passed. Several had open doors. They could see boxes and luggage that lay strewn and open all over the lot as if someone had hurriedly searched through the belongings.

"What were they looking for?" Wes wondered aloud, eyeing a box that lay on its side, its contents spilled on the pavement. He could see shiny gold chains and a pile of cash that blew around, littering the lot with the faces of long-dead presidents.

"Whatever it was, I don't think they were here too long ago." Steve watched a suitcase teeter and fall off the hood of a car as the breeze caught the lid. A couple of very small shirts and socks fell to the ground. The tires crunched over another half empty suitcases on their way to the front of the building. Kate eased the car to a stop.

No one spoke a word as Kate turned the key. Silence filled the car for just a moment then the mournful moan of the dead mixed with the distant smell of death caused a shudder in every occupant. The doors to the car creaked open while the three exited. Kate slowly closed her door, making sure the door latched, then quietly pushed it the rest of the way shut with her hip. She scowled at Steve when he slammed his own door.

"What?" he hissed at the look on her face. Wes rolled his eyes, then wandered toward an old Ford that sat close by with its driver's door open. "Wes!" Steve called in a whisper. Wes looked from the car's interior to Steve, his confusion growing. The glove box was open, as was every other container in the vehicle. Everything of value in the old world was still there; the things that were missing were clothes and personal grooming products. On the ground next to the door was a tube of toothpaste. The contents squished out the back, the top and cap crushed as if stepped on. Wes kept looking at the blue paste as he rejoined the other two.

"Should we even bother going in?" Kate questioned.

"We don't know how long they were here. They may have just ransacked the cars and left. There might be something useful inside," Wes stated unconvinced.

"Yeah and we might find out why they left, still hiding inside." Steve nodded at the front door. The three stood watching the doors. Nothing happened. After several minutes Wes and Kate looked at each other across Steve. They nodded and pushed him closer to the door. "Whoa! Whoa, hold on," he grunted, fighting his way out of their grasp. "I still don't know if it is a good...."

"Let's go in or get out of here, but let's make a decision. It is starting to get late and just standing here isn't getting us food or a place to spend the night," Kate admonished. Wes snickered at the over six-foot tall burly athlete who cowered slightly under the glare from the five-foot-nothing woman. He paid for this by being hit hard on the arm by Steve.

"Come on, scrawny, let's check it out." Wes and Kate followed closely as Steve stepped up to the door. He peered through the dusty window at the dimly lit entrance. "Looks okay," he whispered, pushing the door open. Quietly they inspected the empty offices and cubicles. "It's as picked over in here as out there," Steve grumbled. Moving toward the splintered doors that led from the office to the warehouse, Steve turned questioningly to the others.

Shaking slightly, Kate whispered, "This looks bad; is it really worth it?"

Steve pushed the broken door out of his way, glancing over his shoulder. "They may have missed something, or left a note as to where they are going."

"Do we want to know where they are going?" Wes asked, inspecting the broken hinges. Steve didn't answer. Passing through the splintered doors, they looked around at the large open warehouse. In several places it looked like people had set up camp-like areas. These had obviously been rummaged through. Wes sighed as Kate passed him to check further into the warehouse.

"It looks like they really went through this place. I doubt we'll find much of anything." He kicked an empty suitcase in frustration. He was tired and hungry, and someone had beaten them to what he was sure was a place that had held food. Steve ignored Wes' grumblings. Something had caught his eye. He slowly approached an area of the floor that was shiny in the late afternoon light.

Steve knelt down next to the dark liquid, dipping his finger into the small puddle. He quickly wiped it off. It was blood and it hadn't been there very long. Wes stood over Steve's shoulder. "Why the hell did you put your fingers in...HEY! Look!" Wes pointed past the blood to a jacket. He recognized it at once. Steve was barely standing before Wes pushed past him, grabbing up the piece of clothing.

"Wes, man it could be anybody's."

"No! No, this is hers, I know it!"

"Seriously? I doubt it." Looking at the sleeve and the dark stain and hole he prayed it wasn't hers.

"Dude, it is hers! Look, right here," Wes was pointing to a mark just below the shoulder on the right side. "Beth was so pissed when this happened."

Steve moved closer. "Yeah, that is where you wrote on her with a sharpie. It never came out no matter how many times I washed it." Wes raised his eyebrows. "What? Dad was too busy, and Beth did the vacuuming, so what? I did laundry." Wes shrugged and smiled, but his smile faded as he took the bloody sleeve in his hand.

"This didn't happen too long ago." Wes let go of the sleeve. His hand was red with blood, "She had better be okay."

"Guys, I think you need to see this," Kate called. The two looked at each other. Steve let go of the jacket, but Wes grabbed it. They hesitated for a second before Steve nodded and Wes began rolling up Beth's jacket. They raced to Kate's side. She was standing over a blanket that obviously held a body. A makeshift wooden cross lay on the blanket. "That's not all." Kate spoke, pointing to a closed loading dock door. Another cross, bearing the name Matt was resting against it, and a sign that read "DO NOT OPEN."

Wes looked at the blood-stained sleeve then at the blanket, then to Steve. He could see he was thinking the same thing. Kate took a deep breath then crouched beside the blanket. Steve grabbed Wes' shoulder. They held their breath as Kate lifted the corner and peered underneath. She exhaled first and pulled back the edge to reveal a face none of them knew. "Shot through the head, but it looks like he got a hold of someone first." Kate noted pointing at the blood drying on Trevor's mouth. Wes looked at the sleeve again. Steve lifted it up, poking a finger through a small hole.

"I think, I think she got shot." He was relieved, but only slightly.

"Look. there is more blood and, is that... oh God." Kate covered her mouth, gagging slightly. "Is that brain?"

Wes bent over and looked closely. Standing up with a look of disgust on his face, he said, "Yep, that's brain alright." Kate backed away, looking revolted. She was almost at the loading dock door when she turned around.

She looked at the wooden cross. "Did you guys know a Matt?" Neither of them could recall knowing one well. Kate then looked up and out through the window. She gave a yelp of fright that had an instantaneous effect. The warehouse was suddenly filled with the sound of pounding as hundreds of fists slammed into the door. The metal railing gave way, as did the left side of the door. Several hands reached around the edge. Kate ran back to join Steve and Wes. "They're all over out there! And there's a bunch on the dock."

"How did they get up there?" Wes yelled as the first zombie squeezed through the opening. The top rail fell, as did the rest of the door, crushing the zombie that had made it through. Unfortunately, its companions now had free access. To answer Wes' question, the undead had pressed and clawed their way over the other undead, building a ramp of broken and crushed bodies. Kate grabbed briefly both of the boys' arms as she flew back across the warehouse. Steve and Wes glanced at each other then followed as fast as they could. It was if a dam of the undead had burst, and they were everywhere at once. Kate screamed, finding her way blocked by a heavyset woman with a filthy, bloody shirt, half-hanging off her shoulder. The large ghoul lunged at Kate. She dodged and grabbed Wes by the collar to keep him from running right into the creature. Steve grabbed Kate's arm and she still held Wes as Steve pulled her toward the exit.

"Where are they coming from?" Kate cried. Crashing through the broken doors, the three sprinted across the office space then out the front doors. Kate was in the driver's seat with the engine running before Steve had the door open. Wes dived into the back and Steve into the front. The door banged painfully on his leg as Kate threw the car in reverse. Cursing, Steve pulled his leg in, slamming the door as the first zombie stumbled and fell off the step leading to the office door.

"Right. Next time it looks picked over...we just keep going," Steve said, rubbing his bruised leg.

"You're damn right." Kate agreed.

"Absofu..."

"Wes!" Kate laughed nervously.

There

Night had fallen. Beth bounced along in the back of the truck, bumping into one of the boxes they had taken from the warehouse. It took a few moments for her to realize the hard object that kept poking painfully into her rib was her cell phone. She frowned as she tried to angle her uninjured arm to get to the inside pocket of the new jacket she was wearing. It had been the pocket she always carried the phone in, so it just ended up there during the transfer.

"Why did I even keep this?" she mumbled, "There is no one left to call." Opening the phone, she noticed it was 9:30pm. Smiling at the thought of time, and that it could matter, she saw there was still no service and that her battery was almost dead. Thinking quickly, she opened her picture files and scrolled through them. She smiled to herself as the memories filled her mind. Her Dad and Steve grilling in the backyard, arguing over who was a better cook. Wes at the Ren Faire, Steve with his Mustang. The battery icon began to flash. This might be the last time she ever saw these pictures. She studied everyone, trying to burn the images into her brain. She tried to to crowd out all the things she had seen over the last several days, and especially the last few hours.

The screen blinked out at 9:37pm. She looked at the black screen. She started to throw it aside, stopped, and then put it in her pocket. The back of the truck was dark but roomier than it had been. The added space only served to remind her of all they had lost.

She was out back with Steve, Wes and her dad. It was a beautiful day and she was having a great time. She was laughing with Steve, and Wes had just put his arms around her and was spinning her around. She woke with a start. Where was she? What was happening? It all flooded back, and she fought to keep the tears from falling.

Hector slowed as they approached a small truck that was off the road in the median. Gillian was staring blankly out the side window. Devin shuffled to his feet. "What's up?"

"Looks like we need a gas station." Hector frowned. Beth got to her feet and pulled out her gun. Devin followed Hector out to the truck while Gillian hoped over into the driver's seat. Beth exited the passenger side door. Hector tapped the tank of the other truck. "Wow, full. That may mean trouble." Beth was tense, but after several long minutes of filling empty gas cans and filling their own tank, nothing moved.

Returning to the back of the truck Beth put her head on her uninjured arm and rested it on her knees. "I just want to go home. Is that too much?" She wept.

"I think it is...for now." Hector sniffed from across the darkness.

The next day had a lethargic beginning. The sun had risen fully before the group had even begun to discuss their next move. Long silences filled the spaces. Beth could almost hear the silly questions Matt would have posed. The day was half gone before they had gone ten miles from the truck that had given them power. Gillian had offered to drive, stating that it gave her something to do. The problem was she still had tears running down her cheeks from time to time. Beth stretched out in the back and immediately felt guilty for doing so, as if this dishonored the memory of those who were gone. The truck hit a bump and Beth's injured arm hit the wall, "Ow, Jill! Can you watch out for the potholes?"

"Sorry, got distracted." Gillian slowed the truck. She was looking out over the fields to a farmhouse. Devin was roused from the passenger seat. The farm consisted of a large house with a barn and a couple of outbuildings close by.

"No power lines going to it. Must be Amish," Devin pointed out to the others.

"What do you guys think? Want to give it a try?" Hector asked.

"Hopefully they were the more progressive Amish." Beth stated.

"Yeah, but how much better is it going to be, really?" Hector grumbled.

"Well it could be really good, especially in this area." Beth stated. At their confused looks, she explained. "Most people think the

Amish are completely against technology. The truth is, depending on the order they belong to, they can have a lot of the same things we have." Again, she noticed the raised eyebrows. "As long as there are no wires going into the house, they can have lots of things." She looked at the others and knew they didn't understand.

"You mean they have battery powered stuff?" Hector asked.

"Well, yes and no." Beth replied. "Some sects allow propane powered refrigerators and hot water heaters. Battery powered lights for the buggies and even cell phones." She finished.

"Seriously?" Hector asked. "What about guns? Do they hunt?"

"Not that I am aware of," Beth responded.

Devin was still surveying the house. "Well, let's find a way to get there."

"And soon," Gillian nodded, "we can't keep going without re-fueling again." She shuddered at the thought. They had a full tank, but passed up a rest stop. It had been half burned and covered with the undead. She applied the accelerator but kept the speed to around thirty. A mile down the road, they came to an exit. At the toll plaza they pulled to the left-most booth, avoiding several wrecked cars.

"This is a cash only lane," Devin joked, "Anyone got some change?" Romero gave an appreciative bark. Beth shook her head. Gillian started, because she had actually stopped to pay the toll. Shaking her head, she turned left toward the road back to where they had seen the farmhouse. Several more cars littered their path, but there was enough room to pass the truck through.

Passing a school bus, Beth couldn't help but take in every detail. The front was smashed in, and one wheel had broken through the barrier and was hanging over the side of the bridge. The windows were smeared with dried blood. Several of the handprints were very small. In her mind's eye she could see what had happened. One of the passengers or more had been infected and turned. The screams and panic rang in her ears even though she had not witnessed the event.

"Do you think we should stop and check the vehicles for supplies?" Devin asked.

"I think it is best if we just keep going," Gillian responded.

"There might be something we need," Devin argued. Beth noted there was no real conviction in his voice. They rumbled on, Devin staring off across the fields, Gillian at the wheel, Hector rearranging supplies and Beth absently rubbing the palm of her hand on her injured arm. She watched as the daylight began to fade.

Gas and Go

Night had fallen by the time Kate parked the car behind the lone convenience store on the empty stretch of road. They could see the highway they had left just an hour before. They had been able to find a couple of bottles of water and a few scraps of food: snack cakes and some chips. The best part was, in Kate's opinion, the bathroom. The toilets still flushed and the faucets still ran. Each of them took turns standing guard while the other in the group tried to clean themselves as much as possible. Steve found deodorant in one of the isles. "Looks like people don't mind smelling bad when they are on the run," Wes laughed. His smile was wiped from his face as Kate threw him a stick.

"Yeah, but they aren't stuck in a car with you," she pointed an accusing finger at him, "You stink."

"Me? What about monkey boy over there, or you, for that matter?" he demanded.

"Well, Steve does smell. Me? I'm a lady." The three broke out into fits of laughter. They scavenged whatever they could and returned to the car for the night.

Kate slowly woke, the bright light blinding her. Wes grumbled from the driver's seat, until Steve hushed them both. Even though there were dark circles under his eyes, he was wide awake and alert. He pointed to the far corner of the store behind the car. A zombie was shuffling around the trash can, an empty bag fluttering in his hand. The creature would knock into the bin, stumble back, wander away a few feet, then stumble back to the container.

"What is it doing?" Kate wondered aloud.

"Not sticking around to find out," whispered Wes as he turned the key. The powerful engine sprang to life at once. Steve urged Wes to *move* as the ghoul's attention sprang from the trash can to the noisy rumble of the engine. Wes pulled away, watching the zombie get smaller and smaller in the rearview mirror.

"Glad he didn't decide to change the bag last night," Kate laughed nervously.

"He could have been there; we never made it that far," Wes replied.

"Couldn't have. I mean, we were in there for a couple of hours, and we weren't exactly quiet when we returned to the car." Wes had no reply to this, so they drove along in silence for a while. After a few hours they pulled over on a deserted stretch of highway high up in a mountain. The view was spectacular.

"You know, I used to ride up here with my dad. We would go to a biker rally a few towns over," Kate said, staring out over the valley. "It looks so peaceful—it isn't, but it looks nice." She pointed to a small town in the valley. Wes and Steve looked down at the scene. Wes thought Kate was overlooking several things to come to the peaceful idea. Several buildings were blackened and burnt out. Cars littered the streets and the occasional zombie wandered in and out of view. No, Wes thought, that place looked like the exact opposite of peaceful. He exchanged a glance with Steve, who shook his head, as if to say, let her have her moment.

Getting grudgingly back into the car, Steve fired up the engine, then let out a low whistle. "We have a small problem."

Wes looked over Steve's shoulder at the gas gauge "Yep, that is a problem."

Driving for an hour, the three kept glancing at the gauge as it steadily approached the large "E." Wes became progressively frustrated the closer it got to the letter. "Seriously? We saw cars all over the place when we had a full tank and three full fuel cans," he cried out, punching the back seat. Steve didn't say a word. He was watching the sky grow darker, threatening rain.

Distracted by a flash of lightening, Steve jumped when Wes yelled, "Hey. check it out! That's a fuel truck!" Steve slammed on the brakes; Kate threw out her hands to keep from smashing into the dash. Wes picked himself up off the floor of the backseat and hit Steve on the back of the head. "Dumbass," Kate nodded her approval.

"Ow. What do you think?" Steve asked, rubbing the back of his head.

"Well, after that stop, I think we should see if there is anything in there," Kate replied grumpily. Slowly approaching the truck, Steve became uneasy as the three vehicles around the fuel truck became visible. Fuel cans littered the highway, surrounded by a shoe here, a bag there, and there were several ominous stains on the pavement. Steve turned off the key, letting the car coast closer to the side of the truck.

"Maybe we should keep the engine running?" Kate whispered.

"Maybe if there are any around, they'll be like the gas station guy and not notice us," Steve whispered back. Wes' knuckles were white on the back of the seat.

"Stay here; be ready to run if we have to," Kate said shakily, trying to appear brave. She nodded at Wes to make sure he was ready. She eased the door open, just as thunder rumbled in the distance. The first can she picked up was heavy. She gave a thumbs-up back to the car. Wes gave a short whistle, telling her his can was also full. Moving as fast as they could, they emptied them into the tank, Kate lifting the heavy containers while Wes brought more. He was starting to find more empty than full, causing him to venture further and further from the car.

He started gathering the empties around the tanker truck. Kate gave a yelp, jumping back as gas splashed out of the car onto the pavement. Wes looked up. "Full," she mouthed. Wes gave a thumbs-up and beckoned her to him. She grabbed as many empties as she could, running to join him.

In the car Steve kept up a constant mutter, "Come on, come on." Seeing Kate run past with the empties he sat up straighter. "Leave it, we have enough," he called.

The empty gas cans thumped to the ground. Wes was trying to figure out how to get the gas out of the truck. Kate began combining some of the cans that held small amounts of gas together. A sound caught her attention, but she shook her head. It was just Wes messing with the valves. She stepped back, tripping over one of the empty containers, and losing her balance, she continued to fall. Wes lurched forward to grab her, knocking several empties noisily out of his way. The moan thet heard told them they were in trouble.

Wes held Kate's arm as she regained her footing, and they stood rooted to the spot, terrified. Steve screamed from the car, firing up the engine.

The undead poured out from behind every vehicle. They came up out of the tall grass and ravine. Everywhere Kate and Wes looked, the dead were closing in around them. "Shit! Shit! Shit!" Wes was muttering, searching his pockets. Kate looked left, then right, but she couldn't see the car through the throng of the dead. Wes was kneeling down suddenly, and heat and fire rose up behind her. The zombies bounced off the hood of the oncoming car and were thrown in front of them. Steve slammed through the once-human wall.

Wes dived into the back and Kate slammed the door as soon as she was in. Hair was ripped from her head, left in the clinging hand of one of the undead. Flaming zombies stumbled through the fire Wes had set from emptied gas cans. Fists pounded on the windows; angry faces peered in. Steve threw the car into reverse. Bodies crunched against the trunk and popped under the rear tires. As rain began to fall, a gas can ignited, showering the undead in a flaming rain. Steve put the car into drive to plow through the ghouls and the flames.

Home

The truck rumbled to a stop along the dirt ruts to the huge farmhouse. Beth looked from the back door of the armored car to the dried blood on her hands and shirt. "Hey, it's going to be okay. We are going to find a safe place," Devin did his best to reassure her. Silence filled the cab, both thinking of all the friends they had already lost. Beth's attention was caught by the front door of the truck opening. Hector jumped out and glanced back at them.

"Time to go," Beth whispered.

The thought that every time they stopped it seemed they lost someone weighed heavily on her mind. With each step toward the wide wraparound porch, her heart rate increased. Panic fought to take over and she struggled to maintain control. She stopped and closed her eyes for a moment, thinking, I want to be home! I want to be home right now, I don't want to be here, I want to be home in my bed. She chanted this several times in her head, getting it out of her system. Opening her eyes, she took a calming breath as she looked at the porch. A light breeze rustled the remains of the corn harvest in the nearby field. Somewhere in the barn a horse whinnied. Some of the calm Beth had been able to restore ebbed away. Romero whimpered and ducked down into the back of the truck.

"Where are they?" Devin asked in a carrying whisper. Hector waved his arm to quiet everyone. His heavy boots creaked on the wooden porch. Hector peered through one of the large windows near the front door. Cautiously he turned the doorknob. It turned easily in his hand. Motioning for the others to get ready, he turned the knob fully and pushed the door open. Seconds passed like hours. Nothing moved inside the house. Hector motioned Devin forward to cover him and for Beth to keep watch around them. The two men disappeared into the darkness through the doorway. Several seconds later, Devin hissed and waved for Gillian and Beth to follow.

Entering the front room, mustiness met Beth's nose. It didn't have the stench of death, but of disuse, as if the place had been empty for a long time. The cleanliness of the room told a different story. Devin closed the door, letting only the late-day sun light the room through the windows. The small group stood and listened. The only sound was a set of wind chimes softly tinkling on the corner of the porch. Devin shrugged at Gillian, who looked over at Beth. Hector was looking through the room toward the kitchen, his rifle relaxed but ready. He snapped it up when Beth called out, "Hello!"

Hector glared at her while the room held its breath. Nothing responded. Beth had expected to hear the tell-tale thump and bump from upstairs telling them they were not alone, but nothing came. "Still, we are going to check this place out room by room, together," Hector whispered.

"Yeah, I don't particularly care for a repeat of the dance studio," Beth commented, rubbing the side of her head.

"Where to first, the creepy basement, or the upstairs, or the possibly even creepier attic?" Devin asked, trying to keep his tone light.

"We sweep this floor, then go top down," Hector explained. The group moved as one through the downstairs of the house. They found a nice large kitchen, living room, dining room, toilet, and two bedrooms. Upstairs they found another bathroom and four more bedrooms. None of the rooms showed signs of violence. The beds were made, the rooms were clean; everything was in its place. Gillian was reaching for the pull rope to the attic stairs when Beth wondered aloud, "I think maybe they were gone before any of this started." She looking into one of the bedrooms at an old-fashioned glass eyed doll. "Why are those things always in old houses? They are seriously creepy." She returned to the room and snatched up the doll. Gillian pulled down the attic door and the stairs unfolded. Hector pointed his weapon up the stairs and listened. Holding the doll in her injured hand and her gun in the other, Beth mounted the stairs. "I don't care what else is up here, this creepy thing is finding a new home."

Thin strips of light filtered through dust from a vent at the far end of the attic. The boards were mostly bare, save for a few trunks and a couple of chairs. Hector's flashlight illuminated the corners from behind Beth. She reached the top of the stairs and placed the doll on one of the chairs. She avoided its gaze as she and Hector searched the open space. Dust lay thick up here, so their footprints were easily seen on the floor. "Kinda reminds me of a cartoon," Beth said, pointing at Hector's boot prints.

"We still need to check this place out," he grunted.

"I didn't mean to say we shouldn't, it just looks funny," she grumbled. Clearing the attic, they rejoined the others at the bottom of the stairs. "Just the creepy basement left." She smiled, but her sense of unease was building again.

"I think the door to it is in the kitchen," Devin said, a definite strain to his voice. As they proceeded down the stairs he added, "I should say. I noticed the door was bolted shut."

This caused Beth to pause, forcing Gillian to give her a little push down the stairs. Beth did not like the prospect of unbolting the door in the kitchen, as they had no idea why it was bolted in the first place. Reaching the kitchen, no one stepped forward to the locked door. Finally, Beth huffed and approached it. She gave the military man a disgusted look, then pressed her ear to the wood. She heard nothing. Mustering her courage, she knocked on the door and quickly took a step back. Everyone collectively held their breath, waiting for the banging to start on the other side. Nothing happened.

Beth reached for the bolt. Behind her Gillian was anxiously chanting, "Oh man, oh man," and bouncing on the balls of her feet. Beth was reminded painfully of Matt. Turning to Hector, she nodded, and pulled the bolt free. Taking another deep breath, she turned the knob and threw the door open. Something fell forward, and she jumped back with a scream. Hector raised his gun, Devin pulled Beth further back, Gillian squeaked. A broom hit the floor.

"Who the hell deadbolts a broom closet?" Hector gasped, out bending over and catching his breath.

"What?" Beth jumped around the corner and stared into the shallow cupboard containing three more brooms and a dustpan. "So where is the door to the basement?"

"Maybe there isn't a basement," Gillian stated hopefully.

"Naw, I bet it is one of those you can only get to from outside, you know, with the doors that open up." Hector gestured opening two doors at a low angle.

"Aw, crap. I don't want to go back outside. It's getting dark," Devin said, looking at the long shadows starting to creep across the yard.

"Well, we have to, to hide the truck," Hector reminded him. "The barn should be okay. I mean, we heard a horse in there."

"Yeah, but the horse wasn't what bothered Romero. We need to check the barn before it gets dark," Beth noted, "and we need to get Romero inside."

"How do we do this? Check the barn, then move the truck, or move the truck into the barn, then check it?" Gillian looked out the window. "The barn door is open."

"I'm thinking we move the truck in, then we can use the headlights. Remember, this place doesn't have electricity, and it is getting dark," Devin said.

"No place has electricity now," Beth reminded him.

"Doesn't matter, it is getting dark! Let's get this moving."

The group cautiously opened the front door, checking the surrounding area; it was still clear. The clouds were getting grayer as the light faded. The smell of rain was carried to them on the increasing breeze. "We'd better make this quick. It looks like rain over there." To emphasize Beth's point, a low rumble crossed the empty field.

"Come on, I don't want the storm to mask any sound in there," Hector said, pointing a thumb over his shoulder at the barn.

Romero barked happily, seeing his friends exit the house. Beth smiled, seeing the little dog's excitement. "I'll get the doors," she stated. Devin nodded and joined her on foot to the barn.

"You doing okay?" he asked, glancing at Beth.

"I guess I'm just waiting to see who we lose next," she muttered. More thunder sounded, closer this time. Devin and Beth increased their pace to the great red barn. Behind them the truck growled to life. "I think we're going to have a problem," she whispered, reaching the door.

Devin smelled it too, the distinct odor of death. He waved the truck to stop while Beth rechecked her weapon. Hector turned the keys and grabbed his rifle. Romero whined when he was told to stay.

Beth was peering through the gap in the door when Gillian joined the others. "What do we have?" she asked, holding her own gun pointed down at the ground, but in both hands, like Hector had taught her.

"I can't see anything. I mean, I see a horse and several stalls, but I don't see any of them," Beth responded.

"This isn't going to be good. Stalls, and two floors, man, this is gonna suck," Hector noted.

"Should we skip it? If any are around, they don't seem too concerned over us," Gillian whispered.

"So far. No, we need to get this hidden. I really don't want anyone trying to take it. Or any more trouble like Ryan."

"Do you think that is going to happen? I mean, do you think people would just try and take the truck without seeing who owns it? This might be a great way to find more survivors," Gillian asked.

"From what I saw at the ballpark and back at the warehouse, I'm not really willing to go out on a limb and trust anyone at the moment," Hector replied, giving Beth a nod. She returned it and pushed the door open further. She struggled, grimacing as her injured arm pressed against the wood. Devin jumped quickly to help.

Gillian was looking at Hector's back as if she wanted to continue the discussion, but Beth felt Hector had made a fine point. This did not feel like the time to trust first and hope for the best.

The smell of decay mixed with damp straw intensified but did not overpower. "Can't be too many; I can still breathe," Beth whispered. She cautiously moved deeper into the barn with Hector on her right and Devin and Gillian behind. The horse whinnied and stamped in a stall halfway along the barn.

Hector held up a hand to halt the party. He pointed to a place just across from the occupied stall. A pair of black shoes could be seen; they lay on the ground at odd angles. Approaching the shoes, Beth saw they were attached to a pair of legs covered in black pants. As she drew nearer, she could hear the grunting and thrashing of an undead. Peering around the corner she saw a bearded man in a white shirt with two large bloodstains on it. The creature's back was broken, its legs useless. One of its arms appeared to be shattered as it flung it around, the appendage whipping through the air. Hector grimaced, then grabbed a pitchfork from nearby. As he advanced on the man, Beth turned her back on the scene. She should have been used to it by now, but she still cringed at the crunch as the implement was thrust through the eye sockets, crushing the bridge of the nose, destroying the brain.

"Let's check the rest of the barn quickly. It is getting dark and that storm isn't going to wait on us," Hector stated, backing away from the dead man.

"He must have been trying to take the horse," Beth said as she walked over to the stall. The horse reared and whinnied. She held up her hands, speaking calm words, trying to get the animal to relax. She glanced around and spied a feed bag nearby. She grabbed it and returned to her slow approach.

"Beth, we need you," Devin hissed.

"This will be easier if this guy calms down. Plus, we have no idea how long it has been since he has eaten." She spoke clearly. Gillian hushed her, but Beth spoke up again. "What? If I talk normally, it will draw them out. If they don't come out, then we are sort of safe." She raised her eyebrows as if to invite a contradiction. No sound came.

Devin noticeably relaxed, but Hector seemed agitated. "We are going to have a talk soon," he pointed at Beth. The others spent a few minutes checking things over while Beth coaxed the horse to eat. Cautious at first, the animal began to eat greedily.

The headlights from the truck were the only light now. The wind was picking up and lightning began to flash. "Okay, that is enough. Let's get back to the house and set up a barricade," Hector said to the others. He eyed the loft above him uneasily.

Placing a hand on his arm, Beth said, "Hey, if they are up there, they'll probably break their legs when they fall off trying to get to us." She smiled at him, and he nodded. Quickly they pulled the truck in, locked it, then struggled to get the barn doors shut against the increasing winds. Running back to the house, their feet hit heavily on the porch. Beth tried to look through the window but couldn't see anything. "It was clear before," she shouted over the thunder.

Hector pushed the door open, flicking on his flashlight he scanned the room, and then motioned for the others to get in, just as the heavy rain arrived. Closing the door behind them, the room felt eerily quiet. "Okay," Hector whispered, "we barricade the bottom of the stairs, then more at the top, and we lock the bedroom door."

"Are we all going to stay in one room?" Gillian asked.

"Safety in numbers?" Devin suggested, grabbing one end of a side table.

Beth grabbed the other end, "I don't know, those rooms are rather small. It might be more of a hindrance if we have to move around to escape."

"Two to a room? We could take rooms with opposing views. One person sleeps while the other keeps watch," Gillian suggested while helping Hector move some chairs.

"Now that is a good plan," Hector nodded.

"Well, here is a *not* good plan." Beth said, looking at the stack of furniture at the bottom of the stairs. "We're on the wrong side of the barricade."

Devin slapped his forehead, Gillian swore, but Hector caught Beth's eye and started to laugh. The four spent the next several minutes trying to move and rebuild the structure through fits of giggles. At the top of the stairs the group built another barricade, then paired up, choosing rooms at opposite ends of the house. Beth and Gillian took the east side, Devin and Hector the west. Everyone muttered good nights and retreated into their rooms. Beth gave a smile to Hector as she closed the door and he returned it with a wave.

"Not sure I like the separation, but I am so looking forward to a night without Hector's snoring," Gillian said when Beth turned around. "Who gets the first watch?" she asked.

Beth eased her way to the window, watching the rain and lightening. She pulled a chair over to it and sat down. "I'll do it," she said, still watching the storm. Gillian sunk to the bed with a sigh of gratitude. Two thumps announced Gillian's shoes hitting the floor.

Beth sat in the dark room, staring out of the window. Occasionally she would check through the other window, which looked out over a different portion of the lawn. The storm started to pass, and Beth's mind wandered to thoughts of Steve and Wes. Resting her head against the glass, she tried to imagine their faces, tired to remember a time over the summer.

The sun was warm, and the smell of the barbeque filled the air. Wes and Steve were laughing, trying to drench her with a water balloon. Lightning flashed, illuminating the expanse outside her window. She blinked, staring into the darkness. It was a tree, swaying in the breeze. Another flash told her it wasn't a tree. "There's a zombie on our lawn. We don't want zombies on our lawn," she hissed, jumping to her feet.

"Wazamadder?" Gillian mumbled.

"There's one out there!"

Gillian sat up instantly. Beth hurried to the door, in a rush to get to the other room. "EEEP!" she squeaked, running into Hector's chest.

"There's one out there," he whispered, holding Beth by the shoulders.

"How did you see him?" she asked.

"Him? No, it's a woman."

"No, definitely a man."

"We have more than one? Shit." He released her.

"Maybe they'll just pass us by?" Gillian whispered.

"There is another one out there." Devin pointed back to the room he had just left.

Lights flashed across the hallway. All four stared, from one to the other. A horn sounded, then a gunshot. Hector and Beth ducked, but then Beth turned, running to the window. Crouching to look over the sill she saw headlights gleaming through the rain.

A zombie lay motionless in front of the car, and three more were approaching it. The vehicle backed up slowly. Another gunshot, and another zombie fell.

All Together Now

Rain fell so fat and heavy against the window that the wipers were barely able to keep up. Steve's hands still shook on the wheel even though he had been driving for almost an hour. The fuel truck escape still played over in his mind. It had been far too close. He'd almost lost Kate and Wes. He glanced in the rearview mirror. Wes' head was lying on the back seat, but his eyes were open, watching the dark landscape slide by.

"You okay?" Kate asked from beside him.

"We need to find a *safe* place to stay," he grumbled.

"Hey! Hey, over there," Wes called from the back seat. Steve looked in the direction Wes was pointing. For a moment he had no idea what he was supposed to be seeing, until lightning lit up the silhouette of a large farmhouse with a barn not too far away. He began looking for a ramp off the highway. A mile or two later he found what he was looking for. He almost missed it, as the exit sign had been knocked down by a pickup truck that lay buried in some trees just off the road. Wes grabbed the side of the car as it fishtailed wildly over the rain-drenched pavement.

"Okay, we just, um, need to find a way back to that house," Steve said, trying to calm his nerves as he slowed the car to take the turn at the end of the ramp. He glanced over at Kate, who was still clutching the seatbelt in a death grip.

"Yeah, but let's get there in one piece, okay?" she said, relaxing her grip. Wes grunted something from the back seat that Steve ignored, but it made Kate snort. Steve weaved in and out of the detritus on the road, finally finding a turn that seemed to lead them back in the direction of the farmhouse.

After several minutes they came to a small house close to the road. Steve slowed the car, "What do you think? You want to try it?" Lightning lit up the area; a zombie was standing on the porch. Steve pulled the car into the driveway, throwing light over the front of the house. The porch zombie stumbled and fell off the front step, slowly rising to approach the car. "Only one. We can…"

"No good, dude, look." Wes pointed over his shoulder. The front door to the house hung off its hinges, and several undead were staggering out of the blackness. One, two, three, "forget it!" Steve agreed, reversing out of the drive as the first of the undead's hands found the hood.

"Let's find that other place, shall we?" Kate said through a nervous laugh.

For a few miles the only sound in the car was the wipers and the tattoo of rain on the windshield. Finally, Steve slowed the car again. A break in the fence line showed him where the long drive to the large farmhouse began. He stopped at the end of the drive. He turned to look at his two passengers with a "whaddaya think?" look. It was met with shrugs. He eased the car down the bumpy, muddy track to the house.

"Damn it," Steve shouted, pounding the wheel. Four undead were roaming around the lawn and field.

"Look, the door is shut. This looks like an Amish place, and these guys don't look Amish. Check out the trucker hat and that hideous nightdress," Wes pointed out.

"You think they just wandered here?" Kate asked.

Steve honked the horn. Kate's head spun; her face demanded an answer. "To draw any more out," he replied, then pulled his gun. He opened the window and shot a zombie that was in front of the car. Kate glared at him for a second, shrugged, pulled her own gun and shot at a zombie several feet to the right. Steve slowly backed up.

"Where are we going?" Wes demanded.

"We'll draw them away from the house, then come back after we deal with them," Steve answered. Kate fired again, this time finding her mark. Two zombies continued to approach the car through the rain. Thunder rumbled and another shot rang out, this time fired by Wes from the back seat. Steve was halfway down the drive now. Only one undead still pursued them. Steve shook his head, hit the brakes, put the car in park, swore, opened the door, walked up to the zombie, and shot it in the face. Rain poured down on him as he stood over the ghoul, its corpse glistening with rain in the glow of the headlights. "I'm going to find a safe place and I am going to get some sleep!" he shouted at the dead heap at his feet. Wiping the rain from his face, he returned to the car.

"Feel better?" Kate asked him.

"For a second. Now I'm just cold and wet."

"Brilliant." Wes laughed.

Could It?

Beth watched as the car backed slowly down the drive. Several shots rang out, until the driver finally got out to execute the last of the undead pursuing the vehicle. Beth stood up, placing both hands on either side of the window frame, unconsciously holding her breath.

"Oh, that isn't good," Hector said from beside Beth, making her jump. "That does not look like someone we want to deal with."

"What? What happened?" Gillian asked in a fear-laced voice.

"Guy got out of the car to shoot one of those things in the head. He looked pissed."

Beth was only slightly aware of the conversation going on behind her. The car had started pulling forward again. She jumped and spun around bumping into Hector again. They did the left-right dance before she was rushing past him. She ran into Devin. He grabbed her arms to keep her from getting around him. "Where are you going?" he hissed. She yelped as he grabbed her injured arm. "Sorry! Where are you going?" he asked, letting go.

Footsteps thumped on the wooden porch. Gillian, Hector and Devin froze, listening. "Did anyone think to lock...." The question hung unanswered. The sound of rain increased for a moment, then several voices drifted up the stairs. Hector held a finger to his lips.

No Way

Wes shook the rain from his soaked hair, and Kate yelped when the water hit her. Steve hushed them as he looked around the room. He pointed to the barricaded stairs. The three tensed, raising their weapons slightly. "You think they are still here?" Wes asked.

"Should we call out, and see if they are...friendly?"

"Or alive?" Wes suggested.

Steve stood thinking. A sound upstairs made him look up and raise his gun to the ceiling.

"I know it is him! Let me go!" a familiar voice cried out from above them. Steve dropped the gun to his side. He turned to look at Wes. Wes' face showed total disbelief.

"Hello?" Kate called from between the stunned men.

"We are armed," called back a gruff voice.

"Oh, for crying out loud!" Beth turned, stamping her foot and glaring at Hector. "Steve!" she called from the top of the stairs.

Steve stood stunned for a second, then he turned, gaping at Wes. He cried, "Beth? BETH! OH MY GOD!" Wes' gun clattered to the floor as he threw himself at the barricade. Steve watched for a second, tears streaming down his face. He joined Wes at the bottom of the stairs. Thumping from the top told them another barricade was coming down.

"Wes! Steve! Please be you!" Beth cried, tears almost blinding her eyes. Hector moved the mattress and Beth flew down the stairs. The sideboard was cleared from below, and someone with long brown hair flew into Steve's arms. Her small fist pounded on his back as Beth's muffled voice repeated into Steve's chest. "I knew it, I knew it, I knew it." Kate smiled, with her hands over her mouth. Three people appeared on the stairs. Steve put Beth down. She cried and smiled. Slowly she turned to Wes.

The room vanished, and they were alone. Wes gave a little wave. "Hi." he said.

Beth stared at him. "Hi." She stood still as he ran to her. He stopped, putting a hand on her face. She closed her eyes at the touch. He grabbed her and pulled her into the tightest hug she had ever felt. He pulled back, looked her in the eyes, and kissed her. After several seconds they became aware of introductions around them. Beth grabbed Steve and pulled him to her and Wes.

"I knew you were okay. I knew you were," Wes sobbed into Beth's hair, his hand running up and down her back, then pulling her to him tight. "You had to be okay."

Beth's shoulders were shaking as the tears ran free from her eyes. She pushed him back and stamped her foot. "Don't you ever do that to me again!" she screamed, then turned to face her brother. "Either of you!" She pulled Wes to her again. "Don't you ever leave me again," she whispered into Wes' ever-dampening shoulder.

New Start

Beth woke with a start. The weight on her chest was unfamiliar and terrifying. Dim light filtered through the boards covering the first floor windows. It took a moment for her to realize where she was, and that the weight was Wes' arm across her. They had fallen asleep holding each other. Her heart rate slowed and a smile spread across her face. Her stuffed bunny sat staring at her, a little worse for wear than she remembered, but it smiled at her all the same. She thought back to the night before, the storm and the reunion. After tears and tales, Wes had pulled the bunny from his backpack. Now she had her brother, her bunny, and her boyfriend back. Rolling over to face him, she watched his eyes slowly open. He returned her smile.

"Good morning," he said. Behind them Steve mumbled in his sleep. Beth quickly shushed Wes. He covered his mouth but kept smiling. Beth moved his hand and gave him a quick kiss.

She was suddenly aware of how stiff and sore her back was. The mattresses they had pulled down from the upstairs were old and lumpy. At some point in the night she had moved so much of the down filling that she was basically sleeping on the floor. Sitting up, she stretched and leaned forward to touch her toes. Wes groaned as he stood, stretching. Steve muttered a threat at Wes to keep quiet. Kate was now awake, smiling at Beth and shaking her head, pointing to Steve. "Not a morning person," Beth whispered.

The others began to wake now. Hector yawned and stretched while moving to the stairs to relieve Devin from watch duty. Kate watched him go. She leaned over Steve, gave him a quick kiss on his cheek, then followed Hector to relieve Gillian. Steve tried to stay asleep, but he gave up when the floor began to creak with movement. The smell of coffee brewing and eggs cooking wafted into the room. Beth laughed as Steve sat up. "I'll need to remember to tell Kate that the only way to get you out of bed is with breakfast." Steve just waved her off as he stretched and stumbled toward the kitchen.

The group sat drinking coffee and looking out over the fields. "It's a good start. This is as good a place as any to set up in." Devin yawned, then thanked Beth for a plate of eggs. "We can use Matt's idea and create a fort. Then maybe we can start to raise crops and such."

Steve looked at Devin, still in his wrinkled dress shirt and pants. "Do you know anything about farming?" Devin admitted he didn't.

"Looks like we'll need to find a library." Wes shrugged while grimacing at his coffee.

"We'll need to fortify this place and figure out how to get information and supplies." Gillian remarked, walking into the kitchen. "I guess we need to start working on a plan."